ALSO BY JOHN WRAY

The Right Hand of Sleep

CANAAN'S
TONGUE

CANAAN'S TONGUE

JOHN WRAY

Alfred A. Knopf New York 2005

THIS IS A BORZOI BOOK
PUBLISHED BY ALFRED A. KNOPF

Copyright © 2005 by John Wray

All rights reserved. Published in the United States by Alfred A. Knopf,
a division of Random House, Inc., New York, and
in Canada by Random House of Canada Limited, Toronto.
www.aaknopf.com

Knopf, Borzoi Books, and the colophon are registered trademarks
of Random House, Inc.

Library of Congress Cataloging-in-Publication Data
Wray, John, [date].
Canaan's tongue / John Wray.—1st ed.
p. cm.
ISBN 1-4000-4086-8
1. United States—History—Civil War, 1861–1865—Fiction.
2. Fugitives from justice—Fiction.   3. Slave trade—Fiction.   I. Title.

PS3573.R365C36 2005
813'.6—dc22   2004064902

Manufactured in the United States of America
First Edition

I

He appears to have been a most dexterous and consummate villain, this "Redeemer" . . . The stealing of horses in one State, and the selling of them in another, was but a small portion of [his gang's] business; the most lucrative was the enticing of slaves to run away from their masters, that they might sell them in another quarter.

This was arranged as follows; they would tell a negro that if he would run away from his master, and allow them to sell him, he should receive a portion of the money paid for him, and that upon his return to them a second time they would send him to a free State, where he would be safe.

The poor wretches complied with this request, hoping to obtain money and freedom; they would be sold to another master, and run away again, to their employers; sometimes they would be sold in this manner three or four times, until they had realized three or four thousand dollars by them; but as, after this, there was fear of detection, the usual custom was to get rid of the only witness that could be produced against them, which was the negro himself, by murdering him, and throwing his body into the Mississippi . . .

—Life on the Mississippi

Geburah Plantation, 1863.

T HERE IS A HOUSE, Parson says.

There is a river. The house, built of the corpses of historic oaks, leans toward the river as if parched. The grounds stand vacant and abashed. A finger-bowl of bare red clay surrounds the house, which seems more desolate even than the grounds. But there are seven men inside of it, and one woman. They are faithful to the house—; they are beholden to it. They could make their home no other place, as no other place would have them.

They are wanted for blood-crimes in eleven states and their lives are held in forfeit. They are wanted by the Union for the murder of ninety-seven slaves—; they are wanted by the Confederacy for destruction of private property. The War the rest of the nation curses has sheltered them, till now, in its great and ample shadow. They are free and at liberty to take their ease. The War rolls past them on the river, and makes the woods unquiet in the evenings—; no more than that. The War is an entertainment. But now a thing has happened that flushes the War from their thoughts like a sparrow from a thicket.

A body has been found. Virgil Ball has found it. Virgil Ball, the most skittish of them all, the most inquisitive, the most tender. He hovers above the body like a bucket above a well. Three other men are with him. The men look at Virgil, then down at his feet, where the body lies stiff and equitable and naked. They draw closer and squint. It is a particular body, known to them by sight. They are each of them killers and well used to unpleasantness but the sight makes them curiously restless.

A question has begun forming in their minds.

Virgil Ball.

MY LIFE'S NOT WORTH A PIG'S KIDNEY, Virgil says.
Everyone knows I murdered the Redeemer, driving a
sliver of pier-glass through the back of his neck and stuffing him, with the help of the house-nigger, down the hole of the
privy—: everyone knows it, and now another of our gang's been
snuffed.

The three holy horrors beside me know it. They know it because I
told them—; I told them because I'm a donkey. And now another of us
is killed. Goodman Harvey, a lisper, whom nobody liked much, and I
liked less than anybody. They suspect me, of course. How could they
not suspect me? The thought sends a tear guttering down my cheek,
but I'm not such a fool as to look anybody in the eye. I keep mine fixed
on this morning's cadaver, once a man I knew well, laid out like a cat-
fish at my feet.

The story I mean to tell will be a right cameo of this nation, truer
than a daguerreotype, more telling than the Constitution. It's the story
of the Trade, and of my twists and turns inside it—: the crimes that I
committed, the blasphemies I abetted, the passions I conceived. I speak
as of the past, but I am frying in it still. How the devil, then, to tell it?
Frontwards, like a Roman history, or backwards, like a Mandarin
scroll? From all sides at once, like the Gospels of the Christ? I'm an
educated man, but also something of a ponce. I have ever balked when
left to my own counsel.

Ever, that is, except once. Once I did not balk. Best to start there,
perhaps—: back at the height of my achievement. Best to start at the
beginning of the end.

I might begin it as a rhyme, a scrap of school-yard doggerel—:

Virgil Isaiah Dante Ball
Murdered the Redeemer in the fall.

"The Redeemer" was what we called him, out of devotedness—; but his given name was Thaddeus. Thaddeus Morelle. A plain-faced dumpling of a man, remarkable chiefly in his smallness, like Alexander the Great, or Bonaparte. He was set to eat America like a biscuit. He was set to make princes of us all.

Instead I cut his wind-pipe, and he died.

The War for Southern Liberty had just turned a year and a half—: that fixes the date at October 12, 1862. The house-nigger and I hauled him to the privy (his favorite part of the grounds, in life) and forced his little body, after a brief eulogy, through the square-cut opening in the planks. He fell without fanfare, hit the bottom with a *whoomp*—: the hole was freshly dug and deep. After the service I sprinkled a bit of quick-lime after him and answered nature's summons. I took my time about it. Then I went back to the house and brought the rest of the gang together and told them what I'd done.

It was the worst hour of my life. The Redeemer had been our Washington, our Robespierre, our Jenghis Khan. I fully expected to be torn to pieces, wept like a Frenchman and had to pinch my right ear-lobe to keep from dropping in a faint. It took a goodly while to tell it—: I'm a coward at the best of times, and on that occasion I warbled like a goose. To my astonishment the gang heard me out in silence, then went off to the privy, one by one, to pay their last respects. By supper the bucket of quick-lime was empty and I'd moved my carpet-sack up—wonder of wonders!—into the master bedroom. I went to bed that night a reinvented man.

That, however, was then. Today is the twelfth of May, and the Natural Order again prevails—: a cleverer man has slipped into the Redeemer's britches, easy as you please, and I'm once again the Jack Fetchit to them all. Down, and up, and down again, like the India-rubber ball I am. Such is the tendency of heaven, at least with regards to me—: the occasional blessing followed by a shower of shite.

I now sleep in a narrow cubby under the attic stairs. There is a little port-hole window—; I am not ungrateful for that. And I murdered the Redeemer, that oily-faced, cane-twirling, preening sport of nature, just as I promised that I would.

I'm not ungrateful for that, either.

A QUARTER-HOUR HAS GONE BY. We remain clustered together, my three associates and I, adoring the deceased. The silence is thick enough to poke. I'm desperate to say something—anything at all—but my cowardice keeps me mute. Elsewhere (*everywhere*, in fact, in this part of the country) men are shooting at each other from shell-holes and river-beds and fields of winter wheat, debating the future of our Union. I'm here at Geburah, miles from the nearest battle-field, watching a body blanch and stiffen.

When I think of it that way it almost seems a privilege.

The body was called "Goodman Harvey" last night, when it still spoke and strutted—; I'm not sure what to call it now. It was a Mormon by birth, a nigger-runner by accident, and an arse-kisser by profession. I stare down at it enraptured. Its undeniable *deadness*, chalk-white and utter, reminds me again of the Redeemer. (The Redeemer's face, as I pushed his eyes shut in the light of the nigger's lantern, wore the same tender look—as though he'd just been given a present—that poor dead Harvey's has.) In the honeyed morning light that cleaves to every object Harvey's features seem settled into an expression of serenity—even of wisdom—that I never knew them to wear in life. Alive he was a fidgeting, sot-brained schemer, and I don't calculate I'll miss him. But his dying *at this moment*, hip-deep into the war, in this rotting house the eight of us are packed into like so many Christmas hams, comes as an advertisement, a calling-card of sorts—: a reminder I could just as well do without. The noose is tightening hourly about this house and not a one of us can forget it.

We were brought here to Geburah, after all, for no other reason but to die.

I WANT TO GIVE AN ACCOUNTING of the Trade, of the Gang from Island 37, and of the Redeemer most of all. I want to puzzle him out, if only for my own security of mind. The only way to get free of the past, I've decided, is to eat it—: to chew on it, digest it, and deposit it in pellets. So I mean to do just that. But first I have to get out of this room.

Colonel Erratus D'Ancourt, interim chairman of our Trade—a stuffed frock-coat of a man, as much like the Redeemer as a diaper is to a dinner-jacket—shuffles forward and gives Harvey a jab with the tip of his ash-plant. The body lies at a peculiar angle to the bed, its feet just shy of the foot-board, its speckled skull pointing toward the room's south-east corner. The flesh of the shoulders and neck is still yielding and the head turns readily, with a barely audible popping of the vertebrae. I decide for myself that it was poison. The raw, strophed markings on the nape, likely made by his own fingers, and the fan-shaped bloom of broken vesicles under the skin point to permanganate of potassium, which I often laid out for prairie foxes as a boy.

A small amount of this same unctuous powder, sealed in a cut-glass vial, was given to each of us by the Redeemer at the Trade's first meeting. He had a weakness for the trappings of dramatic theater, and we sought to ape him in this, as we did in everything. No gesture of ours was extravagant enough, no brutality too baroque. Looking down at Harvey, however—his eyes closed in parody of ever-lasting rest—I can't help but marvel at the inappropriateness of this latest tribute. It doesn't sit right, somehow. Harvey was not a man given to over-doing things.

It's likely, then, that he was murdered. Each person in the room must now be suspicious of every other—: fresh killings will spring from this like flowers from a cow-pat. The Redeemer would have been delighted.

A sketch—:

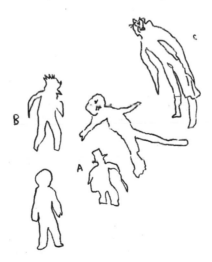

We stand about in an assortment of stiff-necked postures, the sorry remains of a once-great enterprise, each wanting to slip away but feeling himself watched by all his fellows. Since the collapse of the Gang and our exile to this god-forsaken tongue of bayou, we've been gathered like this only once before, when I made my grand confession. The Colonel (A) crouches to my right, as low to the body as his lumbago will allow. To his left is Stutter Kennedy (B), who'd as soon stick a knife into your eye as look at you—; to *his* left skulks our Parson (C), who'd gladly sup upon your sweet-breads after Kennedy was done. These, then, are my peers—: the last three heads of the illustrious, blood-caked, gospel-sucking Trade. Colonel the bureaucrat, Kennedy the assassin, Parson the intriguer, Virgil Ball the fool. I wonder which of us did Goodman Harvey under.

Why kill Harvey at all, come to think of it, and leave *me* cozy as a pup?

The Colonel clears his throat and squints down at his liver-spotted knuckles, a sure sign that he's about to launch into some new foolery.

"Boy come up at six from the depot," he says, arranging Harvey's shirt with the tip of his ash-plant. His expression is one of aggrieved nobility.

The "boy from the depot"—in fact a toothless, ageless Creole—is our last connection to society. One day soon he'll turn us in.

"Did he bring any soap?" I ask.

"The news is in from Chancellorsville," the Colonel says, ignoring me. "A Dixie victory, praise Jesus, after five days' butchery." He sucks in a melancholy gulp of air. "Our Stonewall Jackson's sadly killed."

"Not *our* Stonewall puh!—puh!—pissing Jackson," Kennedy spits out. "Remember that, you damn butternut."

It's a gall to Kennedy that the Colonel (who was born and reared in Indiana) should treat the Confederate cause as his own—; Kennedy hates the South and all it compasses. The Colonel bites his lip and hushes.

From his position at the foot of the corpse Parson raises his left hand, holding it aloft in the attitude of the Magnificat—: "Magnificat anima mea Dominum."

Parson's contempt for papism is well known to me, and I do not mistake his tattered Latin for a performance of last rites. He is simply having his regular fun with Kennedy.

"Kind of you, Parson," I murmur. "He'll sleep better now, God rest him."

Parson grants me his customary grin, one that leaves his eyes free to regard me coldly. "Thank you, Virgil. I try to match the verse to the occasion. Stonewall Jackson, after all, was birthed out of an Irish whore."

"You shut your muh!—muh!—*mouth*," Kennedy hollers. "God-damn organ-grinder's monkey—"

"Steady, Mr. Kennedy!" the Colonel says, bringing his ash-plant down between them like a gavel. "That's a lie, Parson. It was my privilege to know General Jackson well."

"You knew bollocks," Kennedy mutters, his eyes trained on Parson like a pair of cudgels.

Parson says nothing, content to honor me with a silent wink. I look at him a moment—at his black-robed bean-pole of a body, his cat-like face, his womanish gray hands folded piously together—then allow my sight to travel from point to point in the room, in the hope that I might find one single object that is not hateful to me.

I fail.

"Without Stonewall, I just don't see it clear," the Colonel says. When this draws no reply, he says again, more shrilly—: "Without Stonewall, the South may end up—no more than a *place*—"

"All the same to us," Kennedy says. "Or should be. It weren't ever but a place to me."

The Colonel gathers in a breath. "But the Confederacy—"

"Will hang us as quick as the Federals will," Parson cuts in. "Quicker. Let's hope the trouble drags on a good while yet."

"Hear, hear," I whisper.

To my relief no one pays me the slightest mind.

MOST OF US, like the departed, are still in the clothes we passed the night in—; only Parson is fully dressed. He wears a floor-length soutane, clasped closely under the chin, trimmed with crimson satin at the hem-line and cuffs. He looks like a crypt-keeper to the Vatican. In ten years of working with him on the river, much of that time on flat-boats and tar-bottomed nigger rafts, I've never once seen him out of his Sunday silks. In his cadaverish way he's more terrible than Kennedy—: Kennedy is a killer, plain and simple. Parson is anything *but* plain. Each time I look at him I see a different animal.

"Poor fat Harvey," Parson murmurs. "The Latter-days have taken back the most oblong of their saints."

The Colonel gawks down at the body, running two tobacco-stained fingers through his beard. The rest of us keep mum and stiff. Parson plays with the window-sash, whispering to it fondly from time to time. I let my eyes fall closed. Sweet silence, oblivion, death-in-life—

"Was it you that found the body, Virgil?" the Colonel barks out.

I nod. "I sleep across the hall, Colonel, as you know."

"Messing about, were you?" Kennedy sneers. "Poking your puh!—puh!—*peck* into other people's knickers?"

"No, Kennedy! I wasn't. I—"

The Colonel gives a low, choked cough, as though he's swallowed a crab-apple. "*Look* at me when I address you, Virgil. Did you shift anything about?"

"I locked the door straight-away, Colonel. Then I came to your room and roused you."

"Locked the *door*, you say!" This piques his senile interest. "With what key?"

I hold up Harvey's room key, identical to every other on its gut-string loop. "This one, Colonel. I found it by the bed."

He makes a low harrumphing sound. "What did you do next?"

"I rapped on everybody's door. Then I came back here and waited."

"I was awake already," Parson whispers to the sash.

The Colonel looks hard at Parson. "And where were *you* sequestered, Your Saintliness, might I inquire?"

Parson turns lazily about to face him. (The Colonel is a parakeet—; Parson is a cat.) "I heard the fuss and come on downstairs," he says.

"You were gone from your room all night, sirrah. I heard you as you left."

Parson simply shakes his head. He looks at me and smiles. "Poor fat Harvey," he says. His voice is sweet as clotted butter.

A new fancy strikes me then. We stand gathered about the body like delegates to a mock Confederate Congress—: the Colonel playing the part of Robert E. Lee, Harvey standing in for Stonewall Jackson, Parson for the blessing of the Lord, and Jefferson Davis, that paragon of Southern gentility, being played (of course) by—

The thought strikes each of us at once. Oliver Delamare is missing. The Colonel raises his head with a jerk and his eyes dart from one of us to another. I do my best to avoid his look.

"Where is the mulatto?" he demands.

"Back in Huh!—Huh!—*Hominy*ville by now, most likely," Kennedy answers, letting out a snort.

"See if you can find that mulatto, Virgil," the Colonel says tightly. "Tell him to get himself up here."

"As you like, Colonel," I say. But I say it too eagerly. Kennedy's lips pull back from his teeth and Parson shoots me that look of his. No matter, I think—; in another moment I'll be gone. Gone from the room, gone from the sight of them, out into the un-cankered air.

The Colonel crooks a finger at me as I go.

"You bring him straight up here, Virgil! No dallying! Do you hear?"

BY VIRTUE OF OUR DAILY WALKS TOGETHER, it's supposed that Delamare and I are friends. The truth is that I adore him. My love for Delamare is not like the love I feel for my Clementine, of course, though his beauty plays a part in it. (Clementine Gilchrist! My catastrophe! My life!—No. I won't think of her. Not yet.) Delamare possesses what the rest of us are desperate for—: Delamare possesses grace. He draws on it at whim, effortlessly, like a hawk tipping on the wind. The adoration I feel toward him is in no way returned—: he feels a lack of revulsion toward me, at best. But even that is no small miracle in this place.

I step out into the hall, force myself to take a breath, then shuffle in my heavy-footed way downstairs. The Colonel knows where Delamare is as well as I—: out on the verandah, dressed in his immaculate city clothes, gargling his Mississippi mud.

Each morning at six Delamare goes to the river, dressed as if for a banker's holiday, then wades into the current and ducks his body under. He stays under-water until his sight goes black and the water clambers up his brain, until he forgets himself and Geburah, until death comes and tickles him on the ribs. Then he brings a jarful back to the house and sits cradling it in priestly silence, breathing in carefully plotted patterns, waiting for the breakfast bell to chime. Often the whites of his eyes are red with broken veins and his face is as yellow as the mud he sips. He swears by this ritual, and occasionally performs it a second time at dusk.

I've been in the water exactly once, and that by accident. The last thing I want is that damned river in my skull.

Delamare is not sitting as I pictured him, with his boots propped against the rail and a jar cradled in his kid-gloved hands, nursing his heroic spite. Instead I find him leaning out over the lawn, not so much to get a view of the river as to distance himself from the house at his back. The look on his face is that of complacency beatified by bitterness. He glances at me and I find myself straightening, waiting for him to address me—: there are moments when he inspires, quite carelessly, a behavior that borders on the courtly. For a time I thought it arose from his nobility of spirit—; for a time from his natural refinement—; for a time simply from his youth. After thirty weeks together in this charnel-house, however, I know that it can be traced to the calm disdain in which he holds each of us without exception, and to the violence that hovers about his perfect body like a cloud of bees over an exotic flower.

"Ah! It's you, Virgil," he says, as though I were bringing him out his slippers.

"Goodman Harvey is dead."

He blinks at this. "Poisoned?"

I nod. "Permanganate of potassium, rules the inquest."

He scratches his chin. "Kennedy's my guess."

I say nothing for a moment, considering. "I might reckon it a suicide."

"Might you?" He grants me a smile. "And on what would such a ruling rest?"

"He was a sorry son of a bitch, that's all. Perhaps he realized it."

Delamare sighs. "By that logic, we should each of us be laid in our respective plots, Mr. Ball." He winks at me. "Excepting present company."

I make a courtly bow. "I might excuse Asa as well, the poor cracked egg."

This proves a mistake. Asa Trist, mad-man and heir to this estate—both the gang's protector, therefore, and its protégé—was born into everything Delamare covets, and has grown into everything Delamare hates. His madness has never been enough to excuse his wealth and pedigree. Delamare's face goes dark and tight-cornered as a closet.

"Your generosity does you credit, Virgil. Historically speaking, however, young Asa has more blood on his hands than all the rest of us put together."

I tip my head to one side, trying to catch his eye. "Look him in the face, Oliver, the next time you see him. He's paying for the sins of his fathers every waking minute."

Delamare looks out at the river. "That may be," he says, in a voice drained of all humor. "Yes. I expect he is working at his atonement."

From the kitchen-house comes the sound of old Dodds, the house-boy, busying himself with breakfast. I watch Delamare patiently, waiting on a sign. All traces of calm have rolled off his features like river-water from a bluff.

"I'm sorry, Oliver," I say.

"Nonsense!" Delamare sing-songs, getting to his feet. "Shall we take our ceremonial turn through the grounds?"

This is less a proposal than a decree. He gives me a mock bow and glides elegantly away, out from under the shadow of the house and off toward the orchard without a single wasted movement. I think of my promise to the Colonel and hang back a spell, gazing over the red clay lawn at Delamare's gracefully retreating form. The next instant I'm off the porch and gone, shuffling after the Redeemer's prodigy no differently than I shuffled after the Redeemer himself, faithfully and doggedly, those seven swift years that led me down into this hole.

II

The Law is a ass.

—William Bumble

Horse-Thievery.

IT BEGAN at a respectable camp-meeting, Virgil says.

I first laid eyes on the Redeemer in May of '56, just up-river from Natchez. I was passing the head of Lafitte's Chute in a pine-sap canoe I'd paid for honestly in Vicksburg when the immaculate white of a revival tent caught my notice, fluttering bravely at a spot that had been wilderness only a fortnight before. I banked my canoe in the shade and climbed up the muddy, stump-littered slope, aiming to satisfy my curiosity at the tent-flap. A water-stained bill stuck to the canvas by what looked to be a lady's hat-pin caught my eye—:

> THADDEUS II. MORELLE
> REDEEMER OF LAMBS
> "The Same Came For A Witness;
> To Bear Witness Of The Light"

On the far side of the tent, past a cluster of traps and wagons, thirty-odd horses stood tethered in a row. There were a few skiffs and bucket-boats farther up the bank, but not many. Most of the congregation looked to have come on foot. Up close, the canvas was frayed and weathered—: peering in through a thumb-sized gash, I saw the tent was already amply filled with lambs. I hung back a moment, overcome by a fit of bashfulness (I was a rather timid vagrant in those days) and looked straight above me at the sky. It was sapphire blue, I remember, and wonderfully calm. A warbling rose up now and then inside the tent, punctuating the reedy exhortations of the preacher. Even through the heavy cloth his voice had something queer about it, something out of place, as though a chimpanzee were lecturing a learned assembly.

My prudence did battle with my curiosity, fired a brave volley, then collapsed in a heap of dust. I parted the tent-flap and slipped inside.

In doing so I sentenced my Christian self to death, though at the time I felt nothing but astonishment. Through a breach in the crowd I saw the preacher on his crate pulpit, gasping and spitting and proselytizing and weeping—: a delicate, sallow-faced, limp-haired dwarf, in a suit that looked cut out of butcher's paper. I mumbled an oath and passed a hand over my eyes. Was this some manner of vaudeville? Had I mistaken a curiosity-show for a bona-fide camp meeting? I stood stock-still for a spell, my right hand clutching at the tent-flap, my left hand in front of me as if in expectation of a fall. Then I found a place for myself at the back of the airless, man-smelling tent and listened.

The preacher wore a bi-cornered hat of brushed black silk, the kind Napoleon favored at Waterloo. His left fore-finger rested lightly on a Bible, and he was declaiming in a tremulous voice, a voice riddled with earthly suffering—:

TRULY GOD IS GOOD TO ISRAEL, EVEN TO SUCH AS ARE CLEAN OF HEART. BUT AS FOR ME, MY FEET WERE ALMOST GONE; MY STEPS HAD WELL NIGH SLIPPED. FOR I WAS ENVIOUS AT THE FOOLISH, WHEN I SAW THE PROSPERITY OF THE WICKED.

He paused the briefest of instants and raised his rum-colored eye-balls to survey us. I'd been to revivals before, and was used to their choked-back burlesqueries—; delighted in them, in fact. This was altogether different. The few women in the crowd clutched at their bosoms and wept in silent misery—; the men stood together in a clot, staring at the preacher with a look of unleavened murder. They did their best to drive the notion from their minds, of course, as the killing of a preacher is no small matter in the eyes of God and society. But the urge was there, and unquiet—: you could read it in their faces. And it was this very same urge held them in his power.

"'For there are no bands in their Death,'" the preacher continued, lingering affectionately over his *t*'s and *s*'s in an unmistakable shanty-town lisp. I smiled a little to myself—: this sport of nature had come—of all places!—from the nigger-townships along the delta. But he was all the more marvelous for it.

THEY ARE NOT IN TROUBLE AS OTHER MEN: NEITHER ARE THEY PLAGUED LIKE OTHER MEN. THEREFORE PRIDE COMPASSETH

THEM ABOUT AS A CHAIN; VIOLENCE COVERETH THEM AS A
GARMENT . . .

He leaned slowly forward, the trace of a frown on his damp, rat-like face, and glanced up from the book as though he'd just recollected us. "This puts me in mind of an episode from my own life," he said in a wistful voice. Planting a finger on the little book, as if to keep it from escaping, he began—:

"I was raised on an acre of black peat in Virginia, youngest boy to a simple, scripture-loving planter of plug tobacco. There were thirteen of us all told, minnowed into two eight-by-seven-foot rooms. But we lived modestly, and praised God nightly in our prayers." The crate creaked angrily beneath his feet. "Up the lane lived a great patriarch, Yeoman Dorne, with his wife and seven sons. The youngest of them, Ezekiel, was my equal in years."

His eyes grew melancholy and fixed. "Lord knows, our lot was not a disburthened one," he said.

A chorus of anticipatory sighs.

"Hejekuma Morelle, my grandfather," said the preacher, "was, to put not too fine a point on it, stricken with the pox" (assorted gasps and mutterings). "Contrary-wise, Yeoman Dorne—a Bostoner—was a wide-breasted squire of sixty-five, arresting in person and boisterous in manner. The cries and frequent imprecations to our Lord by my grandfather, who raved and cursed us in his misery, took their toll not only on my grandmother, Odette—who developed in consequence a nervous palsy—but also on my mother, Anne-Marie, who grew pro-gressively weaker from lack of sleep, and presented an easy mark to the cholera which swept through the country in the winter of '29" (brighter, more plaintive whimperings from the choir). "Morelia Dorne, wife of our neighbor—whose boots we buffed, whose wheat we threshed—never suffered the least complaint of health and bore seven healthy, plum-cheeked sons and daughters."

The preacher regarded the assembly dolefully. Not a word was spoken during that very lengthy pause. The breeze rustled the canvas and moved the tent-poles from side to side, giving the illusion of a ship at sea, or at least of a barge in a heavy current. At last he cleared his throat.

"The premature end of my sweet mother sent my father, who'd never been entirely right in the head, into antics of filth and violence undreamt of by Christian man. My eldest brother, Thaddeus Everett—

whose left side was withered from birth—made the error of repri-
manding my father one evening for his profligacy, calling on Saints
Peter and Albert as his witnesses. My father brained him with a cast-
iron chimney pan." The preacher paused again. "The sight of *that*
drove my sister Sophia clean out of her wits, and troubled all of our
sleep for six months thereafter. My grandfather's blubberings, needless
to say, continued without abatement."

The preacher had not so much as blinked since the commence-
ment of his narrative. His face was placid as a saint's. Ignoring the
mounting disbelief of the crowd, he continued—: "The eldest Dorne
boy, Patrice, excelled at hunting, fishing, and the steeple-chase, in
which last he took particular pleasure on account of the Libyan thor-
ough-bred with which his father had lately furnished him. *Contrary-
wise*, my second sister, Margaret, a bed-ridden cripple, witnessed the
unrelenting recession of our family's fortunes stoically from her pallet
by the coke-stove. My younger brother Thaddeus Benjamin had the
skin slowly peeled from his body for the sole offense of stuttering at
the supper-table—; Ezekiel—my counterpart in the Dorne house-
hold—was never, to my knowledge, so much as shat on by a pigeon.
My third sister, Isabel, was set upon, while still quite young, by a hungry sow and horribly disfigured. Each of the Dorne boys, contrary-
wise, received a trained jacarundi at their confirmation, with a
pearl-and-moleskin collar on which the Declaration of Independence,
in its entirety, had been embroidered in platinum thread. Esperanza,
our youngest, was seized by my grandfather in a fit of syphilitic delir-
ium, taken hold of by the ears, and repeatedly, mercilessly—"

At this instant the preacher's litany was cut short by the sobs of a
woman to the left side of the pulpit. With a wink to the assembled
crowd, he turned to her.

"You there," he said. "You, little mother! Would you venture to
affirm that you know your scripture?"

I could just make out the back of the woman's head, if I stood on
tip-toe. It shook a little, but she answered confidently enough—:

"I believe I do, preacher."

"We'll see what you believe," the preacher said. His voice was low
and reverent. Holding his right hand aloft, he intoned—:

THEIR EYES STAND OUT WITH FATNESS:
THEY HAVE MORE THAN HEART COULD WISH.

"Who is being discussed here?" he asked, looking not at the woman but over her black-bonneted head at the rest of us. A light was beginning to kindle in his eyes.

"The wicked," the woman answered promptly.

"The *wicked*," the preacher repeated for our benefit. He coughed once into his sleeve. "Recognize them, do you, from that description?"

"I haven't—beg pardon, I recognize their manner from it," the woman said. "I'd know them by their *ways*, sir, yes."

"Your familiarity, sister, with the ways and manners of the *wicked* is duly noted," the preacher said. A ripple of laughter ran through the tent. "Pray continue your declamation for us."

The woman said nothing, shaking her head more resolutely now.

"No?" said the preacher, frowning. "Nothing? Shall we give you more? Good—; we'll give you more." He ran his finger slowly, almost coquettishly, down the page.

THEY ARE CORRUPT, AND SPEAK WICKEDLY CONCERNING OPPRESSION: THEY SPEAK LOFTILY.

He paused again. The tent was as silent, in that moment, as a genuine church might have been. The woman was one of a small, severely clothed handful at the very front who looked to be the only persons there to have opened the Holy Book—; the others, by the look of them, were in the habit of passing their Sabbath-days in decidedly looser collars. The preacher smiled and shifted his balance on the crate.

"I don't follow, sir," the woman said, looking to either side of her in perplexity. "I don't see that I warrant—"

"'They set their mouths against the heavens,'" the preacher hissed, glaring down at her as though the Antichrist were hiding in her bonnet—: "'They set their mouths against the heavens, and their tongue walketh through the earth.'" There! What is the lesson in *that*, little mother-in-Jesus?" He stepped—or rather teetered—back from the edge of the crate as he spoke, holding the small glossy book above him like a tomahawk. I saw now that it was a cheap brush-peddler's copy, the sort passed out at every river-landing. "'Their tongue WALKETH through the earth,'" he sang out, slapping the binding smartly with his palm. "Psalm 73, one–nine!"

The woman made no attempt at a reply. The bonnet hid her face from us, but it was plain that she was weeping. The preacher looked down at her contentedly. He was a puzzle to us all, and an entertainment—; but he was more than that. He was a revelation. To the woman in front of him, of course, he was no less than a scourge.

"'Their tongue walketh through the earth,'" he said once more, almost too quietly to hear.

Just then a scuffling began outside the tent. No-one else seemed to take note of it, though the sound was irregular and bright. Perhaps the preacher did, however, as he suddenly stood bolt upright and sucked in a solemn breath. In spite of his exceeding smallness—or perhaps because of it—this act had a tragic nobility that was irresistible. It seemed as if he were about to embark, with gentility and grace, upon a long and sweetly rendered discourse on human suffering.

Instead he hurled himself down at the stricken woman, buffeting the air with the little book, his thin voice sharpening to a shriek—:

"It's ME, of course, little mother-in-Jesus! *Me!* Can't you find me in that scrap of doggerel? Can't you make out my silhouette? Do *my* eyes not stand out with fatness? Does pride not compass *me* about? Have *I* not set my mouth against the heavens? Answer! Have I not spoken loftily?"

He tossed the book aside and caught the woman about the waist, pulling a pocket-mirror from his coat and bringing it within a hair's-breadth of her face—:

"The lesson, little mother, is not to go rooting about for sweet-meats when your bowels were meant for oats."

The woman's body slumped forward slightly, as though the wind had gone out of it. The preacher's next words came out very like a hymn—:

LOOK UPON YOUR CUD-CHEWING NATURE,
BLESSED OF JAHWEH, AND BE CONTENT.

The image of him in that instant is graven onto my memory like acid onto copper-plate. He stood stock-still before the woman, one arm hidden among the starched pleats of her dress, the other holding the mirror aloft that the entire tent might peer into it. He was a good deal smaller than his victim and there was something about him of the supplicant and the school-boy even as he stared up into her eyes, his face a patch-work of malice, exultation, and heaven knows what species of desire. The rest of the women buried their faces in their shawls—; the men howled at the pulpit like heifers at a branding.

No-one had made a move as yet, however. All stood looking on abjectly, stiffly, breaking away in a great show of disgust only to look back at once, helpless as babes in their curiosity. Some of the men had begun, without being aware of it, to leer. The sermon had done its work—: in the space of five minutes the assembly under the tent—which at first had borne at least a skin-deep resemblance to a gathering of the faithful—had been exposed as a carnival of mawkishness and lust. A dream-like stillness overcame me, the stillness of astonishment, weighing down my awareness and my limbs—; I turned back sleepily to face the pulpit. The preacher was now clutching the woman's head by its tight, revivalist bun and fumbling with the fly-button of his britches.

In the blink of an eye the crowd swung shut on them like a gate. I fought my way forward with all my strength—; just as I reached the pulpit, however, shouts rang out behind me and the gate swung open as inexorably as it had closed. The preacher and his catechist had vanished. A tide of bewildered faces swept me out onto the grass—: it was the better part of a minute before I was able to get my bearings. When at last I did, I couldn't suppress a laugh—: along the edge of the tent lay a row of cast-off saddles, ranged neatly side-by-side in the weeds. Of the thirty-odd horses there was not the slightest trace.

Neither, when I made my way back inside, was there any sign of the "Redeemer." A throng of bloodless-looking men stood packed together at the pulpit, cursing and whispering to one another—; it was impossible to guess whether he'd escaped or been bustled off to the nearest fork-limbed tree. A deep and righteous violence prevailed. A number of suspicious looks were directed toward me, on account of my ragged river-clothes—: I came to my senses, turned my back on the lot of them, and slunk quietly back to my skiff. Only when I was well out on the water did I notice the thick, oily throbbing of my brain, as though I'd spent the last hour drinking mash.

From Parson's Day-Book.

What is America? What is it for?

America is a covenant, John Bunyan said.

America is a race-horse, Robert E. Lee said. A fine proud dappled horse, with a silver harness.

America is a balloon, Abraham Lincoln said. If you cut one piece out of it, the rest sputters out the gap. No piece shall be cut out of this balloon.

America is a cutlet, the Redeemer said.

Certain of us agreed.

A Pair of Boots.

I T WAS A PAIR OF BOOTS THAT DAMNED ME, Virgil says.

After the camp meeting I spent two days out in the middle of the river, drifting in no particular hurry toward Fort Pillow, Mississippi, where a cousin of mine had recently been elected rat-catcher. That thimbleful of destiny which is portioned out to each of us, however, had finally been bestowed on me, and there was to be no side-stepping it. On the third day I laid up in the little cropper's hamlet of Stoker's Bluff, whose landing lolled darkly out over the water—: I was reminded, pulling in, of the passage in Asaph's psalm about the tongues of the wicked. Perhaps it was this that enticed me to put in there—; perhaps it was hunger. No matter. At the first house I called at I found the Redeemer.

The house was in fact a plain buck-board hotel, unpainted and porchless, with a bar of sorts giving out onto the street. I saw him at once behind an unmade table in the corner, stockinged feet stretched lazily toward the fire. I mistook him, in the gloom, for the bar-boy—; as I passed him, however, he turned to face the fire and the room was suddenly flooded in a cold, pale light.

"Preacher—?" I mumbled.

He gave no reply. The bar was empty save for the Redeemer, the bar-keeper, and myself. The object of my fascination was so fascinated, in turn, by our host's least interaction with the bottles, steins, and barrel-heads of his trade that for a good stretch of time he took no notice of me at all. The table in front of him was not so bare as I'd supposed—: three wooden cups were set diagonally across it. Every so often he'd select one of the cups, seemingly at random, and raise it dreamily to his lips. When at last he marked my stare, the eyes he turned on me were the same two glittering poke-holes I remembered from the revival tent, his face the same blend of austerity and malice. There was no mistaking the Redeemer. It spite of this, it came as a surprise when he opened his mouth and, seemingly without moving his lips, said deliberately and slowly—:

"What are you gawking at, google-eye? Never seen a child of six sucking on a dram?"

The bar-keeper snorted belligerently. I mumbled something unintelligible, skittish as a fawn under the Redeemer's sudden scrutiny. I'd never felt a thing to match it—: a cold, ill-meaning, stone-faced glare, but far from an indifferent one—*passionately* interested, in fact, with a school-boy's curiosity suffusing his yellow, puff-cheeked school-boy's face. Returning his look, I was struck by a vision of myself laid out naked on a pallet, my hands bound or pinned behind me, in mute anticipation of a surgery performed with the dullest possible tools. The effect of this waking dream, which fled as suddenly as it came, was terrifying beyond words.

The Redeemer registered it all without surprise.

"Struck dumb? Don't fret, google-eye—; you're not the first. I'm a curious-looking whoreson, heaven knows."

"I've seen you before," I said at last.

For an instant this seemed to discomfit him. "Is that so?" he said, glancing toward the bar-keeper. "Whereabouts?"

"At Lafitte's Chute. I saw you preach."

At first he seemed not to have understood me—; then, very gradually, a smile gathered at his mouth-corners.

"Lafitte's Chute, you say?" His voice had a new quality to it now, one of sly bravado. "Tell us about it, pilgrim. Did you care much for our sermon?"

I broke with his look, struggling to compose a suitable reply. Already I was coming under his influence. "I liked your sermon well enough," I said, venturing an ironic smile. "But then, I didn't come on horse-back."

"What?" said the Redeemer. His face was blank as milk.

"I reckon it served its purpose."

His expression grew slightly pinched. "Ah! And what purpose was that, by your reckoning?"

My smile began to wilt. "I reckon, sir, that those horses—"

"Now look *here*, you cripple-faced river muck," the Redeemer bellowed, slamming down his cup like a gavel. "Did you *once* look me in the face when I was on that pulpit?"

"I looked—; yes," I managed to reply.

"You *looked*! Well, then! Didn't you see me?" He was standing up now on the ricketing bench, swaying from side to side like a squirrel on its hind-quarters. "Didn't you see me weep?"

The bench teetered frantically under his weight—: he was obliged to flutter his arms wildly to keep from falling over. He looked for all the world on the verge of weeping *now*. I kept my eyes fixed on the bench. It looked to have been pilfered from a school-house, or possibly even from a church.

"I saw you make your introductions to that poor spinster," I said, mustering my last courage.

"I'll tell you *once*, and once only, google-eye," the Redeemer said, sitting reluctantly back down. "I meant every word I preached at Lafitte's Chute."

"To be honest, sir, I wouldn't care a damn—"

"I'll thank you not to use *curse-words* in my presence!" he shrieked at the top of his voice, his face going purple and white by turns.

This last utterance so bewildered me that I was unable to make any reply to it at all.

"Who was this spinster, then?" the bar-keeper called over after a time. Though still a young man, as far as I could judge, his face was creased like the skin of an old potato. He moved stiffly and drunkenly. "Put the fear of Guh!—Guh!—God into her, did you, Reverend?"

The Redeemer laughed. "I made the Word flesh for her passingly, Kennedy—; that's all it was." He turned to me and winked. "What's your drink, pilgrim?"

"Rye," I said cautiously, expecting some new paroxysm. But the Redeemer simply kicked a stool toward me. I sat down on it gingerly.

"Where do you hail from?" he asked, pushing a pint-flask across the table.

"Kansas," I answered. In his last question I'd again heard the patois of the river-flats. I poured myself a middling swallow. "Yourself, sir? I'd guess from your accent—"

"*Kansas!*" he crowed. "Well, I'll be a bare-assed injun! I'd have taken you for one of our own, God's truth!"

For some reason I blushed at this. "I've been on the river for quite some time, Mr.—"

"How old are you, Kansas?"

"Twenty-five."

He nodded. "And what was your father, in the territories?"

"A distributor of the Holy Writ." I stared down into my cup. "Not unlike yourself."

"Ha! Of a different caliber *altogether*, by your way of talking, sir." He grinned. "Quite a thing, in these parts, to come across a river-rat that talks like a king's bishop. Eh, Kennedy?"

The bar-keeper waved a hand, whether in agreement or indifference I could not have said. The Redeemer's eyes bored into me as before. I felt sullen and restless under their attention, like a cow in need of milking—; there was a quality to the Redeemer's interest, however, that was more flattering than any compliment could have been. Question followed question in a fevered rush. He was not simply curious about my life—; he was intoxicated by its most trifling detail. As terrifying as his interest was, it was as undeniable as the packed-earth floor beneath us. My loneliness—the steady companion of my last years—cooked away, as we spoke, like hot oil on a skillet. I'd not have got up from that table for my weight in Spanish ivory.

"Your father, Kansas," the Redeemer said, raising his cup to his lips. "What might have been his church?"

I'd not spoken of my father since the night I'd left his house. "Methodist," I said.

"Meth-o-dist," he echoed, still holding the cup suspended. "What rank?"

I hesitated a moment. "Prelate."

The Redeemer sat forward and whistled. "A *prelate*! Tidy house and garden attached to *that*, if I'm not mistaken." He regarded me narrowly. "Am I mistaken?"

"You are not."

He smiled at me. "Not much of a talker, are you, Kansas."

I shook my head, trying not to redden.

"I assume that's *your* church, then? Methodist?"

I'd been expecting this question—been looking forward to it, in fact—and drew myself up with my best attempt at dignity. "I belong to *no* church, sir. I am a student of Spinoza and Descartes."

To my chagrin this entertained him mightily. "A *rationalist*! Well, I'll be dipped in butter!" He studied me even more intently than before—: some new thought seemed to have crept into his mind. "A firm believer in *God-in-man*, then, I suppose?"

"I am a believer, sir, in the scientific method." I straightened in my seat, painfully aware of my sack-cloth shirt and britches.

His gaze, if possible, grew even keener. "And nothing else besides?"

"Nothing, sir. I consider myself a scholar."

"Been away from your books for some time, by the look of you."

I took a sip of whiskey. "Six years."

"Had much luck, have you, in that time? Got your little pile together?"

I spread my arms. "You see before you, sir, the whole of my estate."

He clucked his tongue and nodded. "That doesn't surprise me, Kansas. The teachings of Descartes are well and good for the *old* country—; but here they just don't churn the butter. This nation was founded on belief—credulity pure and simple—just as the great French Republic was founded on skepticism. Faith, whatever clothes you put it in, is the corner-stone of our Union. You're an American, sirrah—; not an Egyptian or a Swede. Without an understanding of belief—without a *sympathy* for it, a talent for it—you will never make your penny." He shook his head. "No, my friend! The Enlightenment is not for us."

"Evidently," I said faintly.

The Redeemer held up a hand. "Not because it isn't *interesting*—; don't get peevish. I'm sure it's a rare delight, this rationalism of yours. It's just not useful—; not to me." He leaned forward till his chin rested on the table. His voice, already mellow with drink, dropped to a satisfied whisper. "*Belief*, contrary-wise, is. Belief flows through this country like a river. There's not a thing to match it. Compared to belief, Kansas, the Mississippi is a trickle down a pant-leg."

I smiled at this—; how could I help but smile? The Redeemer's face, however, showed no hint of its earlier mischief. I took a careful sip of rye.

"That's all it's ever been to me," I said.

He sat back on his bench and nodded, a nod that carried over at some point to a slight, nervous bobbing of the head. "Tell me something else, prelate's boy," he said after a time. He raised a finger tentatively, almost shyly, and pointed at my left eye. "Was it Papa knocked that eye-ball of yours crooked?" He took my cup from me and refilled it. "Was he no follower of Descartes?"

This question, so simple and direct, made the floor shift subtly beneath my feet. I'd gone so long without thinking about my father that even his face had grown vague to me—; I hoped, one day, to forget it altogether. The Redeemer had asked the history of my eye, however, and I was helpless to refuse him. It took three cups more for me to tell it—; when at last I did, the words had a dry, uncertain sound, as though the years had leached the meaning out of them.

"My father endeavored—to corrupt me, you might say. I refused to be corrupted."

"*Corrupt* you?" the bar-keeper said, leaning brazenly over the bar to gawk at me. "Come at you, did he? Come at you with his stiff little Muh!—Muh!—Methodist—"

"I was born a doubter," I said quickly. "I had no use for my father's eschatologies. That's all it was."

The Redeemer squinted at me. "His which?"

"His views on the end of the world."

"Ah!" His squint changed, subtly, to a grin. "You preferred that the world *not* end, I take it?"

"Not just then."

"And that's when he stuck his foot in your eye?" the Redeemer said blithely.

In six years no-one had mentioned my eye at all, let alone asked its whyfores. The topic was skirted around with no small measure of distaste by everyone I met with on the river, on account of its being my left eye, white as a boiled egg, and terrible to look at—; it was taken for a hex by old and young alike. Before me, however, was a man who not only considered my disfigurement fit subject for a fire-side chat, but plainly wanted to talk of nothing else. As I related the history of my escape from my father's house, ploddingly and with no end of pauses, it became clear that he held my eye in the highest possible esteem. Again and again his attention, diverted by this or that trifle, would swing back to it like the door of a saloon—:

"That *eye* of yours, now, Mr. Ball—: can you see aught out of it?"

"Very little."

"But you *do* see?"

I gave a deprecatory shrug. "If it pleases you to call it seeing."

His eyes moistened with excitement. "Describe it for us."

I hesitated. "I can't make out anything at all, stupidly, unless the other's closed—"

"The hell you say!"

"—and when I do close it, I see only in a shadowy sort of way, as if through the bottom of a bottle. Not much light gets in." I tapped the side of my head forlornly.

"No shapes?" said the Redeemer. He went quiet a moment. "No—forms of any sort?"

I shrugged. "Sometimes I can make out forms. The *idea* of forms, better said." I smiled at him. "As in Plato's cave."

"I see," he murmured. "Perhaps, however, your vision will improve?"

For the first time since I'd left home, a man of intelligence—however eccentric—had taken an interest in me. And what an interest! In my loneliness and gullibility I practically did the work of seduction for him. The Redeemer had only to open his mouth, like a crocodile, and let me totter in. What's more, in some back larder of my brain, unconquered as yet by his whiskey and his guile, I knew this full and well. Had I guessed what lay in store for me—the killings, the privations, the final apocalypse in Memphis—I might have recovered myself in time. Or perhaps not. It was clear enough, staring into his narrow, sharp-eyed face, that he didn't mean me well.

"Where are your shoes?" I asked, pointing at his feet. His stockings were dusted with ash from the fire.

"Lost," he said flatly.

I grinned at him. "However will you preach?"

"Don't fret on account of my *stockings*, Kansas. My boys are bringing round a pair of boots directly." As he said this his eyes fell, seemingly idly, to my own feet—; but he found nothing there to tempt him. "With luck, they may have something in your size," he added. He jerked his chin toward the bar. "Kennedy's already placed his order. Haven't you, Kennedy?"

"Just so they pull the fuh!—fuh!—feet out of them first," Kennedy said. The Redeemer guffawed. Looking from one of them to the other, it seemed to me that I was in the company of two boastful and precocious children.

The Redeemer stared down into his little cup of rye, seemingly forgetting me altogether. For the first time it occurred to me that he might possibly be drunk. There was a candle between us and he brought his own left eye close to it, holding it open with his fingers, as if to demonstrate its beauty and its health. An instant later he sat up with a start. His greasy, half-fermented breath seemed to stain the air between us.

"Come in on a boat of some stripe, did you, Kansas?"

"Yes," I lied. Why I did this I can't say—; there was only the conviction that the canoe, the one thing of value that I owned, should be kept from him.

"What boat?" the Redeemer said, still studying his cup.

"A stern-wheeler from Natchez." I took a breath. "Put me off at Thompson's farm."

His eyes met mine. "I didn't hear of any boat passing," he said. "What landing was it?"

"I told you," I answered hurriedly. "Back up the river—three miles or so—family name of Thompson—"

At this moment the door was shouldered open and three men entered, shambling and sullen-faced, dragging a fourth between them. Catching sight of the Redeemer, they stopped and laid their burden, whose head was wrapped in a muslin sheet, down in the middle of the room. One of them called out to Kennedy in a tired voice and he commenced drawing drafts of beer. All eyes came to rest on the Redeemer.

"You—: Harvey. Take off that swaddling," the Redeemer said, rising from the table.

The man on the floor was arching his body with a languid, reptilian slowness, like a snake crushed under a cart-wheel. His head in its wrapping looked like a ball of fresh-ginned cotton waiting to be spun. Where the cloth met his shoulders a circlet of blood, the thickness and consistency of pig-suet, glistened in the fire-light. The man the Redeemer had spoken to pulled the cloth away in three easy jerks.

"This was Tull," the Redeemer said thoughtfully.

The face thus revealed was split from forehead to chin like a kindling-wedge—: the two halves fell away from the wound as though forswearing any knowledge of it. Blood welled and receded in time to the body's tiny, bird-like breaths. That there should be life behind that face was unthinkable—; but there was more than life. There was understanding. To either side of the gash, at its profoundest point, blue eyes looked out through a film of milk-white tears, blinking and trembling and rolling, flitting from one of our faces to the next. But always and again, as if at the tugging of a wire, they interrupted their circuit to fix beseechingly on the Redeemer.

With what emotion the Redeemer returned Tull's look I couldn't tell. I'd turned away from them both by then, fighting the urge to faint, holding on to the table for dear life. When at last I dared look, I saw only the Redeemer's girlish back, and the faces of the three men watching him. They were cowed, spiteful, worshipful faces.

"Some manner of hatchet, was it?" the Redeemer said blandly.

"Shovel," the man called Harvey mumbled. He spoke with a high, cloying lisp.

"Ah!" said the Redeemer. He chewed this over for a moment. "Where was he done?"

I could see only the left half of Harvey's face in the fire-light. It was a weak-looking face, soft and all but chinless—; a tendon along his jaw-line tensed, relaxed, then tensed again. "Lawson's farm," he answered. His voice was brittle as a biscuit.

"Lawson's *farm*," the Redeemer said, turning the word over in his mouth. "What were you looking for at Lawson's, boys?" He turned to look at each of them in turn. "Not my boots, I take it?"

The faces assumed identical shame-faced looks.

"It's been near on a month," a stooped-over man to the left of Harvey said. "We'd thought possibly to pick up—"

"What you'll pick up at *Lawson's*, Johnson, is a dose of the private sorrows," the Redeemer said. "And if that's all you catch, consider yourself blessed of the Lord."

"You left your own boots there," the third man said in a quavering voice.

"What?" said the Redeemer, spinning about to face him. "What was *that*, now?"

The man's mouth opened and closed to no discernible effect. The Redeemer took a few steps toward him, stared up a while into the poor fellow's face, then reached quickly up and caught hold of his nose. The man let out a bright chirp of terror.

"Crangle, isn't it?" the Redeemer said quietly.

"It is, Your Honor," the man managed to reply.

"Don't neglect the small hairs that project from your nostrils, Crangle—; or those that grow about the apertures of the ears. Such small matters of the toilet are often overlooked." He let the man loose and glanced over his shoulder at the bar. "Am I right in saying so, Mr. Kennedy?"

"Ay," Kennedy answered without looking up.

The man kept quiet for an instant, then took a deep breath and pointed at Tull's feet. "Beg pardon, sir, but them's your boots, I think."

The Redeemer spun back toward the man, raising a hand to strike him—; then he stopped short, cocked his head, and looked at Tull. "Fry me for a chitterling!" he muttered. "Those *are* my little mollies."

"Tull took 'em off Lawson," Harvey put in. "Lawson took offense."

The Redeemer was already pulling on the first boot. "What happened to Lawson?" he said, bracing a foot against Tull's groin.

The third man made an indecipherable gesture with his hand. *"Pffft,"* he said. Harvey shook his head sweetly.

"Lend us a hand, Kansas," the Redeemer said, tugging at my sleeve. As he did so I saw a vision of myself springing to my feet, throwing him aside and dashing head-long out the door. My skiff lay just at the bottom of the bluff—; I might easily have reached it. But I sat quiet as an owl.

"Ball!"

I looked up at him in alarm. "Present!" I stammered.

He smiled at me benignly. "Feeling a bit green?"

Before I could answer I found myself kneeling on the floor, holding Tull by the shoulders while the Redeemer worked a boot free. Tull was utterly unresisting now—: after a moment I realized he was dead. As the boot came away, exposing a filthy, butter-colored calf, a network of intersecting blue lines caught my attention. I raised the cuff of Tull's trousers a half-inch further, disclosing the following design, not much larger than my thumb—:

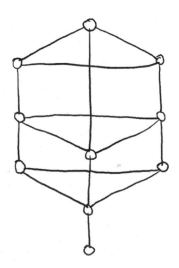

"Ball," said the Redeemer softly.

"Yes?"

"I asked whether you were feeling green."

I passed a hand over my face. "What's that mark there, on his leg?"

"Ah! *That*," he said, stifling a yawn. "That's an old Choctaw figure. They were fond of scratching it into boulders, I believe."

The figure was familiar to me somehow. Its pedigree hovered playfully along the margins of my thought, refusing to come forward into the light.

"Who told you it was Choctaw?" I asked.

"A colleague of mine—; a parson," the Redeemer said, spitting on the boot and polishing its uppers with his sleeve.

"I've seen that figure before." I endeavored in vain to catch his eye. "Do you know anything else about it?"

He sniffed at the boot's lining and made a face. "Some consider it an ideograph for 'ladder,'" he said distractedly.

"What sort of ladder?" A moment more and I'd remember. "Leading where?"

The Redeemer stopped fussing with the boot and frowned at me. "There are more things on heaven and earth, Kansas, than a one-eyed prelate's boy can see."

But I'd already remembered. "The Tree of Life!" I said, a good deal louder than I'd meant to. Kennedy and the others turned and stared. "The Tree of Life. That's what that figure is," I said again, more quietly. "My father had a picture of it. In a book."

"That may well be what it spells for *you*, Kansas," the Redeemer said crisply. "For Tull, contrary-wise, it spelled something else entirely."

"I know that symbol, sir," I said, surprised at my own stubbornness. "It comes from the kabala. That's a book of Jewish scripture."

"You *have* done some book-reading, in your time," the Redeemer said, taking a boot in each hand and banging them together. "Nevertheless, you're up the wrong tree altogether."

He set the boots down and climbed into them. They were much too large for him: he wore them as a boy might wear his father's slippers. He stood up, a good four inches taller than he'd been, and did a pirouette in front of me, kicking the boots up gaucho-style for me to admire. "What do you think, Kansas! Hey?"

I thought he looked like a trained raccoon. "They're very fetching, sir," I said.

He smiled at me with genuine affection. "You're not too proud a man. I'll say that much for you, Virgil Ball."

"I've done nothing to be proud of," I replied.

He stamped his foot at this. "For *shame*, Kansas! You're a philosopher and a scholar, are you not? A veteran of six years on the Mississippi? A rationalist? A man of the world?"

"The world might dispute it, sir."

"Never mind the world, then," he said, taking me by the shoulder. "Let's confine ourselves to this stinking crick of ours. There's not much call for an educated man round these parts, as you well know. A *worldly* man, on the other hand . . ." His eyes twinkled into mine. "Can you read chicken-scratch, prelate's boy?"

"I've been schooled in it," I said, unsure of him again. I sensed another question hidden behind the first.

"You can cipher?"

I nodded.

"And you're a Jew by birth?"

This confounded me anew. "What on earth makes you think so?"

He jerked his chin at Tull. "You saw a Jewy symbol on the man's shin-bone. I saw nothing but a doodle."

I cleared my throat. "With due respect, sir, my recognition of that figure—"

"You are a Jew by birth?" he said again, narrowing his eyes.

I kept still a moment longer. "My mother was born Jewish, sir—; so I suppose I am, by the scriptures' definition."

"Excellent!" the Redeemer crowed. Why this was excellent to him I never understood. He extended a finger in the direction of the body stretched out at our feet and gave me a solemn wink. "Tull, here, was the scholar of our little company. Gracious knows you're a hard man to look at, Mr. Ball, and as handy with cadavers as a box of smoke—; but you evidently know your letters, and we're in dire need of a scribbler. You'll fill old Tull's boots, given time." He reached up, grinning like a possum, and took hold of me by both ears, squeezing them till my eyes watered—:

"If you behave yourself, Kansas, I might even let you *wear* them."

Samuel Clemens.

Jesse] James's modest genius dreamed of no loftier flight than the planning of raids upon cars, coaches, and country banks. The R—— projected negro insurrections and the capture of New Orleans; and furthermore, on occasion, this R—— could go into a pulpit and edify the congregation. What are James and his half-dozen vulgar rascals compared with this stately old-time criminal, with his sermons, his meditated insurrections and city-captures, and his majestic following of ten hundred men, sworn to do his evil will!

In a Brothel.

LOVE CAME TO ME LATE AND HATEFUL, Clementine says. I was standing at the bed with my arms held toward the door when he came in. A cart had tipped over on Chartres Street making a fearful racket and I'd raised my arms to close the shutters, so when he walked in it was as if I'd put them out to receive him—: as if I'd been schooled in the service of that moment and no other. He stopped and mumbled some odd thing and colored. He was passable to look at, comely in his way, but for that eye of his—; that eye made a fright of him. The R—— was just behind him in the hall.

He stood bolted to the floor turning his hat in his fingers, like so many of them do on their first come-round. After a piece he stepped to one side so the R—— could come in. But the R—— stayed where he was.

"Clem," said the R—— in his sham-lofty tone of voice. "This here is Virgil Ball, from Kansas. You two get familiar."

"I'm half-dead, Your Holiness," I said. "I petition you for clemency."

"And I petition you for Clemen*tine*," the R—— said. He laughed.

I shrugged my shoulders.

"I'll be needing the whist room tonight," he said. Then he turned with a squeak of his high leather heels.

"The whist room?" I said. I'd just got up from bed and was barely loused and powdered. It was always that way with the R——: he had a way with the darkies downstairs and liked to come up unannounced.

"You'd best ask Madame!" I said. But the R—— was already down the hall and gone.

That left the two of us to look each other over. There was plenty to look at, Jesus knows, with his dead eye knocked backwards in his face and his queer way of shuffling about. There'd been a time, when I was yet a girl, that I'd have sent him off with nary but a laugh. But that was once.

"Sit down off your feet, Mr. Ball," I said.

"I'm beholden, miss," he answered, putting down his hat. That voice of his gave me a turn. Like the voice of an attorney-at-law, or a gentleman poet, but given over to a fool. I'd made a game of finding a thing to hate in each man who came to Madame Lafargue's quimhouse but that voice of his, like the rustling-together of fancy parchments, got inside of me and settled. I hated that voice straightaway.

"Sit where you like," I said, going to the shutters though the racket had largely stopped.

"Thank you kindly, miss."

I looked at him sharply. "My name, sir, is Clementine."

"I know," he said. He pointed back over his shoulder. "He's told me most of what there is to tell about you, I reckon."

I gave him a smile that would have frighted away any but a first-timer. "Mr. Myrell is a great visitor to this house, Mr. Ball—; but he rarely visits *me*. I can't see what he could have told you." I went to the vanity, keeping my front toward him so he'd not see me from behind without my stays. "Why don't you sit?"

"Beholden," he said in his fuddled way. He sat down on the day-bed and began taking off his boots. Now here's a man, I thought. Already pulling his gear off like a share-holder. The boots were spattered with muck from the street, but I saw that they were new and of a fine, creamy leather.

"Will you be needing help with your britches buttons?" I asked, thinking to see him turn colors again. But no such thing happened.

"He told me I'd find you lovely," he said, kicking his boots under the bed. "He told me that."

"Don't go trifling, Mr. Ball."

"I think you are the most beautiful thing I've ever laid eye on." He covered his blighted eye, then, and grinned at me with the other.

With the leer on his face he looked like a Red Indian. I thought—: If your talk was as ugly as your face, Mr. Ball, or your face as pretty as your talk, we might pass an easy hour. I suddenly found him pleasing to look at, save for that eye of his. "And that's why you're in such a hurry to get out of your pants, Mr. Ball—; is that it?"

"It is," he answered. "You do a brisk business here, don't you, miss?"

I looked at his face. It was grave as a deacon's. "Brisk enough," I answered.

"Then I should get out of my britches briskly," he said. "Before you might be called away."

I had my back to him just then, touching perfume to my neck and bubbies. Turning round I saw him looking at me as I knew he would—: squintish but keenly, out of his good blue eye.

"There'd be another girl in here before you could say Jackson," I said quietly. "If I was called away."

"Other sins for other sinners," he said, giving me the leer. It was then I could see he'd passed time with the R——.

The R—— came less than some, but from the day he'd first climbed the filigreed steps he'd carried on as if the house was his own green acre. He paid in coin always, never in paper. And he was free-thinking with his money. Some girls were amused on account of his smallishness but it never discouraged him and they forgot it quick enough. He'd come to me but once, and then only to watch me get fixed. He must have been thinking of me for his darling Virgil even then.

"Did you bring your French letters, Mr. Ball?" I asked.

His eyes went wide and starting. "I don't speak French."

"French *letters*. Envelopes. For your—" I made a gesture.

His eyes went wider yet. "What would *that* need an envelope for?"

A farmer's boy, I thought. Or a brother from St. Benedict's. "Just bring one along next time." I winked at him. "Or two."

He was still staring down at his britches. "France must be a singular nation," he said at last.

"I wouldn't know to tell," I said. I went and pulled the shutters closed. "Have you ever been with a working lady, Mr. Ball?"

"I don't recall," he said, avoiding my look. "Virgil, miss, is my Christian name." So saying he undid his britches and let them drop.

I stopped short in the middle of the room. "Mother of Providence," I murmured.

His face went flat. "I can't help the way I'm fashioned," he said quietly.

I laughed at him then! I couldn't help but laugh. He'd never been with any sort of girl at all—I knew that now. "Don't curse your lot too hard, sirrah. The Lord might reconsider."

He blinked both eyes at this—: his blue one and his white. "Do you mean to say—"

"Pay me no mind," I said, throwing back the bed-covers. They'd not been aired and as I parted them they gave off a sour, pricklish smell—; but he made no gesture or remark. I smiled at him. "Step out of your trappings, Virgil, if you're ready."

But my laughter had unsteadied him and he stood mute and stone-bodied by the bed. Had he not dropped his bottoms I might have found reason to laugh again—; but there were qualities to his naked self would have commanded respect in any house of fun in Louisiana.

"This room has a peculiar smell to it," he said after a time. He turned about in a circle, sniffing. "Is it coming from the street?"

As I watched him the memory of my first day in that house came out of the dark and brushed me. The smell of it. A chicken-yard smell, sourish and stifling. The noises half-muffled by the thin cane doors. I'd sat on the iron steps for half the day, tracing the arabesques and curls. I was a girl even then—; I knew I was. But a little girl no longer.

"It's the smell of the house," I said. "You'll get adjusted." I patted the sheets. "Come over here to me."

When he came to the bed he seemed to remember why he'd taken off his pants. He reached out and slid the night-shirt off my shoulders. "I don't mind a bit of laughter," he said. "I've been laughed at before. I'm well out from under my mother's skirts."

"How old are you?" I asked, pulling him down.

"Twenty-seven."

A moment passed, no longer than a breath, and I was ready.

He was lying beside me now and I undid the rest of the buttons. "Kiss me, Virgil," I said, laying his hands on my belly. He obeyed with a singular will and the hour passed quicker than many I'd spent in that house. He was one of those whose first pass is slow and arduous and nearly without release, but he had a patience with himself that took me quite aback. I'd expected a rough time of it from the look of him, but he handled me as though I was one of his fancy parchments. When it was done he asked, as so many of them do, what was my reckoning of it and I said I imagined there to be some small hope. He seemed satisfied with that for an answer.

DIRECTLY HE'D FINISHED I went to the night-pot and had a wash. He watched me like I was turning pig-shite into beer. I made a face at him. "Find this very appetizing, do you?"

"It's an education to me, miss," he said.

"Come over here, then. I'll educate you something more. Bring that bottle with you. There—: that one, from the night-stand."

He did as he was told.

"Unscrew the top of it." I turned a cart-wheel then, and stood up on my hands.

"Catch hold of me now!" I said. "Catch hold of me with your hand. There! Keep the bottle in the other, mind."

"Do you do this with every caller?" he asked, gawking down at me.

"With every one that forgets his envelopes," I answered. "That's poison in that bottle, Mr. B."

"Poison?" he stammered. "Ma'am—I mean to say, Miss Clementine—"

"It's a *caution*, you silly man! That's all." I opened up my legs. "Now! Pour it on my shemmy."

And he did.

"There," I said. "Now you've gotten your degree."

"I have at that," he said, and kissed my heel.

I was beginning to see his merits.

As there were no further callers that day we lay back down in bed, sipping rum-and-bitters, watching the afternoon roll over.

"I'd not have thought it was like *that*," he said.

"What?" I said. "The befores or the afters?"

"All of it." He smiled. "You'll laugh at me, miss. My ideas about it came from Byron."

"Who?" I said.

He looked at me. "George Gordon, Lord Byron," he said very slowly.

"I see," I said. "A *lord*. Is he another of your crew?"

He gave a little cough. "Byron is the bravest of our poets."

"We've never had any lords here, that I can remember. Some as claimed they were lords. I'll ask the girls—"

"Do you not read poetry at all?" he said. He sat up in the bed. "I have a book for you to read." His eyes were bright. "Books. I have several volumes—"

"Pray don't leave your volumes *here*, Mr. Ball. I want nothing with any volumes of yours, I'm sure."

"What?" he said. "What's that?" He looked as though I'd caught him at something. "Do you not read books?"

"You could teach me," I said. I said it the way I might have said—:

You could bring me my lousing-powder from the cupboard. But I said it just the same.

He went quieter than before. "Have you never learned at all," he said at last.

I rolled my eyes.

"But you speak elegantly," he said. "I wish I could speak half as elegantly as you."

"I'm not half-witted, Mr. Ball."

"No! Decidedly you aren't." He grinned.

He said nothing for a piece after that and when he did it was with the voice he'd used when he'd first stepped in. Could we have another try, he asked me, and of course I let him. But I wasn't to be fooled. Something had started him to thinking. He was thinking on it all the time he was having his way and when at last he'd spent, more properly this time, he still hadn't done with it.

We were lying just as we'd been before. From the hall came sounds of the whist room being readied for the R——.

"Why bring his fancy friends here?" I asked. "There's many finer accommodation-shops in the Quarter."

Virgil opened his good eye. "Ask me no questions, miss," he said.

I cursed him. "You've got no idea yourself," I said, hoping to shake an answer from him. "Your sweet R—— hasn't told you jack-all."

He looked at me sharply. "Why ask me, then, if you know his ways and means so well?"

I sat up very straight. "You have no idea? Really?"

He shook his head.

I laughed at him. "I see the kind of gang you've got. Does he tell you anything at all?"

He didn't answer straightaway. The noise of a trap and harness carried brightly up from the street. "It's me who tells *him* things," he said at last.

"What's that, Mr. B?" I laughed again. "Are you his privy counselor?"

"Look here," he said, and held his blighted eye open. "Closer." He took me by the shoulder. "This is how."

I looked into the eye, or what little I could see of it—: most of it was tucked under the lid. It peeped out at nothing like a new moon, jet-colored and set. I was in Tennessee once, where there was snow on the ground, and the meat of that eye was that very same color—: snow over a dark, empty rabbit-hole. I looked closer and saw my own pale face reflected.

"How like a piece of glass it is," I said. "A fine black aggie."

"That's what he keeps me for, miss," he said, giving me a wink. "I'm his champion marble."

I kept quiet and let him tell it.

"Once a day the R—— sends for me. He takes me somewhere dark, strikes a match, and holds it to my eye. When the match goes out I tell him what I see. I have to tell him straight off, without an instant's pondering. That's all. Once I've told him he goes off." Virgil rolled onto his side. "That's why he always keeps me by."

I stared at him. "And you believe in that? In what he puzzles out?"

Now his face did a funny turn—; I suppose he was trying to look dignified. "I'm a rationalist, miss," he said. "I have no faith in witchery."

But I was more curious about the R——. "The R—— tells you nothing?"

"Nothing I can use." He let out a breath. "I write things down for him—; he never learned to cipher."

"What sort of things?"

"I'll be in the whist room tonight," he said. "Taking the minutes."

It was my turn to give a crafty look. "So will I."

"The pox you will!"

"The whist room is *my* room on Thursdays."

"The R—— asked you?" His hand ran nervously along the coverlet.

"That room is mine on Thursdays, Mr. Ball. Your R—— comes here often enough to know."

But he wasn't to be quieted. "I wouldn't think we needed to be waited on, at this particular meeting," he said in a careful voice.

So he knows more than he tells, I thought to myself. He looks a fool but isn't.

"The R——'s not declined my services before," I said.

"He comes here often?" His voice went thick. "He comes to you?"

I smiled. "Why, Aggie? Would you mind?"

He straightened on the bed. "I don't mind dividing your attentions with—with the *rest*," he said. He rolled over to face the wall. "But I'd prefer—*not* to share you—with that particular man. I would prefer not to. Uh—"

"You're nothing but a horse-thief's opera-glass, Mr. Ball. You've no call to dictate anything to anybody. Least of all to me."

He got up fumblingly from the bed. "You understand me, I see," he said. His voice was flat and bloodless.

I felt pity for him then. I should have taken that for a sign. I should have known already.

"I'm sure I don't," I said. "Not yet." I held my arms out to him. "Come along back, Aggie, and explain."

He looked hard at me for a spell. Then he passed a hand over his face and sat down on the bed. We stayed like that a while, listening to the bustle from the street—; I might have fallen into a nap. When I opened my eyes he was watching me like a dog would watch a plate of marrow. A look like that ought to have riled me—; instead it made me feel as light as flax. Another sign. I found that I was pleased to have him by.

"How long have you been with the R——, Aggie?"

He smiled. "How funny that you call him by that name."

"We call him by whatever name he wants," I said.

"Yes, miss. So does everybody."

I laughed. "We get well paid for it." I gave him a coquettish look. "Can you say the same?"

He only sighed.

"How does the R—— make his money? Is it only horses?"

Virgil gave me a thoughtful look. "No," he said. "Not only horses."

The skin on the back of my neck prickled in a way that has never done me any good. "What else, then?" I said.

My eyes were closed but I could hear him fumbling for his shirt. "The whist room is yours?" he said.

I nodded. "That's where I receive my callers. If they don't ambush me, Aggie, in my private chambers."

"And you'll be receiving there tonight." The bed-springs squeaked as he got up.

I opened my eyes and watched him go. "I will."

He stood an arm's-length from the door, buttoning his shirt with slow twists of his thumb. "You'll have your answer soon enough, then, Clementine."

Asa Trist.

IN THE BEGINNING AMERICA WAS EMPTY, God said. There were no horses, God said. There were no cabins, God said. The air was quiet. The land was stupid—there were no noises in it, God said. There were no corn-fields, God said. There were no rice-fields, God said. There were no niggers.

There were no *Asas*, God said, to own them.

There were no women, God said. There were no horse-flies, God said. There was a quiet all around. There were no steam-boats, God said. There were no skiffs. There were no fathers, God said. There was this quiet, Asa. It was very black.

There were no armies, God said. There were no sparrows, God said. There were no serpents, God said. There were no catfishes in the river. The river was there, but it flowed quiet. The comings and goings were not in it. The air was stupid, God said. There were no sounds in it. It was a dead air, God said. And it was very sweet.

Sweet, I said. Yes! It was very sweet!

Then came the Asas, God said.

The Whist Room.

I GOT MY ANSWER THAT NIGHT, says Clementine. But not the way Virgil thought I would.

I'd expected a right crowd, what with all the to-do, but the whist room when I came in with my tray of chitterlings and beer held only seven men. I put the tray down on the felt-covered table and sat on a fainting-couch by the door. I recognized Virgil and the rough-neck Stuts Kennedy, who'd come to see me once. The rest were strangers to that house.

The R—— was speechifying—:

"A simple proposal, gentlemen, though you may find it hard to picture. It might be best, in beginning, to summarize the commerce in slaves and bondsmen as it functions this day and hour."

"We know that well enough," Kennedy said into his scruff.

"I wonder if you do, Mr. Kennedy," the R—— said. He was the same bundle of piss as always, the same little peacock, but no-one else seemed to see it—; and suddenly I found that I couldn't see it, either. He leaned back in his high-chair, gave an elegant sigh, and set his hands on the table. He might have been Napoleon on campaign.

"The states along the Mason-Dixon," he said at last, "have a marked glut in man-power—; the lower South, contrary-wise, suffers a desperate lack. For this reason, the slave trade, almost without exception, runs north to south. Although there's a demand upriver, the few-odd head required are not worth the dealers' trouble and often as not go unsupplied. In times of need, such slaves are acquired after much trouble and expense downriver in Natchez—; or, even more commonly, here in New Orleans." He smiled. "This, of course, is why our city has grown so fat."

He turned as he said this to a pallid-faced man whose eyes were as quick as Virgil's were quiet. "Not from your sugar plantations, Asa. Though not for want of every good intention."

"My father poured his blood into this ground," the man replied. His eyes went from face to face as though he expected to be laughed at. He hushed a moment, hiding under his ruffed black hair, then sputtered out—: "We are all of us Asas tonight, dear sirs! Every one of us in these chambers—"

"To the slaves *themselves*, however," the R—— interrupted, "nothing could be more dreadful than this fate of being barge-hauled down the river. The death rate on sugar and rice land is exceeding high, and this knowledge has managed to trickle north, with the consequence that most niggers would rather die the same place they were born."

Kennedy snorted. The R—— waited patiently for him to hush.

"And among those that *do* get shipped, there are more than a few who'd give their last breath for a chance to reverse the above-mentioned flow of trade."

Nobody gave a peep. The R—— settled back in his chair, fussing with his glove-tips. Finally a well-preserved specimen to the R——'s left sat forward. His hair was coiffed and silverish and he looked more like a country squire than anyone I'd seen outside of a penny-theater. I'd expected him to weigh in with quite a speech, from the look of him, but once all heads were turned he said only—: "Is the horse trade not going well enough for you, Mr. M——?"

"The horse trade is going *gloriously*, Colonel," the R—— replied. "So well, in fact, that there are some—or so I'm told—who'd be content to spend the rest of their lives dealing in other people's horses." He cocked his head. "Might you, perhaps, be such a man?"

The Colonel took a breath. He thought of an answer, swallowed it, and sat back in his chair.

"This question—," said the R——: "this question of *whether* to try our hand at reversing the flow of trade, is the least interesting of the questions I'm prepared to address this evening. Allow me to pass over the 'should we,' for the moment, in favor of the 'how.'"

"By all means, let's have it!" the Colonel said quickly.

The R—— nodded and began rifling through a stack of papers. Sitting behind him as I was, I could see what only Virgil and the R—— himself could see—: that they were blank as bed-sheets, every one. Here's a crafty sort of blackguard, I thought to myself. We're marbles to him, all of us—; to be tossed for and collected.

"Each of you may play a role in the effort I'm going to describe," he said, still studying the papers. "Some of you have already given me your pledge."

"You have my thupport, Thir—you know *that*," said a lisping, wheedling fellow at the table's near corner. His prim little face sat on a plump round body that looked to belong to a different man entirely. His chin was drawn into his face as though he was chewing on a lemon.

"Thank you, Harvey," the R—— said. "Now, gentlemen. Kindly permit me to detail the logistics of our plan."

"Whose plan, now?" came a hard-sounding voice from behind the Colonel.

"*Ours*, I hope, Lieutenant Beauregard," the R—— said politely.

That one's not his marble yet, I thought.

"I've no doubt that you *hope* it, M——; who *conceived* of it was my question."

To my surprise the R—— took Virgil by the arm. "Ah! In that sense, *ours*, Lieutenant. Young Mr. Ball's here and my own."

Though I couldn't see Virgil's face I saw his neck go pale and heard him commence to groan and stammer. All heads turned to look at him.

"I've heard tell of this idiot of yours," the lieutenant said in a comfortable way.

I sat up then and looked the lieutenant over. He sported a gleaming black moustache and a canary-yellow waistcoat. His face was cruel and prideful.

"D'Ancourt tells me you read him something like a compass," he said.

"Good lord, Pierre! *I* never said so," the Colonel wheezed.

The R——'s face crimped together. "Ah! Mr. Beauregard. You are new to our little company. I assure you Mr. Ball is anything but an *idiot*, as you express it. Quite the opposite."

Virgil was still scratching busily with his pencil, his nose all but pressed against the table. He was taking the minutes even then. My hands balled together at the thought of it and my tongue thickened in my mouth. I wished the lieutenant every earthly evil. But a part of me wished Virgil even worse.

The R—— heaved a sigh. "Such japes, if you'll pardon my saying so, waste precious minutes. We've still a great deal to discuss."

That said, he went back to shuffling his papers. My eyes wandered about the room. There's every kind of citizen here, I thought. One of each kind of American, like on board of Noah's ark.

The room was poorly lit and the backs of the chairs threw great heavy shadows into the corners. There, where the dark was closest, I saw a man I hadn't taken note of before. He was dressed in some manner of long black nightshirt and his body was as narrow and ganglish as I ever thought to see, with hairs on his face and forehead exactly like a possum's. His mouth was bent sideways and his body was stiff and bristly as a broom. He came piece by piece out of the dark and when his leer fell upon me I went shivery right through. I shut my eyes and said a quick Our Father. When I opened them I saw that the R—— had a map open on the table.

"The *method*, friends, is simple—: it can well afford to be because we have great means at our disposal. Ample means." He smiled at each of them in turn. "A body of mulattoes in our service, apprised only of the initial phases of our enterprise, will visit plantations and shanty-towns in the outlying country and offer aid to any able-bodied slave inclined to run. The capital, it will be explained, to finance the passage north to freedom, is to be raised through the re-selling of said escapee at a plantation farther up the river. A second liberation will follow after three months, resulting in safe passage into Canada. The bond of this covenant, which must be kept secret from all, upon *pain of death*—" (here the R—— gave a dramatic pause)—"shall be a plain and unworked silver ring, much like this one here."

The R—— laid a hoop of silver on the table.

"Which ring the slave shall, *and must*, present to his liberators when his term comes due. As some of you may know—"

"Trust a nigger with a piece of silver?" Kennedy said, showing us his gums.

"Bear in mind, Mr. Kennedy, that this piece of silver will already have been balanced by two hundred dollars in gold, as we'll have sold him once already. If the escapee should fail to produce the ring, it shall be taken as proof of a breach of faith, and said escapee will be left to his druthers. *We*, contrary-wise, will be left our *profit*."

Kennedy rubbed his nose. "I don't ruh!—ruh!—rightly see—"

The R—— all but rolled his eyes. "The man who comes for the runaway at the end of the three-month period, Mr. Kennedy, may not be the same man who deposited him. Some mark of identity is required. A slave is very respectful of a piece of silver, as you may know."

He privileged the lot of us with an easy grin.

"What happens after?" said the lieutenant, twiddling his whiskers. It was clear he was disgusted by the others' way of buttering the R——'s cake. "Your scheme seems of greater interest to the Abolitionists, Mr. M——, than to any natural son of Dixie."

The R—— laughed. "And yet *you* are interested, Lieutenant Beauregard, are you not."

"I'm interested to have you *answer* me, sirrah," the lieutenant growled.

"A horse-thief steals horses, Mr. Beauregard—; an Abolitionist steals bondsmen. I see no difference between the two, aside from the margin of profit. It has simply never occurred to your Abolitionist, as near as I can tell, that he is in possession—ipso facto of having liberated it from its owner—of a highly remunerative piece of property."

General laughter from the assembly. Beauregard was neatly put away. Virgil could have done that much, I thought. But Virgil was still scratching at his notes.

The R—— smoothed the map out with his palms. "Abolitionizing for profit, gentlemen—: such is my proposal. I consider it no less grand for its simplicity. What's more, I have fifty-seven share-holders—both here and in Memphis—who agree with me whole-heartedly." He looked about the room. "I foresaw, of course, that some of you might not. That's why we're not going to steal the above-mentioned slaves."

The Colonel sat up straight as a rod. "*Not* steal them? Do you mean to tell us, M——, that we've come all this way—"

The R—— raised his hands and the map closed with a snap. In this pose, tidy in his costly clothes, he put me in mind of a well-scrubbed toddler waiting on his Sunday porridge. He brought his palms together then, as if saying grace, and the likeness was complete. But it bewitched me regardless.

"What I mean, Colonel, is that we're going to borrow them."

OVER THE NEXT HOUR each guest learned the reason for his being at table. *No end of cash*, it was said and repeated, had been put behind the venture. The stock-holders would know next to nothing of the goings-on—; only that slaves were being dealt in for a profit, and that the profit, in this case, was near one-hundred percent. The rest, the R—— said with a wink, would be left to their fancy and leisure.

The R—— himself would recruit the mulattoes—"strikers," he called them—whose names would be known to him alone. A ramshackle property of Asa Trist's on the Cane River would serve as a *concentration point*, as the R—— called it, before the shippage north. Kennedy and Virgil, who'd spent time on the river, would manage the passage, each in their own boats—; Beauregard would see that the army left those boats alone. The Colonel, who made his home in Memphis, would deal with the up-river buyers. When sprung the second time, the run-aways would come out of the boat's hold expecting to see St. Louis, or Cincinnati—; instead they'd find the plantation they'd run off from. Goodman Harvey—the lisper—was to minister to the runaways—: the R—— spoke of him as a doctor. He'd played some role, it seemed, in the conception of the thing—; but the R—— made a point of paying him no mind.

At the end they'd all been accounted for except the ghost in the corner.

"What'll *hith* job be, then?" Harvey said, pointing at him. The ghost gave a grin. He might have been grinning at anybody, his eyes were so flat. But he was grinning at nobody but the R——.

"Me?" said the ghost.

"Gentlemen—: our Parson," the R—— said. "Parson's handy with niggers."

Nobody gave a coo.

"Well!" the R—— said. "Are we ready to adjourn?"

There was never any yessing to the plan, but they were for it just the same. Every one of them was for it. They'd agreed in themselves, before they came, to whatever the R—— would offer them. The reason was different, each to each—: some were spiteful, some were greedy, some were cowardly, some were sly. But each had a hollow part that this business would fill.

One by one they got to their feet, straightened their cravats, and went downstairs. Some of their glasses were empty, some were full. I marveled at the coziness of it all. All of them kept quiet except for Beauregard, who was set on having sport with the R——.

"Neat enough, M——, I grant you," he said. He stopped as he passed and took the R—— by the shoulder. The difference in their size was fit to laugh over, and Beauregard savored it in a way that showed the weakness in him. "Neat enough," he said again. "If no war breaks out, it should turn a pretty profit."

"War?" squawked Trist. "What war? With Mexico?"

"I think the lieutenant is thinking of a war between the states, Asa," the R—— said, looking up at Beauregard. "An Abolitionist war."

"I can't see how that would affect *us*," Virgil said. "Such a fight would center on the territories, surely. We'd have breathing-room regardless."

Beauregard raised his eyebrows. "Does it speak?"

The R—— made a subtle movement and Beauregard's hand fell off his shoulder. "Mr. Beauregard, there is something I wished to mention to you," he said. "But I'd forgotten it till now."

Beauregard kept his eyes on Virgil. "Of course, M——. What was it?"

"Your waist-coat. It's exceeding pretty."

Beauregard gave a laugh. "A happy accident, sir—; I can't take credit for it. There's a tailor in Exchange Alley, Christian name of Jessup—"

"Don't, in the future, wear apparel with decided colors," the R—— said, holding up a finger. "Or with pronounced patterns, either. What have men to do with pretty things?"

Beauregard blinked at him a moment. "And what the devil, sir, have *you* to do with my choice of—"

"It's true that a waist-coat should be *becoming*, Lieutenant—; but also that it should lend dignity to the figure. A man's costume should never be ornamental, pretty, or capricious, except at a fancy-dress ball."

Beauregard let out a breath. Then he took a half-step backwards and put his right hand into his pocket. I looked from one of them to the other, thinking there'd be an affair of honor under the oaks next morning sure as I breathed. Then a long gray hand came to rest on Beauregard's shoulder and he spun about as though a wasp had stung him. Parson stood behind him, as tall again to Beauregard as Beauregard was to the R——.

"What do you want?" Beauregard said, stepping back. His voice was no louder than a sigh.

"Have you ever laid eyes on a true idiot, Lieutenant?" Parson said. "A true idiot is a creature of heaven, and as such casts no shadow upon the ground."

Beauregard opened his mouth and shut it. "I'm afraid," he said at last. "I'm afraid that I don't—"

"Can you describe your own shadow for me?" Parson said, the smile fixed slant-wise on his face.

"No, sir, I cannot," Beauregard said. "Now, if you'll permit—"

"By all means, Lieutenant," Parson said. "But attend to what I tell you—: there is a second world alongside and atop the one you cherish.

And if you think I am speaking of the kingdom of *heaven*, then you, Pierre Gustave Toutant Beauregard, are but a finger-puppet."

God help me if I understood this, but I laughed anyhow. The R—— looked at me and winked. Beauregard nodded once, vaguely, then slipped from Parson's hold.

"I'll be in the bar, M——," he said into his whiskers. He gave me a hard look as he passed.

When he was gone Virgil and the R—— and Parson stood close together. "Thank our Parson, Virgil," the R—— said.

"I'm grateful to you, sir," said Virgil. "If not for your intercession, I fear—"

"If he speaks of you that way again, kill him," Parson said.

"Sir?" said Virgil. His neck went paler still.

The R—— laughed. "Our boy would never. He has our best interests in mind."

"Kill him," said Parson. He smiled at Virgil in a motherly way.

"Pay no attention, Kansas," the R—— said, leading Parson off.

That left me alone with Virgil. He stood stock-still, staring out the door, opening his hands and closing them. But at last he condescended to remember me.

"They think I wouldn't," he said in a small voice.

I took his hand in mine. "Have you ever killed a man, Mr. Ball?"

"One thinks I'm too clever," he said. "The other thinks I'm too dim."

"Both think you're too weak," I said. Lord forgive me now for saying it. I was young then, and full of spite, and thought cowardice the most shameful of men's failings. "Are you as weak as they think?"

"I'm a servant," he said, turning his dull face toward me. "I told you that."

"I didn't believe it," I said. "But I believe it now."

He seemed not to hear me. "It's a wonderful thing to have a purpose, Miss Gilchrist—; to know what it is, and to follow it." He hushed a moment. "My purpose is to serve."

"And mine is to take your masters to bed," I said. "I wish you a pleasant evening."

I gathered up my gown and left him. I had no gentlemen to wait on, only the rabble at the bar—; but his humiliation had worked itself under my stays. It had dug itself into me like a tick. Perhaps I felt a kinship to him already—: perhaps I felt it most when he'd been made a fool of by his betters. Love and shame both make your body hot, then chill it as the years pass near to freezing. Virgil tells me I loved him, and he may well be right. I know of no better word to describe the shame I felt—feel even now, remembering—than that word so abused by all who touch it.

"I'll go down and find that lieutenant of yours," I said to him.

And so I did.

The bar was well stocked with gentlemen, but I had no trouble finding Beauregard. He was seated at a corner booth, flanked by two great Araby ferns, talking quietly with the R——. The tiff upstairs looked to have been forgotten. Here and there, at tables or along the bar, I made out the others—; all were making a great show of being unacquainted. Virgil hadn't followed me downstairs.

I came and sat down between them, pretty as you please. My anger made me bold. Neither looked at me. Beauregard was trying to get something out of the R——.

"Don't condescend to me, M——," he said.

"I'd not dream of it, Lieutenant. Drink your sherry."

Beauregard scratched at the corner of his mouth. "You'll have to kill those niggers," he said. "That much is sure. They'd bear witness against you."

"As I understand it, the bounty on escapees applies whether alive or dead," the R—— said in a comfortable way.

A silence fell. I looked from one of them to the other. My mouth was dry as parchment.

"Good God, sir," said Beauregard.

The R—— did not blink. His mouth was straight and solemn but it was not impossible to imagine it in a grin.

"You mean to carry this through, I see," Beauregard said at last. "I appreciate that now."

"You've never doubted my resolve in the past." The R—— sipped at a glass of rye. "Or my discretion."

"No," said Beauregard, the dash gone from his face.

"I have your support, then?" the R—— said, letting his eyes drift idly across the room. They found Kennedy, hunched over at the bar, and settled.

"You have it," said Beauregard. He looked weak and disbelieving, but there was something else in his look besides—: a flicker of excitement. "You have it, M——! You have it. Let your Irishman drink his porter."

A Baptism.

THE HOW OF IT WAS SIMPLE, Delamare says.

I came in on a packing-boat, by foot if the place was set back from the river, found myself a room or a corner someplace in the nigger-town, and stayed there. I might stay for a day, I might stay for a week. Sometimes one afternoon was enough to see I wasn't welcome. But if the mood was right, if there was the slow, suspicious eagerness in their eyes and in the way they talked, if they stopped to say good-night as they came in from the fields, not looking me in the face but only at my clothes, my hair, my skin, I'd know the lay of the land was fine, and I'd stay on.

First I'd lay my clothes out on the cot, or on the pallet, if that was all I had—: jacket at the top, pressed shirts underneath, linens at the bottom. My second pair of boots I'd set at the open window, as if I hardly cared whether somebody ran off with them in the night. I'd sit on the stoop (if there was such a thing) and black them in the early evening, when it was still light. When they asked me about the boots and the rest, about the sweet blonde tobacco that I smoked, about the tonic for my hair, I'd say I'd got it up in Louisville, or Baltimore, or Cincinnati. No more than that. But that was all it took.

I looked about as much like them as a sherry-glass looks like a plate of beans, but anyone could see that I had nigger in me. That and the clothes, and the way I carried on, light-hearted and conceited, was enough to put the thought into their heads. I did no *selling* of it—: no prompting, no whispering, no missionary work. I let the idea do my whispering for me.

They came when it got toward dark, full and ready to receive. One or two might want to hear details of life in Boston, or Sandusky, or Ottawa, if only to hear those names spoken aloud. But by the time they asked they were as good as struck already. A white man, however nimble, would have held no sway for them—; but I was living, preening proof of freedom's alchemy. The South they knew could never have engendered me.

Finding shelter was the hardest part of it, and that was no great work. I arrived in the early forenoon, when the men and a good deal of the women were in the fields, and looked for a cabin apart from the rest, neatly kept, with a woman inside it. Whether she was fat or thin, bright-eyed or stony-faced, made no difference to me at all. I looked for signs of children, and if I found any I moved on. If not, I stayed. Sometimes I was traveling for religion—; sometimes I was peddler—; I could have told them anything I liked. By the second or third night the men would start coming round and I'd bring out the idea and let it loose. Once I started I worked quick, pausing only to sleep, so that by the time word reached the big house I was back out on the river. I learned that early, about the quickness. I had marks on my back and on the soles of my feet to keep me mindful. By the end of a week—if I'd stayed that long—the marks would begin to itch and I'd light out within the hour. But not before I'd looked in on each of the men I'd struck. Not before I'd left each of them a token.

Often as not a woman would be waiting for me when I called, sitting with her arms crossed in the middle of the room, mute and blank-faced as a cinder. My man would be sound asleep beside her, half-covered by a quilt, or hid behind a dirty sack-cloth curtain.

"The wind's up, auntie," I'd say to the woman.

"Then get you gone," she'd say. "Gone back down under the river."

"Get him roused, auntie," I'd say. "Wake him, or I'll take him tonight."

"I'll wake the marse, that's who. I'll wake his hounds."

I'd say nothing, looking at her as I might at a cow laid in the middle of the road. It was always the same. After another stretch of dullness she'd get stiffly to her feet and walk out of the shack without a word.

I was sixteen years old when I began as a striker, reckless and full of bluster—; I was caught on my very first strike. A foreman and two boys tied me to a fence-post with a length of hemp and laid into me with a switch for a while, but their hearts weren't in it. They'd heard of the Trade by then, heard of it and feared it, and they had little regard for the master of the house. He came down himself after a time, looked me over indifferently, then dismissed his men. I could smell his

anise-scented breath as he examined my cuts. I can't abide anise to
this day.

"You a right fortunate little coon," he whispered. Then he cut me
loose. I learned later he was one of our share-holders.

Once the husband, or the son, or the lover of the cinder-faced
woman was roused from the bed, I'd refuse whatever hospitality was
offered—a slice of cold scrapple, perhaps, or a wedge of boiled yam—
then press a silver ring into his palm, holding it there until his fingers
closed on it. I'd remind him that he must have the ring on the first finger of his left hand when my associates came for him, and that they'd
come for him within a fortnight. Then I'd have him repeat what I said
word for word.

"If you don't have that ring, they'll shoot you in the belly," I'd say.
"These aren't patient men."

And he'd look me in the face at last, sober and respectful, and
swear to me he understood. I did my work well—; I did as right by
them, each one, as I was able. Not a one of the niggers I struck failed to
turn out for his rendezvous. Not a one of my strikes was wasted.

I began to build a name for myself, in circles. But the more I grew
inside that name the tighter it became, and the more I wanted to slip
out of it like a cicada from its shell. I was bigger than my name already,
and I knew it. I was not yet nineteen years of age.

THE REDEEMER HAD BEEN PARTIAL to me from the start, and had
talked to me long and lovingly about the Trade—; in reality, however,
the sum of what I knew could have fit into a pipe-stem. One afternoon,
when I was sitting with him in his quarters, he leaned back in that
high-chair of his and sucked musingly on his pipe. "You've been a capital striker for us, Oliver," he said finally. "Capital."

"Thank you, sir."

He squinted at me then. "What's that you're wearing?"

"Broad-cloth, sir. A recent cut." I smiled at him. "They call it a
smoking-jacket."

"Don't wear black cloth in the morning, Oliver." He pursed his
lips. "Don't wear evening-dress, of any kind, on any occasion before six
o'clock. The French, of course, wear evening-dress on ceremonious
occasions at whatever hour they may occur—; here, however, we follow the English custom."

He shuffled some papers about on his desk. He'd said things of this sort to me before, and I wasn't too put out by them. "The exception is New Orleans, of course. Follow French custom in that city."

"I will, sir. Thank you."

He studied me for a time. "You've never been to pick up any of the niggers you've struck, have you?"

"No sir," I answered. My throat tightened with excitement.

He flipped idly through a stack of ledgers. "There's one by the name of Bosun, not too far down-river. His time is nearly due. Perhaps you and Mr. Kennedy—"

"Not Kennedy," I spat out, helpless to keep still. The Redeemer looked up sharply from his desk, not so much in anger as in surprise—; his surprise, however, lasted but a moment. When he spoke it was clear that he knew how Kennedy had found me, and what had happened after.

"No—; not Kennedy, of course," he said.

I said nothing then, waiting for some reference to my disgrace. But instead he struck a match, took another pull from his pipe, and said in an amicable voice—:

"It *is* strange that it was Kennedy, of all people, who brought you to us. You two are so very disalike." He looked at me. "Your mother must have been *une femme sans pareil.*"

"Beg your pardon, sir. I never knew her."

He nodded at this, his coy little mouth running over with smoke. "Of course, Oliver. Yes. I mean the woman you were—*indentured* to, when Mr. Kennedy came across you."

"Mrs. Bradford was never a mother to me, sir," I lied. "She was the woman who took me and put me to work."

"She did a good deal more than *that*, as I understand it," the Redeemer said warmly. "She fed you, she clothed you, she taught you to read and cipher—"

"She'd been a school-teacher," I answered, cutting him short. I cleared my throat and continued, if only to keep him from saying any more—: "It was more for her pleasure, sir, than for mine."

"All right, Oliver—; yes." He smiled indulgently. "You'd know *better*, of course." He made a clucking noise with his tongue, the same noise that I'd often heard Parson make. "Mind you," he said. "I had no school-teachers to give me my finishing, when I was of tender years."

"You had Parson," I said.

To this day I wonder at my imprudence. The Redeemer froze in mid-puff and glowered crookedly at his pipe, as though it, not I, had spoken out of turn. Then he went on cheerfully—:

"You looked like the Dauphin himself when Kennedy brought you in, dear boy. I remember it well. All done up in sashes and chenille—"

"She made good money with that still," I said hoarsely. "But you know that, of course."

He raised his eye-brows. "Why the deuce should I?"

"Because you own it now."

He laughed heartily at this and turned the talk to trifles. We spoke no more about my history, then or after—; but a small, true thing had happened. Out of my shame I'd rebelled, however briefly, and the Redeemer had indulged me.

Two nights later we set out for Bosun's rendezvous.

THE RAFT WE RODE ON was a modest one, little more than tree-stems lashed to a birch-plank floor. The Redeemer and I were the only riders—; I didn't know, then, of the years he'd spent flat-boating, and was amazed at his skill with the steering-oar and pole. As we drifted, seemingly without effort, just in sight of Louisiana, he pointed out banks, chutes, and snags to me with a confidence born of a lifetime spent on the river. He took particular pleasure, I remember, in identifying the stars. The commonest constellations were known to me, of course, but the Redeemer mapped out dozens upon dozens across the sky, many of which I've never heard of since. One in particular seemed to delight him, a dim cluster to the left of Cassiopeia that he called Herod's Ladder—:

"It's an entertainment to me, that one," he said. "I've pointed it out to any number of our boys, and each of them sees something different in it."

"Beg pardon, sir, but that's natural enough."

He set the pole aside and took me by the shoulder. "Listen closely, Oliver. Belief is like a river—: you can channel it any way you like. Channel it as easily as water." He watched me a moment. "Do you follow?"

He'd lost me utterly. "Yes, sir. Belief is like a river."

"That's right, boy." He grinned. "Belief in anything is a kind of madness—; and there's nobody so gullible as a cracker." He made a face. "Look at poor Asa Trist."

I grinned back at him. "Yes, sir."

We hushed for a time, our eyes on the firmament.

"Well?" he said finally.

"Sir?"

"What do *you* see in it?"

I looked up at the stars. "A ladder," I said.

He laughed loudly at this. "A ladder! Truly?"

"Yes, sir. Isn't that what you called it?"

He laughed again. "That's right, Oliver. Herod's Ladder. And you'll climb that ladder yet, boy. Just you wait."

THE PLAN WAS THIS—: to collect Bosun at an out-of-the-way landing (little more than a damp tongue of earth jutting east from Louisiana) and keep on down-river to the old Trist estate. Bosun was an enormous man, with hands the size of shovel-tips—; we'd sold him twice already for a mint. I spent the better part of the journey asking myself what he'd do when he found himself headed south yet again, rather than north, as arranged—; but the Redeemer was absolutely free of care. It had been years, he said—*years*—since he'd had cause to work the river. I wanted desperately to ask him what the cause was that particular day, but I sensed it had something to do with my future, and kept my wonderment to myself. We rode the last few miles in silence.

"By gum!" the Redeemer said suddenly. "If this ain't just the way to run the river!"

I nodded and fussed with the collar-buttons of my coat. I'd drifted off for a time, but my sleep had been troubled. The nearer we drew to our rendezvous, the more the thought of Bosun began to harry me.

When we'd last met, seven months before, I'd all but promised him Cincinnati.

"I'm pleased it brings back bygones for you, sir," I muttered. "I'd much prefer the state-room of the old *Vesuvius*. Or even the *Hyapatia Lee*."

"That's the dandy in you, Oliver," the Redeemer said fondly. He was managing the raft entirely by himself, darting from one corner of the platform to the other. "Look lively, now!" he whispered. "There she is! To starboard!"

I couldn't have found that landing to save myself from drowning, even in perfect daylight—; and yet in the next instant it emerged, dark and undeniable, from the gray vagueness around us. Bosun was there as well, not ten paces off, panting and cursing and grappling with the tie-line, pulling us in hand over hand—; the next thing I knew we were off again, the weight of his gargantuan body adding a good two inches to our draft. As the landing fell away, Bosun looked about him as I feared he would and, ignoring the Redeemer altogether, said in a dubious voice—:

"This gone carry me to Cincy, marse?"

There was no sound for a time but the Redeemer's steady working of the pole. "Bosun," I said at last, with a rush of self-importance. "I should introduce you to the pilot of this run. You have the privilege of sharing this flat-boat with none other than—"

"I don't mind a damn if it be Ezekiel himself," Bosun said. I noticed now that he was naked to the waist, that his lips were slick with blood, and that his left arm hung lifelessly from his shoulder.

"Why we headed down this river?" he said very slowly.

"There's a keel-boat waiting two miles on," the Redeemer put in, busy with the pole. "We'll part ways in less than an hour, Mr. Bosun."

Perhaps it was the exotic sound of being called "Mr." by a white man, but Bosun took a sharp, shallow breath, gave a loud guffaw, and turned toward the Redeemer. "Two mile on?" he said.

"At Druthers Crick," said the Redeemer, nodding. "Step a bit to port, Mr. Bosun, if you please."

Again Bosun let his great laugh loose. "You artful courteous, marse!" he said to the Redeemer. I could see now that his arm was pulled clear of its socket. He jerked his head toward me. "You ought to give this niggra of yours some finishing."

"Mr. Delamare is not my negro," the Redeemer said, stopping in mid-pull. "He is a free man, Mr. Bosun—; as free as you or I."

Bosun took a little step to one side, as if to get out of the way of something rushing past—; when he spoke his voice was tentative as a child's.

"As you or *I*?" he murmured.

"That's right," the Redeemer said, his voice as mild as Bosun's. "The hour of your emancipation, Mr. Bosun, has arrived. The hour to put your indentured self behind you." He gave a courtly bow. "Mr. Delamare and I humbly recommend that you savor it."

For a minute, perhaps longer, Bosun gave no answer. I'd begun to wonder whether he'd understood the Redeemer's little oratory when I saw that he was trembling throughout his great body, gasping with slow, hard heaves of his tremendous shoulders. The raft spun and drifted at the current's pleasure—; we were out in the black middle of the river.

"What gone come of this?" Bosun said at last. "What gone follow?"

"I suggest you choose a name," the Redeemer said.

Bosun gave his head a shake, as though a fly had landed on his brow. "A name?"

The Redeemer passed the pole to me now and stepped over to Bosun. "That's right," he said. "The name you carry was given to you by your first master, Benjamin Thomkins Grady, that you might come to him when he called. He imagined that by giving you that name, he himself, and no other, had called you into being. The name your mother chose to call you was the name of a play-thing, the name of a house-pet, just as Grady's name was a name for a champion ox. The name you *yourself* choose, contrary-wise, will be the name of a new-born child." He smiled. "And whether you *answer* to it, sir, will be nobody's business but your own."

That said, the Redeemer stretched up his arm and touched Bosun gently on the mouth. Bosun bowed his head to receive this touch, bashful and not a little bewildered, like Mary before the archangel Gabriel. His expression shuttled back and forth between exultation and dismay, as though he'd been found guilty, through no fault of his own, of some especially noble crime.

"Tell me your name, pilgrim," the Redeemer said softly. "Tell it to me and I'll baptize you here and now."

A measure of silence passed—I know not how long—then Bosun raised his head. "I should be called 'Simon,' after Simon from the desert," he said, his voice full of wonder at itself.

If that was not the sound of religion, the sound of spirit given voice, then I have never heard it in my life. Nothing earthly was real to Bosun at that moment—: not the Redeemer, not the raft we rode on, not the river at our feet. There was only his own body, the fact of all that it had suffered, and the new name hovering before him in the air. Of his own accord Bosun sank onto his knees.

"I baptize you Simon Morelle," the Redeemer intoned, splashing a palmful of water over him. "Stand up, Simon, and be counted!"

Bosun got to his feet and ran a fist across his eyes. "Simon Morelle," he repeated, as if to get the fit of it.

"Holler it out now! Out across the river!" the Redeemer said, his own voice cracking with excitement. "Holler so they can hear you back on Benjamin Grady's land. Let them hear your name, Simon! Let them hear your name and *know* it!"

Bosun hesitated for the briefest instant—; then he smiled and sucked in an eager breath. "*Simon* Bosun *Morelle*!" he shouted, laughing as the raft spun slowly clockwise.

"'And I am a free man!'" the Redeemer crowed, tapping Bosun on the shoulder.

"I a new-born child! A god-damn baby *child*!" Bosun yelled at the top of his voice. All hurt and weariness seemed to have left him. To my full and perfect amazement he brought his hands together and clapped. "Mr. Benjamin Grady! I be Simon Once-Was-Bosun and Morelle!"

"So be it," the Redeemer said.

The next sound I heard was of Bosun's backside crashing against the planks. The echo came after, by way of the far side of the river, turning over on itself and whipping against my forehead like a switch. The sound was loud enough to have come from a brace of cannon—; the weapon in the Redeemer's palm, however, was no larger than a bottle of perfume.

I gaped at him a moment, then looked down at Bosun, heaving and jerking at my feet. Bosun, whom I had come across one day coming in quietly from the fields. "Merciful Jesus," I said.

I passed the back of my hand over my mouth, then turned toward the Redeemer, fully expecting to be next.

"You asked me what became of them, Oliver," he said, handing me the pistol.

Sweet bloodied world, I said noiselessly, pressing the barrel to Bosun's temple. Sweet blood-besotted life.

OVER THE NEXT QUARTER-HOUR, still drifting with the current, we stripped Bosun of his clothes, ripped his belly open, and pulled the guts out of him so that he would sink. In the blink of an eye he was gone under the river. My new and vulnerable understanding was plunged into bewilderment yet again by the fact that the Redeemer was weeping freely. When I finally found the courage to ask why in heaven's name he'd done it, he clucked and laid a finger to my lips.

"I'd meant for you to *look*, Oliver. Not to avert your eyes."

"But why? Why kill Bosun, sir? What had Bosun done?"

"Bosun did *well*, God bless him. Bosun played his part."

I waited the better part of a minute for him to say more. "What of us, then?" I asked, when I could stand it no longer. "Did we play ours?"

"We did, Oliver." He sighed. "We gave our Simon the only freedom he could ever know."

I let my head sink down against my chest, just as Bosun had done at his baptism. Even as I sensed that the Redeemer was speaking to me as though to a child or an idiot I believed his words implicitly. More than that—: I *knew* them to be true. The look on Bosun's face as he sang out his name had not yet left my thoughts, nor would it ever. I myself was never to know such freedom.

"I suppose that I should choose a name, as well," I said. I said it hopefully.

The Redeemer brought a finger to his lips and bit it. Then he gave a laugh.

"The one you've got works well enough, Oliver Delamare."

Dearness.

VIRGIL KEPT COMING, Clementine says. Regular as clap. Regular as my monthly worries.

He came in spite of Lieutenant Beauregard, who called on me now as well. He came in spite of all my regulars and happen-bys. I showed him no special care, made no great fuss over him, the R——'s poppet though he was. But he came every night that I allowed him. Every night that he wasn't in Natchez, or Vicksburg, or up some back-alley of the river. He told me about his dealings when he came, but so did all the rest. All of them with their beloved and priceless secrets. Virgil paid Madame, same as anybody, before he came up to see me. Or he paid her after. But the things he told me he told no other soul.

Get used to listening, Madame said back at the beginning. Listening is part of it. And so I did. I listened to every caller that felt inclined. I discovered that I had a talent for it. I heard enough complaints and anecdotes and humorous asides to put a unit of infantry to sleep. I listened to Virgil no different than the rest—; I listened to him because of the Trade and the R——, and because I was used to listening. I listened the same way I carried myself straight and lady-like, or let my hips move side-wise when I crossed the room, or rouged my cheeks and nipples. Listening was money in my purse.

Telling, however, was different. Telling was not a part of it, I knew that. I'd have been caned for it, or worse—: burnt with match-tips, locked away, fed on sugar-water for a week. Telling was not a part of it. But I began to tell him just the same.

I told Virgil everything I knew. In the early morning hours that were my own I'd feed him scraps of what I'd heard or seen. What Beauregard had told me, and Kennedy, and the R——, and all the rest.

I taught that half-blind bumbler his own business. I educated Virgil in the Trade.

I should have known, from that, that he was dear to me. I did. I'd have left him to his blindness otherwise. I'd have left him to it gladly. I'd have kept to my own counsel, and been well.

As it was, however, Virgil kept coming. He would come in the spring and bring cut peaches in a bowl—; he would come in the summer and take me out on promenades. He'd walk me down the levee pridefully. This is Clementine, my cousin, he'd announce to all and sundry. Down from Kansas on a visit. Many of the men had been to Madame Lafargue's and knew me but they bowed to me just the same. "Charmed," the men said. Or "delighted." He would come in the winter, and bring me hot buttered rum from the bar. As the years went by I watched him prosper and grow clever. He was a gentleman now, in a proper suit of clothes. I saw to that.

He was dearest to me when I was bitter. I took comfort in him then, which made me bitterer still. Dearness had no equity in that house. I resolved to put an end to it, hoping to recover my fortitude of mind. I changed in my manner toward him. Directly he came in I'd put on my working face and commence to treat him coldly. I dealt with him more coldly than with callers I abhorred. I made the visits bitter for him, as bitter as I could, but he would not be turned aside. I adore you, Clementine, he'd say. I love you truly. His certainty was something to behold. His certainty was a marvel and he grew dearer to me still because of it and I grew ever colder. It was all very well, his loving. I knew what would come of it in the end.

Once a month the R—— came and asked about his darling. Each time he came I expected to be punished, but the R—— would only take me by the hand. Success has made me gentle, Clem, he'd say. Then the questions would begin. How does Virgil seem to you? Is he comfortable in his mind? How is his appetite? How is his spend? Is it copious, or scant? Does he make a great noise, or a sigh? Does he speak to you, or cry out? And so on, like a sheriff, or a grand inquisitor—; but also like a boy of fourteen years. Everything I told him he approved of. Sometimes he scribbled marks into a book. That boy is meant for great things, Clem, he'd say to me. Expect great things from that dear boy of ours. A fear would come over me at this and I'd go quiet, watching the R—— scribbling and muttering to himself. Is that all? he'd say at the end of it, helping me out of my skirts. That's all, I'd say. Capital! he'd say, and kiss me on the lips. If he knew Virgil was dear to me he took care not to show it.

After each of the R——'s visits I went colder than before. Have I offended you, dearest? Virgil would say, looking at me fit to die. His suffering gave me pleasure of a kind, as I was suffering over him.

Yes, Aggie, I'd say to him. You've offended me. Come to bed.

"A Made Man."

THE NEW VIRGIL BALL was seven years in the making, Virgil says. But it took a single trip to Memphis to destroy him.

Seven years, to the day, after helping the Redeemer with his boots—and four after my first night with Clementine—I was steaming up the great brown muck-a-puddle on board the *Vesuvius*, the third steam-boat ever to clear the whole run of the river and still the most gaudy of the old "floating palaces." I was a made man now, dandified and whiskered. If the nature of the wares I traded in disquieted me now and then, the fruits of my position quickly put my mind at ease. I was a courier of other people's goods—; no more than that. The fleet of barges I managed might have carried barrels of beer, or barleycorn, or even pocket Bibles. I'd never once had to raise my voice, let alone fire my pistol. The Trade watched over me like a mother hen. I had no faith, as such, in my sooth-saying eye—; but I couldn't deny that the Redeemer had made good use of it. The proof was all around me. Slowly, steadily, like a wine-stain working its way through wool, belief was colonizing me.

As the stream of flat-boats, rafts, and tar-bottomed pirogues slid by, I'd doff my hat, if I happened to be on deck, with all gentlemanly sympathies. Occasionally I'd catch sight of the odd colleague or share-holder in the Trade—: the greeting might be a slight nod, or—if the boat passed close by—a bar or two of "City of the Sun," a shanty-town hymn that the Redeemer favored. It was easy at such moments, standing in the sun and the wind on the open deck, to think of myself as Fortune's darling. I was the *Redeemer*'s darling, after all.

Only once did anyone catch me at my game—: a well-fed Calvinist from New England, round as a river-buoy, who passed the hours pacing the deck and swilling great jarfuls of quinine-water. Just below

Island 30, less than an hour from my port of call, he cornered me against the starboard rail, his face a veritable milk-jug of fraternity—:

"Allow me to congratulate you, sirrah, on the architecture of your waist-coat!"

I stopped in mid-whistle and returned his bow—; the raft I'd been signaling passed quietly down-stream. "My waist-coat?" I replied.

"Yours and none other," said the man. "A properly detailed waist-coat, to a man of refinement, is as a draught of cool water on a summer's day." He squinted at my belly. "Dibbern & Alexander, Jackson Square?"

"Chez Restoux, Paris," I said, regarding him coolly. The quality of my wardrobe had done its share, in recent years, to offset the particulars of my face—; but I was unused, even now, to being addressed by strangers. Most people avoided me as they had always done, albeit with more civility. This plump little Yankee, however—who introduced himself as Barker—seemed to find my lack of politeness scenic.

"Glorious day to be on the river," he chirruped.

"Quite," I said, staring out at the dung-colored water.

"I deduce from your manner, Mr. Ball, that you've spent enough time on the Mississippi to be inoculated to its charms."

I shrugged. "Twelve years this September."

"*Twelve!* That's long enough, by God." Barker rested his elbows on the railing. "I'll bet you've seen your share of devilment along this old creek."

"Devilment?" I said, smiling at his choice of phrase.

"Which poet was it, Mr. Ball, who wrote—: 'Skirt if you can its ebon tongue, its languid, fluvial curls . . .'?"

"I know nothing about poetry," I lied. In fact I had a volume of Blake in my pocket at that very moment.

Barker rolled his eyes at me. "I'm *sure* you remember—it was set to music—quite a popular ditty, in its day—" He stopped in mid-sentence and rapped me fiercely on the chest—: "What tune were you whistling just now?"

I looked at him sharply. "Tune?"

He nodded. "You were torturing it to death against the rail."

"Some old gospel or other," I answered as casually as possible. "The name of it escapes me, I'm afraid."

He took me passionately by the arm. "You *must* sing it for me, Mr. Ball!"

"I have no voice for singing, Mr. Barker," I said curtly. "You've said as much yourself. I've only just now tortured—"

"*Blast* you!" he cried out before I could finish. "No matter! I remember it now." Climbing three steps up the port stairs, so that our faces were level with one another, he began to croon, in a reedy but not unpleasant voice, tapping a lively accompaniment on the rail—:

> Be-*hold*, the Lord of *E*-gypt comes riding on a cloud,
> The *i*-dols all shall *trem*-ble, the *pha*-raohs cry a–loud—;
> Five ci-ties down in *E*-gypt shall talk in Canaan's tongue,
> The first of these is *Mem*-phis, the *City* of the *Sun*!

He paused to catch his breath. "Shall I push on?"

He was a step above me now, staring down at me with the same moist-eyed glee he'd previously directed at the river. He was about to begin the second verse when I caught hold of him by his sleeve—:

"You sing charmingly, Mr. Barker—; but that song is a melancholy one to me." I fixed my dead eye on him as balefully as I could. "A matter of the heart."

He gave an impish little laugh. "But you were just now whistling it yourself!"

"It's the words, sir, since you press me." I took hold of his elbow and led him down into the bar, away from the river, out of public view. "As to the tune, it's not so very different from 'Bringing In the Sheep.'"

Barker let out a gasp. "Great *Josh!* I suppose it isn't!"

We chose a table with a clear view of the river, and Barker sat down with his back to me, content, it seemed, to brood upon its evening majesty. Here was a chance to slip quietly away—: Barker seemed to have forgotten me completely. Instead I found myself sipping quinine-water mixed with bourbon. My mind was a puddle of confusion.

"What do you do for a living, Mr. Barker?" I asked. "Are you perhaps a waistcoat-merchant?"

"Hardly that," said Barker unperturbedly. He turned and looked me frankly in the eye. "I'm a ferreter by trade, Mr. Ball. I ferret things out."

Another long moment passed, during which the cogs of my brain came grudgingly into rotation. "You're a Pinkerton," I said at last.

"Not in the *general* sense!" Barker said cheerily. "You might say I'm a specialist of sorts." He lowered his voice. "The nigger question, actually."

"Runaways, you mean?" The urge to bolt was full upon me now.

"Correct, sirrah! That's it exactly. Runaways." Barker's round head bobbed like the buoy it so resembled. "Runaways are my purview." He tittered. "I shouldn't *tell* you that, of course."

I set my bourbon-and-quinine down carefully. If this man was a bounty-hunter, as he claimed, then he was the most wretched bounty-hunter ever born. One met with no shortage of naturals, jackasses, and madmen on the Mississippi—; the possibility could not be ruled out, however, that he was speaking to me in some manner of code. I racked my addled brain for a reply.

"My dear fellow," Barker said after a time, "don't look so stuffed and gutted! Have you never met a nigger-man before?"

"Not of your caliber," I answered, truthfully enough.

He heaved a sigh. "They run off regular as clock-work, poor desperate creatures—; and if they stay out long enough, I find 'em. I find 'em, I catch 'em, and I coffle 'em together. Then a courier takes them back down-river and collects the bounty for me." He gave me a wink, an action that lifted his left ear a good two inches above his right. "Often as not, I have to track *those* sons of Samuel down and recover my commission." He lowered his voice. "Between you, me, and the mud on your shoe, it's barely worth the effort!"

I stared at him in silence. He was taking on a supernatural quality for me now. "Sounds like a tiresome business," I said at last.

"It *is* that, Mr. Ball. Very tiresome, and taxing. It helps to have a hobby-horse—anything at all—to wick away one's worries." He turned to look out at the water again, smiling at it as if in benediction. "Mine's a trifle childish, but it seems to turn the trick. I study the kabala."

"A privilege to meet you, Mr. Barker," I said, already on my feet. "I get off in a quarter-hour, so if you'll kindly excuse—"

"In a *quarter*-hour?" Barker squealed. "Where, for pity's sake? There's nothing up ahead of us but cottonwoods and muck!"

"A cottage, belonging to a relative of mine," I said tightly. "On Island 37—"

"Island 37!" Barker sang out, slapping the table-top in triumph. "I *knew* you lived a life of intrigue, Mr. Ball!"

"Sorry to disappoint you," I mumbled, backing out onto the deck. "My aunty's boy, Thaddeus, has a tubercular hip—"

"Don't slink off like some sort of *pick-pocket*, Virgil!" Barker said, jumping up from the table. "I *may* call you Virgil?"

"Not slinking—begging your pardon—my cabin—"

"Favor me with your card, at the very least!"

"No card either, damn you!" I snapped, struggling against the urge to pitch myself into the river.

"Take mine, then," Barker said, pressing a moist wad of paper into my hand. Before I could answer him he'd disappeared, quinine-water and all, like a jack-rabbit into its burrow.

I reeled back to my cabin in a daze. Who in Christ's name was this Barker? I did my level best to know each member of our fraternity by sight, if not by name—; but I'd never before laid eyes on him, I was certain. On the other hand ("contrary-wise," as the Redeemer would say), the Trade was growing more byzantine by the hour. It was just conceivable that Barker *was* a colleague—; but if so, what the devil was he playing at? I forced myself to walk measuredly about my cabin, taking deep, deliberate breaths, and in time I recovered my calm. There was nothing for it, I decided, but to carry on. Either the man was as pudding-headed as he seemed, or he was sporting with me masterfully—: I'd discover which, most likely, when I tried to dis-embark.

When the landing arrived, however, there was neither hide nor hair of him. As the steamer pulled up and the hitch-ties were thrown, I remembered the paper he'd given me and dug it out of my pocket. It was bare of print save for this device—:

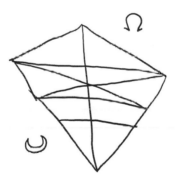

Underneath was scribbled, in a loose, excitable hand—: MORRIS P. BARKER, RUNAWAYS. That was all. Barker did not appear out of the shadows to whistle at me or to clap me in irons, and I stepped off the *Vesuvius* not so much like a thief in the night as a school-boy who's been told by his teacher to run along home and hunt squirrels. I all but cart-wheeled down the landing in my relief. But the thought of Barker—Barker blustering, Barker winking, Barker singing "City of the Sun" in his shrill, squirrelish voice—buzzed about me like a horse-fly. It followed me up to the Redeemer's quarters, worrying me cruelly all the while—; then, all at once, it settled on the Redeemer's brow and bit him.

Samuel Clemens.

June 8, 1860.

My Sweet Leah,

    You may or may not care to hear about a rare type of character I met yesterday on a pack steamer out of New Orleans—I will tell you about him anyhow. The boat was the Culpepper, *bound for St. Paul, Minnesota (don't you have an aunty there, my little cockrobin?) and I discovered him drinking sweet coffee and rootbitters in the pilot-house with none other than Horace Bixby, whom I cubbed under on the* Paul Jones. *Bixby's new cub was at the wheel, sweating and mumbling to himself like I did on my first run, but Bixby payed him no attention. In fact it took that old eggbeater a good quarter-hour to privilege your Sam with so much as a nod, so immaculate was his devotion to his guest. There wasn't much for me to do but take a seat on the bench and wait my turn. Thankfully I had the visitor to goggle at; and that passed the time for me nicely.*

    I'll try to describe him for you.

    The man who held the monopoly on Bixby's attentions wore a three-quarter hat buffed to looking-glass brightness, a shirtfront entirely appropriate for a visit to the "Opéra de l'Epoche," a carbuncle breast-pin, gloves of white kid and boots of the butteriest patent leather. I nearly took him for the "Dauphin" of France when I first caught sight of him. He sat perched like a dove on the opposite bench; his English was fine, if a bit Creole in the delivery; he supported his palms on a cane of lacquered teechee-wood. From top to bottom, hat included, he was no more than four and one-half feet in height.

    At this point you're sure to think this no different from my other sketches, but I petition you (pussums!) for a half-dram of patience. Bixby took notice of me at last, and answered my smile with a granitic nod, evidently with the idea of sending me about my business; the dwarf, however, let it be known that he *would tolerate my presence. Now: when I cubbed under Horace "Gomorrah" Bixby, damned to perdition if anybody got comfortable on his watch, let alone (by Jesus!) presumed <u>to direct traffic</u>; Bixby's pilot-box was his Eden. To see the old tyrant dictated to under his own steam—by a frock-coated Tom Thumb, no less!—was too much for me by half. I made a small, confused noise, loosened my neck-tie, seized a lock of hair behind my ear and twisted with all my might. I was not, judging by the result, asleep; neither was I in my cups. Meanwhile, the conversation—such as it was—continued. All I could do was listen in astonishment.*

The talk ran along the usual channels for a time; by and by it turned to negroes. Bixby said something to the effect that a darky's worth proceeds from the weight of sack he's able to carry without discomfort; he imagined himself, quite reasonably, to be speaking for us all. But Tom Thumb begged to differ.

"Some men of note, Mr. Bixby, equate the black race with the renegade angels mentioned in <u>Leviticus</u>, who lusted after the daughters of Men, and were cast out of Heaven on account of it." He raised his coffee-cup thoughtfully to his lips. "From that point of view, the best measure of a <u>darky</u>—" (he lingered over the word, rolling it about on his tongue, delighting in it) "—would be the number of our daughters, mistresses, and wives that he has bedded."

A slack-jawed silence fell. The sound of the paddlewheel rose up loud as thunder through the floor. I tried to guess, from the dwarf's expression, how he meant this speech to be received—; but I found his face expressionless. After perhaps a minute's time, with no small expenditure of effort, Bixby stammered:

"I can hardly concur with such—" (here he fell silent for a moment, gnashing his teeth) "—I could never—" (another splenetic stammer) "—Never conscience such a—"

"I quite agree, Mr. Bixby," the dwarf interrupted. "No penalty could be too severe in such cases."

"Certainly not," said Bixby. His face was the color of a pomegranate.

"I don't believe I've met your young associate. . . ?"

Bixby took a breath. "That's Clemens, sir. One of my old cubs."

The dwarf winked at me. "What's your opinion, Mr. Clemens?"

As I was incapable of rational speech by then, I simply shrugged my shoulders. He nodded and set his cup back on its saucer.

"I apologize, gentlemen, if I've led us into muddied waters. Theology is an inexact science, I'm afraid." He sighed. "Perhaps a dose of chemistry might help us in our quandary."

"*I* see no quandary," Bixby murmured, staring off into the distance. "A gallows is quickly made."

"An acquaintance of mine—Asa Trist, of Cane River—you know him, perhaps, Mr. Clemens? He is about your age."

"By name, sir," I managed to reply. In fact Trist is well known on the river as an epileptic and a fool.

"As I was saying: this young man, since his earliest boyhood of a scientific bent, has made an exhaustive study of the human dermis, taking samples of about *so*—" (he held his thumb and forefinger perhaps a half an inch apart) "—from financiers and flatboatmen, priests and prostitutes alike. Some of his samples were taken in the grandest houses of New Orleans; a sizable number come from his own slaves. Immediately on taking a 'cutting,' as he terms it, he places it in a solution of one part saltpeter to two parts extract of albumen." He paused to examine his glovetips. "A preservative solution, he informs me. I wonder if either of you can guess what happens next."

Bixby and I remained speechless. The cub made a great show of interest in the river.

"No guesses?" said the visitor, in a voice that made it clear that he'd expected none. "Permit me to enlighten you!" His round cheeks puckered with excitement. "Mr. Trist has found, in every case, that the sample sheds a fine— one might almost say, a _negligible_—layer of particles into the astringent mixture, exposing a fundamental pigment that is blacker than the night your mothers, gentlemen, were so fortunate as to conceive you."

This was too much for Bixby at last. "Nay, sir—; nay. I will not _tolerate_—"

"Tut, tut!" the little man said, holding up a finger. "We are each of us a darky, gentlemen; science has spoken. Au revoir!"

He hopped nimbly from the bench, snatched up his cane and disappeared down the ladder. Bixby immediately turned the whole of his attention to the efforts of his cub, not so much as twirling his whiskers at me for the remainder of the run.

Picture my surprise when I discovered, that same afternoon, that I'd been exchanging pleasantries with the notorious slave bandit Thaddeus Murel, and furthermore that he _owned_ the boat, from the boiler to the watch on Bixby's fob!

The Punch-Line.

ISLAND 37 WAS THE CRADLE OF THE TRADE, Virgil says. But the Trade had no need of a cradle any longer.

The island was a much-fabled port of call—; not every steam-boat would put in there. When the state of Louisiana was chartered, it laid claim "to the mid-point of the river," and the state of Mississippi "to the channel"—; a simple enough division, on the face of it. Six years later, however, a rogue thumb of current carved a long, flat sliver out of the Mississippi mainland, well out into the river but short of the mid-point by half a mile. The new-born island belonged as much to one state as to the other, and owed allegiance, by law, to neither. It was a country to itself.

Decades passed, and the residents of the thirty-seventh island up-stream from New Orleans—an overnight passage by steam-ship—grew down-right cozy in their solitude. The absence of law, not to mention tax-collectors, made it a haven for fugitives of every stripe. For the Redeemer, of course, it was paradise itself. In no time at all 37 had become his play-pen, and he—as a matter of course—had become its Lord Regent. He had no further need to scour the country-side for suckers, he was fond of declaring—; on 37 the suckers came to him, and they came politely.

The sailing-bell rang behind me and the *Vesuvius* hove off. The pilot's name was Henderson—a Scotchman—and he'd been a share-holder from the beginning. The Redeemer had got ahold of him the same way he'd gotten all of us—: partly by blind chance, partly by design, feeling his way like a crawdad toward his present empire.

No-one was waiting to meet me on the freshly white-washed pier, which didn't surprise me much—: it was going on six, and the flesh-pots at the top of the bluff would be packed to overflowing. The neat white shacks along the water glowed prettily against the bank, their shuttered porches flickering like paper lamps—; here and there a sullen-faced boy or an old woman would nod to me as I passed. For all one could see or hear from the landing itself, 37 was a sweet-water hamlet like any other.

The sleepiness of the water-front never failed to charm me. As always, I felt a quiet temptation to find some ragged pallet in an empty room, hang up my coat, and delay my interview as long as possible. Had I examined this desire, my reluctance to keep my appointment might have struck me as curious—; but I did not examine it. After a few instants' hesitation I went on up the slope to meet with my Redeemer.

I found him in his usual warren in the basement of the "Panama House" saloon, holding court before six or seven flat-boat roughs of the sort you'd be more likely to stumble over in some piss-soaked alley than meet with on the river. The week before, it had been a clutch of Presbyterian clergy-men—; the week before that, Mandarin Chinese. The clambering vines of our "corporation"—as the Redeemer had come to call it—left no patch of light uncourted. Rumors had even begun to circulate that some of the finest houses in the South—and above the Mason-Dixon Line, as well—were serving as its trellises.

You'd never have guessed it, however, from the gathering in the Panama House that night. The boat-men were sitting in a clump on the straw-battened floor, passing a pail of rotten-smelling shine between them—; a riper bunch of gallows-apples could not have been got together. The Redeemer sat cross-legged on a padded stool he'd had specially made in Baton Rouge, presiding over the goings-on like a wax saint in a crèche. Smoke from Chinese incense and skunk-weed cigars closed the room in like a tent—; whatever compulsion I'd felt to present myself vanished completely. I was about to turn to go when the Redeemer caught sight of me.

"Virgil!" he sang out, granting me that particular smile—at once conspiratorial and shy—that never failed to convince me that my most private thoughts were known to him. "Come sit down with our friends from the Butternut Society."

"Beg pardon, sir—; I'd rather not."

He'd developed an acute sensitivity to my moods over the years, and an even stronger indifference to them—; tonight, however, proved a rare exception. Leaning to one side, as if to get his head around the smoke, he studied my face for a moment, then slid down off his stool, bowed to his guests, and led me wordlessly upstairs. We passed through the bar like spirits, side-stepping the first bowie-fight of the evening, and continued up to the second floor, where a small suite of rooms had been set aside for Trade affairs. The Redeemer lit a candle, motioned to me to shut the door, then guided me by the wrist—as one might lead a debutante in a quadrille—to a table flanked by two low chairs.

"Well, dear Kansas!" he said at last. (We were both still on our feet—: the table and chairs had a definite purpose in our ritual, and its moment had not yet come.) "Well!" he said again.

"How runs the Trade, sir?"

"Weakly, Virgil. Totteringly."

This answer took me quite aback—: the usual response was "ineluctably," "indefatigably," or some equally luxurious term.

"What is it, sir? Have the returns let up?"

"Oh, the *returns* are right enough! It's nothing *fiscal*." He smiled in a melancholy way, and tugged once—pensively—on his right ear.

My alarm deepened. "Tell me, sir! What is it?"

He made a delicate gesture of regret. "Politics, Virgil, since you press me." His eyes met mine for an instant, then slid dolefully away. "I have it on good authority that we're to be voted out of office."

"What—! The Trade?" My voice rang out stupidly in the empty room. "I wasn't aware—beg pardon, sir—that we'd ever been elected."

A look of genuine bitterness crept into his eyes. "A poor choice of phrase, Kansas. Forgive me." He went quiet for a time, then added softly—: "You can leave a man hoeing in a field his health, his hoe, and his liberty, *mon frère*. But that won't do much good if the field's pulled out from under him."

I said nothing for a time, attempting, as I so often did, to sift for meaning in his blather. "The Abolitionists, sir?" I said at last.

He nodded. "Between those righteous angels above us, dear K, and the plantationers below, this *confrérie* of ours"—peppering his conversation with Frenchisms was a recent affectation of his—"may soon run out of runaways!"

I blinked at this a moment. "How, for God's sake?"

"Through the complete and utter abolishment of slavery, both in the territories and the states."

I let out an uneasy laugh. "Respectfully, sir, you can't believe all the rubbish that gets talked downstairs. You've been holed up in this backwater too long. Nobody I've come across is ready to toe the Federal line—; not yet." I shook my head decidedly. "They'd prefer to die."

"They may have to," the Redeemer said. When I tried to speak again he hushed me with a flutter of his kid-gloved hands.

"Enough talk. Let's proceed."

"But you can't actually credit—"

The hand flew up again. "*Repose*, Virgil! Cultivate repose." He frowned at me a moment. "I may be 'holed up' here, as you say—; but the world is so obliging as to come to *me*. It tells me things, on our little tête-à-têtes, and I listen very closely." He stepped up to the table and motioned to me to sit. "Those boys down in the cellar, for example. Six butternuts from Indiana, and they're saying the same thing as associates of ours in Boston, Baltimore, Louisville, even the capital itself—; everywhere, in fact, but in these god-forsaken swamps. Do you understand me, Virgil? *Word for word.* Sit down, now—; there's a boy. I'll be back *tout de suite.*"

I did as I was told. The notion of abolition, however—the *possibility* of it, better said—had worked itself under my hide. "You seem to be listening to everybody but the people around you, sir," I said at last. "The South will never stand for it. The idea that anyone would endorse—"

"They won't need to endorse so much as a theater ticket," the Redeemer replied. "The country we fatten ourselves on thinks of itself as a *democracy*, Virgil. Have you forgotten?"

"You know as well as I do, sir, that this country is a—"

"Nebraska and Kansas are to come into the Union as free states," he said, cutting me short. "I received word this morning."

I sat back in my chair, dumb-struck. I'd just come from New Orleans, and would certainly have heard such news down there, if anyone had known it—: there would have been rioting in the streets. "You got *word*—?"

The Redeemer nodded absently, as if the fact held little interest for him. "Don't get into the habit, dear K, of letting your mouth hang open. An open mouth indicates feebleness of character—; it is also well known to affect the teeth."

"I should very much like to know, sir, who you're getting these reports from, and whether they're in any position to give reliable, well-founded—"

But the Redeemer only turned on his heels in that odd pirouette of his, and said to me melodiously as he waltzed out of the room—: "So long as the present constellation of states persists—the Yankees fat and nimble, the South condescended to at every turn—then our way of *life*, dear K—" (and here he winked over his shoulder, as a vaudevillian might to an offstage admirer) "—remains permanently *en péril!*"

With that I was left to my disbelief. The fight over the territories had been raging for years, and I'd stopped paying attention long since. But the Redeemer was right on one score, at least—: the admittance of Kansas and Nebraska as free states would tip the balance of power irresistibly, irrecoverably toward the North. In time, the holding of slaves would be outlawed throughout the Union. It would take years— perhaps even decades—for the change to come about—; but come about it would, sure as pox and watered beer.

The Abolitionists were the cause of it—: the Abolitionists with their mirthless, glassy rhetoric, their funerary tastes in clothing and amusement, and their Bible that resembled our own in every outward respect but seemed the testament of an entirely different deity. The Trade ate away at the foundations of the South, of course—; but it took care only to nibble. That the Abolitionists (whose existence—irony of ironies!—made our enterprise possible) might actually *succeed* was an idea I'd never once credited. They'd always seemed too starched, too prim, too shrill to catch the fancy of the country. But things were changing everywhere you looked—; you felt it even on Island 37. The country itself was getting shriller, and the Abolitionists fervid speechifying was taking on the ring of prophecy.

I was floundering in this and other worries when the Redeemer reappeared, carrying a quill, a palm-sized note-book, and a penny-box of matches. He set the matches beside the candle on the table.

"Is it right?" he asked, as ritual required.

I shook my head. "It's not right," I replied.

Deliberately, silently, he moved the candle to the left, rotating it counter-clockwise as he did so.

"Is it right?" he asked again, more softly than before.

I took in a careful breath. "Yes," I said. "It's right."

He smiled and snuffed the candle with his fingers. The room fell at once into a heavy, violet darkness. I made no effort to clear my mind of its usual clutter, to compose myself, or to locate the Redeemer in the room. I simply sat as I was and waited. The sound of the bar below us gradually fell away. The darkness thickened and set.

"I'm ready," I said, straightening.

No sooner had I spoken than there came a sharp *pop!* and the head of a match flared to life a hand's breadth from my left eye. If a powder-keg had caught fire in my left eye-socket the pain could have been no greater. I cursed and gnashed my teeth and cried aloud to heaven. The flame remained as it was for perhaps three seconds more—; then it sputtered and went out.

For a time there was only a hexagram of light in my left eye, and a rhombus of vaguer color in my right—; then, creepingly at first, but with ever-greater speed, a net of green sparks spread across my sight.

"What is it?" came the Redeemer's voice.

"A six-pointed star. With a net drawn across it."

"What color is the net?"

"Green."

"Green? You're sure?"

"Yes. Green and rust-colored."

A pause. The sound of a quill being scraped against a cup. The smell of India-ink.

"And the net? Also green?"

"Yes. The net is fading now."

"Does the star remain?"

"Yes. It's beginning to turn."

"Clock-wise?"

"Yes. Wait—: there's a cloud behind it."

"What color?"

"Yellow."

Another pause. The rustling of paper. "Yellow, you said?"

"Yes. It's already gone."

"What now?"

"Nothing. Gray lines on a grid."

"Is it the old grid?"

I opened my eyes with a sigh. "Same as ever."

"I'll be the judge of that," the Redeemer said smugly.

Now the candle was lit again, and slid closer to me, and I bent slowly forward till my eye was at its flame.

"What is it?" the Redeemer whispered.

I brought my eye closer still, so close that my brow began to prickle from the heat. The brightness was so severe that I could feel the flickering and bucking of the flame, like a curious finger-tip, on the lining of my brain.

"The net," I said quickly. "The flare. The yellow cloud." I paused a moment. "The same star as before."

"What else?"

I sat back with a groan. "That's all."

The Redeemer nodded and closed his book. "Was there pain?" he said, touching my forehead lightly with two fingers.

I cursed him silently. "You know there was."

"How much?"

"There was pain," I said. I brushed his hand away.

"You're becoming more sensitive," he murmured, touching my face again. Something I'd seen had excited him—; that much was clear. "More pain with the candle, or more with the match?"

"More with the candle," I said. "With the candle it was as much as I could bear."

This pleased him better still. "A *full* reading!" he crowed, holding his notes aloft. "Fuller than most, at any rate. *Four* signs!"

Usually he said nothing when we'd done, and asked me no more questions—; the reading must have affected him profoundly. "Will it take long to puzzle out?" I asked.

"Don't be impatient, Kansas. Bide here for a spell." He snatched up his notebook and spun away again.

I sank wearily to one side, covered my eyes with my palms, and tried to make my own sense of what I'd seen. The result, as usual, was an over-powering urge to sleep. There was nothing wondrous, to my mind, in our sessions, other than the amount of pain they caused me. I had as much confidence in the power of my left eye to foretell the future as I had in my right ear's ability to predict rain. From the next room, as if across a great body of water, the rustling of folio pages could be heard. A familiar voice intruded on my repose.

"A yellow cloud, Virgil? *Yellow?* Are you quite sure?"

I sat up with a start, as though prodded awake, to find the Redeemer sitting next to me at the table. His arms were folded tightly against his belly and he was watching me with violence in his look—: at first I thought I'd somehow spoiled the reading.

"What is it?" I asked. "What's wrong? I did my sovereign—"

"You're to leave tonight," he said, cutting me short.

I frowned at him. "Tonight, sir? But I haven't—"

"You've heard about the trouble up in Memphis?"

"I've heard there's some manner of epidemic making the rounds," I said, pressing my fingers to my temples. "Pulmonary grippe. Catarrh."

"Not catarrh," the Redeemer said, his eyes brighter than before. "Yellowjack."

"The fever?" I said hollowly.

"The same."

I watched him for a moment before I spoke. Something in his manner made me circumspect. "They've certainly kept it quiet," I said at last.

"There's no keeping it quiet any longer, Kansas." His voice was sedate and teasing, as though withholding the punch-line to a joke. "Eighty-score are dead—; thousands flee the city every hour." He clucked his tongue against his teeth. He and Parson both made that same sound, usually as a sign of satisfaction. I began to grow skittish in my seat.

"It's the seventh day of Judgment up there, according to the Colonel," the Redeemer said finally.

"The Colonel's in Memphis?"

The Redeemer shook his head, toying with two burnt matches on the table-top. "He left the day before yesterday, after finding his cook face-down in a pan of hopping-john."

I tried in vain to catch his eye, hoping to guess the joke before he made it. "As good a sign to jump ship as any, I suppose."

"Black bile and blood-puddles everywhere," the Redeemer said, still twiddling the matches. "*Rivers* of it in the streets."

I said nothing. My skin was going hot and cold by turns.

"Not everybody's cleared out, though," he added playfully.

Blearily, as if through a the bottom of a bottle, I began to see.

"Stacey's clearing-house, for example, is still open for business. Goodman Harvey's with old Stacey, managing things on our end." He scratched his nose. "At present, of course, there isn't much to manage."

Goodman Harvey, I thought. Naturally. The only boot-licker in the whole chain of command more eager to please than I was. I knew exactly what the Redeemer wanted of me now. Seeing this, he said nothing more, content to watch me struggle against my better judgment—; the struggle, as always, was a brief one.

"How many?" I asked in a bloodless voice.

He closed his eyes, one after the other, like a tom-cat in a patch of sun. "How many what, dear K?"

"You know damned well, sir. How many niggers."

He arched his back, cracked his finger-joints against the table, then settled down more comfortably into his chair. He was too content even to chide me for my language. I'd seen him take pleasure in his power over me before, but never with such ruthless, careless coziness. When finally he spoke I learned, in no uncertain terms, just how little I was worth to him.

"Fifty-seven souls," he said coolly, pushing a dog-eared ledger toward me. I recognized the hand-writing—curlicued, girlish—as Parson's. Fifty-seven Christian names were listed, each of them male. The list was divided into four columns—: (I) age, (II) weight, (III) disposition, and (IV) marketable skills. A fifth column, labeled "Sold For," as yet remained blank.

The most I'd ever taken on a single run was seventeen head, and that mostly women. I should have bowed to him politely, walked down to the landing, and dog-paddled all the way to New Orleans.

"Why so many?" I asked. My voice was thick as custard.

"Because we *can*, Kansas! We can—; and we have the yellowjack to thank for it. It's the fourth birthday of the Trade, and the fever has given us a present—: enough panic to run a herd of bison through. If Jefferson, or Rush, or even old Baron were still receiving, we'd ship every last darkie off this island *tout à fait!*" He quieted himself, with an obvious effort, and gave me a sober look. "But Pop Stacey—blast him!—won't take more than fifty-seven."

"You'd need seven barges to hold them, sir," I mumbled, fighting the urge to fall blubbering at his feet. "And seven idiots to run them."

By way of an answer he held up his fingers for me to look at, cracked them again, then bunched them together into dumplings. He regarded me a moment, brought the dumplings to his mouth, and blew across them once, twice, thrice in quick succession—: then his right hand opened. A ring of worked silver glinted in his palm. A tired trick, of course, but he had need of nothing better. I was already long since brought to heel.

He laid the ring before me on the table. "As it *is*, though, Kansas, I need only one."

AND SO THE PUNCH-LINE arrived at last. The Redeemer meant for me to take fifty-seven grown men into a fever town and sell them. I sat up straight, arranged my collar and cravat, then slumped face-down onto the table. I wept in a series of dry-eyed little gasps. It was tantamount to a death-sentence, after all.

"Will I be running them alone?" I said. I saw nothing but the thick green felt covering the table. For some reason its blurry coarseness soothed me.

"I've sent across the river for Parson. I don't expect you'll require more camaraderie than that."

"Parson," I said, grinding my chin into the felt. I'd have preferred to make the run in a butter-churn.

"I've explained my scheme to him, of course. He's given it his blessing."

"I wouldn't be surprised if Parson had invented yellow fever."

The Redeemer smiled at this, indulging me. "A once-in-a-decade's chance, Kansas. Once in a *lifetime*, possibly."

"Once in mine, you mean," I said. But I said it meekly. The more I learned about the Redeemer's tricks, the better they seemed to work on me. He was capable of appearing entirely at your mercy, meek and vulnerable as a school-girl—: you pitied him, especially if his plan was flawed, while still trembling at the least thought of his displeasure.

A silence fell—: the silence of the tomb. I stared morosely at the matches the Redeemer had been fiddling with, then all at once noticed that they'd fallen, quite by chance—one straight, one broken—to form an arrow pointing out the door.

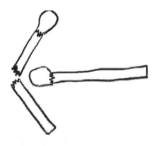

For some reason this jarred me from my bedazzlement like a blast of snuff. Memories of yellowjack victims I'd seen, the image of Memphis filling with bloated, black-tongued corpses, and the thought of myself in the thick of it all brought me suddenly to my feet.

"I won't do it, sir."

He shook his head at me. "Of *course* you will, Kansas! You've already told me so!"

"*I've* told you? I don't follow—"

He covered his right eye, winked at me with the other, and my boldness disappeared like spit into a puddle. I knew what his pantomime meant, of course. My blighted eye had told him.

"What was it?" I said dully, sitting back down. "The star? The yellow cloud?"

The ghost of a grin played about his mouth-corners. "You *could* say it was the star, I suppose. Better yet, it was all the signs in sequence. Better *still*," he said, his eyes narrowing to two coal-colored slits, "it was everything you've done since you stepped off the *Vesuvius*. And perhaps a bit before."

My thoughts flew about in a panic, darting from one imaginary betrayal to another, and settled at last on the little Pinkerton I'd met. Quietly, gingerly, I slipped a hand into my coat-pocket, looking for the card Barker had given me.

It was gone.

"*Everything* I've done? What the devil does that mean?" I said at last. But my voice was as guilty as an adulterer's.

The Redeemer picked up the ledger-book, by way of an answer, and laid it triumphantly in my lap. "It means you leave in half an hour, Mr. Ball."

"YOU'LL HAVE ANOTHER WHITE MAN WITH YOU, *en passant*," the Redeemer said as he walked me to the Panama House landing. It was dusk, and we made our way by the weak light that fell from the windows of the bar.

"Is that so?" I murmured, sunk in my misery like a carcass in a bog.

"More of an *observer*, really, than an active participant. *Un spectateur objectif.*" He coughed into his hand. "Young Asa Trist."

I laughed aloud at this. Let them all come to Memphis, I thought—madmen, naturals, epileptics, amnesiacs—what possible difference could it make? "You mean to put me to death, sir, I take it?"

He quickened his pace. "I needn't explain the *importance* of the Trist family to the Trade, I hope. That boy's been badgering me since the day he arrived. He's harmless, really—; practically a child—"

"Kennedy's told me what a cracked egg he is," I said.

For once the Redeemer looked genuinely pained. "Asa wants to follow this delivery, that's all. To get acquainted with the business. Does that seem so very cracked?"

"Everything to do with this run seems cracked," I said. "Why is Trist so interested in the business, suddenly? He's never cared a crumb before."

"He fancies himself a *scientist*, Virgil. A rationalist, like yourself. *Un homme de recherche.*"

He was leading me about by the nose now, and I knew it. "So Trist's not coming along to learn the business, then," I said. "It's something else entirely."

He shot me a plaintive look. "Don't ask me to explain the ways of the *gentry*, dear K."

"I swear to you, sir, if that loony mucks in my affairs—"

"*Touché!*" the Redeemer cried, as though I'd reasoned him to his knees. His manner had become steadily more theatrical as we walked, as if he were performing for a hidden audience. He passed his arm through mine almost bashfully, and proceeded to recite at the top of his lungs, as one might at the edge of a cataract—:

"It's the same run as *always*, really—; just a bit more freight. Aim to pull in at sun-up, so you'll have light to get them coffled by. Lafitte & Dobbins have left for St. Louis—; you can tie up at their berth. You know Stacey's clearing-house, of course—"

"That is my privilege, yes."

"Of *course* it is. But they've moved two streets westward." He stopped again, watched me closely for a moment, then handed me a peach-colored envelope, embossed with letters of strident blue—:

STACEY & TALON
DEALERS IN NEGROES & BONDSMEN
21 COURT STREET, MEMPHIS

I was to take one of three new boats the Colonel had commissioned for us, sleek twenty yarders that ran on steam against the current and floated back down-river like a barge. They showed less profile than a decent-sized pirogue, and drew less than half a yard of water when full—: perfect craft for smuggling. The Colonel liked to joke that if the Abolitionists had thought to invest in half a dozen, Canada would be an African protectorate by now.

When the Redeemer and I reached the landing, I could see straight-away from the lay of the boat—low in the water, canting subtly aftwards—that the slaves were already in the hold. This discovery caused me pain, though it took me a moment's reflection to understand why.

"You knew *before* looking in my eye that I'd make this run," I said.

"Parson'll be along soon," the Redeemer said airily, leading me up to the pilot-house. (He took a childish pride in these new skiffs of his, though he himself had never run one.) "You've piloted her before, if I remember rightly. Do I remember rightly?"

"Never with fifty-eight head on board."

"Fifty-*seven*, Virgil."

"Fifty-eight, sir, counting that cracked egg of yours."

He tut-tutted with a finger. "Don't fret on Trist's account, Kansas. Parson will be on this run, remember. Has a way with dilettantes, as you may know. He takes the stuffing out of them."

I made a face. "Who'll take the stuffing out of Parson?"

"Parson thinks very highly of you, Virgil. *Very*." He touched his finger solemnly to his nose. "You might say he's your biggest backer, just now, in our little circle."

For no reason I could name, Barker came to mind again. He and the Redeemer were of a piece, somehow. Some invisible thread connected them.

"I met a curious sort of Pinkerton on the boat," I said, as off-handedly as I could. "Made a production out of being a bounty-hunter. Practically wore it on his hat."

The Redeemer made no answer for a spell. "Name?" he said finally.

"Gave his name as Barker."

"Barker," the Redeemer said. Bar—*ker*," he repeated, as though the name were Flemish, or possibly Japanese.

"A student of the black arts, apparently."

"Morris P. Barker is familiar to me, thank you," the Redeemer said curtly. "A known quantity." His tongue clacked three times against his palate. When next he spoke, the words came out regular as playing-cards—:

"Morris P. Barker Is No Student Of The Black Arts."

Just then the sound of rowing reached us, cautious and hollow-seeming in the dark, and a pirogue slid into view. A figure was standing in the bow like the prophet Elijah, his hands clasped fervently together—; the set of oars behind him looked for all the world to be managing themselves.

The Redeemer was still looking at me closely. "Have a chat with Parson, Virgil, the next time you're feeling mystical. Mind the company you keep."

"Shall I ask Parson about Barker, sir?"

"You'll do *no such thing*," the Redeemer hissed, seizing me by my collar. "You'll leave Parson to watch over those fifty-seven *niggers*, Kansas, and you'll see this run through—; then you'll come straight back to *me*." He let go of my collar disdainfully and turned away from me, struggling to catch his breath. I'd never seen him so distressed. "You'll do no such thing as talk to Parson about Barker," he said again, more evenly. "*No such thing*, Virgil. Do you hear?"

The Redeemer was afraid of this Barker—; that much was plain. An idea—perhaps even, without my intending it, a plan—was beginning to take shape within me. "And Trist, sir?" I asked. "What am I to do with him?"

"I don't give one cat's *diddle* what happens to that sport of nature," the Redeemer muttered. It was as near to a curse-word as I'd ever heard him use.

The pirogue pulled in soon after. Two shirtless niggers stood behind Parson in the bow. "Hey the boat!" the Redeemer sang out, stepping past me with evident relief.

Parson didn't answer until he had firm land underneath him. "Fifty-seven souls?" he said, gathering up his skirts. His eyes were like two stones from the bottom of the river.

"Fifty-eight," the Redeemer answered, giving me a wink. "Ziba Goss will be coming on this run."

I breathed a quiet sigh of gratitude. Goss was one of our mulatto strikers, a sturdy sort, the first I'd ever shipped with—; with him along there was a chance, however slight, that we'd actually complete the run.

Parson only nodded. The two rowers turned the skiff about and glided off into the gloaming, stiff as undertaker's dummies. Their manner didn't surprise me terribly—: I felt much the same in Parson's presence.

"Ziba Goss," said Parson, furrowing his downy brow. He turned and started up the path, drawing the Redeemer in his wake. "I've heard old Ziba's getting notions."

I groaned aloud at this.

"Ah! Is it Virgil?" Parson said, squinting back over his shoulder.

"I made a run with Ziba two weeks ago, Parson. There's no trouble with him at all." I fixed my eyes on the Redeemer. "I *need* Ziba on this run."

"Oh! There's no trouble with Ziba, Virgil," the Redeemer said. "You're perfectly right. There's no *trouble* with him, as such, but neither is there—"

"You'll give me Ziba Goss, sir, or the run to Memphis can get buggered."

The both of them regarded me silently for a time, their eyes identically narrowed. But I neither begged their pardons, nor averted my eyes, nor amended my declaration in the slightest—: I was determined to hold my ground at any cost. In doing so, I have no doubt that I confirmed their worst suspicions, and thereby sealed and ratified my fate. My fate was sealed already, of course—; but I didn't know it then.

"Ziba might not be three-quarters *dead*, sir, like the niggers Parson scares up from God knows where to paddle his funeral barges—"

"Here's our Asa!" the Redeemer said brightly, looking up the hill.

The figure in question was already half-way down the bluff, his limbs a blur of antic jerks and twitches. I'd met him only once before—in the whist room, at the Trade's first meeting—and remembered him as little more than a brittle, anxious voice and a shock of coal-black hair. Clearly his condition, whatever it was, had worsened. His lips fluttered pauselessly, sometimes in accompaniment to a smile, sometimes an indignant tossing of the head—; his right hand clutched a hat-box, his left a parasol. He was less than six paces off before he noticed us. Never have I seen a man look more like the wretch that gossip and calumny would have him be.

"Mr. Ball!" he squeaked, stepping past the Redeemer and Parson and taking my arm eagerly in his. "I understand you're my passage to the City of the Sun."

"I'm bound for Memphis, as per our Redeemer's orders," I said, freeing myself from his grip.

But Trist took no notice of my manner. Turning back to the others, he exclaimed—:

"One sees the Jew in him, it's true. There's a sallowness to the skin, a richness—; a biblicality, in short. I'd die for the least scrap—?"

"You'll have to ask Mr. Ball himself, Asa," the Redeemer said, looking as though he'd bit into a peach-pit. Parson watched the two of us contentedly.

"Ideally, I'd take a cutting from the praeputium," Trist continued. "However, in this case—"

"The which, Mr. Trist?" I asked, taking a step backwards.

Trist gave me a beatific smile. "The *praeputium*, Mr. Ball. The foreskin."

"Quod ergo Deus coniunxit, homo non separet,"* Parson intoned, holding up a finger.

WITH THAT I WAS LEFT to the readying of the boat. Ziba Goss appeared not long after, and we stretched ourselves out on the lee deck, passing a tin of tobacco back and forth. Goss had always been my favorite striker, largely on account of his extraordinary greed, which kept him sober and level-headed at all hours. Knowing exactly what he liked and how to get it made him a personable companion, rarely out of temper—; what's more, he was possessed of common sense, an almost unheard-of quality among river-men. I asked him, after a time, what he thought about the run—; he simply shook his head and grinned.

"I don't think *nothing* about it, Mr. Virgil. Not a thing."

"You're happy, I expect. There'll be a fine cup of gravy on fifty-seven head."

His answer took me by surprise. "Oh! I ain't thinking about *that*," he murmured. He beamed out sleepily at the river.

Ziba had a secret, and I guessed it soon enough—: chaw always quickened my wits. "You're set to leave the Trade, aren't you."

His eyes fell closed. "Got me a new address, Mr. Virgil." He began to grin. "A beef-steak-chewing woman, now! A full-on roly-poly."

"There's a term for men like you, Ziba," I said, spitting over the rail. "A sacrificial lamb."

Ziba laughed. "You won't tell?"

I shook my head, yawned, and looked up toward the Panama House. To my surprise, Trist was already half-way down the path, waving his arms as though the boat might steam away without him—; Parson followed just behind. Both were traveling with all the speed their respective dignities would allow. Not surprisingly, Trist reached the landing first.

"Do you have any difficulty with leeches, Mr. Ball?" he called out in place of a greeting, clutching his battered hat-box to his chest.

I stared at him a moment, weighing all possible answers to this latest piece of poetry. Parson kindly answered for me.

"He wouldn't be ferrying you to Memphis, Asa, if he did!"

---

*What God has joined, let no man rend asunder.

Being a Brief History of T. Merryl & His Trade

by Frank S. Kennedy.

IT WERE THAT COZY BASTARD G. Harvey thought it up, Kennedy says.

I were hunched back there slopping the evening's cups, passing the time of the day with T.M., when be darmed but that fat cherry-popper comes waltzing in, a yaller silk jacket on him fit for the privy-master to the royal house of Brunswick.

It's His Grace, Goodie Harvey, says I to T.M.

So it is, says he. I'd thought it was a banana.

Good-day to you both, says Harvey, lisping as he done. A pint of thith or that, Mithter Kennedy, if you would.

You'll get as much as can fit in your eye till you pay debits out-standing, says I.

You're not square with me either, Goodman, T.M. puts in.

The very aim of my vithit! Harvey chirps. Firthtly! Kennedy—: your two dollarth fifty.

And bedam but he pulls five chits out from his pocket and lays them on the counter.

I must of look like a monkey's butler cause T.M. lets out a laugh and slaps me on the back. There's an easy enough answer for it, Stuts, says he. I just heard the angel Gabriel sound his trumpet.

Thimpler than that, even, Harvey says. Gentlemen—: I have found me an eathy mark.

They are all of them easy to a snit of your caliber, Goodie, says T.M.

Christ, but that little rounder blushes. Thank you, thir. But thith one I can't take no credit for. Thith nut ith cracked wide open. He leans forward on his hands. I thuppoth you have both heard tell of the Tritht thugar empire.

T.M. looks him hard in the face. You haven't got hold of Sam Trist's idiot son, says he.

Harvey says nothing, twiddling his mug.

Mister Harvey, says T.M. You aren't come in here jabbering and japing to take the vow of silence on us now. Give out.

Harvey digs at the corner of his gob with his tongue. I'm blue moldy for the want of a drink, says he.

T.M. grins. Give the man his due, Kennedy.

I could always tell it when something were cooking with T.M. Harvey takes up his mug and sucks it and the story comes out of him like piss from a horse's croppers.

It happened thith way, says he. Tritht the father is getting on, and our dear boy ith hith one and only. Deedth him three old family parcelth to keep in running order, for to learn the rigging of it. Thee? And young Atha barely out of thort panth, and crazy ath a beaver into the bargain.

He stops a bit.

Lets hear it, Harvey, you dithered little shite, says I.

All right, says he. What do you reckon our nutter planth on doing firtht?

Enlighten us, says T.M.

He meanth to let em *go*, Harvey yells, slapping both hams on the counter.

Who? says I.

HITH NIGGERTH!

What, to liberate em? says T.M., frowning.

Harvey hops and titters. You heard rightly! Every ounth of plucked cotton up the old River Jordan. Fare thee well, ye thport of thpring and nature . . .

You must be off your parsnips, Goodie boy, says I.

True ath I live and breathe. Thomething about *puckerth* in their thkin. Harvey rubs his face. Thinkth blackneth ith an ailment. Or the cure for one. Taketh *cuttingth* from 'em.

He what? says T.M.

Harvey nods. Cuttingth, he says again. He did all manner of fiddling, and now he'th decided to let 'em go. But not out of brotherly good-feeling, mind—: he'th afeared of them. He told me.

So he's no liberationist, then, says I.

Elbow-litionist, Stuts, T.M. says. He goes quiet for a bit. Well, Mr. Harvey—; I would recommend—

I reckon we could *thell* 'em, Harvey whispers. The lot. Up in Memphith, maybe. Or Natchez.

I look down at the cups in front of me. Seven wet cups in a row.

That's D'Ancourt's godson, says I. The old Colonel who drinks down at Cheney's. He'll not be very keen.

He'll be keen ath a cricket, says Harvey. I know him.

T.M. tips his head back and lets out a cluck. Harvey! says he. You're forgetting Trist senior. You think old Sam Trist can't keep count of his niggers?

If he can't, there's plenty on his payroll knows better, says I. There's no way we could peddle those niggers and live.

Tritht would put a bounty on em, that'th all, Harvey says. We thell 'em here and there, one or two niggerth at a time. Around Memphith. In the townth.

Or take them back to Daddy Trist and collect the bounty on them ourselves, a voice says from the corner booth.

Goodman, I believe you know our Parson, says T.M.

Harvey suckles on his beer for a time. I know him, says he.

T.M. has his head cocked toward the booth. Would it work?

But the old bogey is done for talking. T.M. turns it over for a spell.

Mister Harvey, says he. Run along to your nutter and ask him when he'd like to loose his niggers on the world.

A Sacrifice.

THE RUN TO MEMPHIS ENDED IN A BUTCHERY, Virgil says. It cured me of airs and fancy clothes forever.

We weren't three hours out of 37 when a commotion started up in the front hold. It was pitch-dark already—: aside from Trist, asleep beside me on the pilot's bench, I was entirely alone. I called for Ziba Goss and Parson, listened a moment, then called out again. Neither answered. The noise from the hold carried up in swells, now harsh and cutting, now strangely musical and mild—; within a quarter-hour I was desperate to know its cause. I resisted my curiosity as best I could, knowing the danger of giving the wheel over to Trist. It was not uncommon, after all, for the niggers to sing or pray together on a run. But this was neither the sound of singing nor of prayer—: it was a small noise, solitary and beseeching, that rose every so often into a chorus, then quickly fell away to nothing. At times it was so unearthly, so melancholy, that I questioned whether it was made by human tongues at all.

Soon I could no longer bear not knowing. Shaking Trist awake, I propped him up behind the wheel, ordered him to keep us hard into the current, and left him to the questionable charity of the river.

That was the first of my mistakes that night. I was fated, within the hour, to make two more.

I stepped out onto the star-lit deck and listened. No sound could be heard but the hissing and stuttering of the boiler. I felt my way along the rail to the front hold, listened another moment, then pressed my ear against its cast-iron shutters. For the space of a breath I heard nothing but the churning of the current—: then the current seemed to hush, the sound from the hold came up terrible and clear, and I was running back to the pilot-house as fast as my legs would carry me.

A man was being tortured in the hold. I had a trap-door Derringer in my vest pocket, little or no confidence in its kick, and none at all in my ability to put the fear of God into a boat-ful of death-crazed niggers. Such things fell under Parson's jurisdiction. I shouted his name, and Ziba's, again to no avail. Where in heavenly blazes had they gone? Were they still on board at all? Had they perhaps heard the sound in the hold themselves, weighed its credits and its debits, and jumped head-first into the river?

I found Parson soon enough, as it happened, but it brought me little comfort. He was leant stiff as a musket behind the boiler-house door. I lit a match and held it toward him—: he neither twitched nor blinked nor shed a tear. His face was ungiving to the touch, like a plaster-of-paris mask—; for his final, immortal expression he'd selected a thin-lipped leer. That was not all, however. His tongue protruded a good half-inch from his mouth, slack and slate-colored and fat, like the tongue of a yellowjack victim.

At the sight of that tongue I lost my last crumb of composure. I screamed and cursed and abused Parson's name every way I could think of, jumping up and down in front of him, slapping him, throttling him, shaking him back-and-forth by the collar. Parson remained effortlessly status quo. The sound from the hold was eclipsed, for the time being, by the workings of the boiler, and by my tantrum—; but the *idea* of the sound was more terrible than the sound itself. I screamed Parson's name one last time—I could think of no worse insult—and left him as he was.

When I returned to the pilot's house the sound was shriller than before, more plaintive, more severe. I couldn't stand it another instant. I knew better than to send Trist down, and I'd found no sign of Ziba—: for all I knew Parson had swallowed him alive. There was no commandment set down in the scriptures of the Trade, of course, that the cargo need be ministered to at all, let alone at night-time, out in the black middle of the river, under a topping head of steam. But I was not interested in the Trade and its protocols just then. I was not acting out of sympathy, or humanity, or even out of fear—: I was spurred on by my hatred of that noise, by a passionate desire to kill it off, and by a curiosity that admitted neither of caution nor delay. I had good reason to hurry. Acting in concert, even a dozen men could easily have forced the hatch—; I'd seen it done before. This, at least, was the rationale I gave myself while I fumbled with the padlock and the bolt. I was to repent it bitterly, and soon.

When the bolt slid open the sound stopped short, leaving a sudden vacancy in the air, as though a piano-wire had snapped. A humid silence met me as I raised the hatch, broken only by a rasping—or a *wheezing*, better said—in the far corner of the hold. The smell of piss and sweat and excrement seized me by the throat and commenced to wring the breath out of me slowly. A step-ladder extended two rungs downward, perhaps three, before vanishing into darkness. The stench and the dampness and a steady tightening of my bowels, as though in anticipation of a blow, were all there was to tell me I was being watched by two-score pair of eyes.

I could not say how long this spell of quiet lasted. Finally there was a scuffling below me, and a single clap of hands—; then a low, easy whisper of command that frightened me worse than all the rest combined.

"We at yin chopping-block yet, Savior?" a voice said mellowly.

"What's your name?" I called down. My own voice seemed grotesquely high and quavering.

A silence. "John yin Baptist," the voice said at last.

"You take this, Johnny, and you light it," I said, throwing down a match and a candle-stub.

This was my third error of the night.

A dull click followed, as of a jack-knife being opened—; then a scraping along the bottom of the hold. The match flared to life and was brought up to the candle. So dark was the hold, so much darker even than the night outside, that the match-flame all but blinded me. When I recovered my sight, I was dumbfounded by what I saw—: no more than an arm's length down the ladder, near enough to touch, two dozen head stood crushed together like kippers in a jar. A white-haired titan of a man stood just below me, balancing the candle on his left shoulder and watching me out of bolt-steady, ginger-colored eyes.

His look took me so aback that I was unable to speak for a moment, let alone to act—; but I saw, looking past him, why the hold seemed packed so tightly. There was a gap half-way back, the size of a bale of cotton, where nobody wanted to stand.

"What have you got back there?" I asked the white-hair. My voice cracked as I said it, like the voice of a pubescent boy, and I knew in that instant that all was lost. "Well? Give me an answer, damn your eyes! What are you fussing with?"

"Nobody *fussing*, Savior," he answered, his eyes widening as he spoke. All at once I saw the fear in them—: the fear, and the unmistakeable death-knowledge. My throat began to close, then, and my legs commenced to buckle. I had no intention of going down that ladder. There was a brightness, now, to every pair of eyes, the kind that comes to men with violence fermenting in their mouths. Those niggers knew what was waiting for them in Memphis. They didn't reckon, or suspect—; they *knew*. All that could be done was to close the hatch and leave them to their knowing.

Toward the back of the hold, at the edge of the mysterious gap, someone shifted his weight and a sharp cry of agony rose up. The man with the candle took a deep breath, smiled sorrowfully at me, and let his eyes fall closed.

I took my pistol out and brought it forward to catch the light. "What the hell was *that*, you lying sons-of-bitches?"

The man looked up at me again. "Nobody trying to fraud you, Savior," he murmured.

"Move aside or *Christ-help-me* I'll unload into the middle of you!" I shrieked. My voice was tremulous and slight. I marveled at how far from the Redeemer's easy bark of command it sounded. Panic was run through my voice like fat through a strip of bacon.

For perhaps the space of a breath all was quiet. Then came a shuffling and a scrambling and a falling of body over body and I made out a man pressed flat against the floor, his arms pinned beneath him, his face so badly beaten that I couldn't have guessed his age within thirty years. I saw at once that the remainder of the poor wretch's life would be measured in hours, if not in minutes.

A more prudent man would have let the hatch fall closed at that instant, stumbled back to the pilot-house, and let them pound their victim into pudding. The difference between fifty-seven head and fifty-six, after all, was not worth quibbling over. It was not prudence, however, that held me fixed above them—; nor was it Christian feeling. The only means of quieting that hold, I knew, was to make a show—however laughable—of sovereignty.

I leaned away from the square of candle-light, looked above me at the sky, and cursed the Redeemer, Parson, the Trade, and my own servile nature with a passion that was altogether new to me. Then I brought my face back into the light, wearing what I hoped was a look of homicidal ecstasy.

"You bring that man over here or so help me the Father, the Son, and the Heavenly Spirit," I said.

Two things happened as I spoke—: (I) the white-hair began to laugh—a deep, unhurried laugh full of scorn and melancholy, and

(II) the pulped and mangled body was carried forward to the ladder. I could tell from the way this was done—playfully, almost coyly—that I'd never be allowed near it. My panic was replaced at once by an overwhelming drowsiness. I wanted nothing more than to curl up next to the hatch and go to sleep.

"Who is it?" I said, once the body had been set down. I could see now that he was not a young man—: a bald spot was just visible at the crown.

"Just one of yin *angels,* Savior, sent down here amongst us," the white-hair said. As he said this he rose, raised his right foot in the air, and came down with all of his great weight against his victim's chest. I saw who it was in that same instant. It was Ziba Goss.

His shirt was ripped clean away, one of his feet was bare, and his breeches were in tatters—; but I saw, to my amazement, the butt of a one-shot pistol peeping from his boot. By some perversion of chance no-one had come across it in the dark. I knew then that I had to go down to them. So down I went.

The white-hair was so astonished to see me tumbling toward him that he simply stepped aside to give me room to fall. No sooner had I hit the floor than I snatched up Ziba's one-shot, giddy at my own folly, and pulled the hammer back. The entire hold hushed at once. It took them a moment to accept this newest offering—; but a moment only. I turned to the white-hair just in time to see him nod to me respectfully and tip the candle from his shoulder.

My life in the Trade ended with that gesture. I could taste my own death, luke-warm and ferric, against the roof of my mouth, and my past was taken from me like a hat in a gust of wind. As the candle went out I emptied Ziba's pistol at its after-glow and felt a jet of brackish liquor strike my cheek. The first pair of hands was already at my shoulders when I fired the second pistol, this time without any effect at all. Both guns were torn from my grip soon after and I heard furious curses when they refused to discharge. But even as I smiled at this my body was being tossed about and fought over and awareness was slipping out of me like a cat from out of a burning house.

My first sensation on awakening was pain—: my second was disbelief that I was still in my own body. For a time my eyes refused to clear, and when at last they did I shut them again at once. A great number of people were about me, muttering to one another and moaning, and behind them was the curved wall of the hold. This knowledge sickened me and gave the pain free run of my brain and body. I was not so well off as I'd thought. After a very great while, in which nothing whatsoever happened, I heard Parson's voice behind me.

"I prefer my baptisms the old-fangled way, Virgil. I prefer them to be done with water."

A drawn-out, comfortable sigh.

"People are *amenable* to it, you understand. They trust it—; they think of it as clean. I can see, of course, how such orthodoxy might bore you, free-thinker that you are. I'm often bored with it, myself. But *this*, Virgil—this *display* . . ."

I kept as quiet as a fish. Never in my life have I felt such a reluctance to come back to my senses. As understanding returned, so too did the memory of the struggle in the hold, and a good idea of what I'd see when I finally looked about me. Or so, with my last scrap of innocence, I believed.

Eventually I could stand it no longer and let my eye-lids flutter open. The sight that greeted me was the following—:

Parson sitting Indian-style in the middle of the floor, swaying to and fro like a hindoo snake-charmer. Trist just behind him, fiddling with something or other in his hat-box. A power of black bodies to every side, twitching and shuddering and weeping.

I thought, at first, that there were fewer niggers in the hold—; then I saw that they were simply pressed back even more impossibly against the walls, as far from Parson as their tangled bodies would allow. I took a careful breath and tried to move my fingers and my toes. All appeared to be in working order.

"How goes it, Captain?" Parson said, seeing me awake. He straightened slowly as he spoke, closed his eyes and smacked his lips together. His vertebrae clicked against one another like dominoes in a paper sack.

I shut my eyes at once. I took a breath, then rolled over onto my belly and tried to stand. My legs seemed to answer, for which I mumbled a silent hosanna—; when I made to push myself up, however, the room went all the colors of the rainbow and my face smacked resoundingly against the floor. "Christ preserve us!" I gasped. My right shoulder felt as if it had been chewed away by ants.

Parson's left eye opened. "Collar-bone's broke, Captain."

I could only sob in answer. Parson regarded me in his cold, contented way, keeping his right eye closed, shifting his weight every so often with an indolent little coo.

"We're past due for Memphis," he observed after a time.

"Bugger Memphis!" I hissed, trying a second time to rise. I must have looked for all the world like a pilgrim genuflecting in front of a wax effigy of the Pope.

"Tell me, Captain," Parson said, looking down the crook of his nose at me. "That *eye* of yours—: that blessed far-seeing ball of jelly." He turned his head clock-wise until his neck cracked. "Did it show you many wonders, as you quit this life?"

The pain in my shoulder lessened for a moment and I staggered to my feet. "It showed me all manner of things, Parson," I said, struggling to keep from falling backwards. "I saw the cloud you travel under, for one. Your own portable saintly nimbus." I spat onto the floor. "It was the color of rotten bile."

"You *do* have the gift," Parson said admiringly.

"It's the Jew in him," Trist offered.

Slowly, painfully, I worked the fingers of my right hand into a well-known gesture of contempt.

"He's giving us the fig!" Trist said, pointing at me delightedly.

"The yellowjack take the both of you," I croaked.

Parson bit his lip in mock concern. "You'll have to get us a fair piece up-river yet, Captain, for us to honor *that* request. "

I spat at him and made wobblingly for the ladder. I'd not taken three steps, however, when a new thought struck me. I glanced back at Parson.

"How did Ziba come to be down here? He had no business in the hold."

Parson raised his eye-brows. "Didn't you know, Virgil? Our commander-in-chief had him stowed for safe-keeping. He'd gotten flighty, it appears."

So this was Redeemer's doing. His by order and design. Why it should have surprised me so, why it should have washed my mind clear of all else, I can't rightly explain—; but it turned me irrevocably on my head.

I kept silent for a time, finding a place for this latest revelation in my thoughts—; relating it, slowly and painstakingly, to the history of my tenure in the Trade. The fact that I'd not been told about Ziba did not bode well for me, of course—; but I had no thoughts for the future. The present was more than enough for me. The *Redeemer* had brought this hell-on-earth about—: my own Thaddeus Morelle. My own.

"Where are the pistols?" I said, looking about me on the floor.

"Ah!" said Parson. "Trist has one of them—; you're welcome to it, I'm sure. As for the other—"

He planted his palms lightly on the floor, lifted himself without untwining his legs, and slid a foot or so to his left. Trist stepped away as well, and thus three corpses were exposed, stacked one atop the other like sacks of rice at market. At the bottom was the white-hair, his immense frame loose and slack-boned now, Ziba's pistol clenched in his left fist. Ziba himself was next, laid the other way round, with his battered head resting against the thighs of his executioner. Both were arranged neat as funeral-house cadavers, their arms bound tightly at their sides.

At the top was a third body, much slighter than the others.

"Ah! Jesus," I said weakly.

The body was that of a rail-thin boy, perhaps eleven years of age. For some private reason of Parson's he was arranged exactly as Parson was himself, with his legs crossed loosely under him and his back supported by the hold. His mud-colored eyes hung indifferently open. In the center of his forehead was a small red hole, a clean and perfect circle, its edge lightly speckled with powder-marks.

"Who shot that child?" I whispered.

Trist gave a guffaw. "*You* did, Captain!"

"Neat shooting, that, for a hand-puppet in the dark," Parson said silkily.

It was then I decided to murder the Redeemer.

III

The rising People, hot and out of breath,
Roared around the palace: "Liberty or Death!"
"If death will do," the King said, "let me reign;
You'll have, I'm sure, no reason to complain."

—Ambrose Bierce

The Yellowjack.

W̲E PULLED INTO MEMPHIS AT NOON, Virgil says. A day and a night had passed since Ziba's killing.

I'd never delivered contrabands in daylight before, but Parson promised me not a soul would care—: the Yellowjack had the keys to the city now. The look on his face put me in mind of the mayor of Sodom returned home after a holiday. He clapped me on the back—which caused me to gasp aloud with pain—and breathed deeply of the air. "Look yonder, Captain," he said sweetly, pointing up the bluff. At the top of it the customs-house was burning.

I brought us in slowly, easing up to the pier so that Trist wouldn't strangle himself in the hitching-rope. Since my vow of murder two nights before, I was resolved to become a model citizen in my associates' eyes. My chance with Morelle would come quickly enough, and I was not impatient. I could no longer quite conceive of the world without him, I discovered—; and I was in no great hurry for apocalypse.

Apocalypse, however, chose not to wait on my convenience.

Having tied and weighted the line, we pulled out the gang-planks and laid them flat, as with any other delivery. The niggers had been quiet as deer since the uprising, taking the water Trist brought them but refusing all food. I knew Parson well enough to expect no great help from him, but I reckoned the lingering effects of his hoo-doo might yet be strong enough for us to finish the run, provided he accompanied us to Stacey's. Even this small hope, however, proved a vain one. As I stepped onto the pier I caught sight of him, already well up the road to town, moving with swift, bobbing strides, like a silk-skirted daddy-long-legs.

Trist and I watched him steal away. "Sure you wouldn't rather follow Parson, Asa?" I asked. "He'd show you a livelier time than I ever could. Just look at how he prances."

"Not a bit of it, Captain!" Trist sang out, clicking his heels together. I was once again, apparently, the apple of his eye. My scalp prickled at the merest thought of it.

"I'm sure you could teach me more than *he* ever could, about the business-end of things," he said, raising his skittish eyes to mine.

"I've seen the business-end of things, all right."

He gave a squeal of delight at this. "You mean—you mean it would be *acceptable* to you—if I—"

"Get that mid-hatch open," I muttered. "Go on!"

The truth of it was that I needed him direly. With Ziba dead, my collar-bone broken, and Parson off God knows where, I stood as much chance as a one-legged man in an arse-kicking match.

The twenty-three head stowed amidships came up readily enough. Two hung back below deck, cramped and exhausted from close quarters, but Trist coaxed them up the ladder smartly. A few minutes later they were coffled together and ready to march, and the same held true for the stern hold. There was no delaying it any longer.

Slowly, ruefully, I walked with Trist up to the bow. I stood by the front hatch a moment, then gave him a stiff-lipped nod.

"Look lively now, Asa," I whispered, gripping the butt of my one-shot. "Christ knows what they'll do when they see it's just the two of us."

"Oh! *They* won't be any bother," Trist said breezily.

"Won't they?"

He smiled down at the hatch. "You saw as well as I did. Parson put the fear of God into them."

I looked past him at the river. "That wasn't the fear of God, Asa."

"They'll be gentle as lambs, Captain. You'll see." He threw the cross-bolt open and stepped aside. "Call the all-hands down to them, sir. They'll come to heel!"

Trist's faith in Parson's good works proved to be well founded. All twenty-two head came up orderly as you please, with their heads bent low and their wrists held out in front of them, as though positively eager for the chain. In a matter of moments the queues were coffled-up and ready. The faces of the niggers from the aft two holds looked sleepy and bewildered—; those from the bow looked as dead as cobble-stones. They moved like dead men, too, once we got them moving. It took us the better part of an hour to reach the top of the bluff, but I can't say I objected. If the Yellowjack was all it was rumored to be, most of them would breathe their last in old Pop Stacey's pens. Who could fault them for regretting it a little?

The nearer we came to the top of the bluff, the more wooden their movements grew—: man followed man so mechanically you might have taken them for soldiers at a drill. "Quiet bunch," Trist said as we rounded the last bend. I said nothing at all. The customs-house was close enough now that we could hear the flames lapping at its timbers and smell the sharp cloy of the boiling sap. I'd passed the house often on my visits, and had fallen into the habit of peering in—not a little enviously—at the clean, square parlor, and watching the customs-master's wife setting the table for breakfast, or for supper. I'd taken a fancy to that woman, and to the family I'd assigned her. Now they were dead, either in their rooms or on the street—: it was the custom during the worst bouts of Yellowjack to set afflicted homes on fire. As the coffles passed the house, its high slate roof commenced to shudder and bow, sending great hissing embers down onto the street. I began, with a calm born of my exhaustion and my pain, to weigh my odds of surviving the afternoon.

I was a different man than I was used to being. Nothing struck me as familiar, my own behavior least of all—; but that was only fitting. That day was to be the levering-point, the very pivot of my existence, and I knew it even then. This day must not be wasted, I said to myself. This day must be played out. I was both patient and resolute. I was, in a word, *decided*. I'd been brought back from the dead for a reason, after all—; and I intended to make good use of my reprieve.

If the fire in the customs-house had been set as a warning to passing boats—an illustration, however crude, of the disaster up in town—it might as well have been a match-flame. The sight that met our eyes as we came out onto Shelby Street could easily have been wrought by Moses. Hundreds of houses were in flames, and countless more had burnt down to their cellars—; the smoke from the combined conflagrations turned the mid-day sky the color of sodden brimstone. The citizens went about in perfect indifference to the smoke, to the fires, even to one another. Mountains of pulverized window-glass, roofing-tile, dry-goods, offal, evening-gowns, gunny-sacks, and every other conceivable article of trade smoldered in the streets, festooned with the carbonized remains of shop-ledgers, mastiffs, bed-linens, saddles, daguerreotypes, and various other objects I did my solemn best not to recognize.

We'd come only four streets when we saw our first corpses—: three of them—another trinity—propped together at the intersection of Shelby and Union Streets like the legs to a looted end-table.

Their bodies were set back to back, each supported by the others, in a deliberate parody of wakefulness. I was reminded straight-away of Parson's handiwork in the hold. Two were men, perhaps fifty years of age, and looked to have been dead for quite some time—; the third was a woman in the first flush of her youth. Her body had been stripped naked and doused with kerosene and an empty lantern lay beside her in the mud. The kerosene was freshly poured—: her belly and breasts shone under its glaze like preserved fruits in a jar.

"Damned waste of lamp-oil," a passing citizen said tonelessly. He was dressed as if for Sunday service, all in pressed silks and linen, except that his feet were bare and caked up to the ankle-bones with ash. I made to speak to him but he walked away from us, into the looted skeleton of a shop, closing the shop-door conscientiously behind him.

I was staring after him, trying to puzzle out some sort of explanation for the man, the bodies, indeed for everything we'd seen, when Trist gave a tactful cough behind me. "Our charges seem to be coming to," he said.

And so they were. The desolation and the stink hadn't seemed to trouble them—; the sight of that trinity, however, laid out so artfully in the middle of the street, was beginning to do its work. I was certain now that it was Parson's doing. Guessing the route that we would take, he chose, for some obscure reason of his own, to render it more scenic. But how had he found the time to assemble this little tableau? And why would he want to sabotage the run, so shortly after saving it from ruin? Out of contrariness, perhaps, or simply on a whim? Or possibly as a warning of some kind?

The thought struck me then that none of the fifty-seven head had been told about the Yellowjack, or even that the boat was bound for Memphis. Parson's hoo-doo had sloughed off at last, and now the fact of the fever was breaking over them like surf.

Parson surely knew that this would happen, and decided it should happen here—: here, in the middle of a ruined city, with only Asa Trist to help me. Was this entire run, down to its last detail, only a baroque form of punishment for me, a penance paid out in advance against future crimes? Had the Redeemer guessed at my betrayal before

I'd even thought of it myself? Had he *seen* it, plain as porridge, in my left eye?

The men in the nearest coffle were beginning to move nervously from side to side and to glance, almost shyly, into one another's faces. A tinkling rose up along the coffle-chain as the hands grew restless in their shackles—: an innocent enough sound, on the face of it, but terrible in portent.

Trist, by contrast, was care-free as a dove.

"Doesn't this put you out, Asa?" I whispered.

He grinned back at me. "No, Mr. Ball! It doesn't. Not as such."

"'Not as such,'" I said to myself, turning the words over in my mouth. The phrase lingered in my mind, adding to my disquiet—; its blitheness was so wonderfully ill-suited to the Golgotha on every side.

We managed to get the coffles moving again, but it was tricky going. A few streets farther on, I found the perfect complement to Trist's expression—: a bamboo-handled polo mallet, lovingly waxed and polished, lying in a puddle of iridescent yellow filth.

I glanced side-wise at Trist, meaning to point the mallet out to him, but what I saw made the words curdle in my throat. Trist's eyes rested neither on me nor on the coffle nor on anything on God's earth. They seemed less like eyes at all than like chips of milky bottle-glass, washed up by some caprice of the sea.

The rumors I'd heard about him came rushing back to me in a torrent. "Mind the coffles, Asa!" I said sharply, hoping to call him back from wherever he'd gone off to.

In place of an answer he held up his hat-box for me to admire. His face was flushed with a look of secret pleasure, as though he were sucking on a lump of sugar.

I gave a quiet curse and seized him by the shoulders. "We can't have this, Asa! Not here! Do you hear me?"

"Dilly?" Trist said politely, turning as if to someone passing by.

"Who the devil are you talking to? There isn't any—"

"I'll be your Dante, Virgil!" Trist said, giggling into his hand. His eyes were back on mine, and they were lucid again—; he looked at me fondly for a time, then gave me a coquettish wink.

I decided, with all the force of desperation, that he'd simply been playing me for a fool. He was less an hysteric or a madman than a molly-coddled planter's son—: he had to be. The alternative—at that moment, and in that place—was impossible to consider.

"No time for the classics just now, Asa, I'm afraid." We'd halted at the crossing of Jefferson and Main. I looked back at the coffles, to see if any of the head were watching us—: all of them were, closely and intently.

"Take out your pistol, Asa," I said quietly.

I smiled as I said it, hoping to give our audience the impression of business-as-usual. But even as Trist returned my smile—uncertainly, as though he were hard of hearing—the wistful look began to bloom again behind his features.

"No-one gets shot *today*, Captain!" he said, holding up his hands.

The change I saw gathering in his eyes was more frightening than the corpses in the street, than the coffle behind us, or even than the Yellowjack itself. I found myself gazing over Trist's shoulder, unable to return his stare, desperate for something else to look at. On the far side of Jefferson Street three school-boys were smashing the windows of a rice-and-grain-depot—: their tools were a U.S. Army bugle, a dress-maker's dummy, and the leg of a snow-white pianoforte.

"Give me that pistol, Asa," I said, forcing my eyes back to his. "Where is it?"

A scrap of sobriety returned to him then—: his smile slid to the right and disappeared, like the moon on the face of a clock. "Is it—is it not in the case?" he stuttered, pushing the words across his tongue as if they were clots of dirt. No sooner had he said this, however, than both his eyes went perfectly blank—: I saw the pupils flare a final time, spasm, then seemingly vanish altogether.

This is the end of me, I thought, watching Trist sink to his knees. The Colonel had described his fits to me once—with obvious discomfort—and Kennedy had gleefully filled in the specifics. I prayed that the fifty-five niggers behind me hadn't heard tell of them—; but it made not a whit of difference. What was happening to Trist was plain for all to see.

He gave a side-long jerk of the head, as though shooing away a fly, then set the hat-box down and undid its clasps. Keeping my good eye fixed on the coffles, I motioned to him to throw it open, thinking I might find his pistol there. The coffles still stood more or less in file—: only the first ten or fifteen head could see what he was about. I wondered how much longer they would bide. Not long, by the look of them. I'd just resolved to get them moving again, to make one last push to Pop Stacey's, when Trist got the hat-box open and I stopped thinking about the Stacey, the coffles, and the entire city of Memphis altogether.

Packed together in the box's velour-lined recesses, in neat, Linnaean rows, were vials and bottles of every conceivable color and description. Some were old kölnisch-water bottles—; others had once contained balms, perhaps, or menthe liqueurs. Each of them now held a dram of yellow fluid with a neatly cut square of what I first took to be oil-cloth suspended within it. Trist's pistol was nowhere to be seen, but that was trivial to me now. The box had already yielded up its secret.

The squares were samples of skin—of human skin, to be precise— in every imaginable shade of brown.

I closed my eyes a moment. "Listen to me, Asa. You get that collection of yours as far away from here as you can. We can't let the coffles see it. Do you follow me?"

But Trist was already on his feet.

"In the beginning America was quiet!" he announced to the coffles. "There was this *quiet*, children! It was very black!"

For a moment all was still. Then—mutedly at first, but with greater and greater vigor—the coffles commenced to laugh. Soon they were all but rolling on the ground.

The interior of the box was, as yet, hidden from their view.

"There were fine white women of savory looks," Trist continued. "They were good dollies of the river escaped up from the water, and they went down to the cellar and upset casks of lemon-punch, and drank to the river-maid, and got well and rightly liquored, and were sent by force to strip quite naked, and farts occurred and many, many wets! And all sang in joy to their favorite of hymns—: 'Fill to the rim that which stitches the bed—; fill to the quim that which bitches the dead. That which bitches and *foals*!'" Trist cried, laughing along with the coffles now. "'*Dearest Elohim! Amen!*'"

Then he curtsied to them all.

With the end of Trist's speech the laughter died down somewhat, and a weak and abject wheezing could be heard. It was the better part of a minute before I recognized it as my own. There was no way on heaven or earth to hold them now. Trist was standing with his arms akimbo and an earnest, benevolent expression on his face—: the learned speaker pausing to collect his thoughts. I stood slumped over beside the hat-box, fingering Ziba's pistol, which lay heavy in my pocket. It brought me precious little comfort.

The coffles, which ten minutes before had been the very picture of despair, now waited good-naturedly for Trist to resume his lecture. Even the boys from the depot had broken off their fun to listen.

Trist, however, appeared to have concluded.

A few blocks south of us, on Shelby Street, the roof of a burning store-house began to buckle. I felt keenly, in that egregious silence, how thin the tissue is that separates this life from the next. The sensation, while it lasted, was a pleasant one—: I felt the satisfaction one might get from looking down onto two converging valleys from the ridge of land between. A cold comfort, granted—; but a comfort nonetheless. The gentle satisfaction of perspective.

Taking advantage of this charmed moment, I kicked the hat-box shut, turned back to Trist, and struck him hard across the temple with the butt of Ziba's pistol. He turned toward me as he fell, the smile still hovering about his mouth, and hit the ground with a wallop that brought me a distinctly different satisfaction. An appreciative "Ah!" rose up from the coffles. Incredibly, all fifty-five head still stood rooted to the spot. It occurred to me, then, that we were only three streets removed from Stacey's—; I might yet, by some miracle, manage to complete the run. I made an elaborate show of cocking the pistol, realized the lameness of this gesture at once, then let the gun fall slackly to my hip. I accompanied this action, if I remember rightly, with a quiet warble of defeat.

For perhaps ten seconds the coffles studied me carefully, as if committing my face to memory. Then—all in the same instant, as though in answer to a bugle—they about-faced and shuffled back the way we'd come. I raised the pistol in the air and shook it at them forlornly. I might as well have been brandishing a feather-duster.

I looked down at Trist, at the hat-box beside him, then over at the rice-and-grain depot. The boys had vanished without a trace. Memphis looked as desolate, and very near as ruined, as its Egyptian namesake. I returned the pistol to my pocket, gave the hat-box a punt that sent its varicolored bottles flying, then walked the last three blocks to Stacey's clearing-house, leaving poor barmy Asa to his fate.

LITTLE WAS KNOWN about the Yellowjack, other than that it traveled through the air on tiny motes of dust, something like a jockey—; niggers got it less than white folks did, and Indians got it less than niggers. To stave it off, men dined on cloves of garlic chased with cre-

osote, or swallowed chips of pulverized house-brick, or poured granu-
lated strychnine down their boots. In Natchez-on-the-Hill, the time-
honored custom was to fire a brace of cannon at a forty-degree angle
into any and all suspicious-looking clouds. Not surprisingly, none of
these prophylactics proved reliable, and soon everything short of suicide was being indulged in. Nothing short of suicide, however, ever
truly seemed to turn the trick.

I was mid-way across Washington Street, nearly at Stacey's door,
when I suddenly stopped short, as though someone had tapped me on
the shoulder, and took a quiet, cautious look about me. The city before
me was pristine as a doll-house—: the buildings were spotless, the
curbs freshly washed, the window-pots brimming with well-tended
flowers. There were men on the street again—dapper, courteous men—
and the ladies dipped their bonneted heads to me as I passed. Most of
the shops were open, and though carts stood before some of them,
piled high with luggage, the general atmosphere was one of cheerful
industry. So great was my shock that I felt a need to look behind me—:
there, not two streets back, the eastern half of the city lay charred and
ransacked and abandoned. A woman in a shift could be seen walking
from one side of Main Street to the other, wiping her face with a scrap
of cloth that looked, from that distance, like a funeral shroud.

A vision of Clementine overtook me then—: irresistibly and without the least warning, as it always did. I'd spent an entire night with her
only two days before, an almost unheard-of privilege. She hadn't once
let me touch her, preferring instead to prattle on about all manner of
trifles, reveling in the sway she held me in. Her silhouette rose up
before me, thin-limbed and fairy-like, with palings of shuttered light
behind her—: the way she held herself languidly but proudly, unmoved
by me but moving always for my benefit, stopping now and then that I
might admire her better. She was still, four years after our first meeting, the most beautiful woman that I had ever seen. I stood a long time
in the middle of the street in that pest-ridden city, letting the idea of
her sequester me from ruin.

Inevitably, however, my thoughts declined from Clementine to
Morelle. I hung back a moment outside Stacey's shop-window, thinking of my secret vow and of the chances that I'd actually live to keep it.
A reading would be the best time to make my attempt, I reckoned—:
Morelle always insisted that we be undisturbed. He was lost in his
charts for long stretches afterwards, paying as much mind to me as he
did to the candle-stub. Simple enough to put a bullet in him then.

When I tried to imagine the killing itself, however, the breath stuck and clotted in my throat. I was the Redeemer's opera-glass, as Clementine had put it—: his bauble, his play-thing, to use howsoever he chose. I could no more picture myself assassinating Morelle than finding a cure for yellow fever.

Such, then, were my thoughts as I loitered on Stacey's door-step. When at last I stepped inside, my heart sank further still. There he was, indefatigable as ever—: Julius Jurisprudence Stacey, the most self-contented profiteer ever to dip his hand into the muddy waters of the Trade. Goodman Harvey sat on a bench just inside the door, grinning from one of us to the other like the insufferable ponce he was. In the absence of Morelle, he directed all of his cloying, lisping humility at Stacey. Stacey's sweet-potato-shaped paunch was in its customary place, gently astride the corner of his desk—; an evil-smelling meerschaum dangled from his lip.

"Mr. Ball," he intoned, after a drowsy pause.

"Mr. Stacey," I answered, ignoring Harvey altogether.

"Am I right in assuming that you come empty-handed?"

This caught me very much off-guard—: I'd expected, and dreaded, the necessity of accounting for myself. Was failure writ so plainly across my face?

"You know already, then?" I mumbled.

"Bechair yourself, gentle traveler," Stacey said, digging idly at his nose. (Stacey, it was clear, had no health complaints to speak of. I wondered which of the fever cures he subscribed to.)

I did as I was told.

"That's better." He set his pipe down decorously. "Now, then—: how long since you and my property *in derelictum* parted ways?"

"Fifteen minutes," I answered, staring dully at the floor.

He consulted a hide-bound ledger. "Since the corner of Shelby and Union, was it?"

I practically swallowed my tongue. "I must tell you, Mr. Stacey—"

"That I astonish you?" Stacey beamed side-wise at Harvey, who in turn leered mincingly at me. "I'd like nothing better, Mr. Ball, than to prolong your wonderment—; my conscience, however, won't permit it." He gestured over his left shoulder, to the corridor that led out to the pens. "We've had a visit from a confederate of yours."

"Parson," I said at once. My stomach began to knot together.

Stacey nodded smugly. "Go have a look in the yard. You may find that you are amazed anew."

"I don't have to look," I said. On another day I might have cursed, protested, cried out that it was impossible—; it *was* impossible, after all. "He brought them all in, didn't he."

Stacey only scratched his nose.

"I suppose I ought to feel indebted," I said.

"You're upthet, of course," Harvey put in solicitously.

"Nobody enjoys surprises," Stacey agreed.

I glared at them both in stony silence. "Where's Parson now?" I said finally.

"Gone off." Stacey waved a hand, as if the question were an idle one. Harvey grinned at me and shrugged his shoulders.

All of my impotent anger and disgust settled on Harvey in that instant. If he had a purpose in the Trade other than to annoy me, I had yet to discover what it was. What in hell was he up to? Why hadn't he met us at the dock? Why in Jesus' name was he grinning at me that way, like a pig dipped in shite and honey?

"Where was Parson headed?" I said, keeping my eyes on Stacey.

Stacey gazed up at the ceiling, as if to say—: How for us the ways of the clergy?

"He mentioned Jew-town," Harvey offered. "The houtheth of fun down along the river."

For all I cared, Parson could have been summoned to the Vatican—; it mattered only that he was well away from me. "In that case I thank you gentlemen very kindly." I turned to go. "Is there any paperwork to sign?"

"Everything is quite in order, Mr. Ball." Stacey was looking at me in a way that made me feel uneasy in my skin. Harvey beamed at me me insipidly. The urge to flee was full upon me, but I compelled myself to move toward the door as slowly and lackadaisically as possible.

"Mr. Ball!" Stacey said, just as I took hold of the latch.

"Mr. Stacey," I answered, turning back to him with a sinking heart.

"There is *one* thing you might do." He fussed with a pouch of shag tobacco as he spoke. "A buyer stopped in this morning, asking for you expressly. Amiable sort—; neatly got together. All the trappings of a sucker. He requested that someone fetch him when your coffles got to town." A wad of leathery-looking leaf was worked free of the pouch, inspected with care, then jammed into the meerschaum's grimy bowl. "He's staying at the Pendleton. Bring him round for me, would you? All my boys seem to be under the weather."

"Why not send Harvey?"

Stacey took a moment to light his pipe. "He asked for *you*, Mr. Ball. He asked for you expressly."

This puzzled me not a little. "How did he know I was due?"

Harvey gave a nervous cough. "Because we *told* him, of course! He knew the path-word, after all."

"Pass-word?" I said, frowning.

Harvey glanced at Stacey, fiddled with his collar, then gave me a grudging nod.

"That's the first I've heard of any pass-word," I said tightly. I was beginning to lose my temper. "What in blazes is it?"

"You are," Harvey said, and coughed again. "That is to say, your *name* is. Virgil Ball."

I passed a hand over my eyes. The whole of Memphis had evidently lost its wits. "If I bring this sucker round to you, Mr. Stacey, do I have your permission to quit this wretched place?"

"Your colleague seems in a frightful hurry to *absent* himself, Mr. Harvey," Stacey said, squinting at me sharply through the smoke. "One might almost suspect that he was prejudiced against us."

"I feel nothing but affection for your fine city, Mr. Stacey," I said sourly. "But there's a touch of yellow fever going round. Have you perhaps not noticed?"

Stacey regarded me blankly for a moment. "Yellow fever?" he said.

Had I felt one crumb less indifferent to the world, less bone-tired and defeated, I might have wondered at this reply—; by that point, however, I had less curiosity in me than a teak-wood Indian.

"Does this sucker have a name?" I said, already three-quarters out the door.

"Morrith Barker!" Harvey chirped.

THE PENDLETON STRADDLED THE BOUNDARY between the east and west halves of the city—between the stricken and the hale—and as such should have found itself balanced precariously between its customary function as a glorified brothel and the more novel one of a charnel-house—; whatever force it was that kept the Yellowjack at bay, however, had been magnanimous to the old hotel. Aside from the inexplicable presence of seven tame white ducks, I saw nothing out of the ordinary as I stepped into its tastefully gas-lit lobby—: only tradespeople sipping grandiose-looking drinks, and grandioser whores beside them, tittering and dipping their cigar-ends into brandy.

I found Barker crammed between two buffalo-hipped octaroons who outweighed him by at least a hundred pounds apiece.

"Evening, Your Honor," I said to him, doffing an imaginary cap. "You like your chicken frying-size, I see."

"Guilty as charged, Virgil—; guilty as charged," Barker said quickly, freeing himself with no small amount of effort. "I was *hoping* you might find the time to call."

"Wanting to purchase some niggers, were you?" I said in my most professional tone of voice. The two octaroons glared at me, unmoved. I could only guess how much they'd soaked him for already.

"Not *precisely*, Mr. Ball—; no," Barker said, taking me by the arm. "Would you be so kind as to accompany me upstairs?"

"Only to talk business, Mr. Barker. None of your French amusements."

Barker flushed deeply. "Naturally, Virgil. Yes. I'm up this way." His voice dropped, for no apparent reason, to the flimsiest of whispers. "The *mezzanine*, you know."

I followed Barker's neatly attired back-side up the stairs, wondering what he wanted of me, how he could afford to stay at the Pendleton, and why in heaven's name I'd agreed to come at all. There'd been nothing in our first meeting, certainly, that led me to think I'd stand to profit from another. I'd have written him off as a moderately cunning fool, best kept clear of, if not for the Redeemer's reaction to his name—; it was this mystery, I decided, and nothing else, that kept me climbing the Pendleton's gilt-trimmed stairs.

And yet, even as I recall that day—that fateful day which was to invert my life, which had up-ended it already, leaving me kicking helplessly in mid-air—I see that I had a second motive, more telling than the first. My confidence in Reason, under slow but relentless siege since my admission to the Trade, was suddenly on the verge of full extinction. That the Yellowjack should lay waste to one side of the city, then stop short, as if held back by surveyor's tape, leaving the other side chaste and industrious and bright, was too much for my battered brain to fathom—; but I'd seen beyond all doubt that it was so. I'd begun to question the evidence of my clear, hale, unwavering right eye, the eye that had never once endeavored to deceive me.

The ascendancy of my left eye had begun.

Barker's room proved to be a modest one, surely the least frilly in the place. Its windows faced due east, toward the plague-ridden precincts of the city. Since the hotel straddled the east–west line exactly, this meant that the room itself lay within that quarter. For some reason, however, I felt easy and secure. I went to the small bay-window while Barker made a show of fixing drinks. The view was all I expected it to be. In the alley-way below us, a man lay on top of a limp, shirtless woman, weeping and running his hands over her face and shoulders. They were perhaps ten yards below us—: I could see droplets of sweat on the man's sun-burnt nape, yellow stains on his collar, and flakes of drying mud on the woman's bare breasts. Her lips were slick with charcoal-colored bile.

"Remarkable, isn't it?" Barker enthused, joining me at the window. "Close enough to spit on! Yet we feel absolutely safe." He tapped the pane of beveled glass with his thumb. "There's not been a single case of Yellowjack in the Pendleton, you know. The dividing line between quick and dead is straight and unswerving, from one end of Washington Street to the other—; the solitary exception is the east portion of this building." He went back to the table, gulped down both the drinks he'd fixed, then poured out two plain snifters of whiskey. The room's only chair had been brought to the bed-side—; Barker gestured toward it solemnly, then offered me a glass.

"Join me in a peck of nature's restorative, Mr. Ball?"

I took the snifter from him warily. "Your good health, Mr. Barker."

"Nothing to joke about, sirrah! Not in this sweet town." Licking his lips, he added—: "I have my *own* theory about it all, of course."

I took a sip of the whiskey and set my glass down immediately. Something had no doubt been distilled to make it—; what, however, was a mystery for the ages.

"What might your theory be?" I said once I'd recovered my voice.

Barker's flat, pink eyes began to take on life. "Only *this*, Mr. Ball—: in Exodus 8, when the plague of flies is visited upon Egypt, it is mentioned—in passing—that a single land is spared the devastation. The name of that land, of course, was Goshen." His eyes, if possible, turned pinker and flatter still. "Do you remember that much scripture?"

"My father was a minister," I said.

This took him quite aback. "Was he, by God! What church?"

"Methodist."

His face grew sly. "A comfortable church to serve, they tell me."

"Not for me it wasn't."

"I don't doubt that for an *instant*!" He fumbled a bit, unsure how to proceed. "The Methodists are, as they say in Cincinnati—"

"Exodus 8?" I said, cutting him short.

"Exactly so!" Barker cried. "You're a *listener*, Mr. Ball! That's capital." He took a quick sip of his whiskey. "The land of Goshen, as we know, was spared because it had earned the particular favor of the Lord. But what would you *say*, Mr. Ball, if I told you that there was a second town, omitted mention in the Gospel, that was spared the plague as well?"

I watched him for a moment. "I'd ask you how you came to know of it."

"Never mind *that*," Barker said, affecting a merry grin. I saw, however, that his plump little hands were trembling. "Can you guess *why* the town in question—which, for convenience sake, we might refer to as 'Sun-town'—was excused from duty, so to speak?"

To hide my interest—which by now, I confess, was keen—I picked up my glass and held it to the light. "I haven't the slightest notion, Mr. Barker."

"It was the center of a profitable trade," Barker whispered, his breath tickling my cheek. "A very profitable one. So lucrative, in fact, that the dividends extended in all directions—; even unto the houses of greatest wealth and influence. Even, perhaps, unto those few—those *elect*—owed a favor from the Most High Himself."

He took a long sip from his glass, cocked his head to one side, and spat the whiskey out onto the carpet. "A *case*, to put it coarsely, of Ammon collecting from his most hallowed Debtor. But I ask you *this*, Mr. Ball—and reflect a while before you answer—if that city existed in the current age, where, in your opinion, might it be?"

"Here, of course," I answered blandly. But my heart beat furiously against my ribs.

Barker sat back with a gasp, as though I'd poked him in the belly with a stick. "You are a *wonder*, Mr. Ball! A natural wonder."

"It *is* Memphis you're dithering on about?"

"In a sense," Barker said. "In a sense." He held his glass to the light and peered into it intently, as if it were the oracle's pool at Delphi. "Can you guess what I saw this morning, waiting for your steam-skiff to arrive?"

"Something portentous?"

He nodded. "A family of four, Mr. Ball, splayed out dead in the middle of the street. Rats had fed on their remains—: the softest, fattiest morsels only, leaving the rest to rot." Here he paused a moment, pinched his features together, and sniffed at the palm of his right hand.

He couldn't have seemed more rat-like if he'd tried. "Even rats can be choosy, when Providence permits."

"What of it?"

"Those self-same rats lay clustered in a puddle of black filth, not twenty yards away." He tapped the side of his nose. "Dead as casket-nails themselves."

"Must you speak in parables, Mr. Barker?" I said, making as if to rise. "I have very little patience for proselytizing—"

But Barker was already flushed with victory. "Touché, sirrah!" he squealed. "Touché!" He gave a peal of boyish laughter and brought his boots together with a bang—:

"How *does* the poet say—?

> The flabby wine-skin of his brain
> Yields to some pathologic strain,
> And voids from its unstored abysm
> The driblet of an aphorism.

"You'll have no such driblets from *me*, Mr. Ball, I promise you! My meaning is simply this—: those who fatten themselves on the rotten, *ulcerated* matter of society—"

"I thought you wanted to talk about the Redeemer."

Barker's eyes narrowed. "That's right, sir. I do. You appreciate straight dealing, I see." He studied me for a time, then set his whiskey down. "I know you are disaffected with our friend Morelle. With your role in this back-water melodrama of his."

I kept my face composed. "And how did you come by this knowledge, Mr. Barker?"

"From testimonies to that effect," Barker said unctuously. "Acquired in the field."

"I don't believe you."

"Tut *tut*!" Barker said, waggling a finger. "Morelle isn't the only one to take an interest in you, Virgil. I've looked into that eye of yours. *Both* of them, in fact."

There was no hiding my anxiety any longer. "Who are you, Mr. Barker? A Pinkerton? A customs-agent? A missionary? A goblin? What in God's name are you after?"

"Your *cooperation*, Virgil—; nothing more. Half an hour of your time." He drained his glass with relish—a wax-cheeked, jubilant little gnome—and began to pace back and forth in front of me.

"I have no desire to dismantle the machine your Redeemer has set in motion—; never fear. Quite the *opposite*, in fact."

"He did more than set it in motion, as I recall," I said.

Barker spun suddenly about and caught hold of my chair, rocking it from side to side as he spoke—: "Have you not listened to a *word* I've told you? Not a single blessed word? The Trade existed long before Thaddeus Morelle stumbled onto it, sirrah. *Ages* before. It existed before you or I or that misbegotten dwarf—or even the Mississippi *itself*—had wormed its way out of the ether. The Trade, Virgil Ball, is an element—; a humor—; a *pre-condition*." He swallowed once, then took a breath—as if to give himself courage—and continued—: "The Trade is as basic to life as carbon. It's as ancient as the yellow fever, and easily twice as popular. Even you, with your great gift, are less than a *peanut* in the Trade's design."

"A peanut?" I said. "Then what use, Mr. Barker, could I possibly be to you?"

At this he crouched beside my chair and took me by the hand. "You have more and better talents, Virgil, than you know. You or Thaddeus either, blast his eyes."

"Do you know the Redeemer well?"

"*Must* you call him that?" Barker's right eye-corner began to twitch. "I know him, all right. I know old Taddy well enough."

Taddy?

"Tell me about him," I said. "Something I haven't heard before."

Barker gave a pinched little smile.

"As a youngish man, sixteen or so, Taddy overheard some soap-boxer—a disciple of phrenology, I suppose—say that the measure of a man's genius could be read from the height of his brow. That same day he shaved a good two inches from his hair-line, thinking nobody would catch on." He made a face. "That's your 'Redeemer' for you, Mr. Ball."

"That's hardly the revelation I'd hoped for," I said. "You have secrets, Mr. Barker, or you pretend you do. Sweeten the pot a little."

Barker's look darkened. "I need your help, Virgil—; I admit it. But I'll have it from you whether you find the 'pot,' as you call it, sweet or bitter. I've made something of a study of you, you see. And I know even without consulting that magic lantern of yours that you'll set my plan in motion." He turned to face the window. "You'll put down Thaddeus Morelle, for starters."

"I'll put down your granny."

He held up a hand without turning. "You'll kill Thaddeus Morelle—; you'll put your eye at my disposal—; you'll do as I say in all particulars. Firstly, because you're a *follower*, born and bred. It comes easier to you to obey than to resist. Secondly, because I have the power to destroy the Trade, and you along with it, if I must. I have the knowledge and the willingness to do so." He shook his head gently as he spoke, like a world-weary judge. "You have no say in your future, Virgil. Best accept that straight-away."

I stuck my tongue out at his back-side. "Thanks for the whiskey, Mr. Barker. Best of luck."

Barker only nodded. "Come to the window now."

I rose from the chair at once, as if directed by wires, and joined him at the window-bench. He had said that I would obey him, and I did. Together we looked down into the alley. The woman lay just as before—: her companion was nowhere to be seen. Her legs were spread in a wide, awkward-looking V, as though she were passing water. But it was clear from her face that she had quit this life.

Barker took me solicitously by the hand.

"Life is fleeting, Mr. Ball, as any fool or Methodist can tell you. The things a man has *wrought* in his lifetime can, however—in the rarest of instances—bear the stamp of the ever-lasting. You and I could set a great many stones a-rolling, if we chose." He let my hand drop and pressed his face against the window. In that instant he might easily have passed for the Redeemer's twin.

"You'll show me many things," he murmured. His breath made little fleur-de-lys patterns on the glass. "We'll journey side by side, my friend, into the vast and luminous Unknown."

"You first," I said, bringing Ziba's pistol against his temple.

Barker's body went limp at once. "Virgil!" he gasped. "*Listen* to me, Virgil—"

"You'll not look into *my* eye, you dumpling-faced bastard."

His face, reflected in the glass, was the picture of bewilderment. "Your eye?" he stammered. "But surely, Virgil, you understand that I was speaking figuratively—; your eye, as such, means *nothing* to me—; nothing whatsoever—"

"That's right, Mr. Barker. And it never will."

"Don't be an *ass*," Barker managed to squawk, but by then I'd already pulled the trigger. I had no desire to trade one Redeemer for another.

"God Taught It to Me."

G OD AND SCIENCE WERE MARRIED one Sunday in Paris, Asa says. I myself was minister.

At the Académie—: as soon as Mssr. Horseface came up to the labs on his appointed rounds (Sunday morning, 6 May 1853) I flagged him to my table. Mssr. Trist, he said, his horse-mouth hanging open. Have you no other studies? Do you pass every waking hour on these premises?

He was standing at the north-west corner of the desk, width of a lady's palm from my work, but still he did not see it. We might as well be out on the river, in a punt, I thought, and the idea brought a curse-word out of me. But it was a curse-word in English and as such out of Mssr. Horseface's ken. What did you say, Mssr. Trist? he cheeped at me. He looked askance. Would you not care to retire to your dormitory, peradventure, and take a spell of rest?

I might just, I answered. I'm well satisfied with my work.

Very good, Horseface sighed, his eyes gone to the window. In that event, if you'll permit me, Mssr.—

I've made a discovery, I said. A discovery of merit. I might go so far, in fact, as to announce that the merit of my discovery is such that this academy will never be forgotten.

His eyes spun back from that window you can bet. My dear fellow—, he began. I knew then that I had his ear—: more than that. I knew that I had him frightened and this knowledge did more for my pride than if he had stripped himself naked and got onto his thick, blotchy knees and petitioned me to explicate my researches. My pride was such that it spilled over, it over-spilled, I became wild at the merest thought of it. The school would be remembered now (by G*d!) and the unwashed son of an American river planter would have done it for them. They'd hate me openly but the pleasure of their hating would be lost to them. My dear fellow—, he said again. I held up a hand before he could run on and away.

Shall I tell you my discovery?

His eyes fell shut. His mouth fell open and formed a noiseless syllable. I could see it in the air above him—: O—U—I.

I shifted the ocular to one side and pulled the papers closer. I shuffled them a bit, arranging them so he might better follow faith and intellect on their little sack-race. I gave him a few moments but it was all too much and I spoke very sweetly, clipping my s's in the manner of his home province (the Lorraine)—:

The difference between yourself and a nigger, Mssr. LeVertier, is the sum of a single molecule.

I thought at first he hadn't heard me. He stared down at the topmost sheet, the one that outlined my methods and my protocols. The idea came to me that perhaps I hadn't spoken it aloud, and I had just opened my mouth as wide as I could get it when he said—:

This is what you've been about, then, all this time? This is the result of your first term at our academy? His black eyes dug into the paper.

Mssr. LeVertier—

What molecule?

A decatomic protein, I said. The wildness came on as I said it. $C_2H_2Fl_3O_1N_2$. The most beautiful compound I have ever seen.

Preposterous! he muttered. But a hum came out of him regardless. The crease of his lips was peaked and white. It twitched at both its ends.

Where did you find it, Mssr. Trist, if I may pry? May I ask you to reveal so much? His eyes were full upon me now and I could not stomach them. Kindly remove your eyes from me, sir, I howled, but again he did not hear. Did he?

In the blood, I suppose? Is that it? In suspension?

It was all I could do. Not blood, I said. Not blood at all.

What's that? he said. *Not* blood? He was white all over. Speak up, little Asa. Speak. Have you forgotten already? Forgotten how?

Skin, I spat out, the sound cotillioning in my mouth. In the skin the skin the skin.

He went quiet as a pond. In the skin, he said. The wildness had gone from one breath to the next and I felt undressed and afraid. Please, Mssr. LeVertier, I said.

His eyes were gone already. They could barely stand to look. They wandered from my hands to my smock to the microscope to the bottles ranged transparently behind me. The bottles! I must get his eyes away from them.

Look here, Mssr. LeVertier, I said. I pulled the top sheet from my notes. Underneath lay my first sketch of the decatom. I coaxed his eye-balls down to it.

Merely a sketch, I offered.

He took up the paper with a twitch. Blinking slowly, like a horse, he held it high above his shoulder, as a school-master would a dirty drawing—:

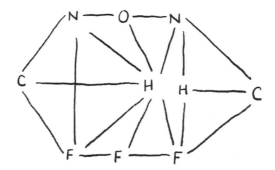

This is the molecule, is it? Your protein molecule? Your pigment?

I shook my head. No, sir. Not a pigment.

Not a pigment, Mssr. Trist? What, then, would you have it be?

I said nothing for a goodly while. I took a breath—:

His mark.

His mark, Horseface repeated. He lowered the paper. Whose?

G*d's, I answered. Stamped in Moses' time onto the flesh of his chosen peoples. The niggers and the Jews.

He laid the paper daintily on the table.

You see God in this, do you, you baboon?

It represents the Passion, I said. I spoke slowly and carefully, so that he might follow. Christ's quartered host, superimposed over the Doric crucifix. It's been tipped to one side, as you can see—: He is about to be taken down from the cross.

He was smitten. In others words, then, Mssr. Trist—

In other words, sir, He is dead already. I paused, seeing that he was not yet satisfied. I said—: Do you see now, Professor? Science and Heaven *do* agree.

Science? he said, staring down at the desk. *Science* taught you this?

G*d taught it to me, Mssr. Horsepiss, I answered, and gave a little bow.

Abduction from the Seraglio.

I CAME BACK FROM MEMPHIS A KILLER THRICE OVER, Virgil says. And I had one murder in me yet.

I arrived at 37 alone, off a stern-wheeler bound for Baton Rouge. My idea was to kill Morelle at the next of our match-and-candle sessions—kill him quickly and with a minimum of fuss—and go straight to Clementine with the news. I truly believed that I could do this—: I'd just put a bullet in his double, after all.

But Morelle was a far cry from Morris Barker. For six days he showed no inclination toward a reading, and I never once caught him unattended. South Carolina had just announced its secession, and his thoughts turned upon this fact like wool upon a spool. I grew more and more restless, more impatient to see Clementine—; on the seventh day I found I could wait no longer. I boarded the next down-river steamer, a new boat christened the *Hyapatia Lee*, though Morelle himself cautioned me that my old rival Lieutenant Beauregard was on it. The date was December 27, 1860.

As there was no hope of avoiding the lieutenant for the duration of the trip, I resolved to seek him out at once. With his uniform and moustaches he was an easy mark—: I found him reclining like Caesar Augustus on a divan in the front saloon, following a game of faro at a nearby table with the bashful fascination of a child. His hair was now distinguished by a romantic sprinkling of gray—; his eyes had a melancholy satisfaction to them. The port wine he sipped was evidently to his liking. He looked at me blankly when I greeted him, then broke into a pearly-toothed grin, clapped me on the shoulder, and motioned to the bar-boy for another glass.

"Lay down your burden, brother!" he said, patting the cushion next to him. "How long has it been? Four years? Six? Aren't you surprised to see me?"

"I'd heard you might be on this boat," I said.

Beauregard squinted back at me with genuine wonder. "How, by god?"

"I'm not the Redeemer's *only* opera-glass, Lieutenant."

This half-hearted joke was lost on him, of course. He regarded me soberly for an instant, then replied—: "Either Morelle's hoo-doo works better than I've credited, or the Trade's grown even bigger than I thought. I myself didn't know that I was going to be on this boat, Mr. Ball, until five o'clock this morning." He pushed the bottle toward me.

"What are we drinking to, Lieutenant?"

His air of satisfied stolidity returned. "You knew I was going to be on this boat, sirrah, and yet you ask me that?"

I poured myself a glassful, took a good-sized sip—it was really very fine—and felt suddenly inspired. Only one thing could have put him in such high spirits. "To your promotion?"

"You're a sly old toad, and no mistake!" Beauregard crowed, striking me between the shoulder-blades three times in quick succession, as though I was choking on a giblet. He seemed to remember me as his dearest, truest comrade—; and I was disinclined, just then, to set him straight. I detected the Redeemer's hand, clear as heat lightning, behind Beauregard's turn of fortune. Perhaps I'd discover something I could use.

I drained my glass and the lieutenant refilled it at once. This, it was evident, was not the afternoon's first bottle—; it was safe to assume that the promotion had been a large one. I wondered which wires Morelle had tugged upon, and precisely which advantages he stood to draw. War between the states—the possibility of war—was at the bottom of it, that much I knew. It had been his sole obsession the last few months.

We drank to one another's health. "It must be quite an advancement, Lieutenant, if they're calling you all the way to New Orleans," I offered.

Beauregard held up a crack-nailed finger. "*Not* New Orleans," he said. "I'm off to Charleston in the morning—; to the battery in Charleston harbor. And guess *why* I've been sent for, Mr. Ball." He scratched his head thoughtfully, as though trying to work out a sum. "Guess in what *capacity*."

"Mess cook?"

He gave a loud guffaw at this—; nothing, it seemed, could spoil his self-regard that evening. "Not on your *life*, sir! Not by half." He wetted the ends of his moustaches with his tongue. "I've been commissioned, Mr. Ball. Three stars."

I hushed for a spell, genuinely stunned. "*General* Beauregard," I said, when I could say anything at all. "I'll be damned."

"Not yet," Beauregard said, grinning like a donkey. "Not until I get to Charleston."

He went quiet after that, focusing, no doubt, on some point in the foreseeable future when he'd be crowned first commander-in-chief, then president, then Imperator of the New World by a diet of generals, congressmen, financiers, and kings. As I watched him, the memory of our first meeting at Madame Lafargue's—his arrogance, his insults, Clem's following him downstairs—came back to me in luminous detail. No sooner had it done so than the desire to murder him stole over me like laudanum.

I resisted the urge, however, potent though it was—: to indulge it would have cost me the Redeemer. Looking back, of course, I regret my decision bitterly. How much might have been different if General Beauregard had never reached Charleston harbor!

At the time, however, I was ignorant of the Redeemer's true design. And so, I soon learned, was Beauregard himself.

"Have you had much contact, lately, with He Who Shall Go Unnamed?" I asked.

Beauregard shook his head sleepily. "The Trade doesn't need me to cover its tracks anymore, Virgil. Mightier personages than myself have its interests in their care." He filled our glasses yet again. "I haven't heard from our benefactor in over a year."

"He hasn't forgotten *you*, though, it seems."

I'd thought this might finally rouse him, or at least put him out of sorts—; but he only pursed his lips. "I *know* he hasn't. I still get my dividend, first of every month."

"That must be a comfort."

"I don't mind telling you, sir, it *isn't*." Beauregard frowned. "I'm a man who likes to work for his upkeep, strange though that may seem." He ran a hand through his thick, bear-greased hair, on which the rim of a lieutenant's cap was still perfectly imprinted. "I'm hoping our little friend won't get wise to my change of address."

I couldn't help but grin a little. "Oh! I think he might," I said.

Beauregard only grunted.

"What's the state of things, by-the-bye, with the Yankees up in Charleston?"

He bit his lip. "Touchy. There's a good bit of—debate, I guess you'd call it—about a fort on an island in the harbor. Name of Sumter. The Yankees have it, you see. And they don't want to give it over."

I'd heard the name of Sumter before, from the Colonel and Kennedy. "And what's your opinion? Should they?"

Beauregard shrugged his shoulders charmingly. "I don't *have* an opinion, actually."

I smiled at him. "You'll most likely have to develop one, General, if you're taking command of the Dixie batteries."

"It won't be *my* decision," Beauregard muttered. I'd finally gotten him riled. "You do comprehend, don't you, that one hasty decision there could start a war? Rest assured, Mr. Ball—: my orders on the Sumter question will be handed down from on high."

"I have no doubt of that," I said.

I was beginning to see the scale on which Morelle was playing, and it robbed me of my breath. Close as I'd been—or *believed* I'd been—to him, I was utterly confounded by this new intelligence. My brain went hot and pricklish, cringing and expanding, trying to get the outline of it clear.

My thoughts ran as follows—: (I) Abolition, if the papers were to be believed, had free run of the Union. (II) Even our new president was rumored to indulge in it, if thus far only in secret. (III) Abolition provided the Trade its cover, but an over-dose would prove lethal—; even secession, that most desperate of bluffs, might not manage to save us. (IV) If bluffing fell short of the mark, what then—?

"What's the likelihood of war, do you think, General?"

Beauregard chewed on this a while. "I don't think it must *necessarily* happen," he said at last. "There's a good deal of talk, on both sides, about preserving the Union. In spite of the all the fire-works—" He paused. "To be honest, I have no idea. If some manner of common ground could be reached on the slavery question—on slavery in the *territories*, at least . . ."

I thought back to my parting words with Morelle. Divided as they were over slavery, he'd said, North and South were united over one thing—: the Trade. The powers that be—all of them—had come to view it as an intolerable evil. "They hate us heartily, dear K," he'd said to me. "We can only hope, for the sake of our little métier, that they hate each other more."

Now those last words had a new import for me. I sat on the divan in awe-struck silence, staring past the faro-tables at the tumbling brown river. The card-players had fallen strangely silent—; Beauregard, for his part, was adrift in a port-tinctured reverie. His exultation had altogether passed away and he looked haggard and remote. I excused myself and retired to my cabin.

I lulled myself to sleep that night by withdrawing into the most private recesses of my mind and gazing in calm fascination at the chaos Morelle had wrought there. My understanding of the Trade, of the country, and of my place within both had changed so drastically since my last visit that I wondered whether Clem would even know me. The shambles Memphis had made of me were terrible to behold. My allegiance to Morelle was shattered, my sense of right and wrong perverted past all remedy. The most fatal change of all, however, remained hidden from me still. My rationalism, which had been faltering for years, had been unseated in a single stroke. I had witnessed things in Memphis that would have sent Descartes himself scrambling for his rosary.

Thus, as Providence—or chance—would have it, Morelle's influence over me doubled when I took him for my enemy. Reason was useless against him—; that much was clear to me after Memphis. To revenge myself on the Redeemer I'd have to enter, naked and half-blind, into the Redeemer's world of symbols.

I awoke that night to a shape unlike any I'd seen with my blighted eye before. A glittering, scintillating sphere, the color of obsidian, revolved above me in the dark. Its surface was cut into facets, and all manner of images danced across them—: ramparts of smoke, rows of sallow, bearded faces, scores upon scores of boot-prints filling up with rain. The shape spoke in a language of trills and clangs and stutters, like the sound of valves opening and shutting in a boiler. Try as I might, I couldn't understand a word of it, but I understood the pictures perfectly. I was being presented with the future—: not harbingers of the future, not abstract portents, but the future itself, in body and in blood. I needed no charts to make sense of what I saw.

It was war.

I sat up in my berth at half-past six, wide awake and grateful for it. To all appearances I was still aboard the *Hyapatia Lee*. I passed a hand over my face, trying to recollect my vision, then looked warily about the cabin. The shape had shrunk to the size of a chestnut, but it persisted in the far corner of the room, throwing off chiaroscuro sparks.

Do what I might, it stubbornly refused to vanish. It kept me company all the way to New Orleans.

The change in me had now become impossible to ignore. For the first time since the start of the Trade, I'd made sense of a vision unassisted. But that was not all. I'd done more than simply make sense of what I saw—; I'd done something stranger still, more remarkable, more dreadful.

I'd believed in it.

IT WAS IN FULL EXPECTATION of calamity, then, that I made my way up the levee to Madame Lafargue's. I moved through the Quarter as if through a stage-set to an opera which, having finished its run, might be struck at any moment.

I entered through the niggers' door on Lime Alley—a trick Morelle had taught me on my very first visit—and slipped up the filigreed iron steps. Clem's door was unlocked, and I pushed it open. She lay fast asleep under her tent of netting, her hair spread over her precise white features like a courtesan's in the Arabian Nights Entertainments—; best of all, she was alone. I eased myself down onto the powder-and-wine-stained coverlet. Her eyes opened and fixed on mine.

"It's you," she said. She seemed relieved.

"Were you expecting someone else?"

She kept her eyes on mine, steady and unsurprised, and let the sleep drain out of them. When finally she chose to return my smile it was with a gentleness I'd despaired of ever seeing in her. I bit back the pleasantry I was about to give voice to—; my tongue thickened in my mouth and my lips went dry as parchment. Something had happened to Clementine while I was gone.

"I dreamt about you just now." She stretched herself and yawned into her sleeve. "That's how I knew to expect you."

I brushed her hair aside with my finger-tips, looping it carefully behind her ears. I ached for a kiss but was afraid, as always, to touch my mouth to hers.

"Did you do me justice in your dream, Miss Gilchrist?" I said. "Was my waist-coat elegant? Were my stockings clean?"

She shook her head. "I couldn't tell, Aggie. It was dark. And you were tucked away in bed."

"Were you tucked away beside me?"

She shook her head. "I was spinning above you in the air. We were in a steam-boat cabin."

My hand must have made a subtle jerk, because her eyes darted toward it. "What is it, Aggie?"

I took up her hand and kissed it. "I've missed you, darling. Terribly."

Her eyes were clear now and she was looking at me closely. "Is that all?"

"I'm tired."

"They work you hard, poor boy."

I bowed to her. "We Jews are like the olive, Miss Gilchrist, as the Talmud says. We're at our best when we are being crushed."

She said nothing for a time, holding tightly to my arm. I savored the pressure of her thin, determined fingers at my wrist.

"How long has it been, Miss Gilchrist? Seven weeks? Thirteen?"

"You know how long exactly." She pressed her knuckles to my temple—: they were cool and white as pianoforte-keys. "To the hour and the minute, you poor crushed olive."

"I can't deny it." I kissed her hand again. "Tell me, darling, how you've lived."

She turned away from me, not unkindly, and pressed her face into the cushions. "Come to bed now, Aggie."

The change had been clear to me as soon as her eyes had opened—: the simple, unbegrudging welcome I'd dreamt of since our first encounter had finally been bestowed. I could think of no earthly reason why—; but I found, to my surprise, that I had no need of one. The fact of it was enough.

I stood and let my coat fall to the floor. My shyness had passed, and I was suddenly in a fever to possess her. She's *convinced*, I thought. After all this time. I knelt and cupped her face in both my hands.

She gazed up at me sternly. "Your hands are filthy, Aggie! Go and wash them." But as I rose from the bed she caught hold of me by my shirt. "We're pieces in a puzzle," she whispered. "We fit into each other. Did you know?"

"Yes, Clem. Something new is made when we come together," I murmured, running a hand along her ribs.

She gave a quick, shrill laugh and brought the bed-sheet to her mouth. "If you only knew *what*! Run along now, Mr. Ball! Go on!"

I shuffled bemusedly over to the basin. She'd come to a decision of some kind, I knew, but my thoughts went no farther than the fact of her on the bed. There'll be no great change, I told myself, with a sudden pang of joy—; only in her manner toward me and in my entire way of living. I did a very poor job of washing and came directly back to bed. She did not seat me at her feet—my usual station—but laid me close beside her, her eyes meeting mine in a frank, approving way that made the teeth rattle in my skull. The blood roared so emphatically behind my eyes that it was all I could do to keep from crying out. I'd never known such a violent and total happiness.

"I want to leave this place," she said, pulling the netting closed around us. "I want to leave this place tonight."

"We can go straight-away, miss," I answered. "Get your garters on!"

"This is no promenade, Virgil." Her voice was hushed and urgent. "We can't simply walk outside, like two children playing at courting." Her eyes moved past me toward the door. "I don't mean to be dragged back to this pit once I'm gone from it. Not ever."

As if by the sudden turning of a corner from sunlight into shadow, the air went cold around me and every object in the room was edged in a clear, transparent light. Clem was not at liberty. Fool that I was, the thought had never crossed my mind—; I hadn't dared to conceive of her running off at all, much less running off with me. But she could *not* run off. The Trade owned this house, this room, this bed. Owned her.

"All right, Clem," I said at last, letting out a breath. "I'll come for you at seven. Don't pack more than we can carry."

She smiled at me—a smile such as I'd never seen her give, the smile of the girl she'd been, perhaps—and drew me closer still. "Can you manage it by six?"

I mulled this over for a bit. "I'll need to find a room for us, firstly. Somewhere out of view."

"Not in the Quarter," she said. Her breath came quickly now. "We wouldn't last five hours."

"Of course," I said. "Not in the Quarter." The realities of our elopement, both its pleasures and its consequences, began to gather outside the netting like mosquitoes. I had no doubt we'd be hunted if we ran. The Trade specialized in runaways, after all. The memory of the shape I'd seen in the night made my eyes and throat go ticklish.

Clem was talking all the while, giving me precise instructions, repeating things often to make sure I understood. She'd been planning her escape for months, I realized—years, perhaps—telling not a soul. I listened closely to all she told me, and when she finished I rose quietly to go. Time was very tight. It would take at least till six to make the arrangements, but Clem was adamant that I return before that hour.

By the time my coat was buttoned, I'd guessed the reason why—: a caller was expected at half-past.

"Who is it, Clem?" I mumbled. I'd never asked such a question before—made a point of not asking, in fact—but something in her voice gave me a queasy feeling. She was afraid of this caller, whoever he might be. A wave of jealousy swept over me, and in the self-same instant I found myself thinking it might be best, after all, for her to keep this last appointment.

The shame I felt at this thought undid me altogether.

"Who is it?" I asked again, more sharply. "Is it somebody I know?"

She rose from the bed and came to me. "Do you know why I've decided to run off, Mr. Ball?"

I gave a crooked smile. "Have you gotten yourself religion?"

"I'm in the way of starting a family," she replied.

When I said nothing to this, she leaned closer to me and whispered—: "And so are *you*, Virgil Isaiah Dante Ball."

The floor dipped and wobbled a moment, as if it were balanced on a barrel—; then it righted itself, and I was able to continue breathing.

Clem waited patiently for me to speak.

"You're sure of that?" I said at last. "You're sure, I mean, that *I'm* the party in question—?"

"It's your doing, Aggie," she answered, her face radiant and mild. Not even that question could jar her from her beatitude. "We take *precautions*, you know. With the paying customers."

I'd been a paying customer myself, of course—; but I forgot it at once. "You mean—with me alone—?" I stammered.

"Don't be angry with me, Virgil," she said softly, misunderstanding the look I gave her.

"I'm not *angry* with you, Clem! It's only—" I spoke without thinking, as I so often did in her company—: "I haven't killed him yet, you see."

She tilted her head at this, squinting very slightly. "Who do you have to kill?"

I cleared my throat. "Half of New Orleans, miss, to be safe."

She smiled at this, her face still lit as if from within—; but there was truth to my joke, and she knew it. I drew her closer still and kissed her. I was calmer after that kiss, and free of all desire—: I wanted, in fact, for nothing on this earth. I felt no fear of the future, or of the war, or even of Morelle. I am ready to die, I thought, then laughed indulgently at myself. To think of dying at such a time!

. . .

I SPENT THE DAY MAKING PREPARATIONS, both spiritual and worldly, for springing Clementine from her Bastille. In spite of my bedazzled state—or perhaps because of it—the day was an unequivocal success. An aged bachelor I'd worked under ten years before, an importer of spices and cigars, had a room to let in the Eleventh Ward—; he expected us that same evening. There remained only the hiring of a cab, the bribing of the old Creole who kept bar at Madame Lafargue's, and the cleaning and the cartridging of my pistol. A host of shapes visited me that day, the first I'd ever seen in day-light—: hoops of lazuli and gold, translucent yellow flowers, varicolored hexagons and stars. They didn't discomfit me in the slightest. I took them, in fact, as great good omens. The world was about to end, I knew, by fire or by flood—; with Clem at my side, however, I wasn't altogether sure I'd miss it.

It was just past three-thirty when I returned to Madame Lafargue's—the middle of the night in that house—and not a soul was stirring. The Creole had spent my money wisely, on a cigar and a pint of cherry brandy, and nothing troubled his repose. I'd steeled myself for a scene with Madame, but there was neither hide nor hair of her. Fortune, it seemed, had strewn our path with roses.

Once her effects were stowed in the cab I'd hired—canvas-topped for privacy, and drawn by two unassuming nags—Clem bade the driver start without a single glance behind her. We made our way creepingly down Dumaine Street—which smelled fouler than usual, on account of the warm weather—then southward along the levee. To my amazement she fell asleep at once, her face pressed hard into the canvas. I laid her across my lap, taking great care not to rouse her, and rode the rest of the way to the Eleventh Ward in the most immaculate state of bliss that I have ever known. Slowly, almost imperceptibly, the change was becoming real to me.

My former employer, a regal, antiquated-looking Jew, was waiting for us on the stoop of his shop with a basket of ginger-cakes and a jug of fino sherry, by way of a wedding-present. Tesla was his name, and I'd done things for him during my tenure at his shop that another stock-boy might have balked at—; the importers of New Orleans subsisted along the margins of the law, and Tesla's little shop was no exception. He wept tears of joy to see us. I began, cautiously and quietly, to congratulate myself on my talent for intrigue.

That night Clem and I stayed awake well into the morning, indulging in our new-found gift for talking plainly with one another. I gave the clearest account of Memphis that I could—: she listened closely, not once interrupting, and at the end of it simply took my hand in hers. I had best leave that same day, she said, to get to 37 before the news of our elopement did. Once again her even-headedness left me speechless. I detailed my strategy of doing away with Morelle at the close of our next reading—with a knife, I said, or something equally discreet—and she nodded at this, too, though with perhaps a bit less confidence. This was enough to halt me in my tracks.

"Should it not be with a knife?"

She frowned. "It's not *that*, Virgil. It's only—"

"What is it, darling? Tell me."

She bit her lip. "You believe in your eye now, you say. You believe the R——"—she always spoke of Morelle this way, as if the mention his actual name might invoke him, as it would a demon—"about the shapes. That they come out of the future."

I hesitated a moment, then nodded. "Yes."

"Why not do it *before* the reading, then? Why give him a chance to see what's coming?"

I hadn't thought of this, of course. We decided that I'd attack Morelle after the session itself, but before the signs and shapes had been decoded. With that the business portion of the night was settled.

We united a short while later in a manner approved of by my faith—if not by hers—to the accompaniment of old Tesla creaking back and forth above us. Clem declared him our minister in absentia, rapped three times against the head-board, and pronounced us man and wife. When at last we fell asleep, the old man was still going about his rounds—; I pictured him patrolling the corridor with a blunderbuss left over from the French and Indian War, hunting for tobacco-thieves and weevils. My sleep that night was free of any visions.

Our parting that morning was not especially grave. Clem had awoken in an almost trance-like state of indolence, sloe-eyed and con-tented, and barely saw me to the door. I'd never seen her so untrou-bled. One reason for this, I flattered myself, was her growing faith in me—; another was revealed to me soon after. As I was buttoning up my great-coat, she beckoned me to her trunk and brought forth two glass vials, the kind sleeping-draughts are sold in, for me to admire.

"If things don't run well, little olive, don't you fret. There's more than one way to serve the R—— his quittance."

I took one of the vials and brought it to the window. It held an ounce of oily liquid and a tuft of light-brown hair. I nearly choked. "Where did you get this, Clem, for the love of Christ?"

She only smiled. "Don't you worry about that. Only remember—: any one of those hairs is as good as a brace of pistols."

"This is *Morelle's* hair? The Redeemer's?"

She nodded, taking the vial back from me and slipping it into her pocket. I looked at her mutely, feeling, as I so often did, that I'd never truly made her out before. Her trust in those bottles was childish, of course, and put me in mind of Asa Trist—; yet hadn't I myself, only the day before, seen the future reflected in a spinning marble?

I kissed her on the brow and left her. I was to return within the week. If Morelle remained alive, we'd sail at once for La Habana—; if he was dead, we'd sail for any port we pleased.

"I'll Take You to Him."

I KEPT MY EYES HALF-CLOSED WHEN VIRGIL LEFT, says Clementine. I hardly missed him.

I hardly missed him because I was full of him. I was filled up precisely, like a measuring-cup. Such a simple thing, and plain! The thought and the smell and the weight and the manner and the notion of Virgil Ball. That he, out of all of them, should have filled me so exactly! Not to overflowing, mind, not gluttingly—; but never a half-grain short. I moved about the room with my head held straight, like a debutante working at her posture, for fear that I should spill a single drop.

I spent the morning ordering my trousseau, which I'd thrown together willy-nilly, and sorting Virgil's heap of clothes. Not since my eleventh year had I folded someone else's linens. What a queer thrill I got, what a half-forbidden feeling, from arranging his sundries on the window-bench! He'd taken nothing with him but a jack-knife and a candle. His shape was still pressed hard into the bed. I took off my shift and my bloomers and laid myself down in it. I felt snug in his outline, like a mouse in its burrow. It was mid-day by then, and hot as blazes already. The old man creaked about upstairs. A chill came up suddenly through the heat, making me feel small and solitary—: then I remembered. I'd forgotten it for a while, as there'd been so much else to think of. But it came back to me just then, and blew the solitariness off like smoke.

I had a family in me.

I woke with a start, dry-tongued and foreign-feeling. A rapping sounded at the door. I opened it on Goodman Harvey.

He looked at me and gave a cry. Had he expected someone else? I wondered. I had yet to come all the way up out of sleep.

"Something terrible hath happened, mith," he said, keeping his eyes screwed downwards.

"What?" I said.

"I'll wait here, on your convenienth, mith," he mumbled, clapping a hand over his eyes.

Then I understood, and gave a laugh. "Just a minute, Mr. Harvey," I said, and went to fetch my shift. He was all but making the sign of the cross when I looked back at him. I laughed again. "Don't be shy, Mr. Harvey! Won't you step inside?"

"No, mith!" he said.

He was sorely in distress. His face was tight and blanched and the spot where a chin would be on anybody else was all aquiver. He stood shuffling his feet, moving without going anywhere, exactly the way Virgil used to do. "Mith Clementine," he mumbled. "It painth me very much to tell you—"

Virgil!

I threw a shawl over my shift and rushed back to the door. "What is it, Mr. Harvey?" I cried. The chill was upon me again and I felt barer than before. I could all but see my breath. "What is it, sir?"

Harvey's mouth worked for a moment to no effect at all. "It'th Virgil, mith!" he got out at last. "I'll take you to him."

The Eagle of History.

THE END OF ME BEGAN THAT MORNING, Virgil says.
After parting from Clementine, I booked passage on the *E. P. Fairchild*—owned and operated by one of our guilds—and landed at 37 the next day. Following me off the boat were sixteen cattle-fixers, two assembly-men from Natchez Township, fourteen mulattoes carrying sackfuls of silver rings, and a dealer in Arabian thorough-breds. None save the assembly-men were there to meet with the great Redeemer, but all came on Trade business—; there was no other business any longer. Local competition had either been eaten alive or given generous permission to emigrate to the United States.

I discovered Morelle, after a long and byzantine search, on the same crumbling pier that the run up to Memphis had started from. Kennedy loitered a few yards down the bank, chucking pebbles at the current. Morelle was staring down the river with a melancholy, abstracted look, the look of a man who's misplaced something very dear. He seemed greatly changed to me. In the dull light off the water he looked frayed and defeated, nearer the Colonel's age than my own. He gave no sign of seeing me. In my confusion I began to wonder if he was waiting for the arrival of the *E. P. Fairchild*.

"The *Fairchild* is tied up across the way, sir," I said tentatively.

"Thank you, Kansas," he said. "I'm not waiting on the *E. P. Fairchild*."

"What are you waiting on, then?" I hesitated. "Parson?"

"Parson? Why do you ask?" Now he turned and looked at me. "Do you have need of religious counsel?"

I hushed at once, studying his face for signs of spite or mischief. He was looking at me squintingly, as though he found me hard to see. He seemed impatient to turn back to the river.

"What were you doing in New Orleans, Virgil?" he said after a time. "You and I were to have a conference."

I stared at him a moment. "But you walked me to the landing yourself, sir! You seemed to have no further need of me. I waited the better part of a week—"

"But you were *impatient*," he said. His voice was low and thoughtful. "Impatient to get to town."

All at once I recollected Clementine. "Let's have that conference now," I said.

Morelle cocked his head at me. "You've never been anxious for a conference before, dear K."

I cleared my throat. "I've had a vision, sir."

He frowned up at me, cautiously, circumspectly—; then suddenly his look brightened and he clapped his hands. "Without the aid of the candle? We're finally making *progress*, Kansas! Now, if you remember the shapes clearly, we can—"

"There were no shapes, sir—; there were only pictures. And I understood them perfectly. I've no need of your charts and mummeries any longer."

Morelle's face went slack for the briefest of instants—; but he recovered himself straight-away. "It's wonderful what one can *understand*, dear K, with the help of a dram or two of port." He scratched at his nose. "How's our little general? Well oiled, I hope? Thoroughly brocaded?"

In spite of his care-free air I saw clearly that he was troubled. I decided to press my advantage. "I'm a different man since I came down from Memphis, sir. I believe in things that I'd have considered sheer madness this time last week."

A change came over him as I said this. His untroubled manner was cast aside—all of it at once, as if it were a mummer's cap—and his face began to redden. "If you've let that *idiot* Barker look into your eye, I promise you—"

"Barker left Memphis in a winding-sheet," I said, cutting him short.

This news had an unprecedented effect on Morelle—: it robbed him, however fleetingly, of the faculty of speech. "Morris Phelps Barker," he said finally, looking past me at the river. "Old Morris."

"I want to tell you how it happened, sir," I said, taking him by the arm. "Let's go up and have our conference. Barker seemed to think my visions—"

"I don't give a *toss* about your visions," Morelle said peevishly, jerking his arm away. Kennedy let out a snort behind us.

My confidence drained away at once. "Please, sir—if you'll but give me half an hour—"

Morelle shook his head emphatically. "I'm standing on this dock for a reason, Kansas. If you've in an itch to share your *pensées fantastiques* with me, you can do so here and now!"

My heart sank into my boots. "Out here?" I said in a whimper. "Where anyone can see?"

"Right here on the dock," Morelle said irritably. "It's private enough, isn't it? You have no need of charts and mummeries any longer—; you told me so yourself!"

I could think of no reply to this. I stared down at the water for a time, then turned to go, abashed. But even as I did so, a new thought took hold of me—: it *was* private enough on the dock, save for Kennedy. In my eagerness to get Morelle alone I'd overlooked the fact that he was practically alone already.

"All right," I said. "We'll do it here. But send Kennedy off somewhere." I lowered my voice. "My vision featured him in a position he might not care for."

Morelle laughed. "What if I want the old sodomite to hear it?"

"You'll grow fonder of him for his absence," I said, turning and shooing Kennedy away.

Kennedy looked at me as if I'd spat onto his shoes. "Do that again, google-eye," he said.

"It's all right, Stuts!" Morelle said, giving me a wink. "Run and find our friends from the Natchez Assembly. Tell them I'll be along presently."

Kennedy said nothing for a spell. "Fuh!—fuh!—*fishing*, ain't I."

"Go on, Stuts," Morelle said, jerking his chin.

Kennedy kept still another moment, then threw a fistful of gravel into the river and stomped off, practically on all fours.

I ambled slowly out to the end of the dock, trusting that Morelle would follow me. Eight steps, by my reckoning, ought to bring him well away from the rushes and snags along the river-bank—; the rest should be easy as passing water. The current was stiff along the west shore of the island, and the bank fell away steeply beneath the pilings. In addition to being illiterate, I happened to know, our exalted Redeemer couldn't swim.

Morelle, however, stopped short after only three steps. "*Out* with it, Virgil! Tell us what fancies you fancied on old Pierre Beauregard's tab."

"I had a vision," I answered, speaking quietly to draw him nearer. "In my cabin on the *Hyapatia Lee*. I saw the future, plain as milk."

"Had a vision, did you? Was I in it, tearing my hair out in clumps?" He took two more steps and gazed up at me forlornly. "I don't mind telling you, Kansas—: our little enterprise is in a dire way."

"Judging by the six-ring circus I got off ship with, I'd have thought we owned a controlling share of North America," I said.

"That's just the *farce* of it!" Morelle cried, taking my hand in his. "We've never been more flush. We've grown too big for our britches at last, dear K. This island is an open secret, a burr in the collective arse, from Natchez Trace to the Capitol Bulge." His eyes widened as he spoke, as if he were describing a natural disaster, an act of God. "We're quite the cause célèbre now, I'm told. Bigger than the territories—; bigger than paper currency—; bigger, even, in some circles"—his voice dropped now to the most gossamer of whispers—"than the question of slavery *altogether.*"

I gaped at him, thunder-struck. Had his paranoia grown so vast? What had Parson and the rest been feeding him? "Bigger than slavery, sir? Beg pardon, but you're talking about—"

"What I'm talking about, Kansas, is a joint Federal Commission. North and South together." Morelle led me three more steps down the dock, his arm slung comfortably in my own. "All the states on the lower river, free and slave, collaborating in our complete demolishment." He seized his collar as he spoke and pulled it up under his chin, sticking his tongue out like a lynched nigger. "A gradual, inescapable tightening of the noose. *Attendez?*"

I shook my head resolutely. "Dixie would never cooperate with the Union now—; not for any purpose. Beauregard told me as much on the *Hyapatia Lee*. We're practically at war."

"That's just it!" Morelle hissed, pulling me closer still, as though we were gossiping in a theater—: "A 'Great Cause' is being sought to re-unify the Union. It may not be too late, even at this eleven-and-three-quarters hour. A universal wrong is all that's needed—: an evil on which every Christian soldier can agree." His fingers rapped painfully against my collar-bone. "A common enemy, Virgil. What the red-coats were for us in 1812, and the red-*skins* were before and after." He let go of my arm and gave me a stiff, unsmiling bow. "You and *I*, dear K, have been judged to fit the bill."

Neither of us spoke for a time. The light was fading from the bluff, and the preliminary noises of debauchery fell to our ears from the Panama House. The current burbled contentedly at our feet, indifferent to history. Morelle stared morosely at his shoes.

"They've deeded this island to Louisiana," he said finally. "They mean to flush us out like pigeons."

I watched Morelle calmly, contemplating his end. I felt entirely capable of killing him now. "So it's ended, then," I said.

He gave a stutter of surprise at this. "*'Ended,'* the man says! 'Ended'! Business such as ours has no beginning, no middle, and certainly no end—; our business simply *is*." He took a small step backward, as though to appraise me better. "Demand is our life's-blood, Virgil. Recollect demand. When there was a shortage of horse-power in my native state, I was the first to meet it. When there was need of honeyed words among the well-heeled farther up-river, I saw to that, as well. Now—: if the demand for niggers slackens, or—heaven forfend!—lets up altogether, I'll be the first to bow out, and move on." He held up a finger. "But not before then, Kansas. Not before my time."

"With all due respect, sir, perhaps that time's arrived," I said. His death was becoming realer to me by the instant.

"Nonsense!" He ran the tip of his tongue along his gums as he spoke, as though he'd eaten something bitter. "Clap-trap, nonsense, and *twaddle*! Has the demand for niggers let up one *centime* along this river?"

I confessed that it had not. "What about 37, sir?" I asked.

"What! *This* place?" He leaned to one side and spat into the current. "We've resided here at the whim of the powers-that-be, plain and simple—; it was convenient for them to find us here. We won't make *that* mistake again."

"And the Federal Commission?"

"The commission?" His look darkened. "The *commission*, dear K, is another matter."

He was just within reach. Soon, I thought, you'll have nothing else to tell me.

"You have a scheme, sir, I suppose?"

He looked guardedly up the bluff, then along the bank, then back to me. His head bobbed very slightly.

"I *had* a scheme—; now you might say it's a policy. In a matter of two weeks, perhaps a little more, it will ripen into a fact. A fact of *history*, no less." He smiled shyly. "I'll tell you about it, if you're curious. I've borrowed a page—or should I say a leaf?—from our pagan brethren-at-arms."

I regarded him blankly for a spell. "The Indians?" I said at last.

He snapped his fingers. "*Exactement!* Now listen, Kansas. The great advantage of being the common enemy is that your opponents carry the seed of dissent within them—; otherwise they wouldn't *need* you. Do you follow?" He waited patiently for my nod. "Good. You are acquainted, I suppose, with the Nauva-Hoo tribe of the Rio Grande head-waters?"

I confessed that I was not.

"What!" He clucked his tongue at me. "You, who were born and raised in the territories?"

"You never see them in the territories," I said. I paused a moment. "I don't think they've been sent there, as of yet."

"Ah! And why is *that*, do you suppose?"

I shrugged. My hands were twitching in my pockets. "Perhaps nobody cares about the Rio Grande head-waters."

He scoffed at this. "Think a little, Virgil. *Think!* Who borders the Nauva country to the east?"

"We do."

"And to the south?"

I considered this a moment. "Mexico."

"Spot of trouble with Mexico a few years back, I seem to recall."

"A spot of war," I answered.

He gave a triumphant little jump. "Do you remember the incident that set it off, Virgil? An unprovoked attack, by the Mexicans, on a unit of Federal infantry?"

"The papers were full of it for weeks," I said, bringing my hands out of my pockets. "There were rumors that it was staged."

"It *was* staged," Morelle said tenderly. "Beautifully staged. But not by *our* army, Virgil. Or by Mexico's."

I stared out at the river in perplexity. What he was proposing was so far-fetched that I felt foolish giving voice to it. "Do you mean to suggest, the Indians—?"

Morelle let out a war-whoop at this and jabbed me in the ribs. "The Nauva-Hoo country is rich in salt-peter and copper, and we wanted it *tout de suite*! Plans were in place for the inevitable rounds of treaties, pacts, and heaven-mandated coercions—; the land was to be carved up like pork-shoulder. A joint invasion would have left the natives with no means of escape. The Nauva-Hoo were finished, Kansas! *Finished!*"

I took a breath. "That's all well and good—"

"*Hssst!*" He put his hand on my nape and drew me gently toward him, as one might a bashful lover—:

"A sudden stroke of genius—a pau-wau before dawn—a clutch of stolen uniforms—a strike at sunrise, with the morning sun behind them—and *voilà*! From enemy to indispensable ally in a morning's work." He beamed approvingly at me, as if the plan had been my own. "The Nauva-Hoo of the upper Rio Grande will endure for a thousand years yet—; mark my words." He clucked contentedly. "And so, Mr. Ball, will we."

I said nothing for a time. "That's a fairy-story," I said finally. "You're farting into the breeze."

"What would you say if I told you I'd heard that 'fairy-story,' as you term it, from the *chief* of the Nauva-Hoo nation?"

"You've never met a Nauva-Hoo in your life," I said. "It's Nauva-*Ho*, first of all. And they've long since been driven into the mountains."

Morelle only shrugged. "Disregard the Nauva-Hoos then, if you like. The *rub* of my little parable is this—: the eagle of history sheltered them, in their hour of greatest need, in the crick of its great black wing. And it will do the same for us, Virgil, if we only let it." His eyes snapped shut. "I see that mighty eagle coming, Kansas. I see its shadow sweeping towards us. Close your eyes for an instant—: both of them. Can't you see it too?"

"It looks more like a buzzard to me," I said.

"A *buzzard* then, if you prefer." He opened his eyes and sighed. "You *do* see that it's the only way left to us, don't you? To the Trade?"

The mention of that word, grown so hateful to me since Memphis, brought my fists out of my pockets. I had only one question left.

"Will it be at Fort Sumter?"

There was no way he could have overlooked the violence in me now. He stepped to one side and gave me a thin, proud smile.

"You *have* had a vision, haven't you! If so, then you must know that there's no way of stopping things—none whatsoever—once the black ball gets to spinning. Things that *may* happen don't appear in it—; once you see them they're as good as done already." His face clouded for a moment. "Not that I can see why you'd *want* to put a stop to things. What's come over you, dear K?"

"Will it be Sumter?" I said again. In my mind's eye he was already at the bottom of the river. A noise had sprung up somewhere behind me—the scream of a steam-whistle, shivering and shrill—but I paid it no attention. One hard push and I'd be free. "Is it going to happen there?"

He chuckled at this and wagged a finger. "Didn't Beauregard explain things, google-eye? Didn't he spell things out for you?"

The whistle blew again, much louder than before. "I'm not here on Beauregard's account," I murmured.

"What?" Morelle said, bringing a hand up to his ear.

"Beauregard never sent me!" I shouted, seizing him by the collar. To my astonishment he was heavy as a boulder.

Morelle looked up at me disdainfully. "Don't touch people, Kansas, when you have occasion to address them. Catching people by the arms or shoulders, or nudging them to attract attention, is a violation of good breeding. It can't help but provoke—"

"I'm here for Clementine! For *Clem*, you ghastly little thing," I cried, meaning these to be the last words he would ever hear. Heavy as he was, I hauled him inch by inch toward the water's edge. He put up no resistance whatsoever.

The steam-boat was close enough now that I could hear shouts coming from its deck.

"Why are you blubbering, Kansas?" Morelle asked gently.

"Shut your mouth!" I gasped. I was weeping freely now.

"Afraid you'll never see your Clem again? Is that it?"

I tried to speak, to shut his mouth, to hurl him into the current—; but all I could manage was a groan of pent-up misery.

"In that event, take heart!" Morelle said brightly, slipping free of my arms. "Turn yourself about, dear K, and welcome her!"

The groan died in my throat. My head turned smoothly, like a weather-vane, to face the approaching steamer. Clem was there on the hurricane deck, her face as empty as a well—; Parson stood to one side of her, supporting her triumphantly by the elbow. Harvey cowered to her left. Clem looked neither at me nor at Morelle nor at the landing, and I saw by the dullness in her eyes that she was looking at nothing on God's earth.

"A precautionary measure, in the event of war," Morelle said, stepping past me. "Try to be brave and accept it, Virgil. As a Nauva-Hoo might do."

William H. Seward,
Sec. of State.

THE MISSIVE WAS BROUGHT TO MY CHAMBERS still sealed in its envelope of foolscap—; I forwarded it to the Butternut's office without delay. That afternoon, when I rapped at his door, I found him reclining in his mole-skin chair with a camphored handkerchief draped over his face. Lloyd Harris, his aide-de-camp, was reading to him with sleepy fatalism from *Paradise Lost*, Book VII. Harris shot me a desperate smile as I entered. From the looks of him, I reckoned they'd begun at Book I sometime before dawn.

Neither of us spoke for a goodly while after Harris left. The handkerchief remained *in status quo* across the bridge of his great Illinoian nose.

"Damn this April pollen," he said finally, pulling it off his face.

"Has there been no change, Mr. President?" I said. "I'd hoped the rain of the past night might have brought some small abatement."

"Abatement your granny," the Butternut said, mopping at his nose. "You've been reading Milton, I see."

"Lloyd's been reading, Mr. Seward. I've been doing my damnedest to drain my ducts." He sniffed and sat forward, keeping his handkerchief at the ready. "Marvelous stuff. We'll have to see to importing it to Illinois."

"Yes indeed, Mr. President. Milton certainly is one of the pillars. At Exeter we had to learn it forwards and backwards, one canto after—"

"I was referring to the *camphor*, Mr. Seward." He sniffed again, more profoundly. "They bring it over here from France."

"Of course, Mr. President." I paused. "I've come to see whether you found a chance to look over the letter I forwarded."

He gathered up a sheaf of colored papers and made a fan of them, holding them up for me to see. He had yet to glance in my direction. "Which of these epics was it?"

"The briefest of them, I'd hazard," I said, keeping my patience masterfully. "The quote from Revelations."

He sighed and sat back in his chair. "I did read that one, as it happens. I was just asking myself which of my cabinet members could have forwarded me such a sterling specimen of the poet's art."

"Respectfully, Mr. President, I hade ample reason to forward it."

He repositioned the handkerchief across his face. "Go on then, Mr. Secretary. Read it aloud."

I took the letter from the heap in front of him and, bringing it close to my eyes, as I was without my enlarging lenses, read—:

A PROCLAMATION FROM THE LOWLY
TO THE PALACE OF THE PROUD.

REVELATIONS 13 : 6 —

AND THEY WORSHIPPED THE DRAGON WHICH GAVE POWER TO THE BEAST. AND THEY WORSHIPPED THE BEAST, SAYING, WHO IS LIKE UNTO THE BEAST? WHO IS ABLE TO MAKE WAR WITH HIM?

AND IT IS GIVEN TO HIM TO MAKE WAR WITH THE SAINTS, AND TO OVERCOME THEM: AND POWER WAS GIVEN HIM OVER ALL KINDREDS, AND NATIONS, AND OVER ALL TONGUES.

WHOEVER HAS EARS TO HEAR, LET HIM.

I let the paper fall flutteringly to the desk-top, and waited in silence for him to hand down a tablet from on high.

He said nothing for a time. I suppose that he was weighing matters to himself. "From our friend, I presume?"

"It would seem to have that flavor."

"He doesn't have his scripture right, I think."

"That's just the flavor I was referring to, sir."

He chortled at this. His breath made the handkerchief furl and flutter. "Well, Mr. Seward? What do you make of his latest?"

"He doesn't seem too pleased with the bi-partisan nature of the new commission," I said, keeping my expression grave.

"Damn right of him. He shouldn't be." The Butternut gave a grunt of satisfaction. "They tell me there was a moment of silence in certain gentlemen's clubs in this city, when news of our commission got round to them."

"I hadn't heard that, sir."

"I can very well imagine, Mr. Secretary, that our friend wouldn't be too pleased."

I cleared my throat. "We expected no less, it's true—"

"You needn't have sent me this scrap of fol-de-rol at all, in fact. We expect to do quite a bit more than *upset* Mr. Murel, with the cooperation of our colleagues in the down-river states." He gathered the handkerchief up in his fist. "I have great faith in this project, as you well know, to heal our legislature's wounds."

I allowed him perhaps ten seconds of complacency. Then I said—: "There were circumstances to the receipt of this letter, Mr. President, that convinced me to send it along to you."

Another grunt, this time of exasperation. "Well? What in Moses were they?"

"The letter did not come to us through the post," I said carefully.

"Not by post?" He was looking at me curiously now, snot-rag a crumple in his right hand, his wood-cutter's features mustering into a frown. "Was it brought to you on mule-back? By carrier-pigeon? How?"

He waited impatiently for my reply, and I took my sweet time framing it. I confess I savored the occasion not a little.

"You'll observe, Mr. President, that there is no stamp—indeed, no marking of any kind—on the exterior. The letter came to me in a cover of cream-colored araby paper, the sort our own memoranda are printed on."

I allowed this clutch of details a moment to take roost in the topmost membrane of his mind, before pre-empting the question that was just then forming on his tongue—:

"That's right, sir. This letter was—if not written, then at the very least transcribed—by a member of our own staff."

"Huh!" said the Butternut. He looked me over for a time. Lloyd Harris ducked his head in—apprehensively, it seemed to me—and the Butternut waved him dourly away. At length he heaved a sigh and spoke.

"Mr. Seward, I know that you are embittered at having been passed over for the nomination, and that you accepted your secretaryship only under protest. I'm acquainted, furthermore, with the assortment of nick-names you've bestowed upon me. I know all this—; and I begrudge you none of it."

I bowed to him politely. "That's gracious of you, sir."

"But if I ever came to believe that you were involved in—*flirtations*, of any kind whatsoever, with these god-forsaken nigger-mongers—"

"Quite so, Mr. President," I said, cutting him short. "I should expect a swift and righteous punishment to follow. I thank Providence each day—to be frank with you, sir—that I have never been so tempted."

I bowed a second time, paying his consternation no mind, and shuffled out of the room, bowing a third time from the corridor, like a mandarin at the Imperial Court of Han. Harris—waiting just outside—looked on in amazement. Let the Butternut think what he likes, I thought. I haven't felt so light of heart in ages.

Ambling back to my office, replaying the scene in my mind, I murmured a quiet thanks to that lunatic midget and all of his doomed confederates. I entreated that the Lord might have mercy on them, insofar as it was feasible—; I was confident that their countrymen would not.

Leaded Glass.

THE WAR CAME TO ME IN STOCKINGED FEET, says Clementine.

I'd been on 37 less than a week when the guns fired on Fort Sumter. It was the R—— himself brought me the news. I was sitting in the room they had put me in, staring up at the rafters. The room had only one window and it was too high to see out of. The R—— came in with Kennedy and bowed to me. "You should have kept your appointment with me, Clementine," he said. "You hurt me by your disappearance. And with Virgil Ball, no less."

"My appointment with you was the half the reason I left," I said. "You turn my guts."

"Yes." He sighed.

I looked up at the rafters.

"We seem to be at war," he said after a moment. "Our nation."

"Who with?"

His face furrowed. "With *ourselves*, Miss Gilchrist, as I understand it."

I raised my eyes to his. I wanted to hurt him, to shame him with my look. I could feel the babe kicking and twisting inside me though it was too early yet by half. I've known for twenty days, I reminded myself, keeping my eyes on the R——. For twenty days I have been a family.

"Where's Virgil?" I asked. I asked this every day.

The R—— only smiled.

"Gone," said Kennedy. He came and squatted at my feet, meaning to frighten me. "Gone as last week. Gone as he can be."

I spat onto the floor. I'd meant to hit him on the cheek.

"Mr. Kennedy doesn't mean to pain you, Clem," the R—— said. His voice was mild as honey. It slid across me like a fiddle-bow and stilled the feeling of the babe, the feeling of too soon. In spite of myself I wanted that damn bow to keep on fiddling.

"Clem," said the R——, "Virgil is away on business. Virgil is away and I can't say, exactly, when he will return. Until that time you must think of us—Mr. Kennedy and myself—not only as your servants, but as your kin."

"I have all the kin I need," I said. I cursed him levelly, my eyes never straying from his own. I cursed old Tesla for letting Harvey come and take me. I cursed Goodman Harvey for his trickery. Then I cursed the R—— again, louder and leveler than before.

"Speak ill of me if you must," the R—— said. "But don't speak ill of Mr. Tesla. He treated you generously, I believe."

"How did you find me?" I said. "So blessed quick. Less than a day. And with so little fuss. You must have paid that damn Jew plenty."

"Of course we paid him," the R—— said. "But it didn't come *too* dear, if that's your worry. And as for fuss, there was none at all. Virgil had explained things in advance."

"Virgil—had—explained," I said. This was a lie, of course. But I could hear from the sound of my voice that I believed it. My face and neck went hot, as they do each time I apprehend a truth. I stumbled in that instant over all manner of ideas, and by the time I found it in me to answer I'd already taken his lie for gospel. He'd convinced me with his child's mouth, wet and round and graceful. I believed what he said before I'd even understood it.

It was always that way with the R——.

So Virgil left me with Tesla as a token to the R——, I thought. A token he'd return. Like the silver hoops he passes out to his niggers. It made no sense, of course ; not then or after. But I believed it.

"The old man, his Jewy uncle," Kennedy said. "He sent word where you were hid."

"And that you were ill," the R—— added.

"Ill?" I said. My head was running over with voices. The echo of the R——'s voice was loudest and behind it was Virgil's voice and behind Virgil's was my own, fear run through it like stitching through a hem. Ill? I thought. Is that how Virgil thinks of it?

The R—— and his monkey-butler of an Irishman said nothing. The R—— stood with his head cocked to one side. Exactly like a spaniel, I thought. But the thought didn't help me much.

I believed that Virgil had given me to them but I didn't understand it. Not yet.

"I'm confident you'll recover, Clementine," the R—— said. He gave me half a wink. "In a matter of six or seven months. *N'est-ce pas?*"

"I'm sure Virgil didn't ask you to keep me locked up in this room," I said.

The R—— nodded.

"What?"

"You've never visited Island 37 before, Mademoiselle—"

"I never was invited."

He nodded again. "That's right. And with good reason. This island may offer refuge, of sorts, from the United States government—"

"Govern*ments*," Kennedy interrupted. "There's two guh!—guh!—governments now. The Union and the other."

"Quite," the R—— said. The honey went out of his voice, talking to Kennedy. But he recovered it for me. "For that very reason, however, this refuge of ours holds an attraction for persons you'd not much care to come across unaccompanied. You might be mistaken for—"

"What I am, Mr. Morelle?" I said.

"What you are, Clementine, is a vision," he said. "And you know it all too well."

The look on his face put me on my guard. Later I'd come to despise Virgil Ball with all my might, but just then I imagined he was dear to me. So I studied the R—— long and hard. I'd never have believed that Virgil would give his family to such a man. I never would have credited it. I sat quiet on my bench and looked at the R——, trying to make out what Virgil adored in him.

His voice, I decided. His voice and the way he moved through the world, sure and full of spite for earthly things. The child Jesus might have moved that way, or John the Baptist. The end of the world in the body of a boy.

That afternoon they brought Parson for a visit. I hadn't caught sight of him since we'd got off ship but I'd known that he was still about. You could see it in their faces when he was.

Parson came into the room and sat Indian-legged on the floor. He sat himself down in a dainty way, spreading his skirts like an old madame. He was so long in the body that his flat gray eyes were on a level with my own. My face began to chill at the sight of him.

"Afternoon, Parson," I said in a careless voice. The R—— and Kennedy stood watching from the hall. From time to time an old woman doddered past with a slop-bucket in her hands.

"Afternoon, Miss Gilchrist," Parson said, taking a fat-bellied mouse out of his pocket.

I kept my face slack, watching the mouse wriggling in Parson's palm, working its wet gray nose into the gaps between his fingers.

"It looks to be in the way of having children," I said.

"I found it on my way to see you," Parson said. His voice was high and matronly. "It was building a nest under the stairs."

I smiled at him. "What do you want with it?"

"For you to see it, miss. That's all."

"I've seen enough of mice, thank you." I made a face. "I've no interest in her, Parson."

"Do tell," Parson said. Without another word he set the mouse on the floor and slipped a cork-soled slipper off his foot. He pursed his shriveled lips and brought the heel down on the mouse's skull.

"Don't! *Oh!* OH!" I hollered, feeling a knot of sickness loosening in my belly. The mouse's head burst and a grayish jelly shot from its mouth onto the floor. I twisted my body to the left and vomited.

"She is with child," Parson announced, sliding the slipper back onto his foot. "Five weeks gone."

I looked up to find the R—— at my side. He took a yellow damask kerchief from his vest and gave it to me. Then he turned on Parson with a face gone gray with anger. "You disgust me," he said. "I asked you to discover if the girl was sick."

Parson heaved a sigh. "I have."

"Abomination!" the R—— shrieked. "Out of my sight!"

"As you like," Parson said. In another instant he'd gone, pulling the door shut behind him.

The R—— sat down beside me and folded his hands as if we were in a church. I hadn't been fooled by his charade but it had pleased me just the same. "Please accept my apologies, Clem," he said. "Parson has a prejudice toward your profession."

I gave him a crooked smile. "If he'd brought a possum to step on, or a suckling pig, you might have found out the name of the father."

"I know his name well enough," the R—— said. He leaned across and kissed me on the nose.

"No!" I said, elbowing him away. "You're wrong. It's Virgil's."

All he did was cluck. "You're sure?"

"I haven't let any other gentleman spend," I said. "Not without precautions."

This didn't put him out a bit. "Virgil Ball is not a gentleman," he said, nuzzling my ear.

That was the beginning of it.

We sat together for a while and I began to feel better. He asked if I felt well enough to go for a walk. A constitutional, he said. A brief excursion. I reminded him that he had cautioned me the island was a dangerous place.

"It is, Miss Gilchrist," he said, helping me to my feet. "It is, to the unescorted."

We went downstairs and I stopped to admire the leaded-glass window above the bar. A scene was depicted on it, in leaves of lazuli and green, and I asked him what it was. He blew out the lantern sitting on the bar-top that I might see the picture better. This is what I saw—:

Two men sat on hour-glass-shaped stools under a low dark sky. The one on the right looked something like a young Simon of the desert, with long matted hair in curls. The one on the left I took for a likeness of Parson. Behind him, in the shadow of a little bush, a lapis-colored man was climbing out of the mouth of a sparrow.

The R—— took my hand and said—:

"That is Nachiketa being interviewed by the Prince of Death."

"It's been some time since I read my scripture," I said. I felt small and mildewish in front of that panorama. The red of the clouds, the high green grass, the blue of the figures on their chairs brought tears to my face and I felt myself to be looking through a paper screen onto a finer world than our own. The colors began to lap together along the edges of my sight and this made the picture more beautiful even than before.

"Scripture wouldn't help you, Clementine," the R—— said. "This story was left out of the Good Book, on account of being too old-fashioned. You might say it comes from the *Old* Old Testament."

I let the light from the picture fall on me. "Tell me the story," I said.

The R—— took a breath. "Nachiketa, the son of a prosperous farmer, is sent by his father as an offering to Death. Death is out when he arrives, and Nachiketa waits unattended for five days. When Death finally returns, he apologizes for his impoliteness and offers Nachiketa a boon. Nachiketa asks Death for the secret of everlasting life."

"Is that what's in the picture?" I asked. "Is he being told?"

The R—— nodded. "Death says there are two choices open to the seeker—: to repeat this life—with all its agonies and pratfalls—in one body after another, or to renounce the pleasant for the good, vanity for the real, and thereby pass into eternity."

I closed my eyes, trying to follow. When I opened them I said—: "Is that him? On the right?"

"Nachiketa?" the R—— said. "Yes."

"Which does he choose?"

The R—— gave a laugh. "The second path, of course. Nachiketa lets all vanity fall away." He turned his back to the bar and rested his shoulders against it. "You might say I had that window fashioned as a reminder to myself." He brushed my cheek with the back of his hand. "Or possibly as a caution."

I'd never before thought of the R—— as having religion. "What do you mean?"

"Only that I, in my life, have never failed to prefer the pleasant to the good. The idea of repeating this existence of ours, with all its countless disappointments, is a delightful one to me. Had I been Nachiketa's father, I'd have wished him god-speed on his voyage to eternity and drunk his health that night at the nearest house of fun."

He tipped the lantern on its side and lit it. The window paled but it was still a glory. I looked at the R—— in dim-witted wonder that he could love the pain of life so dearly, and at the same time I understood that this love was at the root of his power over Virgil, over the rest of his company, over me.

"I have need of a *successor*, Clementine. I may not live forever, but the Trade will—; I'm convinced of that." He turned to me. "That's why I take such an interest in you. In you, *chère Mademoiselle*, and in that babe you carry."

I remembered now who it was beside me. I let out a bitter laugh. "Have you taken to breeding your lackeys now, Thaddeus? Aren't you finding enough in the quimhouses and saloons?"

"Ah! Clementine." He brought the lantern close to his face, that I might better see his eyes. They shone like candle-flames. "*This* child would be no lackey. This child would be master of this country—; master of this country, and of me."

I said nothing, only looked from his face to the beautiful window, then back to his face again.

He took me by the arm and led me out into the dust and the heat of the afternoon. I'd not been out of doors for a week and my eyes went half-blind from the daylight. I'd become happy suddenly, in spite of my anger and suspicions. It was the R——'s doing, I knew, but I didn't care to part with it. I closed my eyes and let him lead me on.

ONCE A MONTH VIRGIL CAME BACK TO 37. After a few hours with the R—— he'd be allowed to come and see me. Now that we were away from Lafargue's—away from the red and yellow lights, away from the window and the bed—I began to see what kind of man he was. The R—— helped me to see it. Virgil was kind in his way, but womanish. When he visited he'd wait till he was sure we were alone—: then he'd stammer out every possible sort of nonsense. From his talk you'd have thought that he was helpless as a child. No power, no money, no say over anything in the world. No say over the sundry burthens that he carried.

"You have the Trade, Virgil," I'd remind him. "You left us here, with the R——, and you went away. You left us here as a down-payment."

That stopped him in his tracks. His mouth would open and close and he'd say nothing. I'd wait for him to speak, to stand up for himself, to explain, but a box of sorts would open in my guts and I'd hear my old voice clamoring, shrieking at his averted face, ordering him to leave me. He'd go off then in a fright, pleading with me to be quiet—; or else he'd start his fool story over from the beginning. Or he'd rush up all at once and hiss into my ear—:

"I can still do it, Clem. I mean to. Once you're in safety with the babe."

By "it," he meant killing the R——.

"I'm in safety *now*, Virgil," I'd say, looking back at him with my eyes half-closed. I said this to punish him at first. But as the weeks went by I managed to believe it.

The days passed easier and easier. I was free to come and go as I saw fit. My body being what it was, it got harder and harder to take my strolls, but I came to know the island very well. Outside the Panama House it was men everywhere but never once did any of them so much as look at me unless I asked them a straight question. The summer was a fierce one, hot and stifling as the tongue in my mouth, but by September the hours of the day were a single gilt delight. The island ended in a narrow spit of sand and reeds and I'd lie there on my back, surprised by everything I thought. The water would rush together into a V and the sound of it would brush against me and I'd close my eyes and remember what it was like before my life, when I had no life at all, only a body, a shape like the one that was fattening itself day by day in the hollow of my belly. I knew it was the babe that kept me in the R——'s favor, the babe and nothing else, and I wished to myself that it should never be born but stay inside me always, sheltering me.

Six weeks before my time Virgil went away and stayed gone. I asked the R—— what had become of him but he simply shrugged his shoulders. I'd always gotten letters from Virgil when he went off, stiff with vows and protestations——; but I seemed to have died to him now, and he to me.

The R—— brought Parson to see me every day. Parson would lay a long hairy ear-lobe against my belly and whisper to me that it was to be a boy. I understood that a boy was what the R—— wanted, and I set my will to it accordingly.

When my hour struck, the R—— informed me, Parson was to be my nurse. "You *must* have a nurse, Clementine," he said. "You can't go birthing the little chap into your night-pot." He smiled at me and I understood that I had to have a nurse and that the nurse I had to have was Parson. I thought of the mouse and of Parson's downy face and I said to myself that before I'd have him as my nurse I'd have the Mississippi River. But I smiled at the R—— and said that Parson was certainly very knowledgeable.

Every so often we'd have news of the war. In those first months there were hurrahs among the men at every Dixie victory, and high hopes for an autumn armistice. I'd never imagined thieves to be such patriots. The R——, of course, was not. He made a great show of support for the South, sporting a magnolia sprig on the collar of his jacket, but in private he fretted that the war might end too soon. When the tide first turned, that autumn, it was all he could do to keep from cutting capers.

One morning in mid-winter I was roused out of sleep by a chorus of yells, followed by all manner of stompings and bustlings on the stairs——: I opened my door to find the entire house filing out onto the bluff. I pulled a shift over my night-shirt and hurried after them. Not a hundred feet below us, creeping steadily up-river, were three of the most hideous monsters I had ever seen. They were as long as a house and covered in sheets of iron——; cannon stuck out of them like bristles from a sow. Each of them looked heavier than the whole D'Urberville Hotel. The men above-decks looked like maggots on a chop.

Goodman Harvey was there, in among the rest, watching them

roll by. He blushed when he saw me and tipped his hat. I'd not seen him since he'd stolen me from New Orleans. My change in feeling toward the R—— had done nothing, I found, to lessen the violence I felt toward that canker of a man. I walked toward him through the crowd, meaning to push him head-first off the bluff. Instead I found myself asking him politely about the ships.

"What are they, Mr. Harvey?"

"Pook'th Turtleth, mith," he said. "Union Navy."

I said nothing. The R—— might cheer each defeat as loudly as each victory, but my heart quaked to watch that slow parade.

God have mercy on the river, I thought.

After that the war became a far-away thing again. I thought of it as I might of a disaster in a foreign place. The island, after all, was a kingdom to itself. What are the United States to me? I thought. The war kept 37 as free and as safe as the chap in my belly kept me.

I knew that time and the babe would change me, and they did. But not the way that I or the R—— or even Virgil Ball had reckoned. A different way altogether. We were all of us quite surprised.

One morning in May I found Virgil sunning himself on the Panama's stoop. I'd come down to the bar for a glass of birch-beer and found him outside the door, clutching his tattered felt cap like a pan-handler's plate. I saw at once that he was not in his proper mind. His mouth moved as if he was chewing on a piece of fat. He stood without a word and led me up to my room, wincing when the latch shut behind us. It was clear from his look that the old fear was on him.

"I want to tell you where I've been," he said.

"Where?"

He stood carefully in the middle of the room, looking nervously about him and pawing at his cap.

His mouth opened.

"Well?"

"Shiloh," he said. His voice caught on the -oh.

I could see he expected the name alone to do his work for him. I'd heard of course about the battle there, from the R—— and sundry others. I'd heard the fighting had lasted two days. I'd heard a goodly number had been killed.

"What's Shiloh to me, Virgil Ball?" I said.

His head tipped back, as though his body was tired of carrying it, and the story hissed out of his mouth-corner like a jet of steam.

Shiloh.

ORELLE SENT ME OUT TO KILL BEAUREGARD, Virgil says. He sent me and I went.

It was the end of 1861. Beauregard had become a burden to him, now that the war was under-way, just as I had become a burden. No doubt he'd have an equally burdensome citizen put a bullet in me at his convenience. I had no doubt of this, but I went just the same. Partly because of Clementine, partly out of habit—; but also because there was no life for me outside the Trade, no purpose, no safety. I'd forgotten this briefly, and it had caused me pain. I was never to forget again.

For sixteen weeks I stalked Beauregard through the hill-country of Kentucky and Tennessee, sometimes trailing him at a distance, sometimes mixing openly with his men. He was a full general now, snake-oiled and brocaded, and from morning till night he was surrounded by a gang of ragged, scrofulous thugs that proved to be his cadre of under-officers. I had no trouble moving about his camp—: I'd brought tobacco and soap and a bottle of laudanum with me, and found a welcome at every camp-fire I called at. There were so many hangers-on—refugees and peddlers and profiteers and whores—that no-one looked at me too closely. My kind had long since grown as familiar to them as chiggers.

Getting close enough to Beauregard to shoot him, however, was a different cut of meat. The good general, I soon discovered, was an accomplished coward. Even during the most fantastic skirmishes he kept himself out of harm's way, if not out of sight completely—; a clutch of his most redoubtable aides-de-camp hovered about him at all times, enclosing him like a tent, to camouflage his dislike of cannon-fire. I was a middling shot at best, and I didn't fancy suicide. It would take a full-scale battle, I realized, and not a little luck, for me to catch my general unguarded.

By the end of March the wait had become intolerable. I'd been scoring the days into the soles of my boots—; by my reckoning Clem's babe had been born not long after I left 37. It would be four months old now, perhaps a little more. I knew neither its sex nor its age nor whether it had survived its birth. The child was the only strand connecting me to Clem, or for that matter to the world. My nights grew steadily more difficult, my days too agonized to bear. With each passing day Beauregard seemed farther away than ever.

A chance was to be offered me, however. On the fifth of April—a wet, cloud-blanched Friday—word came down the line of a new offensive. Beauregard's army had spent the past two days and nights hauling itself into place alongside General Johnston's above the town of Corinth, Mississippi—; the plan was to attack at first light. It was rumored that the Union Army, led by that drunken melancholic, Grant, was hatching attack schemes of its own, and had been joined just that night by a large force under General Buell—; Johnston, however, would not be turned aside.

"Old Johnnie said he'd fight them if they was a million!" a corporal I'd gotten friendly with grumbled between spoonfuls of laudanum. "Even Little Napoleon"—as Beauregard was known to the rank-and-file—"couldn't talk him out of it, the bastard!"

I muttered a heartfelt thanks to Lady Fortune, took a spoonful myself in celebration, and spent the next hour cleaning my revolver.

With the earliest streaks of day-light the order came to move into position. I scrambled forward with the rear line as had become my custom, but the banter and bravado I'd grown accustomed to was scarce. Word had spread that this was to be no ordinary skirmish. The men about me checked their rifles and bayonet-mounts feverishly, barely speaking to one another, discharging powder to test for dampness even though the officers had forbidden it on pain of death. No-one knew how many men were entrenched behind the clap-board church at Shiloh—; the infantry moved fitfully, at times surging forward, at times clumped together like livestock in a pen.

When we came to the forest's edge, however, a cry went up such as I'd never heard before, bright and terrible and heedless, and the men dashed forward with such fatal eagerness that in the space of a breath I was left to myself. There were sounds of rifle-fire close by, and the screams of Beauregard's men as they hurtled down the slope—; but the rustling of leaves under-foot, the sound of my breath, and the wind in the crowns of the trees seemed infinitely louder. I could hear the scraping of my trouser-legs against one another, and the squeaking of my boots, which were very slightly damp—; the other sounds—the sounds of the battle before me—were no louder than my thoughts.

I began to make out flashes of gun-powder now, to hear the report of rifles and the queer, repetitive shrieking of the wounded—; but my mind grew less convinced with every step I took. It seemed that I was walking in place, like a soldier on parade, and that the colors and noises were billowing toward me, growing duller and quieter with each passing moment. When at last the forest parted and I came out into the open, the battle was nowhere to be seen. There was only the sky, the grass, and a vision of the child that Clem had borne me, hanging on the horizon like a moon.

The child was beautiful—; more beautiful even than its mother. No trace of its father was visible, save possibly about the eyes. It was covered in a fine, luminescent down, like the down at the base of Clementine's back—; but also like the fine, pale hair on Parson's cheeks. Its fingers and toes were bunched defensively together, as though it had been rudely roused from sleep. Its eyes were raised knowingly to the heavens, like those in portraits of the infant Jesus. There was something about the eyes, however, that no such portrait ever showed. When I realized what it was I let out a cry of wonder.

Both the infant's eyes were blind.

I shut my own eyes for an instant. When I opened them the child was close at hand—; almost close enough to touch. I began to hear the sounds of fighting again, very faintly, and see shadowy figures about me in the grass. As I reached toward the child a ball from a musket grazed my skull, clipping a penny-sized scrap of flesh from my ear and dropping me lightly to the ground. The fighting was suddenly all about me, full and murderous and shrill, but the child remained exactly as it was, indifferent to the shortcomings of the world. I lay flat on my back, easeful and expectant, and let the vision fall over me like a sheet.

As I watched it, the child commenced to revolve, imperceptibly at first but with ever greater speed, quickening and blurring along its edges, mustering itself into a ball. Blood was running down my neck and shirt-front but I paid it no attention. I felt invulnerable, sacrosanct. My heart and mind exulted, as though a question I'd long been on the verge of asking was finally going to be answered. Looking closely at the ball, I saw that it was not smooth, but rather cut into a myriad of facets, like the bell-weight to a chandelier. I recognized it at once as the shape from the *Hyapatia Lee*.

It made sense that the shape should return to me now—: the future it had warned me of had finally come to pass. I let my eyes fall closed, not troubling further about the connection between the war, the spinning ball, and Clementine's babe. That my child should visit me on the first day of the end of the world seemed altogether fitting.

I AWOKE PERHAPS AN HOUR LATER, blood-caked and bewildered, to a sight no manner of vision could have prepared me for. The grassy slope had been exchanged for a curved wall of mud in which bearded, naked corpses, whole or in bits, were set like crockery chips in an alley. Rain was coming down in sheets—; a man close by, who'd died in the middle of a yell, had a mouth overflowing with it. I recognized him after a moment as the corporal who'd told me about Johnston and Little Napoleon the night before.

I tried to get to my feet, but a heaviness at the back of my skull prevented me. I crawled toward the river-bank on all fours, searching for Beauregard among the dying, knowing that I would never find him there. The fighting ahead of me was as furious as ever—; the farther I crawled, the deeper the shell-holes and higher the heaps of offal grew. The Yankees had two Pook's Turtles anchored in the river, and the explosions from their shells sent horse-cart-sized discs of mud whistling into the sky. Each wounded man I passed bade me desperately for something—a sip of water, a spoonful of laudanum, a bullet in the temple—but I paid none of them any heed. They were none of them my child, none of them my Clementine, none of them my Redeemer. And I had no further business with any living soul.

I kept doggedly on for perhaps another quarter-hour, oblivious to the shells and seemingly immune to them—: then sobriety returned to me. I dashed for the cover of a stand of choke-cherry trees, kicking like a mule, and had only just reached it when the field folded over on itself, bringing the sky down with it, and I hit the ground as heavily as a corpse myself.

I NEVER SAW BEAUREGARD AGAIN. The fighting at Shiloh went on for another night and day, as fierce and rudderless as ever, but by the time I'd recovered my strength I was miles behind Union lines. I spent the next week no differently than a genuine Rebel would have done—: scuttling from bush to bush, searching fallen men for victuals and water, making as straight as I could for the Confederate front. The Confederacy, however, seemed to be retreating faster than I could run.

News of my failure would reach 37 ahead of me, I knew. I was thus returning willingly to my own execution. And yet it was not self-hatred alone, nor desire for revenge, that drew me back to the Redeemer like a tick to blood—; there was also the fact—or the *company*, better said— of my miraculous child.

The child came to me each day, some days more than once, and always suddenly. As the weeks went by I saw it lose the sleek, feral look of a new-born and grow plump and wide-eyed and aware. It seemed a strong child, possessed of a fine, loud voice, possibly given to tantrums. Its eyes remained turned inward, as my own left eye is—; and it remained a child whose every gesture bespoke an other-worldly power. It was realer to me by far than the people I encountered, the battered country-side I traveled through, or my own filthy and bedraggled body. The thought that this child—my child—had been born into Morelle's hands, that he might at that very moment be cooing over its cradle, rocking it to sleep, or looking on as it was fed, never failed to sicken me. By the time I got to Vicksburg I could think of nothing else.

The child would have a hard lot, gifted as it was—; hadn't I suffered for my own small gift? It would have need of a friend, as it grew, to share its troubles with. That Morelle—or for that matter, Clem herself—had no further use for me was clear enough, but the child—? Surely this wondrous creature, blessed and blighted as it was, had need of practically no-one else.

It was with a fierce determination, therefore, to see my child—to see it and to cradle it, however briefly, in my arms—that I made the long and miserable journey south.

Clementine Gilchrist.

HE HADN'T MOVED FOR THE WHOLE TELLING of it and neither had I. He stared down stupidly at his hat. He'd told the story like a fable, or like the history of a saint—; he'd told it like an entertainment. He wasn't telling it to me at all. He was a character in the fable, and so was I. His telling made us flat as paper.

"That's fine, Virgil," I said to him when he'd finished. "But my babe died two hours after she came out of me. On December seventh, at six-thirty in the morning."

A little breath crept out through his teeth. I could see it even though it was close and dim in the little room. He looked at me.

"She—?" he said.

I got to my feet. "That's right, Virgil. Her name was Cecilia Ann."

Conspiracy.

I T ENDED WITH A BETRAYAL, Delamare says. What doesn't?
Soon after the war began, the Trade was interrupted. Not
destroyed (as nothing so profitable can be killed by any war, religious revival, or act of Congress) but temporarily dissolved. Even this
came as a shock to us, however. It was a surprise even to the Redeemer.
He'd done his best to get the war begun, thinking we'd fall comfortably through the cracks, only to discover that war, once got in motion,
was a grander thing by far than our humble corporation. Little by little
our confederates, associates, and stock-holders were caught up in it, to
one side or the other—; a goodly number of them forgot, for a brief
but shining moment, about the usefulness of money. "It's a natural
wonder, Oliver," the Redeemer would murmur sadly, and I couldn't
but agree. In the end, however, it wasn't pollution of the network by
high-mindedness (or by fire-eating) that shut the Trade down. The
river itself—our long-time co-conspirator—betrayed us.

It should have been clear from the start that the Mississippi would
see a heap of action, and that this, in turn, would hamper our own
fleet—; but all of us, especially the Redeemer (whom I came to know
better and better, as Virgil Ball fell out of favor), had a religious faith in
its deviousness. We knew it better than the navy did, we reasoned—; in
any case, it was vast enough to give shelter to us all. And it could have
done so easily, had it chosen to. Instead it took the opportunity to be
rid of us, with no more effort than a horse might make to brush away
a fly.

First came the news that the Confederate forts at the Delta had
fallen—; then, on the first of May, New Orleans itself. New Orleans! It
was impossible to credit, but it was so. Freakishly high water and the
mildest of currents had allowed Union gun-ships to pass beyond range

of the forts and take the city with ease. Similar losses up-river were pushing the Dixie navy southwards—; the two halves of the fleet were being pushed into a corner. Soon they'd meet, back to back, for a last desperate stand.

As chance—or the river—would have it, they met at Island 37.

By that time, of course, the Trade was long since departed, leaving a chosen few behind to sweep dust over its tracks. That I'd been selected for this dangerous task—out of a host of strikers and agents—nearly burst my heart with pride. There was talk of a property of the Trist family's at the mouth of the Cane River, "Geburah" by name, where the inner-most cell of the gang was to have its rendezvous—; the Redeemer wanted to watch the war go by, it was said, with his nearest and dearest beside him. When I'd made so bold as to ask the Redeemer himself, on our last walk together, if I could join him there, he had bowed to me (to me!) and said the idea seemed a right pretty one. The heavens had opened for me in that instant.

As I made my sweep of 37—setting fire to store-houses, dumping perishables into the river—it was all I could do to keep my wits and sense about me. Images of Geburah shone behind everything I beheld like light through a painted window-shade. I saw the property precisely, down to its smallest detail. The great house would be spacious and sunk slightly into the earth, so that as you rode up the long, straight avenue of oaks it seemed to rise out of the ground to meet you, like a ship pulling out to sea. Not a pirogue or a river-boat—; not even one of the iron-clads that had free run of the Mississippi—; a genuine sea-going schooner, fully rigged, its sails already great with wind. My fancy would entertain no less.

The oaks would part reluctantly as you rode up, falling aside in steady pulls, like the curtain in an opera-house—; and there it would stand, revealed to full advantage. A warm pink mass of sun-bleached brick, with a double colonnade in the old Greek style. Behind the colonnade, three paces back, a double run of porches. No different than a dozen estates I'd been chased off of with my bag of silver engagement rings, and all the more beautiful because of it—: this time I'd be welcomed as an honored guest. The Redeemer himself, his face aglow with affection and relief, would rush down to the landing to receive me. I even dared to imagine, in my most private fancy, that he might welcome me as his prodigal son returned.

It was a miracle, as it happened, that he welcomed me at all. From one moment to the next, it seemed, Island 37 was engulfed by the entire Dixie fleet—: the two halves closed over it like two fingers snuffing out a light. I was apart from the others just then, on a wooded spit of land pointing west toward Louisiana—; and it was this that saved me. My escape was effected by dog-paddling between the gun-boats and provisions-steamers, giving a heart-felt thanks to Providence for the time I'd spent on the river as a boy. The others were overtaken on the Panama House landing, and some in the Panama House itself—; I heard the sound of gun-play as I swam. I kept my face forward, eyes fixed unwaveringly on the shore. I pissed myself in fright, like a child of six or seven—; but the river cleaned me and swaddled me in its current, and carried me safely across to Louisiana.

To my true and certain knowledge I was the only one to get clear. I took this as yet another sign that Fortune had weighty plans for me, the details of which I could scarcely divine—; certain was only that the Redeemer featured in them. On the Louisiana bank I found a canoe provisioned and waiting, and I set out at once for the mouth of the Cane River. I had no doubt that the canoe had been left for me expressly. With every stroke toward Geburah my sense of destination grew.

By the time I reached it, seven days later, I was all but swooning with excitement. It took just one glance at the Redeemer's face, however—stiff, surprised, and not a little dubious—to pluck my feathers in an instant. My patron obviously hadn't been waiting with impatience and concern for me to make my journey—; in fact, he didn't seem to have been expecting me at all.

As for the house, it was nothing like I'd pictured it. In place of the pied brick-work and noble colonnades, I found a narrow, graceless box—a glorified casket, or a packing-crate—leaning doubtfully toward the Mississippi out of an anemic swath of park. The woods to either side deadened any prospect of the river, while the lawn leading apologetically down to the water served only to advertise our hiding-place to every passing boat. I couldn't for the life of me understand why the Redeemer had chosen as he did—; and our infrequent strolls together did nothing to enlighten me.

On the day of my arrival, as I've said, he was preoccupied and gruff. In place of a hero's welcome he simply patted me on the shoulder, spun about, took Parson by the arm, and argued with him the rest of the day behind closed doors. From that moment on, he frankly avoided my company, stopping by my room once a week with the air of a school-boy compelled to do his sums. My mood grew steadily darker.

I'd left 37 the very darling of the Trade, or so I'd fancied—; I arrived at Geburah to find myself its butler. How could I have failed? Had I been slandered by some rival? Had my store of good fortune been used up in escaping the Dixie navy? I was hapless for an answer.

The answer, as often happens, proved a simple one. As the weeks passed, I came to see that I'd not so much fallen out of favor as out of step, and the rest of the Island 37 Gang along with me. Now that we'd followed him into exile, it seemed, the Redeemer wanted nothing more to do with any of us. Parson alone retained his confidence. He moved between the Redeemer's quarters and his own, up in the attic, as matter-of-factly as a nurse—; the rest of us, of course, trusted him as much as we would a copper-head. For my part, I felt utterly unmanned by my sudden fall from grace—; but I was clever enough to hide it from the others. They still considered me the Redeemer's favorite, and I did nothing to discourage them. In my mind, however, I was anxious and bewildered as a child.

As my estrangement from the Redeemer grew, so too did friendship of a sort with Virgil Ball, my fore-runner both as favorite and outcast. Virgil was a genius at listening, I discovered—; what's more, he gave excellent advice. When I'd first met him, back on 37, I'd been not a little frightened—; later, as my own star rose, I'd thought of him with something akin to pity. Now I saw him as a kind of cipher, as much a riddle to himself as to the rest of us, but well worth puzzling over. In time, a silhouette of sorts—as in a cameo brooch—emerged from behind the trappings of the fool.

It was plain to see that he was in love with the Chartres Street trollop, Clementine Gilchrist, who kept to herself in a drafty, L-shaped boudoir on the second floor. I considered this the driving humor of his heart until I discovered, a short time later, that love was not what kept him at Geburah at all. He wished the Redeemer—and, by extension, all of us—a speedy and extremely violent end. At the same time, however, he wanted this end to interfere with the workings of the Trade as little as possible. He could imagine no life outside of it, he told me.

This was not the least of Virgil's paradoxes.

His scheme (for of course Virgil had a scheme) was revealed to me through a series of casual asides, so subtly and yet with such insistence that I soon understood them as a deliberate appeal. Without offering anything, on his side, but his stone-faced attention and his trust, he was asking me to harbor his secrets for him—; even, perhaps, to abet him in his plan. And it was one of the greatest shocks of my nineteen years on this earth that I found myself—just as tacitly, at first, and just as indirectly—agreeing to his terms.

Soon his hand lay open on the table. The part I was to play was this—: to convince the Redeemer to look into Virgil's blighted eye. That was all. Virgil had been waiting for a session for months on end—; normally the Redeemer could go no more than a fortnight without one. It was their custom, Virgil explained, that the two of them be alone—completely solitary and immured from the least distraction— when that eye of his worked its wonders. He was sure the Redeemer would choose to conduct him away from the house—; down to the landing, perhaps, or off into the woods. This was all that he lived for any longer—: one half-hour, perhaps less, with the alpha and omega of his hate.

After a few weeks more, when I'd finally come to accept that I'd been left behind on 37 like a half-eaten cup of porridge, I gave my assent to Virgil's plan. Perhaps I acted childishly, out of injured self-opinion—; my pride has ever existed in false proportion to my station. But there was more at play than that. To betray the Redeemer meant to become—if only for an instant—his full and indefatigable equal—; even, in a sense, his better. And I wanted to become the Redeemer's better with all my body and my brain.

ALL OF THE ABOVE IS FOOLERY. I have no idea why I conspired with Virgil Ball to murder that man, who to me was as a pharaoh resurrected from the clay . . .

The Omega and the *Gifle*.

MY CHANCE CAME AT LAST ON THE TWELFTH of October, Virgil says.

I was sitting on a cot in my slant-ceilinged cubby, picking stones out of the treads of my India-rubber boots, when Delamare appeared in the open door. I invited him in but he paid me no mind. His shirt was mis-buttoned, which itself was cause for wonder—: I'd never before seen him with a hair out of place. His expression, however, was tranquil as a lamb's.

"He'll be coming up to see you," he said. "He'll be coming up directly."

My heart spasmed in my chest. "That's fine," I replied. I knew straight-away, of course, that he meant Morelle.

"Watch out for Harvey. I passed him on the stairs."

"I will. Thank you, Oliver."

"No need for that," said Delamare. He lingered in the door a moment, looking neither at me nor away. Nothing about him bespoke conspiracy—; he showed as much emotion as a heifer in a pen. My mind gradually flooded with disbelief. Could Morelle truly be coming, that same damp autumn afternoon, that I might take him into the woods and kill him? The thought was utterly preposterous. No scheme of mine had ever run half so well.

"I'd best be off," Delamare said, stepping out into the hall.

"Stop a bit, Oliver!" I whispered. But he'd already shut the door.

I was woefully ill-prepared to receive my visitor. My revolver had been left behind at Shiloh—; an antediluvian musket, its barrel longer than my leg, was the nearest thing to an instrument of death that I possessed. I turned in a slow circle, giddy and short of breath, in the exact center of the room. How on earth was I to do it?

My eyes finally lit on the grime-covered pier-glass next to the room's sole window. It was dull and cheaply made, but the cypress tree outside was reflected in it like a Turkish dagger. Without another thought I laid it on my bed, threw my quilt across it, and shattered it with the butt-end of the musket. It made no more noise than a tea-cup dropped onto the floor. I threw back the quilt, chose a likely-looking sliver, and slipped it into the pocket of my vest. No sooner had I done so than a knock sounded on the door—: Morelle's knock, swift and self-assured. There was nothing for it but to let him in.

I found him standing somewhat stiffly in the hall, sporting the same Napoleonic cap he'd worn when I'd first laid eyes on him. I opened my mouth—to thank him for coming, perhaps, or to invite him in—but I could manage nothing better than a grunt.

"Virgil!" he said, beaming up at me. He pronounced my name with an odd emphasis, as though introducing me to some other.

"Thaddeus," I said hoarsely. I had never before called him by that name.

He gave a quick nod, as though I'd returned some manner of pass-word, then turned briskly on his heels. "Come along, Virgil! A conference!"

I pulled my boots on as quickly as I could and followed him. He led me matter-of-factly out of the house and across the lawn, making a bee-line for the woods, as if he were impatient to be murdered. I did my best to keep up without appearing over-eager—; I'm sure I failed grotesquely. It made no difference, however. No-one happened upon us, no one got in our way, no-one called after us from the house. The world seemed as ready as I was to be rid of Thaddeus Morelle.

He spoke not a word till we came to a small, damp clearing, oblong in shape, with a fallen tree at either end of it. We were perhaps a mile from the great house and as far again from the river. Dusk had yet to fall, but in that close, somber place it seemed the last minutes of twilight. Morelle sat me down on a moss-eaten stump and stood directly across from me, studying my face. The false twilight deepened. Time shuddered, gave a barely audible sigh, then halted altogether.

I'd begun to think we might remain in that attitude—a *tableau vivant* of mutual distrust—until the last day of judgment, when all at once Morelle thrust his hands into his waist-coat and drew forth a candle-stub and a tin of sailor's matches. His close-set eyes never left my own.

"Is it right?" he asked, as tradition demanded.

The words had a different meaning, in that little glade, than they'd ever had before—; and I had a different answer. "It's right," I said.

I could hear his surprise when at last he spoke. "It's right?" he repeated. "Exactly as it stands?"

Our ritual had been fixed from the beginning. I was to say it wasn't right, no more, no less—; and he was to re-arrange things till it was. I said nothing further now, and he continued to stand stock-still above me, breathing whistlingly through his nose. I might easily have attacked him then—: we were perfectly alone, at least half a mile out of ear-shot, and there was a new quality to Morelle, a sort of dull uncertainty, that did a good deal to embolden me. But I wanted to move through the steps as we'd always done. I believed in my gift now—believed in it as fervently as I'd once doubted and disparaged it—and I wanted to catch another glimpse, however fleeting, of what the future held. Perhaps I'd see the Child from Shiloh—; perhaps I'd see myself, or Clementine. Perhaps I'd catch a glimpse behind the scaffolding of the Trade at last, and see with my own eyes what was hiding there.

I was adrift on these and other musings when there came the dry rasp of wood against wood and a match flared to life within an inch of my left eye. The pain was worse than it had ever been. What was more, I saw nothing to reward me for my suffering—: no figures, no landscapes, not even the customary shapes. Only a pulsing web of faint red lines, the precise hue and texture of my pain.

"What is it?" came the Redeemer's voice, as if from the top of a ravine.

"Nothing," I answered, digging my fists in to my eyes. "There's nothing there at all."

As soon as I'd spoken the match-flame was blown out.

"Of *course* there isn't!" Morelle chirruped. He was suddenly in the very best of spirits. "How *could* there be, Kansas, when there never was before?"

I rose wobblingly to my feet, my eyes and brain still addled from the light. "I'm tired of your parlor games, Thaddeus. If you have something to tell me, tell it to me plain."

He lit another match and brought it to his face. "That peeper of yours *never* had a gift, dear K." He covered his left eye with his hand. "Unless you count blindness, of course. Blindness can be a blessed gift. It prevents *you*, for example, from seeing the *gifle* headed in your direction."

"The which?" I said.

His clapped his hands. "The *gifle*, sirrah! The *gifle*! The custard-pie!"

I felt the old haplessness returning. "But our meetings," I protested. "Your *tables*, Thaddeus—; the matches, the shapes—"

"Were a way of getting you to do the unthinkable for me—; nothing more. And you *did* do the unthinkable, Virgil, didn't you!" Slowly, gloatingly, he worked his thumb into his nose. "It was Parson's stroke of genius, naturally. 'Ball is a believer,' he said to me. 'Use him.' And Parson was right, as always." He gave a low whistle. "I must say, Kansas, for a rationalist you sure were an easy fish to fritter. The development of your mystic abilities took a single afternoon!"

The match-flame sputtered and expired. My thoughts flew back to that star-crossed run to Memphis—: the Yellowjack, the coffles, Trist's box of samples, the Pendleton Hotel. Would I have made the run—would I so much as have considered making it—if my own eye hadn't spoken for me? And there had been countless such instances, great and small, from our meeting at Stoker's Bluff to the present hour. I might never have entered Morelle's service at all, in fact, if he hadn't made such a fuss over my affliction. Over my old, fat, imperfectly blind left eye, ugly as the devil's arse by candle-light.

And yet, I thought, forcing myself to return his pig-eyed leer—: your power over me remains imperfect. There's one point that you haven't troubled to consider.

"I *did* have a vision, Thaddeus. On board the *Hyapatia Lee*. Have you forgotten? I had a vision, and you had no part in it. You were a hundred miles up-river that night, with all your tricks and *gifles*."

"Oh! Not so far away as that, dear K. I had a rendez-vous that same evening, in point of fact." He lit a third match, regarded it a moment, then let it drop. "At Madame Lafargue's."

I must have known all the while, in some back larder of my brain, that Morelle was the caller Clem had been so keen to escape. I must have known, as it failed to move me now. I simply shrugged my shoulders.

"I had a vision, Thaddeus. I saw the world—*this* world, not any other—and it made sense to me at last. I saw myself surrounded by it, engulfed by it, spinning in it like a pebble in a creek. And then I saw the muck about me in the water—: I saw the Trade." I brought my fists out of my pockets. "I even saw the two of us, it seems to me, together in this glade."

Morelle guffawed. "Seen the *future*, have you, and all under your own steam? Far be it from *me* to take it from you. But do me this small favor—: look at your face in the pier-glass tonight, when you shuffle back to your cubby, and ask yourself what blessed good it's done you." He raised a hand carefully, palm upwards, as though cradling a tea-cup—; then he turned it over. "I'll never understand you, Kansas. Your blindness was the only gift you had—the *only* one, do you hear?—and you tossed it in the gutter."

He turned his back on me, then, with a world-weary shrug, as though mortally exhausted by my idiocy. My right hand stole into my waist-coat pocket and took hold of what was hidden there. "I don't think I can look into that pier-glass anymore, Thaddeus," I said.

Something in my voice made him stop short—; but he chose not to turn about. He was never to look me in the eye again.

"I can't say I blame you," he said at last. "You're done for." He ran a finger along his collar. "It's in my *nature*, sadly, to be the end of things. Where I exist no other thing can flourish. No other ambition—; no other intrigue—; no other love." He sighed. "Most importantly that, perhaps. No other love."

This was more than I could stand. "I'm not the only one to suffer from hallucinations, you shanty-town Napoleon," I spat out. "I'm sick of your damn self-religion."

He clucked at me. "*Religion*, dear K? Not at all. Our Lord Christ Jesus, if you recall, proclaimed himself the alpha and omega of all things—; I aspire to the omega only." He shook his head. "You're done for," he said again, stifling a yawn. "But don't fret—: the Trade, dear Virgil, will survive you."

"Contrary-wise, you won't," I said, driving my weapon into the flesh above his collar.

Morelle let out a single bright squeak, as of a mouse crushed under a boot-heel—; then he dropped face-forward into the moss. That was all. I crouched beside him and turned his head toward me. His face wore a look of uncomplicated horror. He spasmed soundlessly for per-haps a minute, spat out a purplish froth, and died. There was no magic in his passing, no nobility, no wit.

For a time I neither moved nor spoke, staring down at the corpse to fix the fact of it in my mind. I was amazed at how convincing, how self-evident his killing seemed. The world had tipped for an instant, had shifted in its cradle slightly to acknowledge the great change, and that was all. That was all—; but it was all-encompassing. The long and blood-besotted reign of that tiny monster over my life was ended. And I myself, bungler that I was, had brought it to a close.

"Who's the omega now," I said into the quiet, "if not Virgil Ball?"

As if in answer, a twig snapped close behind me. An unmistakably human sound. At any other time, my heart would have leapt into my wind-pipe—; just then, however, I felt exalted and serene. The world had shifted in its cradle, after all. Past experience did not apply.

I turned my head slowly in the direction of the sound. A man was there, half-hidden by the nearest trees. He was a clot of heavier dark-ness, a silhouette at best—; but I recognized him straight-away. It was Goodman Harvey.

He said nothing, did nothing, only let himself be seen. His mute-ness was both an overture and a threat. I'm beholden to you, Virgil, he seemed to be saying. I'm grateful to you for ending my bondage—; and you must be grateful to me. Be grateful to me, or I'll tell.

There was nothing for it, I realized, but to kill him.

"Come over here, Harvey," I said. I said it softly. But he turned and disappeared into the pines.

IV

*He that loveth his brother abideth in the light, and there is none occasion
of stumbling in him. But he that hateth his brother is in darkness, and
walketh in darkness, and knoweth not whither he goeth, because darkness
hath blinded his eyes.*

Little children, keep yourselves from idols. Amen.

—1 John, 2:10–11, 5:21

Geburah Plantation, 1863.

O UT FROM THE GREAT HOUSE, Parson says. Into the oaks. Virgil is gone from us. Virgil, the most inquisitive, the most tender. Rebellious Virgil. Sent to fetch the mulatto, Virgil has instead gone promenading. The three of us watch him from Harvey's window, entering the orchard, the mulatto at his side. The beautiful mulatto. The three of us sit and watch and bide, with only Harvey's whitening corpse for company.

The Colonel is for following them, placing them under house-arrest, discovering what they know. Kennedy is for killing them both at once. Poor dead Harvey is forgotten.

What are *you* for, Parson? asks the Colonel.

I keep my face close to the window. Me, Colonel? I answer. I smile at him. I'm for leaving well enough alone.

A Gun-Fight.

I OUGHT TO HAVE LEFT WELL ENOUGH ALONE, Virgil says.
That strange and consequence-less night, the night of the
Redeemer's murder, is bright in my mind as Delamare and I take
our promenade. Since we found Harvey dead, Morelle has never left
my thoughts. I should be locked in the smoke-house at this very moment,
awaiting my hanging-trail for Harvey's murder—: everyone knows
what I did to Morelle. Somehow, however, I remain at liberty. It's as if
they've forgotten what I did, Parson and Kennedy and the Colonel—:
forgotten it, or dismissed it out of hand. It's Delamare they want. I'm a
Jack Fetchit to them, nothing more. Of interest only as an errand-boy.

It's enough to bruise my sense of dignity.

"Fetch the mulatto," the Colonel told me, and I went. I went happily. The sight of the three of them licking their chops over Harvey's
left-overs was beginning to affect me. They were altogether too
pleased to have him laid out like a cat-fish at their feet. It was beginning to put ideas into their heads.

Instead of fetching the mulatto as I was told to do, however, I've
taken the mulatto on a stroll. The fact of it makes me feel dangerous
and sly.

Delamare moves sullenly, fingers working in his pockets. "They all
want me under-ground," he mutters, glowering at his shoes. "I've
come too far in this business for a nigger. They'll hang Harvey on me,
you can bet."

"You didn't kill anybody, Oliver," I say, passing my arm through
his. "Poison—even coyote poison—wouldn't suit your temperament."

We stand together by the orchard gate, at the head of the path
snaking down to the river. On less adventurous mornings the gate
marks the end-point of our stroll—; today, however, Delamare is feel-

ing restless. Watching him worry at the gravel with his boot-heel I make a guess, more or less idly, as to this morning's destination. The cedar park, peradventure, or out to the property line? Farther still, to the old shanty-town? Delamare leans to one side and looks me over, itching to ask about the Colonel.

The shanty-town today, I think.

"I did it, Virgil. By Old Wheezy's reckoning, at least. Why else would he send you out to fetch me?"

"I wouldn't say you're the *chief* suspect," I say, pushing open the gate. I wouldn't say it, but of course he is. It's Delamare they want.

"Of course I am," he says. "Who'll they hang it on instead?"

I hesitate. "Parson left his room last night. The Colonel and I both heard him. Some words were passed between the Colonel and Parson. Funny looks."

"Ha! I don't doubt *that*."

"And Kennedy seemed more bilious than usual."

"Kennedy," Delamare says, looking out at the river. "One day I'll be chief suspect in *his* retirement. I'll say that much."

"Then there's me, of course." I pause a moment. "I found the body."

"That's right, Virgil—; there's you," Delamare says fondly. "Shall we walk on?"

I'm a trained bear to all of them, even to Delamare, who knows me best—: trained and coffled to a stump. Though I stuffed the Redeemer's body down the privy and relieved myself on his remains (and this in full sight of Dodds, the house-boy), I'm not thought capable of murder. I was the Redeemer's opera-glass, his faro-chip, his marble—; and so shall I remain, in the eyes of my associates, forever.

"Where to?" I say, pulling the gate closed after us.

Delamare is already sashaying down the bluff. "I thought possibly the shanty-town," he says. "I'm in no hurry to have my head picked by that old horse-buggerer."

The path to the shanty-town winds down from Geburah through clusters of holly and smoke-bush—: malnourished, anemic-looking trees barely able to make shade. In better days it was a proper road, wide enough for a hitched team of oxen to travel on in comfort. Now we walk in single-file. Storm and high water have swept away all traces of humanity but this narrow groove of earth. The country here feels little tenderness toward posterity.

When the town shambles into view it comes as a disappointment, even a shock, as though the current has left its work unfinished. Each time we take this walk I nurture the hope that the huddle of ugly, bow-backed shacks will have been swept away at last. Finding it there time and again, at ease in its pocket of quiet, is enough to make a man lose confidence in the river.

"This was a Choctaw settlement," Delamare says, leaning against the door of one of the less decrepit shacks. "The darkies put the natives off—; then the Yankees drove the darkies away." He smiles. "*Coaxed* them away, I suppose."

I duck into a shack I've not been inside of yet. This theme has long since become familiar to me from our walks, and I no longer credit it. Anyone can see these shacks have been empty for years, since well before the Union came snaking up-river from the Gulf. I feel a momentary urge to poke at Delamare's self-assurance—; against my better judgment, I give in to it.

"They didn't have to coax them too hard, Oliver, it seems to me."

Delamare's head appears in a window-frame with the morning light behind it. His silhouette, topped by its wide-brimmed planter's hat, is that of the finest Southern gentleman—: as always, President Davis comes to mind. "What would *you* know about it, Virgil Ball?" he says.

The answer I give has a natural, plantation-bred obsequiousness to it that Delamare—whether he'd admit it or not—is grateful for. I taught myself this voice for dealing with men of property up and down the river, but it works on him better still. "Not *much*, Mr. Delamare, I guess."

His face disappears from the window. I find him crouched by a scattering of ash and food-tins, picking through them like a relic-seeker. "Did your Choctaw eat salted okra?" I say, taking up a tin.

He stares raptly at the ground. "This is a recent fire, Virgil."

A moment passes before I take his meaning. "What of it? This has been a fishing-hole for ages. You can't expect the local boys to leave off—"

"This country's been lousy with blue-coats for over a month," Delamare says, his voice dropping to a whisper. "You know that as well as anybody. Now shut your mouth!"

He's right, of course. "I'm sorry, Oliver," I say quietly. "You must think me quite the innocent."

Delamare squints at me an instant longer, then shakes his head. "I don't suppose you are," he says. He takes the tin from my hand and sniffs at it. "Do you have no fear they'll catch us?"

"Oh! They'll catch us, Oliver."

"And that doesn't put you out of sorts?"

"The certainty of it has a calming effect," I say. "You might try it yourself. It does wonders for the liver."

"Not in my nature, I'm afraid," Delamare says, allowing himself to smile. "In point of fact—"

Just then a rustling drops down on us from the trees and two men come into view, framed picturesquely against the slope, scrambling with all possible speed up-hill. Delamare is on his feet at once. "You! Boys!" he calls out in a leisurely voice, as though the confirmation of his fears had immediately quieted them.

The two men are clothed neither in freed-men's rags nor in the sack-cloth britches of the boys from town. They are grown men in open white shirts and trousers of Union blue, and their arms and necks where they emerge from the cotton are the color of fresh-turned soil. Their arms jerk in unison as they make for the cover of the pines.

"Those are your people up there, Oliver," I say, moving to stay Delamare's hand.

But his Sam Colt Peacemaker is already out and leveled. "They'll never know it," he says, and fires three shots in the western style, his left palm fanning back the hammer. The lower of the two figures stumbles as they pass into the trees. Then all is quiet and bright.

We take cover behind the nearest shack, harkening for any sound above the river and the breeze. "You've buried us, Oliver," I say at last.

Delamare grunts. "I have no sympathy for turn-coat niggers."

"They had no idea who we were, damn you! Not the slightest notion."

He puts his repeater by. "They moved as if they did."

"A couple of scullery-boys to the infantry, that's all. Most likely we caught them after a dip." I curse him under my breath. "Now we're partisans."

Delamare privileges me with a look of serene contempt. "Some of us always *have* been, Mr. Ball."

I brush this grotesque utterance aside. "Think what you like. If we'd let them run—"

"*If we'd let them run* we'd have been something less than men," Delamare says, the blood rushing to his face. "Don't confuse my role in this back-water comedy of errors with your own. I suffer invasion no more calmly than the next Confederate."

"The next Confederate won't be *hanged* by his country-men on sight, you blessed ass. There's a price on your head, Oliver. You don't have the luxury of playing Jefferson Davis any longer."

Delamare regards me dully for a time. When at last he speaks his voice, normally so sovereign and mild, is greatly changed. All at once I remember that I'm in the company of a nineteen-year-old boy.

"I don't believe you've talked to me that way before, Virgil," he says. "I was unaware, in fact, that you spoke that way to anyone." The repeater hangs slackly at his side—; his hand clenches and unclenches on its grip. "I must tell you it may jeopardize our understanding."

"You've most likely just doomed us all with that damn fire-cracker of yours," I answer, passing a hand over my eyes. "You'll forgive me if I don't remain in character."

"Of course, Virgil! Naturally." Delamare starts back up the path, to all appearances satisfied with my reply. As I come alongside of him, however, I see that he is knitting his brow together and slapping the barrel of the repeater lightly against his thigh. His face has taken on that expression of noble worry which has served him so well since his adoption by the Trade.

"Have I endangered your cause in the interest of my own, Virgil?" he says finally. "I apologize. But I thought you'd reconciled yourself to the inevitable."

A sigh escapes me. "I thought so, too."

He smiles. "But now you're not so sure?"

"The end will come soon enough, I reckon." I look up the bluff toward Geburah. "It came for Goodman Harvey just this morning."

"Goodman Harvey," Delamare says thoughtfully, pursing his lips. "It's no wonder someone ran out of charity for that little sniveler." He coughs softly into his sleeve. "I nominate Kennedy. He's easily the most murderous of our bunch."

"He'd like to murder *you*, Oliver. That's sure."

"I know it well. It's the Confederate in me."

"It's the nigger in you," I say softly.

Delamare slows a moment, cocks one eye at me, then lets out a melancholy laugh. It's a dangerous thing to call attention to his delusions—; but I've become a practiced hand at it.

"Oh! I know *that* much, Virgil," he says good-naturedly. "But it's not as simple as you think. Were I not aware of my birth-right as the son of a Dumaine Street gentleman, fully and *indefatigably* aware of it—; were I a lazy, whip-scared niggra boy, Kennedy wouldn't hate me half as much."

I mull this over. "It doesn't help your case, I grant."

"It's the Southerner in me, first and foremost, that old Stutter hates. That's why I take such comfort in his loathing." He rubs his hands together. "Now! What other irredeemable whore-son might we hang it on?"

"Well—"

His voice goes grave. "Not Miss Clementine, I hope?"

No sooner has he said this than my sight grows dim and the ground begins to shudder under me. I know what is going to happen next and feel no terror or surprise, only a mute excitement. An instant later a wheel of transparent fire rolls up the path, still steaming and sputtering from the river. It stops less than a pace from us, near enough that I can feel its heat. The wheel turns silently in place, then slips into the gap between our bodies, resolving before my eyes into a quivering, weeping, scintillating heart.

I should have known that the mention of Clem's name would bring on a sign. My eyes begin to water from the beauty of it. The second fire-sign of the day—: this night will end in violence as sure as I'm alive.

"No. Not Clementine," I say.

The wheel sheds a last fiery tear and rolls off into the trees. Delamare grins at me. "Of course *you* wouldn't think to blame her, Virgil. You revere her, after all. But Clementine has her natural share of cunning—; all accomplished doxies do."

If there is malice in this utterance I choose to overlook it.

"Perhaps it was the Colonel himself," I offer.

"Poison doesn't suit old D'Ancourt's character, either—; but I defer to you, of course, being your junior in years."

Delamare's bravado has returned to him completely ; the two colored soldiers have been cast aside like corn-husks. Has he decided, then, that his act will have no consequences? It seems as if he has.

He watches me covertly as we walk. Some queer look must have crossed my face, for he says very softly—: "I've no further interest in your Clementine, Virgil. I give you my word."

I keep my balance admirably. "What interest did you ever have in her, sirrah? I'd thought you were the son of a Dumaine Street gentleman."

But Delamare will not be swayed. "The love of a man for a woman, Virgil, is not to be made light of. I know this, vain and selfish as I am. I won't trifle with it twice." He sighs. "There's little enough to approve of in this nest of vipers."

"I wasn't aware, Mr. Delamare, that you had trifled *once*," I say.

Delamare flinches at this—: an honest flinch. "I must tell you, Virgil, that she courted me," he says. His steady brown eyes do not waver.

The sky behind Delamare pales momentarily. I make a great effort, tuck my hands into my pockets, and manage to return his friendly look. "When was it?"

"This Thursday last." He frowns. "I don't pretend to know what sport she's having with you, Virgil. I do own that it surpasses cruel."

I turn from him and continue up the path. His last words were meant as a question, but I've no strength to answer it this morning. Perhaps another.

"Cruel, Oliver?" I say. Then, quoting from memory—: "'Cruelty is a fable. Every act of violence is a vessel, sometimes clear, sometimes opaque, that carries its justification chaste within it.'" I grin at him. "I thought you knew."

I'd meant for Delamare to recognize this citation, and he does not disappoint me. He curses and kicks at the gravel. "The way you ape his sermons like a smug fat apostle turns my *stomach*, Virgil. Don't make a catechism out of him."

I bow my head beatifically. I am trying to provoke him now. "I do view myself as an apostle," I say. "He raised us up out of the mud."

"He left you exactly as he found you," Delamare spits out. "In the *filth*, the lot of you together. You were useful to him there."

"The filth was changed, however, after he passed through it."

"I'll grant you that," Delamare says grimly.

"Others of us he raised up rather prettily. You won't argue that, I trust."

He sucks in a breath. "What the hell are you getting at?"

"Clem's not the only doxie in this house." I look at him and wink. "We all have our little accomplishments—"

This proves too much for him at last. No sooner have I spoken than I'm splayed face-first across the gravel, red and yellow daisies blooming in my eye-sockets and my brain. Delamare's image is there as well, fist out in front of him, face drawn tighter than a drum-head.

"You'll do as you think best," I say, rolling onto my back with a little groan.

"It's unwise to speak to me that way, Virgil. That eye of yours holds no power over me."

I push myself upright. "Evidently not."

"He never raised me up, that dirty nigger-monger. He never made a gentleman out of *me*." Delamare glares down at me, struggling for breath. "Just the opposite."

"He taught you a few things—; you'll not deny that," I say, keeping my eyes on his fists.

"He took me from my home," Delamare says. "That's the only thing I'm grateful to him for."

"Yes. Your 'home'. I remember about that."

But he's already decided to forgive me. He reaches down a hand. "I shouldn't have mentioned that whore of yours, Virgil. I regret it."

I look up a moment, unsure of him, then take his hand. He helps me solicitously to my feet—; his anger is gone as quickly as it came. Soon I find myself endeavoring to console him.

"Don't feel too poorly, now, Oliver. I had it coming."

"That temper of mine is an awful thing, Virgil—: I know it is." He looks at me contritely. "I shouldn't have fired on those darkies, I suppose."

"Nonsense! It was your duty as a Confederate squire," I say, for some reason liking him better than I've ever done. I take hold of him by the coat and pull him onwards and upwards toward the house. "Come on along, now—; no more dawdling. The inquisition grows impatient."

THE COLONEL CHOOSES to conduct his interview with Delamare in the parlor, flanked by book-shelves stripped to their paper backing, cracked picture-frames, and arm-chairs too heavy or hideous for the Yankees to bother carting away on their last sweep of the country. A bell-jar on an end-table—which once held a porcelain figure, perhaps, or a taxidermied bird—has been fashioned into a thermidor for the Colonel's dwindling supply of snuff. The flock-paper hangs in great drooping folds off the walls, and the French parquet has been gouged in waxy arabesques, each looted heirloom leaving its testament in sawdust. It's a tribute to the Colonel's self-regard that he manages not to look more absurd among this mass of humiliated objects. Seeing him there on the hump-backed settee, dressed as always in his suit of cavalry gray, it's hard not to shed a tear or two for the Confederacy. Any society that succeeds in producing so perfect a caricature of itself should, in a just world, flatter Providence no end.

"You boys sure took your Catholic time," the Colonel growls, looking not at Delamare but at me. "Did you perhaps not understand, Mr. Delamare, that one of our number has been killed?"

"It took some time to find him, Colonel," I mumble.

"Why don't you look me in the eye when you ask me a question, Wheezy?" Delamare says.

The Colonel heaves an indulgent sigh. "You've always been an arrogant little coon, Oliver, ever since Kennedy emancipated you out of that mash-hut he found you in. No doubt the Redeemer was right, at the time, to encourage your airs—: the runaways you dealt with must have been bedazzled by them." He grins at us, showing his snuff-colored teeth. "At *this* point, however—as you must surely be aware— the Trade has been suspended, and the Redeemer, God rest him, has been sent down the privy. So let's share an honest word together, you and I."

"I'll leave you to it, then," I say, turning to go.

"Not at all, Virgil! You stay on for a spell." The Colonel's watery eyes dart back to mine. "We may have need of you to mediate. Isn't that so, Mr. Delamare?"

I curse them both silently. "I'm not sure how useful I'd be, Colonel. Mr. Delamare only recently boxed me on the jaw."

The Colonel nods. "You stay on a while, Virgil."

I shrug and sit on the floor beside Delamare, facing the Colonel across a tea-table set on three cracked, palsied-looking legs. Over the next hour Delamare's whereabouts on the night of the murder are gone over in insufferable detail, exactly as in a legitimate inquiry—: one might almost fancy the Colonel to have served in the military police. I can't help but admire his delivery. Clearly he was paying close attention at his court-martial.

The technique is not without effect on Delamare, either. In no time at all he's gone skittish as a doe. "No-one voted you chief god-damned constable," he mutters. "I know the *Redeemer* never did."

"You owed Goodman Harvey money, did you not?"

"Everyone owed that little badger money." Delamare shoots me an accusing look. "I owed him less than most."

The Colonel keeps his eyes fixed on Delamare's cravat, as though his face—and his answers, for that matter—were but a tiresome distraction. "Did you owe Goodman Harvey money, Virgil?" he asks.

"No, sir."

Delamare snorts. "Virgil doesn't enter into relations with his fellow human beings, grandfather. I thought you knew."

I clear my throat. "That's not entirely true, Oliver. I lent you five dollars just last Saturday."

The Colonel gives an arid laugh. Delamare stares back at him with a look of mute expectancy that puts me in mind of a nigger at auction. On Delamare, however, the look has a very different meaning. Leaning back on the stool, he says softly and melodiously—:

"The Redeemer said as much, before Virgil did him under. He predicted this whole vaudeville, you know."

The Colonel says nothing for a time. Then, blinking his eyes slowly, as a heifer might do to discourage a gnat, he leans stiffly forward. "The Redeemer—spoke to you about the future?"

Delamare nods and points at me. "He could read it, Colonel. From Virgil's smoky eye."

The Colonel's face jerks toward mine, but I remain as I am, looking evenly at Delamare.

"Is this some manner of minstrel-theater?" the Colonel says. "A comedy production of some kind?"

Delamare shakes his head politely. "He said that after he was gone you'd begin to drop, one after the other, like bull-frogs after a spawn. Those were his words, not mine. You'd be pared down, grandpappy. Pared down to the marrow."

"Virgil?" the Colonel says. His voice is pricklish as a pin.

"First I've heard of it," I say, truthfully enough. "Who'd be pared down, Oliver?"

Delamare yawns. "All of you, Virgil. The entire Trade."

"You were part of the Trade yourself, as I recall it," the Colonel says sharply. "An *integral* part. Have you forgotten?"

Delamare says nothing. The floor-boards along the inner wall creak subtly—: someone is listening at the door.

Knowing who it is, I rise. "This puts me in mind of another question," I say, gesturing toward the hall. The Colonel nods—; he's heard the sound as well. By the time I've crossed the room and opened the door she's moved off to a table topped by a vase of bone-dry marigolds. But she makes no show of being busy with them.

"Hello, Clementine," I say, testing the door to make sure it's shut behind me.

Clementine says nothing.

"Where did you sleep last night?" I take a slow step toward her. "It's important, darling, that I know."

She moves away as I approach, keeping an armful of reproving air between us. She's dressed in a shift left behind by one of the maids, billowing in great loose folds from her rail-thin body, black at the hem with the dust of countless floors. That filament of beauty which is left to her is more than enough to make the blood run backwards in my veins. She looks at me in a way I find myself utterly unprepared for—: not hatefully or fiercely, but with a steady, desperate interest, an interest which for a moment I misjudge and which quickens my heart in its envelope of tired flesh.

"Clem," I whisper. Is my long wait at an end?

Something in her look, however, stops me in my tracks. It's an expression I've seen before, but never on Clementine's proud face. In the next instant I've recovered myself and understood her look for what it is.

"You're not *afraid* of me, Clementine?"

"I've always known it when you told a lie," she answers. Her voice is dull as cloth. "It gets into my ear and fusses. Like singing false notes in the choir."

I take a step toward her. "Have you ever once known me to sing on key?"

She stands her ground. Her eyes are fully open, her fists are rigid at her sides. "You were lying just now," she says. "Lying to the Colonel."

"Nonsense," I say quickly. "I barely—"

"All this time," she says. "You never guessed that I was watching, did you? You thought that I was long past seeing you. But I *was* watching, just the same—: watching, and comparing what I saw with all the fine things I remembered. All the fine things I remembered about you, when you were still a living, breathing man."

"Clem—" I say, but nothing else emerges. I've forgotten how to speak to her.

"Here I am, Aggie. Just as you've been hoping. Face to face with you—; close enough to see." She sucks in a frightened breath. "Tell me what you did to him. Was there pain?"

"Who?" I say. My head begins to shake.

"Don't play the fool with me, Aggie. I won't tell Parson or the others." She hushes, then says almost soundlessly—: "He deserved what he got, after all."

A green crescent drifts across my sight, turning to the left and sparking.

"Let's not speak of this, Clem, I beg of you. Not here."

She studies me a while, then twists her neck sharply to one side and spits. Her proud unbending neck, that once reddened and inclined toward me. Her brown incriminating eyes. The spittle glistens stupidly against the floor.

"You're a coward yet," she says in a quavering voice. "Even now, with every last thing taken from you."

Each time we're alone the moment arrives, whisperingly and unbidden, when I forget all that's happened since I first beheld her. I speak at such moments without thinking.

"If I've told lies—" I hear myself stammer, the words rattling in my mouth like cracked seeds in a gourd—"I told them to keep you close to me—; to clear the others out, to hollow out a place for you and I—"

She draws herself up at this and lets me look at her, rewarding me for my foolishness as she has always done. Her face comes near to mine, lit along its left side, and I'm allowed to leap-frog over entire years, and only see—: the wide-set eyes, the narrow freckled shoulders, the Catholic mouth. Her skin has become papery at some point without my noticing but it's still lit as if from the inside, and I know that it's hot to the touch, like the shade to a paper lamp. That is what I remember best—: Clementine lit by a red Chinese lantern on her left side, her arms lifted toward me, her small immaculate body glowing like a lamp itself.

I raise my right hand and she allows it to settle on her shoulder, stricken and hapless, curled in upon itself like the carcass of a bird. Her entire body deadens at its touch. She lets out a breath. The last breath she draws will have that sound—: infinitely calm, infinitely bitter.

"You killed Goodman Harvey, Virgil Ball."

Clementine, at least, believes in me.

The Inquiry Proceeds.

Conducted by Col. Erratus D'Ancourt, L.P., M.M.D.C.
Geburah Plantation, 12 May 1863. Virgil Ball—: minutes.

Colonel—*Mr. Kennedy. Good of you to come so quickly. Another round of interviews, I'm afraid.*

Kennedy—*That's all right, Colonel. You can get stuffed.*

Colonel—*Were you out at the privy just now? Is that where Virgil found you?*

Kennedy—*Why don't you ask huh!—huh!—him?*

Colonel—*Out there all morning, were you? (PAUSE)—Touch of the binds?*

Kennedy—*You can go and get worked, you god-damned—*

Colonel—*You might not think it important that I know where you've been keeping yourself, Mr. Kennedy, but it's of great and pressing interest to us all. (QUIETLY) One of our number has been taken in the night, you see.*

Kennedy—*Is that a fact, you old gasser? And weren't I there in Harvey's room to see it? (PAUSE)—What was it? Something that he ate?*

Colonel—*Answer my question. Four to eight o'clock this morning.*

Kennedy—*Either you tell me cause of death, you old wig-licker, or I'm back on that privy quicker than you can part your nose-hairs.*

Colonel—*Most likely that's where you'll do us the most good. (PAUSE)— It was poison, near as we can judge. (PAUSE)—Harvey himself was our physician, so you see the difficulty. The lay of the body, however, and what we know of Harvey's character tend to rule out self-murder—*

Kennedy—*Ha! That's what you boys reckon. If you was to ask Stuts Kennedy—*

Colonel—*I've asked you a question already. Kindly answer it.*

Kennedy (PAUSE)—*Got up somewhere about six. Couldn't lie right.*

COLONEL—*What then?*

KENNEDY—*Puh!—puh!—put my uppers on. Had a look about.*

COLONEL—*At six o'clock this morning?*

KENNEDY (*NODS*)

COLONEL—*Well? Where did you go, Mr. Kennedy? And what, pray tell us, did you—*

KENNEDY—*Saw your Parson.*

COLONEL—*Where?*

KENNEDY—*In the kitchens. (PAUSE)—He come in from the field. (PAUSE)—Gardens.*

COLONEL—*You saw him come into the house at six o'clock this morning?*

KENNEDY—*Six-thirty. Sun-up.*

COLONEL—*Was there anyone else about?*

KENNEDY (*SMILES*)—*No, Colonel. Just your Parson.*

COLONEL—*Did you exchange words?*

KENNEDY (*NODS*)—*I goes up to him where he were suh!—suh!—standing at the bread-box and says—: Come down from the tree-tops are you, you barbary ape? And he goes queer as always and guh!—guh!—gives me the regular song-and-dance.*

COLONEL—*That's fine, Kennedy. In other words—*

KENNEDY—*No by Christ I mean for you to hear this, you damned tea-sipper. Parson puh!—puh!—puts a biscuit in his gob, pleased as piss with himself and all of his transactions. Tell me Stutter, he says, taking hold of me by the arm. What might your philosophy be?*

COLONEL (*PAUSE*)—*Well?*

KENNEDY—*To get by, says I. (PAUSE)—Yes, he says. But how are you going to get by, Stuts? Let me explain something to you. There's two languages spoken in this country—: the language of livestock and the language of Canaan. I speak both fluently, and I'm going to learn you something of their ways. Listen cuh!—cuh!—closely and attend. (PAUSE)*

COLONEL—*Go on. Well?*

KENNEDY—*For him who speaks the language of Canaan, Parson says, the hid-away life of the world becomes plain. He clucks at me. You've heard, of course, of the miracle of the milk?*

COLONEL—*The which?*

KENNEDY (*SHRUGS*)—*I'm not much of a one for scripture, Your Bristliness, says I. (PAUSE)—He laughed at that.*

COLONEL—*And what was his reply?*

KENNEDY—*Trying to remember it just right. No, no, Stuts, says he. Nothing out of that fine book. I'm referring to the elephant-headed god*

Ganesh and his drinking up of all the milk in London. (PAUSE)—
You're off your lemon, you hairy-faced old fright, says I. He tightens his
muh!—muh!—monkey-grip on my shoulder. I know you, Stutter
Kennedy, to be a Catholic buggerer of tombs, he says. For this reason I
trust you better than most.

COLONEL *(LAUGHS)—He was having you on, dear fellow. Nothing more.*

KENNEDY—*Goodman Harvey tasted of that milk, Parson says, looking dead*
into my eyes. He spoke Cuh!—cuh!—cuh!—

COLONEL—*Easy, Mr. Kennedy.*

KENNEDY—*Cuh!—*

COLONEL—*Give yourself a moment.*

KENNEDY—*Canaan's tongue, he said. Goodman Harvey spoke Canaan's*
tongue sure enough, just before he died.

COLONEL *(PAUSE)—I see.*

KENNEDY—*There you have it, you bed-piddler.*

COLONEL—*Sit down, Miss Gilchrist. Have you been apprised?*

CLEMENTINE—*Not for some time now, Colonel. (SMILES)*

COLONEL—*Strike that, Virgil. (PAUSE)—Have you any notion, miss, as to*
why I've called you in?

CLEMENTINE—*Parson told me Harvey's been put under.*

COLONEL—*Parson told you! When?*

CLEMENTINE—*Early this morning, before the rest of you were awake.*
(PAUSE)—Why are you looking at me that way?

COLONEL—*Have you been eaves-dropping from the hall? Answer truly!*

CLEMENTINE—*Yes. Is that the best question you can think of?*

COLONEL—*Strike that, Virgil. (PAUSE)—What was the cause, Miss*
Gilchrist, of your hatred of Goodman Harvey?

CLEMENTINE—*Hatred! Of that little milk-sop?*

COLONEL—*You were heard to say, this morning, that Harvey deserved*
his end. Had he been troubling you, miss? Persistent, perhaps, in his
affections?

CLEMENTINE—*Goodman Harvey? (LAUGHS)—He was the only one who*
wasn't. Excepting you, of course, Colonel. I imagine you can't be.

COLONEL *(SMILES)—I thank heaven for it daily. At what hour did you*
leave your room this morning?

CLEMENTINE—*I don't know. Five-thirty? Six? I went out to the verandah.*

COLONEL—*Normally Mr. Delamare is on the verandah at that hour.*

CLEMENTINE—*Well he wasn't there this time. Perhaps he was too busy snip-*
ing Yankees.

COLONEL *(PAUSE)—Yankees? How do you mean?*

CLEMENTINE—*Haven't you told him, Virgil? Didn't you note it in your minutes?*

COLONEL—*Virgil is not free to converse with you, Miss Gilchrist. If you have an anecdote to tell, you'd better tell it straight to me.*

CLEMENTINE—*Well. I certainly wouldn't want to keep anything from you, Colonel. But if Virgil hasn't told you I'm just not sure. It might still be a secret.*

COLONEL *(PAUSE)—Miss Gilchrist. No doubt you have a power of admirers in this house—; but I am not among them. I'm a bandy-legged old man, you see. At my age one thing interests me at a time, and that only if I bring my full attention to bear upon it. All trivialities must be excluded—banished utterly—for my dried-up brain to function. And most everything becomes a triviality, from my point of view, when one of our number has been assassinated. Especially the details of your divers fornications. Do you follow?*

CLEMENTINE—*Well. I'd hate to seem trivial to you, Colonel, I'm sure.*

COLONEL—*Good. What interests me now—to the exclusion of all else—is the identity of the person who compelled Goodman Harvey to eat permanganate of potassium between midnight and six o'clock this morning. (PAUSE)—You see, I can't help but wonder, miss, whether I might not be next.*

CLEMENTINE—*You're free to leave this house any time you like, Colonel. Virgil and I will miss you, of course. Won't we, Virgil?*

COLONEL—*You take me quite aback, Miss Gilchrist. Have you no fear of being visited by this avenging angel?*

CLEMENTINE—*None at all. (PAUSE)—I leave my door open for him at night.*

COLONEL—*No use in looking to Virgil, miss. He can't call an end to this inquiry, much as he might prefer to.*

CLEMENTINE *(PAUSE)—I'd like to help you, Colonel. I would.*

COLONEL—*You neither saw nor heard a single thing worth relating?*

CLEMENTINE—*I never said that. I saw your Parson.*

COLONEL *(PAUSE)—Ah. Where and when, exactly, did you see him?*

CLEMENTINE—*As I left my room. I saw him from the window.*

COLONEL—*Which window? On the landing?*

CLEMENTINE *(NODS)—He was crossing the lawn. He'd been off in the woods.*

COLONEL—*As I recall it, that window looks out over the river. How could you know where Parson had been?*

CLEMENTINE—*He was carrying an axe, Colonel. And a sack over his shoulder.*

COLONEL—*A sack?*

CLEMENTINE (*NODS*)—*Or something wrapped up in a sheet. (PAUSE)—Perhaps that's what it was. I called his name as he came upstairs and he blinked at me a moment, then passed me by without a word. Not in a hurry but business-like. I waited till I heard the attic door open and shut—; then I went downstairs the way that he'd come up. Something had fallen from his sack. A hair-tonic bottle.*

COLONEL (*LAUGHS*)—*Hair tonic? For Parson? I'd say the man has quite enough—*

CLEMENTINE—*There was no tonic in it, Colonel. It was—*

COLONEL—*I see. An empty bottle. Which you imagine might, at some time in the past, have held—*

CLEMENTINE—*It wasn't empty at all. There was dirt inside of it. (PAUSE)—Dirt, and a few pine-needles.*

COLONEL—*Pine needles, you say. In a hair-tonic bottle.*

CLEMENTINE—*You see? He was coming from the woods—; I'm sure of it.*

COLONEL—*You assume that he was coming from the woods. You haven't—*

CLEMENTINE—*Do you want to hear about the sack, Colonel?*

COLONEL—*The sack. Of course. But you seem to think it might have been a heap of linen.*

CLEMENTINE—*I said no such thing. You note that down, Virgil! (PAUSE)—There was something in that bundle. The size of a tom-cat. (PAUSE)—A bit smaller than that, possibly. (PAUSE)—A baby.*

COLONEL (*LAUGHS*)—*Is Parson stealing babies now, Miss Gilchrist?*

CLEMENTINE—*You tell me something, Colonel. When you've finished questioning the rest of us till the blood runs out our ears, will you condescend to interview yourself?*

COLONEL—*Certainly, miss. Perhaps I'll do that now.*

CLEMENTINE—*No. Not now. I haven't finished yet.*

COLONEL—*By all means! Disburden yourself entirely.*

CLEMENTINE (*PAUSE*)—*I took a walk with Goodman Harvey yesterday.*

COLONEL (*LAUGHS*)—*Is no-one safe?*

CLEMENTINE—*You'd do well to listen to me, Colonel. (PAUSE)—I was surprised when Harvey asked, of course, as he'd never once shown an interest. A walk through the orchard, he said. It was after supper. Something in his manner made me curious. (PAUSE)—We walked to the far fence. He didn't once look me in the eye, or anywhere else. At the gate I said—: Mr. Harvey, why did you invite me out? Then he turned and looked me over. Mith Clem, you know I am a Mormon by faith, he said. I nodded.*

He gave a little laugh. That'th why he thelected me, he said. Meaning the R——. (MAKES SIGN OF CROSS)

COLONEL *(FROWNS)—The Redeemer, you mean?*

CLEMENTINE—*Who else?*

COLONEL—*Note "R——" as the Redeemer, Virgil.*

CLEMENTINE—*Shall I go on? (PAUSE)—What's why, Mr. Harvey? I asked. And Harvey said—: Because he knew the thtrength—*

COLONEL—*Miss Gilchrist! The fact that Harvey spoke with a lisp does not obligate you to do so. We are not upon the stage.*

CLEMENTINE—*As you like. (PAUSE)—That's why he selected me, Harvey said. He knew the strength of my belief, Miss Clem, and the childishness of it. (PAUSE)—Then Harvey said—: I have a letter to write tonight. A very lengthy letter. You may read it when it's done. (PAUSE)—I laughed at him, of course. Why should I be reading your letters, Mr. Harvey? I said. I thought he might be flirting after all. (PAUSE)—Tell him not to look at me that way, Colonel.*

COLONEL—*What?*

CLEMENTINE *(POINTING)—Him.*

COLONEL—*Virgil, could you—? (PAUSE)—Go on, Miss Gilchrist.*

CLEMENTINE—*Harvey stared at me that same way. You'll be reading my letter soon enough, Miss Clem, he said. You'll find it edifying. Then, so quiet that I could barely hear—: Virgil Ball will find it so. Then he took me by my arm. It was the first time that he'd touched me. He took a cautious hold of me, the way a bachelor will, and led me gently back up to my room.*

COLONEL *(PAUSE)—What then?*

CLEMENTINE *(LAUGHS)—That's all, Colonel. If you're eager for more you'll have to trust to your old man's fancy, I'm afraid.*

COLONEL *(SIGHS)—I assure you, miss—(FROWNS)*

CLEMENTINE—*What is it?*

COLONEL—*Who's that shuffling about outside? Is it Dodds?*

CLEMENTINE *(NODS)—He was waiting his turn when I came in. Looked a bit skittish. Poor old hum-bones.*

COLONEL *(STANDS)—Send him in, Miss Gilchrist. You may go.*

CLEMENTINE—*May I?*

(EXIT CLEMENTINE.)

COLONEL—*Well, Virgil? What do you make of that?*

(PAUSE)

COLONEL—*True. It would seem to clear Parson, or at least to put him well away from the house. I heard him go out just after eleven, by the parlor clock, and Harvey paid me a call not long after, begging a few sheets of blotting-paper—; so Harvey was alive and hale at twelve o'clock. If, then, Parson was out on one of his night-time jaunts, and Clem met him returning to the house at six—(PAUSE)—But only if she can be trusted. She is a doxie, after all. I shouldn't wonder, for example, if Clementine and Parson—*

(PAUSE)

COLONEL—*Of course, Virgil! None whatsoever. I humbly beg your pardon.*

COLONEL—*So, Dodds. Breakfast is put away then, is it?*

DODDS—*Yes, Marse D'Ancourt. Stew's fixin. PAUSE.—Been leavin off yin bed-work—; I know that. Stairs in yin back too narrow to get up with a basket. If you and Marse Virgil would allow—*

COLONEL—*Go up the front stairs if you have to. Just so the beds get aired and made.*

DODDS *(PAUSE)—Thank you, Colonel. It's a case of—*

COLONEL—*Did you have something to tell us?*

DODDS—*Tell you, sih?*

COLONEL—*Something you've been keeping secret from us, perhaps.*

DODDS *(PAUSE)—I mean, I—(PAUSE)—Secrets?*

COLONEL *(SHOUTS)—Why the devil does everyone gawk at Virgil when I ask them something? Virgil is present as my secretary, you rag-picker! Look at me!*

DODDS—*Ah! Well I regret about that, Colonel, I'm sure. (PAUSE)— Maybe you has a question for me, sih? So I know what to tell?*

COLONEL—*I've just asked it, Dodds. Collect yourself a moment. (PAUSE)—It can't have escaped you that Mr. Harvey was taken in the night.*

DODDS—*It hasn't, sih, no. A sad loss it is, if you don't mind.*

COLONEL—*I don't mind at all. Do you know how he died?*

DODDS *(PAUSE)—I heard as he was murthured.*

COLONEL—*Did you murder him?*

DODDS—*Sih?*

COLONEL—*The question doesn't seem to put you out.*

DODDS—*It don't, sih, no. I catch hell for all and sundry.*

COLONEL *(SMILES)—Who was it told you of his killing?*

DODDS—*Marse Delamare told it to me.*

COLONEL—*Ah! Mr. Delamare. I see. (PAUSE)—You have an understanding, then, the two of you?*

DODDS *(FROWNS)—Sih?*

COLONEL—*I mean you talk to one another. (PAUSE)—Share your thoughts about the goings-on. Your views.*

DODDS *(PAUSE)—That's so, Colonel. I suppose we do.*

COLONEL—*You're friends with Mr. Delamare, in a word.*

DODDS *(PAUSE)—I wouldn't properly say—*

COLONEL—*Being niggers you have a natural affection for one another.*

DODDS *(LOUDLY)—Marse Delamare no nigger, Colonel. Not like me. Marse Delamare stand up straight. He a regular son of—*

COLONEL—*I must say, Dodds, you couldn't have made your connection to Mr. Delamare any clearer. Before knowing him you'd never have raised your voice to your betters.*

DODDS *(PAUSE)—No, sih.*

COLONEL—*How long have you and I known each other, Dodds? How long have you been the house-boy to the Trade?*

DODDS *(PAUSE)—Nigh on seven year.*

COLONEL—*And before that?*

DODDS—*Before that I belong to Marse Trist' daddy. You know that.*

COLONEL—*How many people have you seen put down in that time?*

(PAUSE)

COLONEL—*Dodds?*

DODDS—*Never learnt no reckoning.*

COLONEL—*Then let me reckon for you. You've seen a great many people put down, Dodds. People of every stripe. White men, niggers, Indians, Creoles, Chinamen, white women, nigger women—; even, sometimes, little nigger children. (PAUSE)—You served the Trade faithfully and unquestioningly over the whole of your long tenure, because you were the Redeemer's nigger. You were his property, to use as he saw fit. (PAUSE)—No different than any of us in this house.*

DODDS *(INAUDIBLE)*

COLONEL—*What's that?*

DODDS—*I ain't the Deemer's niggra now. (SMILES)—He down the privy-ditch.*

COLONEL—*Whose nigger are you, then? Delamare's?*

DODDS *(INAUDIBLE)*

COLONEL—*Was it Delamare put Goodman Harvey down?*

DODDS—*Marse Delamare say it were Kennedy.*

COLONEL *(SIGHS)—Dodds, I find you a most unmanageable nigger lately. I've half a mind to pitch you in the river.*

DODDS—*You do as you please, Colonel. (PAUSE)—Who be making yin scrapple and greens tomorrow—?*

COLONEL—*Clementine might.*

DODDS—*Hah! That lady got but one ability I know of. (PAUSE)—Beg pardon, Virgil. (PAUSE)—Things I ought be doing—*

COLONEL—*Yes, Dodds. To begin with, you might air the beds. But you're not lifting your back-side off that stool till my curiosity's satisfied.*

DODDS *(INAUDIBLE)*

COLONEL—*That's fine. Now. Did you see, hear, or smell Mr. Harvey at any time last night, after his return from the orchard with Miss Gilchrist?*

DODDS—*I saw him go upstairs. (QUIETLY)—Met with somebody on yin landing.*

COLONEL—*The landing of the stairs?*

DODDS *(NODS)*

COLONEL—*Who was it?*

DODDS—*Somebody. A man.*

COLONEL—*A man?*

DODDS *(NODS)*

COLONEL—*I have always taken comfort, Dodds, in the thought that you knew of each and every sordid event that took place in this house. I've studied you closely in my idle hours, you see. And I know that your simple-headedness is only so much mummery and guile.*

DODDS *(PAUSE)—I don't foller you, Colonel. Beg pardon, but I don't—*

COLONEL—*Tell me who it was, Dodds. With Harvey on the stairs.*

DODDS *(INAUDIBLE)*

COLONEL—*I'm afraid I didn't catch that. Did you happen to catch that, Virgil?*

DODDS—*You no kind of man at all, Colonel D'Ancourt. You heart full of weeds.*

COLONEL—*You'll tell me who it was, Doddsbody, or my heart notwithstanding I'll put a bullet in your eye.*

DODDS *(SOFTLY)—How well you know me, Colonel?*

COLONEL—*Well enough. I'll have an answer out of you or I'll call in Mr. Kennedy. (PAUSE)—There! I thought that might enliven you a bit.*

DODDS *(INAUDIBLE)*

COLONEL—*Speak up a little, old scrapple-and-greens.*

DODDS *(PAUSE)—Can I hisper it?*

COLONEL—*Just as you like. Come here to me.*

DODDS—*In you ear?*

COLONEL—*Yes. The left one, mind.*

DODDS *(INAUDIBLE)*

COLONEL *(SMILING)—Ah! Is that so.*

DODDS *(NODS)*

COLONEL—*I see. (PAUSE)—You can go. Find Mr. Kennedy and send him in to me.*

DODDS—*Don't say I told it, Colonel. Don't say as it were Dodds.*

COLONEL—*Go fetch Mr. Kennedy, and kick up your heels about it! Get!* (EXIT DODDS.)

COLONEL (PAUSE)—*Who do you think it was, Virgil? Can you guess? (PAUSE)—That's right, dear boy. Go on, then! Write it down.*

COLONEL—*Mr. Kennedy! Prompt as always. No, sir! Pray don't interrupt just yet. I have something to say to you. Sit down here and give Virgil a moment to dip his pen into the pot. There! (PAUSE)—Mr. Kennedy, you'll be pleased to know that I've uncovered the identity of Harvey's murderer. (PAUSE)—That brings life to those dull little eye-holes of yours, doesn't it.*

KENNEDY—*Who is it?*

COLONEL—*I wonder if you might be able to guess.*

KENNEDY—*Parson?*

COLONEL (LOUDLY)—*No, not Parson, you dullard. If you can't think—*

KENNEDY (STANDING)—*I've done with this bloody parlor game. You can both of you get—*

COLONEL—*Yes, yes, Kennedy. Forgive me. It was the mulatto.*

KENNEDY (PAUSE)—*You don't mean it.*

COLONEL (NODS)

KENNEDY—*The muh!—muh!—mulatto—Oliver—*

COLONEL—*Dodds was so gracious as to tell.*

KENNEDY (PAUSE)—*That's it, then. (SMILES)—I'm beholden to you, Colonel. I'll be taking a walk, if you've got no objection.*

COLONEL—*May I ask your intentions?*

KENNEDY—*My intentions? (LAUGHS)*

COLONEL—*I should like to remind you of the presence of Miss Gilchrist in this house. And of my god-son, Asa Trist.*

KENNEDY—*Don't you worry about that. Our niggra's well out of doors. I seen him go off muh!—muh!—moseying not half an hour gone.*

COLONEL (SITTING FORWARD)—*Where to? To the river?*

KENNEDY (SMILES)—*No, Colonel. Off into the woods.*

COLONEL (INAUDIBLE)

KENNEDY—*What's that?*

COLONEL—*All right, Mr. Kennedy. Go on. Go about your business.*

KENNEDY—*Young cracked Asa's carrying on outside. Do you want him?*

COLONEL—*Mr. Trist and his trouble are no concern of yours.*

KENNEDY—*What's wrong then, Colonel? (SMILES)—Can't abide me suddenly?*

COLONEL—*Come in, Asa! Please be seated. We won't keep you long.*
TRIST—*What?*
COLONEL—*Sit down, Asa.*
TRIST—*Yes. I'll be seated Colonel, God-father, sir but first may I know will I be answering any questions you may have.*
COLONEL—*Shall I ask you a question now, to see?*
TRIST—*You can ask me, yes. But then? (SMILES)*
COLONEL—*All right, Asa—*
TRIST—*Are there any niggers hereabouts?*
COLONEL—*No, Asa. Only Dodds. You know Dodds pretty well.*
TRIST—*Yes. I know old Dodds. Shall I tell you where he got his color from?*
COLONEL—*I have a different question. Last night—*
TRIST—*Why is Mr. Ball present?*
COLONEL—*Virgil is here to put your answers down on paper.*
TRIST—*Oh! I don't know. I don't know about that, Grand-father. No.*
COLONEL—*How did you sleep last night, Asa?*
TRIST—*Flatly. Straight and flatly as a plank.*
COLONEL—*Did you sleep well?*
TRIST—*I was up early. (SMILES)—I might well have been the first.*
COLONEL—*At what hour did you wake?*
TRIST *(PAUSE)—Very nearly five.*
COLONEL—*Did you get up?*
TRIST—*Ah! Uncle. No. I laid down flat.*
COLONEL—*And did you at any time hear—*
TRIST—*I was sitting on the bed, in fact, Colonel D'Ancourt. Then all at once out of the water came a sort of—(PAUSE)—A sort of beasties, and my black dolly was among them. They were human in part, and a part of them was animal—that much I saw clear. There was witchery in it. Do you follow me, Virgil? I lay down flat. I think my own body was trying to slide into the water—: into the river. Under it. And take me bodily out of this world. (PAUSE)—It still happens to me now, when I lie still.*
COLONEL *(PAUSE)—Oh Asa. (PAUSE)—Leave off your scribbling, Virgil.*
TRIST—*Virgil is looking at me with his fine white eye. He sees the nigger in me plain.*
COLONEL—*Virgil, would you—?*
TRIST—*I did hear a noise, Father. Sometime after dawn.*
COLONEL *(PAUSE)—What's that, Asa? What was it you heard?*

TRIST—*Two voices raised up in anger most foul.*

COLONEL—*Whose voices?*

TRIST—*One of them was black and the other was fair gone Harvey. I got out of bed to see.*

COLONEL—*A black, was it? The mulatto?*

TRIST—*Yes.*

COLONEL—*Are you taking this down, Virgil?*

TRIST—*Virgil is putting it down on paper. Virgil is writing us a novel.*

COLONEL—*And what next? Did you see them, Asa boy? Did you open your door and see them?*

TRIST (PAUSE)—*Yes.*

COLONEL—*Where were they? On the landing?*

TRIST—*They were—*

COLONEL—*Asa! Look at me when I speak to you. Where did you see Harvey and the mulatto?*

TRIST (INAUDIBLE)

COLONEL—*Virgil, take him by the shoulder. Quickly.*

TRIST (INAUDIBLE)

COLONEL—*Asa!—*

TRIST (QUIETLY)—*I'm—it's all right. I'm awake. I'm the first to be awake this morning. (PAUSE)—It's nearly five.*

COLONEL—*What happens next, Asa? Do you get out of bed?*

TRIST—*I should like to. I should like to get out of bed very badly.*

COLONEL—*Why don't you get out of bed, Asa?*

TRIST—*Why? Why? (SHOUTS)—Because Harvey hasn't finished his letter!*

COLONEL—*What letter? What letter do you mean?*

TRIST (SMILES)—*This letter, Uncle. Why—*

COLONEL—*Give it over, Asa—; give it here to me. (SOFTLY)—Take it from him, Virgil.*

TRIST—*I'll give it to you! Here it is, Grandfather. You keep playing at your history, Mr. Ball.*

COLONEL—*Thank you, Asa. (PAUSE)*

TRIST—*Is it addressed to you, God-father?*

COLONEL—*Good lord, Virgil.*

TRIST—*Virgil's busy at his memoirs.*

COLONEL—*Go find Kennedy, Virgil. Go and find him straight-away.*

TRIST—*Yes Mr. Ball leave off now of your papers and fetch that black frightful Irishman. That black black fearful man. (RISING)—Lay down with me now, Colonel. We'll all of us lie down together. Lie down flat.*

COLONEL—*Run and get him, Virgil! Virgil! Do you hear?*

An Encounter.

HERE COMES KENNEDY TO KILL ME, Delamare says. When I come out of the woods he's laying for me with eyes like chips of dead gray mud. He has nothing in his hands, no club or knife or bottle-end, but I know from his far-away look what it is he's after. He brings his left hand up, just slightly, to fix me in his sight. He might be preparing to render me in oils.

"Off chasing Federals, were you, blacks?" he says. "Or was it rabbits?"

I keep my eyes steady on his hands. "Why not get your shot off as I came out of the brush?"

"Ah! I wanted to *look* at you, Oliver." He slaps playfully at his hip. "Besides, I might've dropped a Yank by accident. I'd never of forgave myself."

Now he is holding his hands out for me to see.

"You've looked at me," I say. "Now you can shoot."

"Right," says Kennedy. "Yes." But his hands keep still. In his dirty buck-skin breeches with his dirtier body inside them he seems perfect to me—; consummate. There stands Kennedy, come to kill me. He wears his purpose like a crown.

"Been waiting on this to fall down on us, ain't we, blacks. Ever since I muh!—muh!—mancipated you. And here it is."

"Get your pistol out, Irish." His hands are red, not yellow like the rest of him. They open and close like little bellows. "Get it out, or let me by. I'm late for an appointment."

He laughs. "Ah! I could never let you go *now*, pretty fellow. You're a fugitive of society, on account of murder."

And then it makes itself known, like a pane of beveled glass laid against my chest—: the knowledge that he will kill me. The likelihood was there always—he's put so many under—but until this moment it was no more than a thought. Now it fills my mouth like spittle.

"I had no part in Harvey's death," I say, but my voice has gone careless. Harvey is of no consequence any longer. Here stands Kennedy, come to kill me. Nothing else has truth to me, or weight.

He hears it in my voice, my willingness to let him, but still he makes no movement—: there's a chance I'd get a shot off as I fell. I watch Kennedy consider this. He bunches his face together. He's remembering my repeater and my youth.

"I'm an *old* cunt, blacks, it's true." He chews thoughtfully on his lower lip. "An old Irish." He squints at me, then opens his mouth wide. "Half my tuh!—tuh!—teeth's dropped out. Right? But look at *yourself*, now. You've still got juice between your legs." He shuts his mouth and gives a little groan.

"I didn't do Harvey," I say quietly. "You know I didn't."

His eyes go narrower still, then shut for half an instant. I could have drawn on him just then.

"I'd kill you any-road, blacks," he says. "But we're all good and satisfied you *did*. I'm acting under orders, as it happens."

I take a step. "Whose orders? D'Ancourt's?"

His eyes fly open and his left arm jerks—: not his shooting arm but the other. If killing me were a drink he'd be wiping his mouth already. " 'Tweren't *him* I got my orders fuh!—fuh!—from."

"Who, then? Parson?" I laugh in his face. "Taking orders from Parson, are you, Irish? What would Saints Patrick and Ebenezer say?"

"It were Virgil Ball," he coos.

In spite of myself I flinch. "You're lying. Virgil has no truck with you, Kennedy. Virgil would sooner—"

"Precious *young* yet, aren't we, blacks. Not yet at the ripeness of our years." He sniggers. "Too much white meat. Not enough porridge."

The hinges of my nature begin to creak. I was born unable to hold my temper and God knows it and Kennedy knows it better. It's for this that he's kept me alive, worrying me, goading me, with his hands out in the open where I can't help but watch them—; when finally I drop he wants it to be with foam at the corners of my mouth. And I know that I will drop, that I will give him that satisfaction, and still I can't keep my temper in its britches. Could Virgil truly have sent Kennedy after me? Is he so cankered-through with bitterness? Kennedy is the lowest of God's creatures but I've never yet heard him lie. What does Virgil think he knows? He saw me yesterday arguing with Harvey about the debt and the Redeemer and Christ knows what all else. Everything but that whore Virgil trails after in her calico shift. Might *that* be why—? Her smell's run through my linens even now. I've never sought out her company, God knows, but perhaps Virgil doesn't. Might that be why? It might. But Kennedy—

"I was thinking, blacks," Kennedy says, digging a thumb into his eye. "About the day I come across you." He grins. "Should've known *then* that it would come to this." He coughs. "Perhaps I did."

This, the old topic—: tried and proved. The old item. The house and the fat copper still and the curtain behind it and that filthy soot-stained room. The smell of boiling mash. My fists begin to open.

"I'll not quickly forget that day, little man. Christ! Coming down the steps into that stinking kuh!—kuh!—kennel, saying my hellos to your mother, yanking the curtain back—"

Mother Annie Bradford. Mother Anne. She is coming toward me now in the half-dark of the hall and I try my best with her smell still on my clothes but the smell of the mash is stronger and my fine clothes are off, away, as if they've never been—

"Oliver," says Kennedy. "Oliver De—la—mare." Drawing it out, letting the pieces of it break off and fall steaming and abominable to the ground.

By God that woman was not my mother.

"—and here's little buh!—buh!—blacks with his drawers about his ankles, scarf tied back around his arms. A lady's rag. Why was that, now, blacks? Feared of falling in?"

Dearest madam, you who took my life—

"That *were* the cunt you come out of. Weren't it, blacks?"

The forest lifts before me like a petticoat and I fall sideways into running. My jacket and waist-coat and repeater are nothing but burdens to me now and I cast them aside. The smell of the mash keeps me on my feet and I reel drunkenly forward and all the while I hear him hollering to stand where I am and let him. Blank air opens ahead of me, parts as fast as I can run, a peep-hole waiting to be plugged. My mouth opens and six years tumble out of it and still I smell the mash.

Past the trees is the great house, Virgil and the rest inside of it like mice inside a shoe. Kennedy comes after. The scarf was blue crêpe and it was a reward. Fine things, she said. Which she? She of the fat white belly, the sweet-meats, the sweating copper pipes? She of the sour mash? The Redeemer's she, or Virgil's? She who made me white, or she who made me black? A branch breaks just behind.

I have ever been a poppet for the ladies.

As if reflected in a puddle I see Kennedy's form. More than that—: the cold against my chest tells me. Here he comes. Did I stop running? Did I sink to my knees? I did. I kneel slumped against a tree, the very last before the lawn, letting the mash pour out of my open mouth. I wait on Kennedy's convenience. His shadow crosses against the light and there's no house suddenly, no still, no boiler, no Mother Anne, no Delamare, no Trade.

I'm grateful for that much.

He stands still for a moment, potato-faced and breathless, wheezing and sputtering and cursing me to heaven. And yet pleased to see me—: to see me kneeling in the mud, the bright mess in front of me and down my clothes.

"You called my name," Kennedy says, chambering his gun. He must have fired at least once. "You called it, Oliver, as you run."

The cold climbs up my body like a reward. "I haven't forgotten your name, Irish. You drove it into me. Remember?"

His potato-face pivots. "You shut your muh!—muh!—mouth."

Three steps past him the forest ends. It's raining on the naked ground and I can smell the clay. A pale blue blot, the figure of a man, moves toward us through the grass. Is it my end approaching?

"You dipped into a well meant for niggers, Kennedy," I say. "You dipped into it and drank. What does that make you?"

"Nobody heared of it," he says, thumbing back the hammer. "If nobody heared of it, it never was."

"An honorary nigger, Stuts," I say. "And something else besides."

I look up at him against the trees, branches twitching in the rain, bullets dropping sweetly from the pines. A shout comes from the house. "You surely want to die," he says.

I wait to see his features before I answer.

"Parson knows what you did to me, Kennedy. I told him. So does Dodds."

He strikes me across the forehead with the barrel. My left eye shuts and gushes. "You," says Kennedy. "You little nuh!—nuh!—niggra boy."

I half-believe that he is weeping.

"Kennedy!" Virgil shouts, crashing through the brush. "Leave off it, Kennedy! Harvey left a letter!"

So Virgil was behind it, after all.

"Little boy," Kennedy says, bringing down his boot.

Goodman Harvey's Narrative.

On this the night of 11 May 1863 I make my peace with the Lord my Creator & leave this record of my many errors, trusting in His power to see the causes that are hid to all but prophets. I am no Papist & write these lines not to serve as a confession, for I do not believe in redemption at the eleven'th hour; but rather to reckon with the Angel of Death, pale & luminous as a pearl, who stands attentively at my left shoulder.

I do so easefully, recollecting my forty-two years with the calm of one about to forget them for all time. I have, in fact, been waiting on this night for many months; I find myself embracing the prospect eagerly, almost coquettishly, like a virgin bride. Had I not known my Friend was coming I'd have done away with myself weeks ago; but this end, I believe, is better. My lot has ever been to defer to those greater than myself.

I first heard of Thaddeus Myrell in the spring of my fourth year in the Territories. A born child of Mormon, I'd been sent into the west at the age of eighteen to herald the arrival of the Latter-day Saints to an gross & unwitting nation. Mine was the particular honor of bringing word to the Indians encamp'd in the Oklahomas, one of the fabled Lost Tribes of Israel; from my earliest youth I'd been a passionate believer, & I set out on my mission in the highest of spirits, greatly pleased with myself as an agent of God's will. My cousin Alva & I vow'd not to return home to Nauvoo, Illinois, until seven years had gone by, or the entire country south of the Cimarron river had been brought into the Church. We were happy, unencumber'd boys, younger than our years, who imagined the west as a vast quilt of green gorges & dappled fields—a somewhat grander Illinois. Neither of us was ever to see the country of our youth again.

What happen'd over those first three years is of little relevance to this *accounting. Alva died four months into our mission, of gastric fever; my own trials, though less decisive, were hardly less severe. Important is only that I suffer'd, that my zeal & good works were repaid with mockery & violence in those God-hating swamps, & that my own house of faith was thrown open to the four winds, so that the Prophet Himself was moved finally to abandon it. It was in this fallen state, tired in flesh & sick in spirit, scraping a living together by peddling liquor to the Chickasaws & Kickapoos & Choctaws in the guise of medicinal tonics, that I found myself one evening on the porch of a shabby grain depot, listening to two negroes chatter in hush'd tones about the coming of a new Redeemer.*

"He come to Onadee last week," the taller of them said. He was a thick-set, amicable gossip I knew well from my monthly visits. There were always one or two of his persuasion in attendance, listening slack-jaw'd to some gaudy story or other. His given name was Tempie.

"What he come there for?" the second negro asked. "To preach?"

Tempie gave a knowing chuckle. "He come to serve notice to them dirty Meth'dists up at de mill," he said, glancing side-wise at me. Tempie had long been prisoner to the suspicion that I was a Methodist myself; someone had told him they went about in cast-off suits of clothes.

"It's all right, Tempie," I said, sitting down on a sack of corn. "I won't corrupt your immortal soul this evening."

In answer Tempie shot me a look I'd long since grown used to from negroes & white men alike. "I ain't one you sick Indians, Mr. Harvey."

"Go on, already," the other negro said. "How he sized? Big or little?"

Tempie puff'd his chest out as far as it would go. "Ah! He big enough," he said, spreading his arms wide. "Big as this. Voice like rattling thunder."

His friend looked dubious. "Mr. Wallace say he call himself the Baby of the West."

"He a baby, all right," Tempie said, grinning. "He gonna shake his rattle till them rich folk in Onadee drops they purses & runs."

"A confidence-man, is he?" I ask'd innocently.

At this the second negro looked at me as though I'd crawl'd out of a hole in the ground. "He a prophet," he said. "Come to set the peoples right. Mr. Wallace say he gone sweep the territory clean of heathens."

Tempie snorted & waved a hand. "Mr. Wallace say," he japed, puffing out his cheeks. Turning side-wise on his heels, he privileged us with a shuffling dance in parody of John Wallace, his master, who suffer'd grievously from fallen arches.

It was Tempie's misfortune that Wallace, a hard man leach'd of all generosity by ten years in the Territories, chose that moment to come out of the house. "Tempie," he said sedately. "You come over here to me."

Tempie took off at once in the direction of the granary. His companion back'd himself against the wall & stay'd there, quiet as a beam. Wallace watch'd Tempie go, shifted his weight with a diffident grunt, cuff'd the other negro across the ear & turned his attention grudgingly to me.

"Inciting my niggers to mischief, Harvey?" he said, looking at me with unadorn'd distaste. "Been feeding them your cure-alls, peradventure?"

"Beg pardon, Mr. Wallace," I answered quickly, my voice rising as it always does when addressing men of property. "We've been discussing the new preacher up in Onadee."

"Ah! <u>Him</u>," said Wallace, his manner suddenly much changed. He looked me over for a time; I returned his look with bafflement. In two years of acquaintanceship he'd not once looked me squarely in the eye.

"Come inside a bit, Harvey, if you like."

The depot was no great establishment, cobbled together as it was of planks of every size & pedigree; to me, however, it seem'd a very mansion. The walls were paper'd from top to bottom with news-print, as in a negro's cabin. I found nothing unusual in this at first; but as my host busied himself with a rusted coffee-pot & a lump of cold pork-shoulder, I saw that each wall was cover'd in individual clippings, & that each clipping had to do with the so-called "Indian Question" in one way or another. There must have been twenty years' worth, from any number of papers & bulletins, dating back to the Territories' natal days. My host sat me down at the little tin-topped table, handed me a cup of tepid coffee & said in a close-mouth'd, conspiratorial voice—

"One day, Mr. Harvey, the country hereabouts will be as fresh & unsullied as humanity's first garden."

I said nothing for a time, stirring the coffee with my least filthy finger. The faith of my fathers had sent me in search of just such a paradise four years before; those four years, however, had done their share to educate me. "I find that hard to credit, Mr. Wallace," I said at last. Again, however, my voice grew plaintive: "Of course, you've been here a great deal longer than I have. I'd be delighted, sir, to believe—"

"Believe it then, young man! Believe it." Wallace's breath stank of chicory & rancid butter. "We're living next-door to Heaven out here on these plains. Close enough to smell it, if the wind is right."

At this juncture I felt bold enough to attempt a joke. "That may well be, sir," I answer'd. "But when the wind blows the other way, I smell something else entirely."

"Noticed that, have you?" Wallace said earnestly. "There's some that might agree with what you say."

"I challenge any white man to deny it," I retorted. "Which among us hasn't suffer'd at their hands? They're a godless, joyless, hopeless race of mongrels, in whom the seed of Heaven has grown crooked. You'll find no sanctity in this territory, Mr. Wallace. And no Garden of Eden, either."

I was as surprised as Wallace by the venom in my voice; I'd said far more than I'd intended. The desire to please him, to win his good opinion, was as strong in me as ever; but my tongue was thick with bitterness. Did this flat-footed old ass not see that he was living at the center of a vast grid of human misery? Did he actually think of this waste-land, this spiritual desert, this pissoir of the nation as the next best thing to Heaven? If so, then he believed what my father believed, what my cousin Alva had believed, what I myself had believed when I set out on my mission. The thought was almost more than I could bear.

Wallace regarded me in plump, implacable silence, taking sips straight from the coffee-pot. The image of my father & mother back in Nauvoo, so complacent in their faith, appear'd as though stamp'd onto the news-printed walls. It was all I could do to keep from bursting into tears, and if Wallace had kept quiet an instant longer, I surely would have done so.

But he did not. Instead, he straighten'd in his wicker chair & without the slightest warning slapped me viciously across the brow.

"I've cursed my luck often enough, Harvey, as God's my witness; but I don't curse it now. A _man_ has come into this country—a man with the vision to recover everything we've lost, & a good deal else besides. A man to recover our birth-right for us." He stood up from the chair with a noise like kindling catching fire.

"That man is Thaddeus T Myrell, the Child of the New West."

The old grange in Onadee that night was hung from floor to rafters with gaudy crepe banners scavenged from forgotten fairs, cheap tallow torches & bed-sheets painted with all manner of curious slogans—: WHAT LANGUAGE DO YE SPEAK, YE CHILDREN OF ANTELOPES—IS IT GOD'S? and, nearby, TO THE WEST ITS PROMISED HUSBANDS—TO EACH HUSBAND, NOW, HIS CHILDE!

I was unable to make the least sense of them, but they struck me in my eagerness as full of hidden portents. Most obscure of all was a device stencil'd here & there on the walls of the Grange itself, a figure made of intersecting lines that I took at first to be a cattle-brand—

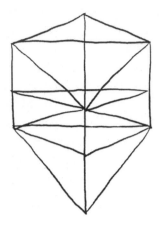

In spite of these trappings, however, & the smoke from the sap torches, the mood of the assembly more resembled a gin-raffle or a country dance than any sober-minded gathering. The laughter, lewdness & commotion on all sides seem'd more in keeping with the medicine-shows I knew so well than with any true revival. But a revival, of a sort, it was. There was the dark, quiet stage—there the wooden lectern; & there, all at once, was the Child of the New West, stepping forward to address the crowd, his pale face glowing in the torch-light. His body was stretched to its fullest in every direction, like a squirrel falling from a tree; as he stepped up to the lectern, holding one pudgy fist aloft, I smiled to myself at how little he resembled Tempie's second-hand accounting.

I'd pictured him in a buck-skin greatcoat, mud-spatter'd riding boots & a wide-brimmed trapper's hat, perhaps with a jay's feather tuck'd into its brim; the man at the lectern—if a man he was, & not a precocious truant—wore a well-iron'd suit of clothes & high-heel'd city shoes. He look'd more like a school-teacher or a claims-adjuster than any Hero of the New Frontier. Everything about him bespoke a quiet reasonableness. He appear'd the perfect gentleman in miniature; so miniature, in fact, that Wallace's hosannas seem'd as laughable as Tempie's. This served the Child well, however; my surprise at his great delicacy disarm'd me.

The crowd had a different notion of the Child. The men about me seem'd to treat him as they would any other beer-hall sermonizer—with beer-hall tom-foolery & cheer. With time, I was to learn that Myrell's great gift was to convince each of his listeners that they'd caught a glimpse of his most secret nature, & that they recognized themselves—their own desires, ambitions, & hid-away beliefs—in what they saw. He'd fashion'd himself into an all-

purpose cipher, perfectly suited in his blankness to take on any meaning, any color, any significance whatever.

For some minutes he tried, as if slightly pain'd, to check the hubbub in the hall. Then, in a low voice, hesitantly at first, he embark'd on what sounded more like a lecture in history than a political speech, let alone a sermon. This departed even further from the bellowing, whiskey-swilling charlatan I'd imagined. At no point did he allow the high spirits of the gathering to tempt him away from his sober tone; in time, out of simple curiosity, nearly everyone in the Grange had quieted enough to hear him. And in fact the Child grew more & more bewitching with every word he spoke.

I've often asked myself, in the course of the unquiet years that followed—what was it I found so remarkable in Myrell's performance that August night in Onadee? Certainly not the substance of his sermon. He was expressing anxiety about the future of white settlers in the Territories—no more than that. Gradually, now, his shyness disappear'd; at times his voice grew strident. He spoke urgently & quickly. The mood he cast over the revelers was heady & violent, & went far deeper than the speech itself; try as I might, I can't recall a single word of it.

But if I can no longer remember specific words, or even clear ideas—I was soon to learn that the fate of the Territories was of less importance to him than a wart on a nigger's heel—I recollect the emotions which fought for dominion over my heart with a vividness born of a lifetime spent under their sway. Our tentative beginnings, the Child explained—our scattering of farms & stores & grain depots & churches—had been built on the very edge of an abyss. What gave the white settler his dignity was not the greatness of his holdings, or the respect of his neighbors, but first & foremost his <u>independence</u>; and this independence, it seem'd, was menaced from all sides. If the hordes of rogue Sioux & Cherokee did not roll down from the west in a mighty purging tide, then the corrupt nation at our backs, with its Federalists, its Pluralists &—worst of all—its Abolitionists, would suck our independence from us like rainwater from a gourd.

What the Child of the New West preached—twenty years before the fact—was nothing less than secession from the Union. The fact that Arkansas & Kansas, not to mention Oklahoma, had not even been granted statehood yet was of little interest to him, or to anyone else that night; by the close of his speech it was certainly of no interest to me. As he stepped back from the lectern with a stiff little bow & the brass donation-trays began to circulate through the hall, my sole desire was to speak with the Child in private.

Once the show was over, the Grange emptied from one moment to the next; the bulk of the crowd simply cross'd the muddy street to the nearest of Onadee's seventeen saloons. A small clot of admirers remain'd to the left of the stage, forming a ring one-to-two-men deep, through which I caught glimpses of the Child's well-groomed head. Wallace was among the men, & I took my place beside him. My plan was to wait until the group thinned out some—what—the Child was reputed to lodge and dine alone. There should be ample time, later in the evening, for a thorough exchange of views.

I can't help but marvel, even now, at my boldness on that apocalyptic evening—it would have served me better on countless others. And yet I understand full well why I acted as I did. I needed the attention of the Child; not to get it was unthinkable. Surprising is only that my gambit worked. But perhaps even that, on reflection, is not so unlikely—my desperation was all the calling-card I needed.

Within a few short minutes only myself, Wallace, & another man—an Irishman—remain'd beside the Child. What had begun as a political debate had taken on an agreeably informal flavor, as though we were attorneys-at-law relaxing after a trial. Wallace, in particular, affected a familiarity with the Child which took me quite aback.

"I've brought some new blood, Mr. Myrell, as you can see."

The Child seem'd to take my measure for the first time. "Duly noted, Mr. Wallace." He squinted up into my face. "Help out at the depot, do you, Mr.—?"

"Harvey," I said hurriedly, cursing my flusteredness. "I have my own small enterprise, sir."

"Oh?"

"In the spirit of the Territories," I added, giving a crooked little smile.

The Child raised an eye-brow very slightly. "Is that so? You didn't mention that to me, Mr. Wallace."

The blood rush'd to my face. When had Wallace been telling the Child about me? It could only have been before I'd join'd the circle. What on earth could he have seen fit to relate? It was all I could do to keep from moaning aloud.

"Mr. Wallace thinks little of my work, & rightly so," I put in, as casually as I could. "I sell tonics to the Indians."

To my surprise the Child responded with amicable curiosity. "Is that so? Which tribes?"

I shrugged my shoulders. "Chickasaw, Choctaw, Seminole, Kickapoo . . ."

"Thirsty devils, the lot of them," Wallace put in sagely.

But the Child didn't seem to notice Wallace any longer. "You make your living off the tribes, Mr. Harvey, & yet you come to hear me speak?"

I had no idea how to answer him. "This is the first speech of yours I've been to, sir. I had no idea—"

He laugh'd at this & I flushed redder than before. He was only having sport with me after all. "Well, Doctor!" he said, striking an academic pose. "What was your opinion of my lecture, as a man of science?"

The desire to please him fill'd me like the need to piss. "I thought it was splendid, sir! Miraculous!"

I could see, in spite of his ironic air, that this pleased him mightily. "Hear that, Kennedy? Some of these beer-swillers recognize the future when it's fed to them."

"Some of them's idjits," the Irishman said, looking at me sideways.

"Nonsense!" the Child retorted. "Mr. Harvey is just the type we're looking for. Just the very type."

"I thought so myself," Wallace put in happily.

The spell of quiet that follow'd, in which each of the three men appraised me in silence, pass'd with a measuredness that drove me half out of my wits. I felt so hungry for some further sign of their approval that I all but bit my tongue in quarters. Was their only aim to torture me? Could they not see my distress? Or could it be, perhaps, that it brought them amusement?

"Well!" the Child said abruptly, taking up his hat. "The time's come for us to repair to Costello's rooming-house. I've a need of putting up my feet."

Instantly Wallace's expression changed to one of pure servility. "Of course, sir. Naturally. You'll be needing your rest. Come along, Harvey." He gave a nod to Kennedy, whose face remain'd slack, & took me by the sleeve.

"I'd like young Harvey to stay behind," the Child said, looking at Wallace with the faintest suggestion of a smile.

For the span of a few seconds Wallace stared back at him in confusion. "Of course," he said at last, in the dullest tone of voice imaginable. Clearly he himself had never been vouchsafed such a privilege.

"& there's one other matter, no more than a trifle." The Child paused a moment. "Have you taken to wearing your hat differently than before?"

Wallace's face went duller still, if possible. "My hat?"

"The angle of it concerns me."

"The angle, sir?" Wallace said. His lips barely flutter'd.

"Don't wear your hat cocked down over your eye, sirrah, or thrust back upon your head. One style is rowdyish; the other is plainly rustic."

Wallace said nothing to this, looking back and forth between my own hat, which was tipped back considerably, & Kennedy's, which hid his pink eyes altogether. Finally he managed to give a nod.

"Good-night, then, Mr. Wallace, & god-speed. We'll be seeing you tomorrow. . . ?"

"You will, sir," Wallace answer'd, but I fancied I saw something more than disappointment in his eyes: they did their best to conceal a rapidly mounting bewilderment, even fear. What in the Child's manner could have brought about such a change in him? Was he out of favor suddenly?

These & other questions were soon to be render'd obsolete. I left Wallace & the Old Grange behind & follow'd the remaining two men—both as yet perfect strangers to me—to a modest rooming-house across the way. Kennedy & the Child, a pace or two ahead of me, gossiped together in affectionate whispers. The Child's carriage & demeanor were already greatly changed. Before, he'd held himself with school-masterly severity; now he slouch'd & shuffled like a flat-boat rough. For the first time since we'd met, I was able to believe that we were near to the same age, & that his parentage was no loftier than my own. If anything, this evidence of his play-acting only awed me further. If you had more of _that_ gift, Goodman, I thought as we entered the rooming-house, you'd have had better luck among Israel's lost tribes.

The foyer was empty & dark & the Child lost no time in crossing it on the toes of his high-heeled boots. Just as we reached the stairs, however, the proprietor appear'd out of the gloom, moving with the unmistakable vigor of a man with money coming to him. "Ah! Mr. Myrell," he said shrilly. "I didn't suppose that _you'd_ retired."

The Child stopped, turn'd slowly about & worked his features into a smile. "I was about to, Mr. Costello. The crowd was a trick to turn tonight."

"I see," said the little man, pursing his lips. "And you, Mr. Kennedy? Will you be retiring, as well?"

"Mr. Kennedy has errands to run," the Child put in before Kennedy could answer. "He'll be sure not to disturb you when he comes in."

"Oh! I wouldn't object to being disturb'd so much," the proprietor said, turning to me—of all people!—& smiling as if to a fellow sufferer. "Particularly if he saw fit to settle his accounts."

"Mr. Costello!" the Child said, making a queer clacking noise with his tongue. "Don't I pay our room & board each week, as regular as church?"

"I was speaking of the bar accounts," the proprietor said primly.

"I like your _crust_," Kennedy growled, stepping around the Child. But the Child caught him deftly by the sleeve.

"We'll have none of that, Stutter. Go & see to your errands."

"I want to stay," Kennedy said, fixing his blood-shot eyes on the proprietor.

"Stutter," the Child said softly.

Kennedy glared at the little man a moment longer, shoved me aside with his elbow, & left the rooming-house without a word.

"You should be careful of that boy of mine, Mr. Costello," the Child said, looking after Kennedy. "He has a temper."

"So do I," the proprietor said. "The bill is fifteen dollars."

I could scarce believe my ears—fifteen dollars was a princely sum at that time. The Child batted his eyes at the proprietor, sniff'd indignantly at the air, then sigh'd & produced a roll of fresh-minted Treasury bills. I'd never seen half as many in one man's hand. "Fifteen dollars to Mr. <u>Costello</u>," the Child said, counting the notes out with great deliberateness.

The proprietor took the bills & inspected them closely, holding them up to the lamp—he'd obviously not expected to see a penny. When he was finish'd he gave a little snort of pleasure & turn'd to me. "And who is this young cavalier?"

"Good-night, Mr. Costello," the Child said, turning his back on him & guiding me resolutely up the stairs.

Once the two of us were alone I found it harder than ever to contain my excitement. The idea that just that morning I'd been no more than idly curious about the man before me, that I'd known less about him than Wallace's negroes did, was almost as incredible as the fact that I was about to enter his private chambers. That the grand suite I'd imagined proved, upon entering, to be a three-penny bedroom, its door held shut by a loop'd length of twine, did nothing to dispel my amazement. My thoughts were set on the coming interview. What questions might he put to me, how on God's green earth would I reply? I imagined nothing short of having to give a complete moral & spiritual accounting of my life.

"The Pharisee's Suite," the Child announced, kicking the door open with his foot.

The room we stepped into was lit by a single window set high in the wall, the kind more commonly found in cellars; by standing on tip-toe I was able to discover that it looked westward, over a jumble of shabby roofs & alleys, toward the better half of town. What scant light remain'd was swiftly draining from the sky, & the room was a tangle of contradictory shadows. I'd just turn'd back from the glass when the wall to my left seemed to fold over on itself; I let out a sharp cry & dashed for the door, nearly trampling the Child in my distress. The Child gave a laugh & caught me by the buckle of my belt.

"Goodman Harvey, hawker of tonics—our Parson. Parson: Harvey."

"Parson. . . ?" I said, staring cow-eyed at the man who now emerged out of the dark, his face tipped sideways into a leer. After a mute, stricken pause, I

shook the apparition's hand; he was one more wonder in a night of wonders, nothing more. His hand was smooth & peculiarly elastic, like the pads on the foot of a pedigreed hound.

"Harvey is an <u>enthusiast</u>," *the Child said, leading me to a straight-backed chair in the middle of the room.*

The apparition smiled.

I sat down in the chair as bidden. My companions remain'd standing.

"Tell us, Harvey," the Child said, laying his palm ever-so-lightly on the back of my neck—"Which portion of our lecture did you find the most affecting?"

I'd not been touch'd by anyone in ages. The warmth of his hand made my mouth go dry. "All of it, Preacher," I murmur'd.

The Child gave a sour little snicker at this. "Did you hear what he call'd me just now, Auntie?"

Auntie? I look'd to every side. Was there a fourth person in the room?

Parson sucked in a breath, as though he'd only just awoken. "I heard," he said.

The Child laugh'd again, more gently. "They ran me out of Louisiana on a railroad tie, Harvey, for giving myself that title."

I squirm'd & fidgeted in my chair, desperate to make some sly rejoinder. The Child gazed wistfully at Parson; Parson's queer gray eyes bored into me in a way that made my stomach twist.

"Those people back at the Old Grange thought of you as a preacher, sir," I mumbled. "They believed every word you said. I'm sure of it."

The Child gazed sleepily at the ceiling. "People believe things in this country, Harvey. Especially if you tell it to them from a well-lit box. Haven't you learned that yet?"

"But surely they won't believe just anything, sir," I protested. "Not from anybody. I see no reason why—"

"Because they <u>want</u> *to, Harvey. That's all. They want to, & it's enough."*

I nodded blankly, looking from the Child to Parson & back again. By some trick of the light it seem'd to be growing brighter in the room. The smoke of the candle crept up the wall behind Parson without the slightest flutter. The Child let his head sink down against his chest, seemingly forgetting me completely; Parson, for his part, neither spoke nor stirred. Seconds went by, then minutes. The silence grew excruciating. Was my interview at an end so soon? I refused to credit it.

Between the Child & myself stood a second chair, distinguish'd by a cushion of yellow silk—a veritable throne in that dilapidated room. I resolved to break the silence. "Won't you be seated, Parson?" I inquired.

Parson's eyes flew open & he straighten'd with a gasp, as though I'd poked him in the side, or broken wind. "You are a Mormon?" he demanded.

"I was, sir—yes," I stammer'd, more astonish'd now than ever. No such information had pass'd between Parson & the Child.

The Child wink'd at me. "Our Parson can smell a believer a mile off, if the wind is right. Can't you, Auntie?"

"They smell like a tart's monthlies," Parson replied.

"Mr. Wallace told me far too little of your history, Mr. Harvey," the Child said, sitting down in the chair himself. "What was it that caused you to drift into this godless country?"

"My mission brought me," I answer'd, wincing at the inevitable rush of shame. "Every Mormon is given one, sir, at eighteen years of age. I came here with my cousin Alva."

"Of course! Your mission," the Child said, shaking his head as if to clear it. "To bring grace to the Indians, was it?"

"We call them 'Canaanites,' sir. Scripture holds them to be the descendants of the sixth of the Lost Tribes—"

A low mewling wail rose up in Parson's throat. "The _Canaanites?_" he hiss'd. "What would you & your clutch of beef-fed bigamists know about _them_, boy?"

The Child heaved a long-suffering sigh. "Let the boy answer, Parson."

"I'll show you Lost Tribes, kitten," Parson said, rising to his full height & opening his mouth wide as an oven-grate. My own mouth flew open at the sight & a thin squeak of terror escaped from it. The freakishness of the two figures before me— the doll-sized man in the great yellow armchair & the rattling skeleton beside him—caused me to go momentarily blind from panic & I heard myself, as if from the bottom of a well, pleading with them both—

"Please, sirs! _Please_, sirs! I'm the man you want!"

This declaration gave them pause very briefly—even Parson clapped his dreadful mouth shut & blink'd. I can account for it only by saying that I'd renounced my previous life before stepping into that rooming-house, before hearing the Child's speech, before so much as setting out for Onadee. I had no intention of returning to Wallace's depot ever again, not even to collect my horse & wagon. What I wanted was a new mission, a new vocation— something definite & profane. I was ready & willing to indenture myself to the Child—all I ask'd was that Goodman Harvey, peddler of chicaneries, constitutionals & penny-dreadful hymns, be burn'd away to ashes.

The Child was suitably impress'd. "So you're Our Man, are you, Harvey? I reckon'd as much." He privileged me with a nod. "Let's not waste precious hours, then, but rather put you straight to service—"

"Just tell me what you want," I said.

The Child look'd me over like a green-grocer appraising a head of lettuce.

"Go & find Mr. Kennedy. You remember Mr. Kennedy, don't you?"

I nodded as frankly & demurely as I was able.

"Perhaps you can be of help to him on his rounds."

I was on my feet in an instant. "Where can I find him, sir?"

The Child looked out of the corner of his eye at Parson. "I'd start at Hennington's hot-house," he said. "That's where he commonly takes his ease."

Being Friday, there were a good many people in what passed for the main street of town, most of them face-downwards in the muck. The street was lit only by a scattering of windows & the coach-lanterns of the saloons; little heaps of men—whites & Indians together—gave the curbs a queer, boulder-strewn look in the dark. Moans arose here & there as I made my way among them, broken by shouted imprecations, laughter & the occasional burbled prayer. I was not in the habit of spending my weekend nights in Onadee. If Kennedy was on the street I failed to find him there.

I spent the next hour looking into every saloon & bawdy-house I knew of. The simple mention of Kennedy's name—or the Child's, for that matter—got me summarily ejected from the lot. By midnight my shirt-front was the color of a stable floor, my face was cut & muddied, & I wanted nothing more than to crawl back to Wallace's depot on all fours. Outside the Palace Hotel I began to weep, convinced in my innocence that a man could sink no farther. It was then that I heard Kennedy's voice coming from the alley.

I shaded my eyes & peer'd into the gloom. The alley, which ran for perhaps forty feet along the south side of the hotel, was lit only by one third-story window. Directly beneath that window two figures stood huddled together. Their faces were hid from my view—it seem'd to me that they were kissing. They spoke & sigh'd together softly.

I moved haltingly toward them. Their voices hush'd as I came nearer. After a long spell of quiet the first voice spoke again—angrily, it seem'd to me now—& I fancied that I understood it.

"Look at us," the voice said. "Look at us, you Jezebel!"

I was certain now that it was Kennedy. I drew closer still, no longer trying to move quietly, confident in my mandate from the Child. Just as I reach'd the alley one of the figures slid onto its knees & let out a soft, wet gasp, like an Indian choking on a drink. The sound stopped me short. I must have made some sort of noise, however—for the standing figure froze. There was no sound for a time but the gurgling of the other.

"Parson?" Kennedy said, his voice oddly penitent.

"It's Harvey, Mr. Kennedy, if you please. Goodman Harvey. The Child sent me to ask whether I could be of service—"

"The Mormon," Kennedy said. Perhaps he said it to himself, perhaps to the figure on the ground. *"Come over here, boy. You'll not help me much in the muh! muh! middle of the street."*

It was a man on the ground, I now saw—a slender-bodied man with a shock of pale hair. He was on his knees in the muck of the alley with his head tilted to one side & his face push'd hard into Kennedy's belly. Kennedy himself was crouch'd stiffly over, his left hand covering the other's mouth. Between two fingers of his right he held a jack-knife, its blade filed down to the merest sliver.

"Mr. Kennedy—?" I bleated. *"Mr. Kennedy, what on earth—"*

"Make yourself handy, Mormon," Kennedy grunted, seizing me by the collar. *"Come around here. Tuh! tuh! Take ahold of him. Not there, you damn fool. There. By the scruff of him."*

I stood still for perhaps an instant longer, fighting the urge to run, then took hold of the stranger's hair. The desire to please, to make a favorable impression, once again conquer'd my reserve—I felt a grown man, suddenly, & bold. The hair was coarse as thatch. *"Here?"* I said.

"Ay," said Kennedy. *"Hold him tight."*

"Look," I mumbled, though my own eyes were half-closed. *"Mr. Kennedy—look here—"*

"I'm looking, boy," Kennedy said gently. *"It's all right."* He nodded his head approvingly as he spoke. *"I see."* All at once he took the man's jaw firmly in his grip & thrust the knife between the teeth, throwing his head & shoulders back, driving the thin blade in with all his strength.

"OUU—GAAWGHH," said the man. *"ORRAAAGHH."* Kennedy pull'd the blade free & clamp'd his hand over the mouth, muffling it as one would a bugle.

"Right! That's fix'd it, you bed-wetter. Back on your mother's milk again."

"Kennedy—" I said.

"Back on her tuh! tuh! tits," said Kennedy, whistling through his teeth. *"Mother's little carrot-headed bundle of piss. Mother's little bread-crumb."*

The man in my arms reek'd of hominy gin, an old stand-by in my elixirs. He made a pitiful attempt to free himself, then sank back against me, senseless. The pants clung to his legs in stiff, jet-colored swaths.

"Let him drop," said Kennedy, cuffing me lightly on the shoulder. *"We've got his thirty bits of silver."*

I did nothing. Kennedy watch'd me for a moment. "Let him drop, boy," he said again.

I open'd my arms & the man slid limply to the ground. To my astonishment he began to snore as soon as his face touch'd the dirt—seeing him splay'd out at my feet like a sleeping calf, untroubled by the violence done him, I suddenly understood the appeal my tonics held for the Indians.

Kennedy was looking at me keenly. "Well, Smith? How goes it?"

"Smith?" I murmur'd.

He nodded gaily. "That's you're name, isn't it? Sure it is. Joseph Smith."

A day before—even earlier that night—such abuse of the Prophet's name might have brought me to my senses. Now for some reason it pleased me. "I could do with a sip of beer," I heard myself say.

Kennedy smiled & clapped me on the back. "Right you are, Joseph!" he said, steering me down the alley by my shoulders. "A pint of plain for both of us!"

"Who was that, Mr. Kennedy?" I ask'd, stopping to wipe my hands against the wall. "I must say, you dealt with him—that is to say, you served him his come-uppance in the most—really, the most efficacious—"

Kennedy shrugged & blew his nose into his fingers. "He was a dirty crybaby, Joseph. Best forgotten."

I nodded matter-of-factly. "What had he done, exactly?"

"He tuh! tuh! traded us, Joseph," Kennedy replied, shaking his fist at me. Something in it made a rattling noise, like pennies clattering in a cup. "He traded us for thirty bits." He scowl'd at me, then broke into a grin. "Thirty-two bits, actually."

We'd come to a door leading down into a cellar. Kennedy duck'd in swiftly, muttering to himself, & I follow'd after. After three or four steps it was black as fresh-poured pitch to every side.

"Mr. Kennedy!" I call'd, stretching out my arms.

"Over here, Joseph. Quietly."

After three more steps I came to a row of barrels that seem'd to run unbroken from one wall to the other. "Mr. Kennedy?" I whimper'd. In the blink of an eye I was dizzy with fear at the thought of being parted from him. I did not question this new-found attachment of mine—this filial affection for a murderer—against my nature though it surely was. I had no "nature" to speak of any longer—there was only the act, the abetting, the decision I had made. Already it fill'd my mind with its finality & sleekness. God could perhaps forgive, but he could never underdo what Kennedy & I had done—of that much I was certain. My fate had been solder'd to Kennedy's own. Had I lost him there, in that relentless blackness, I'd simply have laid down & waited to be lynch'd.

Just then, however, Kennedy appear'd out of the dark & took hold of me by my wrists.

"Have yourself a wash," he said, dragging me to the nearest of the barrels & plunging my hands into a cool, astringent liquid.

"What is it?" I gasp'd. It stung my palms & knuckles fiercely.

"Briarberry wine," Kennedy said, letting go of my arms. "If you've sport to wash off you, Joseph, buh! buh! briarberry wine's your trick."

"Briarberry! But it stains worse than anything," I protested. "& it stinks."

"Clever hen!" Kennedy sing-song'd, still in high humor. I soon heard him splashing it on himself as if it were rose-water. "If the Nick gets ahold of you, all they smell or see's the souse. That's what it's <u>for</u>, Joseph. See?" I fancied I could hear his lips pull back into a grin. "Come along, now! Let's return us to the temple of our familiars."

We made our way back without incident. The Child was asleep in the room's only bed, breathing in soft, melodious whistles. Parson didn't look to have moved an inch.

<u>"Stulti sunt hic,"</u> Parson said as we came in.

"Get pissed, blood-sucker," Kennedy retorted.

"A question," Parson said, unperturb'd. "I wonder, Mr. Kennedy, if you know what a 'priapy' might be?"

"Go to hell."

"A priapy, Mr. Kennedy, is a high ecclesiastic official of the Roman Catholic Church, whose important function is to brand the pricks of the Pope's bulls with the words 'Priapus Romae.' He enjoys a princely revenue & the friendship of God."

Kennedy said nothing for a brief while, during which he appear'd to be asleep. Then, drawing a weary breath, he lower'd himself onto a chair & said—"& a <u>cunt</u>, you clot of puh! puh! pig-shite, is a Baptist of the feminine variety led out to same said pasture by her fancy minister and made to squat down, present arms, &—"

"I don't doubt it, Mr. Kennedy!" Parson said happily. He hummed to himself a moment. "Did you come across our creditor?"

"I did." Kennedy lean'd forward on the stool, dug a finger into his nose, withdrew it, inspected it, then gestured toward the Child. "Rouse him, would you, Joseph?"

I look'd toward the bed. Asleep the tiny creature was so immaculately childlike, so otherworldly in his calm, that it seem'd a shame he didn't go to bed in front of his audience as the finále of his speeches. In spite of this grace about him, however—or perhaps because of it—the thought of laying hands on him fill'd me with unease. Awful as the others seemed, as much as I fear'd them, their significance paled in the presence of the Child—I felt no kinship toward them, no devotedness, no love.

"Go on, Joseph," Kennedy mutter'd, fidgeting with the collar of his coat. It was a filthy, ragged affair, its buttons fashion'd from all manner of odds & ends—bottle-caps, bits of tea-cup, the gnaw'd end of a pipe. A life as one of the Child's retainers clearly didn't bring much in the way of worldly privilege.

Trying to undo one of the buttons, Kennedy put a gouge into his finger & cursed. "Wake him <u>up</u> already, Joseph, for the love of Sam! Up & give him a puh! puh! poke!"

"Mill him vigorously with thy palm, Mormon," Parson intoned.

I took a few steps toward the bed. The Child's breathing had a restless sound to it now, as if he were already half-awake; the notion came to me that he might be shamming sleep, to test me. For some reason this made me bolder. Bending over him, I saw the balls of his eyes flitting back & forth under their glossy lids, his thin lips quivering with each breath. An odd thing happen'd then—suddenly it was I who was powerful, knowledgeable & sly; the Child, by contrast, was as helpless as his name implied. I'd reinvented myself once already that night—the eager sniveler from Nauvoo, Illinois had been quietly put to death. I was free of my old life, burnt clean by violence, like a coal-scuttle pulled clear of the fire. Was any role <u>not</u> mine for the taking, if I chose?

I laid my hand on the Child's shoulder. As soon as I did so Parson darted back into his corner like a mouse into its hole.

The Child's eyes clapped open like two shutter'd windows. "Is it you, Brother?" he said tenderly, his eyes wet with wonder.

"It's Harvey," I answer'd. "Or Smith, if you prefer. Mr. Kennedy and myself—"

Before I could finish the Child gave me a kick that sent me tumbling backwards. He was fully clothed under the blankets, boots & all; the print of his heel burn'd as fiercely against my ribs as if it had been etch'd there.

"Suh—suh—suh—!" I gasp'd, struggling for breath.

"Shut your mouth, boy," the Child said sedately, hopping down from the bed. "Leave the stuttering to Stuts. It suits him better."

I shut my eyes tight, expecting another kick; but instead I heard his voice saying affectionately to Kennedy—"Judging from the reek of briarberry, I would say you found our man."

"I did, the motte-licker."

"Did you come to terms?"

A pause. "Weren't nothing on him. Not a cent."

"And in his rooms?"

"His rooms was in the Puh! Puh! Palace Hotel alley."

Cautiously—simperingly—I open'd my eyes. The Child was directly above me. He was looking past Kennedy now, perhaps at Parson in the corner. "You mean to say that you brought <u>nothing</u> back? Not a blessed thing?"

For an instant Kennedy look'd cow'd; then he broke into a grin. "There's this," he said, opening his hand over the table. A dozen glinting kernels—like gilded pepper-corns—fell softly to the cloth. I stood up to see them better.

"I thought as much," the Child said, bringing one of them to the candle. In the weak light, even the enamel shone like gold—the Child made appreciative little coos as he turned it this way & that, chipping at the dried blood with his nails.

"I <u>knew</u> his family had money back in Baltimore," he murmur'd. "You could tell it by the way he lisp'd." He glanced sideways at me. "No offense, Harvey."

"None taken, sir!" I said brightly. "My own family, back in Nauvoo, Illinois—"

"Shut your gob, Joseph," said Kennedy. I shut it.

Parson reach'd across the table, took the tooth out of the Child's hand & sniff'd at it.

"What the hell are <u>you</u> about?" Kennedy snarl'd, snatching it back from him. "It's your regular flavor, aren't it?"

"He was a chewer of plug tobacco," Parson said smugly, retiring to his corner.

The Child turn'd back to Kennedy and granted him a smile. "You managed it very neatly, Stuts."

Kennedy cough'd into his sleeve. "Joseph were a help to me, of sorts."

For the second time that night the Child looked at me with genuine surprise. "Perhaps you're right, Mr. Harvey," he said, taking my hand in his. "Perhaps you <u>are</u> our Mormon."

An hour later we were well out of town on a cart liberated from Costello's rooming-house, making for Wallace's depot with all practicable speed. The expedition was in the highest of spirits—Parson was whistling under his breath, Kennedy was muttering to himself, & I was standing straight up in the cart, reveling in as perfect a feeling of freedom as I have ever known. The moon was up now, just a sliver short of full, & its light threw quicksilver shadows across the plains. I felt both luminous & invisible. If the image of the man in the Palace Hotel alley return'd now & again, so too did a rush of dis-belief that we'd escaped Onadee unpunish'd. With every mile my sense of deliverance grew.

It was getting on light when we came to Wallace's crossroads. Kennedy stopped the horses & we sat silently for a time. I began to grow restless, & not a little confused, but I managed to keep reasonably still.

"Your team's in the barn?" the Child said finally, keeping his eyes on the depot.

"Beg pardon, sir; not a team. One stippled mare."

Now he look'd at me. "I thought you had a team, Harvey."

"No, sir."

"He said just the mare," Parson put in, gazing indifferently eastwards.

"Huh!" said the Child. "We'll need Wallace's two old bleaters, then."

Kennedy spat. "Might as well ride on the Mormon's buh! buh! back."

"True," the Child admitted, laying a grass-blade between his lips. "But Wallace's pair would give us two teams, with that stipple of Harvey's. Two teams is preferable to one."

"Damned if I think so," Kennedy said, scratching his nose.

"Mind your parlance, Stuts," the Child caution'd.

"Is Wallace not coming?" I said, feeling foolish without rightly know-ing why.

The Child beckon'd me to him, took the grass-blade from his mouth & brought it reverently down to touch my shoulders—first the left, then the right—as though he were knighting me. "Up & after those horses, Goodie," he said, slipping a hand inside Kennedy's top-coat. Still looking at me fondly, he pulled out a little bosom-pistol—an ancient, graceless thing, such as you might find on a doxie's night-table—& toss'd it into my lap.

"Just a tap on the head & a thank-ye, Joseph!" Kennedy said as I climb'd down. "Just a regular puh! puh! poke in the eye!"

So wholly was my lot cast in with them now—so little was left of the self-serving misanthrope I'd been—that I never once question'd the wisdom of entering that depot with nothing but a single-shot pistol from the preceding century. The others hung back in the shadow of the cart, comfortably out of harm's way, while I put one foot ahead of the other down the muddy slope. Twice I lost a shoe & had to hop back on one foot to collect it. A last vain hope—that Wallace's horses would be out in the open, hobbled between the depot & the barn—expired as I came up to the house. The horses & wagons were responsibly lock'd away. I stood on the porch for a time, harkening. There was nothing but the buzzing of flatbugs in the weeds. I coax'd the door open, press'd the pistol to my cheek—for courage, I suppose—and eased myself inside.

The first thing I saw was Tempie lying on a heap of broad-sheets, his sack-cloth over-alls loose around his hips. He snored so emphatically that I could have ridden a mule through the house unnoticed. I stepped over his legs & look'd hurriedly about the parlor for the keys to the stable, but I knew better than to expect to find them there. Wallace was the kind of man who took his keys to bed. I went to his bedroom door & push'd it open.

The bedroom was airless as a tomb & very near as dark. I stood on the threshold for as long as I dared, giving my eyes time to acquaint themselves, keeping my brain & body still. There was a pallet not three feet from where I stood, and a tin night-pot beside it. I'd just noticed a loose heap of clothes on the floor when I heard a soft, melodious sigh & saw a body on the pallet stretch & roll onto its back. The body was long & dark & its skin had the buttery gloss of fresh-tanned leather. It was a woman's body, or a girl's. She open'd her eyes as I watch'd her, saw me above her in the doorway, & sat up without so much as taking in a breath.

If she'd had any feeling for Wallace at all, she'd have lain back down, or made a rush at me, or scream'd; instead she took a deliberate breath, gather'd up her clothes & slipped past me as stealthily as she could. I waited for the sound of the house-door, then bent down & drew the bed-sheet off the pallet. I wasn't thinking about the keys to the stable any longer. The feeling I'd had at the Child's bedside had return'd, & I stood over Wallace's bare, unwitting body in a rapture. Here was freedom of another kind, a kind I'd not yet savored—the freedom to do whatever I liked to the man lying at my feet.

Wallace's eye-lids twitch'd, then flutter'd open. "Goodman Harvey," he said serenely. Then he turn'd and blew his nose into the bed-sheet.

My name had an ugly sound to me now, particularly on Wallace's tongue. I went to cock the hammer of my pistol & found to my surprise that it was cock'd already.

Had I done that?

"About your horses," I said. "Your two mares."

He sat up carefully. "I know how many mares I've got, Harvey." He craned his neck to look past me. "Are the others with you? Parson? Kennedy?"

I shook my head.

"I thought not," he said, & flash'd his teeth. "They would send <u>you</u> to do it! Quite poetic." There was a note of satisfaction—perhaps even of approval—in his voice. "They must think me a sorry old shit-pile indeed, Mr. Harvey." He sat quietly a moment. "They're right, of course."

"You'll open the stable, then?" I said.

"I might," said Wallace, reaching a hand under his pillow & bringing out a key. He did this so promptly, so obligingly, that I didn't think to stop him. If that were a gun, I thought, I'd be blown to Kingdom Come by now. Then I saw the Colt Dragoon revolver in his other fist.

"I'd never have brought the Child somebody I couldn't put to bed myself," Wallace said, rising spryly from the pallet. "You should have known that much. But then, you're new to the Territories. Still in short pants, as it were." He jerk'd his head toward the window. "Out there, is he? With the others?"

I held my peace. Wallace gloated for a time, shifting from one foot to the other; I stared dully back at him, the pistol slack against my leg. He must have expected me to fire, or else to commence pleading for my life; the longer I did nothing, the unsteadier he became. Through my numbness I managed to apprehend that he was deathly scared.

"Don't worry, Harvey," he said after a time, coiling the sheet about his midriff like a Caesar. "You wanted to try on a different suit of clothes, & you got stuck in them; that's all it was. I did much the same thing at your age."

I remember'd vaguely, watching Wallace fidget, that he was said to have ridden with Hall's High Valley Raiders. Now he fears for his life, I thought. He fears for his life—a former outlaw—because of me. The thought did little to encourage me, however.

"What's the Child promised you?" Wallace said, taking a step towards me. "To teach you Canaan's tongue? Is that it?"

"He might have done," I heard myself reply. He'd promised no such thing, of course. But I'd have said anything, just then, to keep the conversation lively.

Wallace roll'd his eyes & groan'd. "You're a bigger idiot than I supposed. You think I wasn't made that self-same offer?" He came closer still—our faces were all but touching. "You don't learn something like _that_, Harvey, without forgetting something else."

"Forgetting what?" I said. I felt unafraid now, almost bold.

"Everything," Wallace murmur'd, bringing his free hand to his temple, as if checking himself for fever. "_Everything_, Harvey. Your entire self."

I closed my eyes & tried to make sense of Wallace's ravings. Could the Child actually help me to forget myself completely? Was he bless'd with such prodigious gifts?

"How wonderful that would be—to forget myself!" I sigh'd.

This cost Wallace his last composure. "You muck-brain'd _ass!_" he yell'd. "Have you not listen'd to a word I've told you?"

I smiled at him benignly.

"*Your entire self, Harvey,*" *Wallace said again, panting quietly. His eyes grew vague & abstracted & he look'd up toward the ceiling. As he did so he let the Colt dangle & I suddenly recollected where I was. I brought the nose of my pistol up against his ribs, silently & smoothly, with no more effort than it takes to point a finger.*

"*My name is Joseph Smith,*" *I said, & fired.*

For a fleeting instant Wallace remain'd unchanged. Then he tilted his face toward the ceiling, press'd both hands to his belly & began to shriek. I threw him back onto the bed & had his Dragoon in my hands & cock'd by the time Tempie came stumbling through the door.

"*Get on the floor,*" *I said. I'd done my best to disguise my voice, to harshen it & slur it over, but Tempie recognized it straight-away.* "*That you, Mr. Harvey?*" *he said, squinting into the dark.* "*This here old Tempie.*"

"*Get-on-that-<u>floor</u>, nigger!*" *I hiss'd, ramming the Colt into his guts. Tempie bent sideways, his eyes gone liquid & enormous. I brought a second hand up to steady the gun, wondering whether the Child and the others might come to my aid, or whether they'd abandoned me long since. No matter, Goodman, I told myself, struggling to keep calm—there are three horses stable'd in the barn. The key is in Wallace's hand, or beside him on the pallet, or somewhere on the floor—*

When the hammer of the Colt slipped I heard no report; my first thought was to curse its light action. Then Tempie let out a high, mournful gasp, like the cooing of a dove, & took a gentle hold of my left leg. I can still feel the slight, determined pressure of his grip.

At that very same instant, as if in answer to a bell, the Child came in from the parlor, took the key out of Wallace's hand, & made to take the revolver out of mine. But I wouldn't let him have it.

"*It's mine,*" *I said. I held the barrel to my chest.* "*Keep the hell away from me!*"

"*Mind your language, Joseph,*" *the Child said, stepping past me with a wink.*

"*I—*"

"*Yes, Joseph? What is it?*"

"*I'm sorry, sir,*" *I stammer'd.*

"*Apology accepted, Joseph. Now let's have that revolver.*"

"*It's mine,*" *I said again, recoiling.*

He studied me a little, click'd his tongue against his teeth, then spun about & left without a word.

If a saint's life is judged by his most wanton moments, might the whole world be saved by the "nay" of one coward?

"Shall I Tell You My Idea?"

THAT SAME DAY I GO TO SEE ABOUT DELAMARE, Virgil says.

The front parlor, until recently the site of the Colonel's interrogations, has been converted into a make-shift infirmary. Delamare lies on a stiff-looking pallet in the middle of the room, staring up at the plaster-work as though the Fate of Man were writ across it. Clementine is with him but she stands to leave at once. She'll be out in the hall in a moment, listening.

Delamare's eyes follow me carefully from the door to the stool beside him. He says nothing as I sit. He says nothing because his lips and tongue are swollen so badly that he can barely take in air. He breathes through his nose in timid, parakeet-like peeps.

"I'm taking over the inquiry, Oliver," I whisper. "I'm putting the Colonel out to pasture. What do you say to that?"

A poor choice of phrase. He gives me a flash-eyed look that I'm reluctant to interpret. Christ knows what nonsense Clem's been feeding him.

"You think they won't let me," I say. "I agree. That's why no-one need know of it, for the present, except you and I."

Delamare lifts his shoulders and lets them fall.

I watch him for a spell. "Bob your head once, Oliver, if you consider me a coward."

Nothing for a time but sullenness. Then a grudging nod.

"I have a reason for asking. Do you care to hear it?"

He closes his eyes for an instant, then opens them.

"I left Harvey's letter in Clem's care," I say. "I suppose she's read it to you."

He nods.

"The last page of it interests me. Do you recollect the post-script?"

Another spell of quiet. Then he nods again.

"'Might the whole world be saved by the "nay" of one coward?' it reads. 'One coward.' That tickles the brain, somehow."

Now his eyes are fixed on mine. The sharp-eyed look remains—; a vengeful look, it seems to me. I'd best be quick.

"I don't think that line refers to Harvey," I say. "At no point does he describe himself as cowardly. Desperate, yes—; even foolish—; but never as a coward. Quite the opposite, in fact."

I've caught his fancy now, I'm sure of it. His eyes are watering.

"I believe that last line, and in fact the entire letter, is a bulletin to us—; to one of us especially. Harvey had no interest in the outside world, and still less in posterity. The letter is a reckoning with the Angel of Death, he says. A 'reckoning.'" I scratch my nose. "What does he mean by that, do you suppose?"

Delamare blinks once, very deliberately, then raises a finger grimly to his mouth.

"Of course, Oliver! I'm sorry. Shall I tell you my idea?"

His sight begins to wander and his head turns toward the wall. Have I come to him too soon?

"It's only this," I say quickly. "On the eve of his murder, Harvey told Clem we'd find his letter interesting—; that it was written for us *expressly*. Why? To justify himself to us? Not very likely. None of us were fit to judge him."

Delamare looks at me coldly, as if to say that he feels fit to judge Harvey and the rest of us besides. But he's listening to me closely.

I clear my throat. "He meant for us to read his account, but more than that—: he meant for us to *decipher* it. Something's hidden in the text, I'm sure of it." I pause a moment. "See if you can follow my reasoning now, Oliver. Firstly—: I take 'Angel of Death' to mean Harvey's killer."

Delamare bobs his head impatiently. His eyes are watering again.

"If that's the case," I say, my voice dropping even further, "then the meaning of 'reckoning' becomes clear. The letter is more than an accounting, more than a confession, more than an entreaty to us to discover his murderer—: the letter itself is the *means* to that discovery, buried somehow in the narrative of Harvey's fall. The story is a cipher, a puzzle, like a parable in the Bible. We have only to solve it." I bend down and say again, close to his ear—: "We have only to solve it, Oliver, to know."

Delamare is staring up into my face, intently, feverishly, but whether in enthusiasm or dismay I cannot tell. Never mind which—; I'll tell my idea to him regardless. Its improbability has made me drunk.

I clear my throat. "It's beyond what I'd have expected from that little ass-scratcher, I grant you. But I'm convinced of it, Oliver. And I'm convinced of one thing more. The letter may well have been written for everyone in this house—; the last lines, however, were meant for one of us alone." I sit back on the stool. "I refer, of course, to the 'coward' of the post-script."

Delamare gives no sign of having understood me. But I know he's understood me. His eyes are wide and starting.

"I daresay you can guess who that coward is, Oliver. You already have. Harvey made particular mention of me, you remember, on his walk with Clementine."

Delamare's lips part slightly and I see the blood-slick tongue behind them. He makes as if to speak. To forestall him, I say quickly—:

"I'm the best suited to take up the hunt, and Harvey knew it. I'm the only one here who puts the slightest faith in reason—; in the scientific method."

Delamare shakes his head wildly. Again he opens his mouth to speak—; again I cut him short.

"Listen to me, Oliver. If one takes the end of the letter—the 'nay of a coward' line—as one's starting point, then one possible approach would be to work backwards from that line." Delamare rolls his eyes at this, but I press on. "I've spent the morning doing precisely that, starting with the killings at Wallace's depot. And something struck me straight-away—: a term I once heard Morelle use. Perhaps you'll remember it, as well. It's the expression 'Canaan's'—"

With a great effort Delamare forces his tongue to speak. "Virgil— *Clementine*, Virgil—"

Nothing could have hushed me quicker. I've just told him something that ought by rights to have bowled him over, to have stunned him, to have stricken him to the marrow—; instead he calls out for his nurse. Is she so dear to him already?

I stretch both arms out, somewhat stiffly, and force him back onto the pallet.

"All right, Oliver. I'm sure that Clem's close by. I'll fetch her."

I get to my feet, ignoring Delamare's burbled protests, and step out into the hall. Clem is there beside the marigolds.

"You'll never manage it," she says. Her face is dull as a chalk pebble.

"Manage what?" I say.

"To play both sides at once. You're not clever enough for it, Virgil." She shakes her head slowly. "You and your blessed 'scientific method.' You're no damned scientist."

"And you're no sister of mercy. But don't let that keep you from playing at one, miss. Not if Mr. Delamare enjoys it."

I take her hand in mine. It deadens, as I knew it would.

"Love makes you erratic, Clementine."

"I feel less love for you than for a spider," she says hoarsely.

"It wasn't of *myself*, miss, that I was speaking." I let go of her hand. "Run along in to your boy."

Regents' Geographical Society, 1614.

T HE CONCEIT—IF IT PLEASE THE SOCIETY—of the "Nyg-ger"—was in broad usage before that Genus, let alone that species, was unearth'd by the excellent Mr. Cleveland, and tax-onomie'd.—Fortunate indeed!—m'lords—that such a beaste was, in fact, discover'd.—It has spared the Chair, in specific;—and the Society, in general;—no small quantity of confusion.

Dodds.

MY NAME CHARLES BALLANTINE DODDS. I standing to the right the grave and Miss Clem throwing in the dirt. Don't nobody else care to, so Miss Clem do it. Rest of them watches her and grins.

Rest easy, Goodman Harvey.

You sure you didn't take that walk with Mr. Harvey, Clementine, Colonel hisper.

That dirty Irish, Kennedy, commence to snicker.

Virgil face go white. He gone say some thing, open he mouth and close it. Kennedy look at him like he dearly hope he say it. Colonel stop he smiling now.

Bottom the grave they no lay-box or casket, just a old cloth strippit off Harvey bed. Harvey always kind to me, account of he religion, so I lookit hard for timber but Colonel say leave off it Dodds get that somebitch under. So I dugged the hole four feet deep. Just four feet, account of the clay. Virgil help some but I tolt where Harvey get placed so it were all right. I say We gone plant him past the stable. And sure enough that where we standing now.

Why lay him here, Dodds? Virgil askit while we digging. Just chat-like, not asking truly. There's a blankety-blank less clay over by the privy.

Mr. Virgil, I say. Please don't vain the name the Lord.

Virgil look at me some. Dodds, he say.

Yes, Mr. Virgil?

Why put Harvey here?

Sih?

Give me an answer, you old fox. This ground's hard as nails.

I tap the side my nose. *Old* Marse Trist, Marse Trist's daddy, tell me something once.

What was it?

One dead nigger smell like peaches.

Virgil look me at me crooked. I don't follow—

Two dead niggers, now, Marse Trist say. *Two* dead niggers, Charlie, smell like the divil's own privy-water.

Ah! say Virgil.

Ain't two white gentlemen gone smell no sweeter.

Ha! say Virgil. No. I don't suppose they would.

And the Deemer down the privy, I say. As you know.

Virgil quiet a piece. Then he rub his face. What did you think of Marse Trist's daddy, Dodds?

I look down the hole. Old Marse Trist a fine man, in he time—

I know what you and Mr. Delamare talk about together, Dodds. You can talk as well to me.

I go right on shoveling. I pay no more mind to Virgil as if he was a haunt.

That were yesterday, in the afternoon.

Now everybody stand about looking down at Harvey thinking what come next.

That's a mighty poor plot, Dodds, Colonel say.

Couldn't dug it any farther, Colonel.

Even the privy-pit were deeper that this, Kennedy say. You getting old awful quick, Doddsbody.

Why put him here, Dodds, if the ground is so mean? Colonel say.

I couldn't be pained, I answer.

What's that, nigger? Kennedy holler.

Problem with Dodds is, say the Colonel. Problem with Dodds is, there's no fright in him. He lost it when our Redeemer passed away.

Let's reaquaint him with it, Kennedy say. L!—L!—Let's—

Leave off it, Stuts, Virgil say. He take hold of Kennedy arm.

Kennedy look at Virgil, then at me, then all the rest. He shake he head three times, slow and murtherish, like a buck-wild bull.

Best let go of me, google-eye, he say.

Colonel smile and step up. *Mr.* Kennedy—

Back away from me, you blankety-blank mother, Kennedy hisper.

He look like he forgotten they anything but Virgil Ball in all the world. Colonel shut he mouth right quick.

I look at Miss Clem. She studying Virgil like she never seen the like. Wouldn't nobody step into Virgil's boots at the present time. Not for fifty Union dollars.

Don't take offense, Colonel, Virgil say. Kennedy's just sore, on account of we didn't let him bugger his mulatto. Ain't you, Stuts?

Kennedy look at Virgil like he half-past dead already. Colonel put he knuckles in he mouth.

Not sore at *me*, Virgil, I'm sure, Colonel say.

Virgil let go Kennedy arm. That's right, Colonel—you *did* let him, didn't you.

Kennedy blink but once, quick, then put Virgil in the hole. Virgil come up with mud on he clothes and he good right eye shut—but they a look on his face like he just got elected.

Mr Kennedy, he say, wiping at he face.

Kennedy whistle and spread both arms wide. Come to me, brother.

Just then Miss Clem make a noise and I look up past the hole and spy Parson coming down from the house. Then I near drop the spade account of I see Delamare alongside him. I can't nearly credit it. Everybody quiet and wait on them to come. Parson give a laugh.

I've effected a faith cure, children.

Delamare look straight at Kennedy. I thought you killed me, Irish, he say.

I'll dig every one of you blankety-blanks *under*, Kennedy shout. Just you come on up!

Everybody hush. Parson stand by with he long coonish hand cross he long coonish face. Kennedy stand twixt of Delamare and Virgil like he can't recollect who need whipping the most.

Nothing doing for a time. Then Miss Clem commence to cuss and start off to the house and Colonel foller right after. That leave Delamare, Parson, Virgil and Kennedy. I keep quiet as a broom.

I thought you killed me, Irish, Delamare say again. Didn't you kill me?

Kennedy don't say much. He look small and crumblish presently, like a crust of weeks-old bread.

All up the sudden he turn and knock me sideways. I smell the mash on you, blacks, he say to Delamare.

And I smell the nigger on you, Irish.

Kennedy laugh, bite he underlip, spit, then off into the woods. Don't nobody foller after. Nobody blink till he gone clear.

Virgil pull me up to rights. If you're on speaking terms with the Death-Angel, Dodds, recommend old Stuts to him, would you?

I give a grin. I will, Mr. Virgil. Sure.

No need for that, say Delamare.

Next time he won't miss, Oliver, Virgil say.

Delamare spits. He had his chance, Virgil. I was ready to get put down yesterday. I was reconciled to it. Eh, Charlie?

Sure, Marse Delamare. Yesterday were the dollar chance.

Men like Kennedy get two chances, Virgil say.

Kennedy is a Catholic, gentlemen, Parson say, making the sign he cross. An idolator of the Heavenly Trinity. As such he always operates in threes.

DELAMARE AND VIRGIL GONE up to the house. Parson watch them like a mother hen. Clucking as he do. In high and blessed spirits.

Is it close enough to the barn? he say after a piece.

I measured it, Parson. I know my business.

Cluck! Cluck! All right, Doddsbody.

I study Parson for a spell. Watch him ruffle he hairy lady face up, then down, then up.

When the next one due? I say.

Parson wave he hand. Tomorrow afternoon.

Where we gone plant him?

Parson give a look. I didn't say as it would be a he.

That's right, I say. I rub my eyes. Where it gone get placed?

Back of the tobacco shed. Three feet seven inches. Measure it from the corner.

I'm a broke-footed old house-boy, Parson. Mind I start on it today?

Parson grin. That might look a bit peculiar.

Don't nobody go back of the tobacky-shed, Parson. You know that.

All right. Anyone asks you, just lay your Doddsbody bit on 'em. Play the holy fool.

Don't you fret on that, Your Honor. Ain't nobody gone know blankety blank, alongside of yourself, C. B. Dodds and that old Holy Ghost.

The Ghost will be pleased to hear it, Parson say.

A Privy Conference.

I'M FIXED TO PASS A CATHERINE-WHEEL, Kennedy says. I'm fixed to pass a oliphant.

Artfer that shite-party over Harvey's remains I go straight to the privy-house and wait for the End to come. I've hardly got the door shut and my pants unknickered when the privy door goes gloomy and I hear the End outside.

You! says I. You've gone and pinched my britches proper.

We've each of us to answer for our own misdeeds, Mr. Kennedy, says the End.

You see what they done to me back there? Did you? I looks down into the hole and spits. Of *course* you did.

The End gives a sad and pityish sort of breath and runs its fingers up the slats. I gave you the mulatto, Mr. Kennedy. I gave him to you and you fecked it.

I works my knees together and groans. I want to kill that checky niggra boy, says I.

He's not for you, says the End. You had your go.

When I gets my two hands on him—

Give your hands a holy-day, Mr. Kennedy. They've earned it.

These bleeding hands have been on holy-days since I come to this darmed property, says I. I've had my share of idle hours. I'm wanting a bit of work.

Mind yourself, Kennedy, says the End.

I'll mind your nobbin, says I. But I says it quiet.

You'll have work soon enough, says the End. For now, use your eyes. You'll see me before you hear me, the next time I come round.

I looks out at the dark. Meaning?

Just that, says the End. Chew on it awhile.

It can't be much longer now, says I. Can it?

The End gives a laugh. That's right, Stuts. It can't be much longer now.

I says nary then. The End breathes up and down in its hennish, endish way.

THE PRIVY WERE THE PLACE the End picked for our chats. I had nary any say in the picking of it. I don't abject to it, however, on account of my time is dear to me and two birds in a bush, et cetera, as they say. And in fact I'm feeling a chick-a-dee coming on.

If you'd step away from the precincts a moment, Your Endfulness, says I.

Work away, Mr. Kennedy, says the End. I don't mind.

That gives me a tickle. Miss the days when you had a body, sir? says I.

The End laughs then but it don't come out proper. It comes out in a sort of a dryness, like wind through standing corn. All up the sudden the memory of my own Marmsie come to me of which I haven't thought in ages. What would the old pussy have said to see me bow-legged in a privy, trading how-dos with the End of All Creation! I give another laugh and the End joins in behind. And that second laugh is dryer still and it turns my guts to hear it.

Dearest Mary, marther of God, says I, doing up my knicks.

Leave it to an Irish, says the End, spitting air. Leave it to an Irish to say his prayers in a shite-house.

You'll have your fun, says I. But remember this: I never prayed to you.

You will, Mr. Kennedy. Give it time.

Give me that niggra, you cotton-mouth! What's he to you? You've got so many. *Give* him to me, Marm.

I'm not your mother, the End say, moving off. The shack goes sunnyish again.

Oh! I know that. I know that full and well. You're just the opposite.

Good-bye, Stuts, says the End. Use your eyes!

What about Ball? says I. I says it quick and tender.

The End stops. What about him?

You don't need Ball for anything. Give me Ball.

The privy goes dark. Dear Stutter Kennedy, the End says. It warms my heart that you've learnt so little from our chats. Bless you, Stuts.

Bless your dear pure heart and your tender brain. Virgil Ball, Mr. Kennedy, is the most important of them all. Expect great things from Virgil Ball.

Ball is a mess-maker, says I. That's all he is. If it weren't for that bug-eyed donkey-pat I'd have got this house in order long ago.

Praps that's why, says the End.

I peep through the slats. Praps *what's* why?

Praps that's why I need him.

That riles me. That shambling cunt? That arse-hole-chafer? What the devil do you need him for? I thought Stuts Kennedy was your boy!

You *are* my boy, the End says. Don't forget it.

Well then, says I. Give me Virgil. Give me Virgil or the mulatto.

Another dry hiss. And what will you give *me*, Stutter, in exchange?

I'll give you killing. That's what you're artfer, aren't it?

The End says nary for a time. The slats go sunnyish again.

Do up your britches, Mr. Kennedy, it says at last. I may have work for you at that.

A Silent Supper.

VIRGIL WANTS TO INTERVIEW PARSON, Delamare says. "Interview" he calls it, though the idea of sitting that old widow-maker down on the settee and exchanging views doesn't bear much looking into. D'Ancourt tried that, and got laughed at and hissed over for his pains. I point this out to Virgil.

Virgil answers that D'Ancourt is a dried-up, flatulent old dog-dropping and I can't rightly disagree. I wouldn't mind seeing Virgil squirm a little, either. So when we come across Parson on our way down to the river—my first morning back on my two feet—I step aside and let Virgil go to market.

"Benedictions, gentlemen," Parson says. "Headed down to your daily dunking?"

"Not me," says Virgil. "I was baptized as a baby."

Parson gives a sympathetic nod. "That's prudent. I've heard tell that followers of Spinoza simmer in holy water like ducks' eggs in a skillet." He smiles at me. "That Mr. Delamare, here, feels no ill effects, is proof of his mental chastity."

"What's your opinion on Harvey's killing?" Virgil says, apropos of nothing. "Might it have been Kennedy?"

"It might have been *me*," Parson says. His snakish spine uncurls till he looks twice the size of us. "I didn't know you were so interested in fat little Harvey's passing. Have you slipped into D'Ancourt's slippers, Mr. Ball?"

"God forbid that," Virgil mumbles. The lack of concern in Parson's voice—and the cold, dry appetite behind it—makes Virgil's head pull back into his collar.

"I haven't taken the Colonel's place, Parson," he says. "Still, I can't help but be curious—"

"No! You can't help *that*, Virgil," Parson says sweetly. "You're a man of science, after all. You couldn't leave a closed box closed if a copper-head was sleeping on top of it. That's what makes it such a delight to have you about—: the world is forever new to you."

"I want to know about Canaan's tongue," Virgil says.

At the mention of that name every last thing hushes—: the leaves cease their rattling and the birds quiet in their shrubs. Parson looks at Virgil as a sparrow might look at a poppy-seed.

"Ah! There's quite a lot to tell, on that score. Where should I begin?"

Virgil takes a breath. "You told Kennedy that Harvey was speaking it before he died. And Harvey himself mentions it in his letter."

Parson looks at me and winks. "That wasn't a question, Virgil."

"What is Canaan's tongue, Parson?" I hear myself asking. My voice is quick and childish.

"Have you soaked up some of Virgil's curiosity, Mr. Delamare? How creditable!" Parson wets his downy lips. "Canaan's tongue, dear boy, is the language of the elect. The language out of whose mash all our so-called 'mysteries' have been distilled. There are thirty-seven words for 'satisfaction' in the tongue, but not a single word for 'sin.'" Parson clucks his tongue at me. "Even dark-skinned men may speak this language, Oliver." He looks back at Virgil. "Even Mormons may speak it."

"Who'd have thought Goodman Harvey was so close to heaven," Virgil says.

Parson's lips give a twitch. "It is *this* world I am speaking of, Virgil. Not some fairy kingdom."

"Then speak English, damn your eyes! Do all of God's chosen eat permanganate of potassium for breakfast?"

Parson shakes his head. "*English*, Virgil, is the entire cause of your confusion. I could explain further about the tongue, but I'd have to use the tongue to do it. And neither of you have the necessary fluency."

"I'll find someone to give me lessons," Virgil says.

"Harvey's tutor might be free," Parson answers. "Shall I put in a good word for you?"

Virgil says nothing, breathing in panicked little gasps. Parson watches him serenely. "You're wondering if *I* tutored him, of course. A reasonable thing to wonder. I can only say that if I had, things might have turned out differently for that little pot of suet."

"I'm sure they would have, sir," I offer.

"Thank you, Oliver."

Virgil hunches forward, struggling for air.

"Short of breath, Virgil?" says Parson. "A touch of ague, perhaps? A bilious complaint? I might have a bottle of something that can help."

Virgil says nothing. Parson moves his head from side to side like a clock-weight, studying him. "Any questions, Oliver?" he says out of the corner of his mouth.

"Nothing but, Parson," I reply.

"I have a question for you, as well." Parson hums to himself. "Have you ever been to a silent supper?"

A silent supper? I shake my head.

"No?" Parson takes me by the shoulder. "I'll tell you about it, then. This is how it's done."

I shrug his hand away. "What I'd prefer to know, Parson, is—"

Parson presses a loose-skinned finger to my mouth.

"*Listen*, Oliver, and attend. Several girls prepare a supper in the dark, doing everything backwards and without speaking a word. When the meal is ready, they put a pan of water and a towel on the door-step, and leave the house-door open to the night. Each girl brings a chair to the table, then stands silently beside the chair and waits." Parson looks from me to Virgil. "The future husbands of the girls will soon appear, wash themselves in the pan of water, dry themselves with the towel, then sit down in the chairs to eat. When they have finished they will leave the house exactly as they came." Parson's gamey old breath wicks along my ear—: "That's how *babies* are made, Oliver."

Virgil shouts a curse. "Who murdered Harvey? Answer me, you damned witch! Do we have to cook a dinner backwards to get an answer out of you?"

Parson pauses a moment, smiling into his collar, then says carefully and crisply, as though reading from a book—:

"While the husbands are eating, they converse with one another. They talk of the things they've seen on their way to the house. And if the girls are clever—if the girls have ears to hear—they listen and attend. For the future will bring every last thing their fiancées describe." Parson takes a step forward and allows his back to settle into its habitual crook. "What language do you think those husbands converse in, gentlemen? Surely you don't suppose it's English?"

Neither of us answer. Parson beckons us closer.

"Canaan's tongue is the language of future things." His voice drops to a whisper. "The future, gentlemen, is its one and only tense. Soon—

very soon—there will *be* no other language. Some will speak the tongue, some will obey it. And each of us will be asked to choose between those two societies." Parson cocks his head at Virgil. "Which will you choose, Mr. Ball?"

"Which did Harvey choose?"

But Parson has already turned his back on us, tipping and bobbing toward the house as if he had paddle-wheels for feet.

"He's a great one for riddles," I mutter as we watch him go.

"He knows who killed Harvey," Virgil says. "He knows everything about it."

I nod. "What's more, he knows you think so. And he doesn't seem to mind."

"But there is something else he minds," Virgil says, keeping his eyes on Parson. "Something he wants us not to see. Behind all his sport there's a living fact—or perhaps only a question—that he's desperate to keep us from discovering. He wants us in the dark, Oliver. Like the girls at that damn supper."

"If that's what he wants, my hat goes off to him," I say.

"Canaan's tongue is the key to it—; that much I'm sure of." Virgil chews on his lip for awhile. "It means what Parson says it does, of course, but it means something else besides." He turns to me. "And so does that cattle-brand. That shape. The one in Harvey's letter."

"Cattle-brand?" I say. "What cattle-brand? Are you speaking Parson's English now?"

"I had a vision this morning," Virgil says.

I give him a good hard look. His face is solemn as an urn.

"Spare me your wheels of fire, Virgil. They become a man of reason poorly."

He takes a nervous breath and clutches at my sleeve, the same sleeve that Parson clawed at not five minutes gone. "Do you recollect that shape in Harvey's letter?"

I think a moment. "That boxy sort of scribble? From the meeting at the Old Grange?"

"That's the one." His voice goes shrill and eager. "I've seen that shape *before*, Oliver."

I look toward the house. Parson is nowhere to be seen.

"So have I," I say.

Virgil all but vaults into the air. "I knew it! I *knew* it! Where was it, Oliver? Did you manage to find out what it means?"

I regard him evenly for the briefest of instants, allowing myself to commit his slack-jawed, slavering look to memory. My satisfaction has arrived, easily and completely, as I knew it would. I take Virgil's full measure, remind myself that he sent Kennedy to kill me, then calmly free my shirt-sleeve from his grip.

"It means 'Suffer fools,' Virgil," I say to him. "And you've been had for one. That sign is a Cherokee fool-catcher."

The Victoria Diamint.

SOON ENOUGH, Dodds says. Didn't it come down on me soon. Virgil come jabbering about that hole. I knew when I dugged it a body might see it and come round fussing. Praps I reckoned it. Praps I reckoned he would come.

Virgil find me by the griddle in the cook-house, pulling cuts off a ham-brace and stewing sundry greens.

Dodds, he say. I'm puzzled by your diggings.

I shake my head. I'm puzzlit by them, too.

Praps we can puzzle it out together, he say. He give a cough. Who said to dig behind the tobacco shed?

Parson, I say, fussing at the ham.

Parson, he say. All right.

I commence to cutting onions.

What for, Dodds? Did he say what for?

He said most likely they was more to come.

Virgil face go flat. More whats? More burials? More holes?

More killings, I say.

Virgil hush.

So, I say. I askit could I get started.

Dodds, Virgil say. He voice gone soft and jumpish. Did Parson give a reason why?

I tolt you it, I say. They likely come more killings—

Yes but *why*, Dodds? Why would there be more?

I pull my shoulders up. I askit that already.

Virgil swallow and shuffle and blink. What did Parson say?

I take in a longish breathe. I grin at Virgil and scratch behind my ears and watch him stew and fret himself. Then I give it to him like a sweet.

Parson said to me, Three reasons, Doddsbody.

Three reasons, Virgil say. He say it slowly back to me, like a lesson.

That's right. Then Parson put three fingers up. Reason one! he say. You know, Doddsbody, that to meet a friend on the street, and to pass him by like a stranger, is a sure and proven death-sign for that friend.

Virgil hush for a time. Well?

Everybody on the river know that, Parson, I tolt him. Right, he say. Reason two! You must also know, Doddsy, that two persons saying the same thing at the same time, in one another's company, means a violent ending for one of them.

Virgil open he mouth and close it.

Yes, Parson, I said. I know it. Then Parson tappit me on the collar. What are the tenants of this *house*, Charlie, but a group of friends living together as enemies, passing one another by without knowing it, and reciting the same words over and over, all of them together, like deaf-mutes at a mass?

Virgil eyes go slantish.

There you have it, Marse.

You ape our Parson beautifully, Dodds. You might have passed for a man of God yourself, just now. You sound positively schooled.

And me just a tom-fool nigger, I say.

Virgil blink and go flushed. I'm sorry, Dodds. I meant no harm by it. Go on.

Well—

Go on, Dodds! Tell me the rest.

All right, I say. That's all, Parson? I askit. That's all, Doddsbody, he say.

Virgil squint again. But—

But you still got one finger in the air, Parson, I tolt him. That were only the two reasons.

Bless you! What did he say to that?

I'll tell you. Parson look at he third finger like he never seen it yet. Oh! *That*, he say. That's just my lumbago, Charlie boy.

Virgil face turn to mush. That's all? That's everything? That's all he said to you?

You know how Parson get, Virgil. When you try to press him.

Yes, say Virgil. Yes. I know.

We hush a spell, looking toward the river.

Dodds, he mumble.

Present!

Has he mentioned Canaan's tongue to you?

Tongue of which?

Never mind, Virgil say. He take a breath.

Right, I say. Well. If you allow, Marse Virgil, they a power of work—

What about this, then? he say. He pull out a paper and fuss it open and hold it under my nose like a kerchief. Have you come across this anywhere? This symbol?

I give the paper a turn. I knew what it was before I seen it. I tip my head at him and grin. Sure, Marse Virgil. I come across it once.

You have? Then—

That the Victoria diamint! I know that much. They got a paste of it in Memphis. I seen it in a show.

Taken Prisoner.

HE'S THERE BELOW MY WINDOW, Clementine says. Virgil is. Walking up and down.

Not too proud to look up and see me—: afraid to. Since he caught me outside the parlor door and I told him what I know he's kept well clear of me. Clear of me but not of the thought of me, not of the part of him that thinks about me six times every hour, which is why he's there. There below my window, not once looking up. Trusting that *I'm* looking down at *him*.

Which I am. I'm watching him, bored to death and thoughtless, in this raggedy old shift that I thought would keep trouble off me, but hasn't trouble risen up just the same. The very same as always.

It has. I might be wearing the clothes I was birthed in for all the peace I've gotten in this house.

He moves hunched and buckled, an old habit. To keep that witchy eye of his from passers-by. There's nobody going to pass him on that old lawn full of blight but old customs die hard, as they say. He's looked people in the face no more than ten times in his life. Poor sly Virgil. Six of those times it was me.

I wonder whose death he's chewing over presently. I wonder if it's mine.

Something's eating at his brain, some puzzle—: his lips are working as they do. Puzzling out his next one. His face is turned away from me but I can guess his look. I saw him digging with Dodds in back of the tobacco-house.

Would Virgil do me under? He would if he was clever. I want him up here suddenly—: up beside me on the bed. I'd call him up here, but. I turn and go back to the pallet.

"He still out there?" the boy says, lolling on his belly. His backside is as perfect laid across the quilt-work as a rooster's tail-feathers laid across a puddle of shit. He sighs. "Why won't that wall-eyed jackass look up?"

I press a finger to his shoulder. "I don't think it was Virgil sent Kennedy out to shoot you, Oliver."

The boy gives a laugh. "You've sure got a power of opinions."

"I know him, that's all. He's never messed with Kennedy before."

The boy is at the window now. Buck-naked, black against the light, waiting for Virgil to look up.

"Why won't he look up?" he says.

The spite he nurses in his heart for Virgil waxes by the hour. He can't think of Kennedy without thinking of Virgil giving him the order. And he thinks of Kennedy with every breath he pulls.

"Come away from the window, Oliver," I say.

He grins. "But you just got yourself presentable."

"Come on over here."

But he doesn't come. He wants Virgil to see him bare-arsed in the window. He fancies that would give him satisfaction.

"You don't know Virgil Ball," I say. "You *think* you do."

"He's proud," the boy says.

"Not the way you are, Oliver. Not the kind to look my lover in the face. Not the kind to come up here, kick the door open, and spit in your pretty eye." I smile at him. "Which is just what you deserve."

"And what do *you* deserve, Miss Gilchrist?" says the boy. He gathers up his clothes. "What, all things considered, should your own penance be?"

"Go play Indian with your Yankees," I say.

He buttons up his shirt. "You're a fine woman yet," he says. He says it grudgingly.

"And what are *you*, Mr. Delamare?" I say. "Are you half what you pretend? Can you get me out of this smoke-house?"

He laughs—he laughs at this!—and shakes his head. "There's men at every cross-roads, ma'am. We'd not make it half a mile."

"I'll get eaten if I stay," I say.

"You might," the boy agrees.

"I can't recollect why we came to this place," I whisper. "Do you remember why?"

"He told us to," the boy says. Referring to the R——.

"He must have wanted us to get to know each other better," I say, and give a laugh.

The boy steps into his boots. "He wanted us to get together in a skillet and fry in it."

"Wouldn't he be pleased," I say.

"At least we've got each other," the boy says. "You and I."

My face is turned into the blanket. The look on it wouldn't suit the boy's notion of himself half a grain.

"You've got a fine back-side," he says.

The boy has no idea what I keep him for, and that's what pleases me. What comfort I scratch together each day comes from that one thing. Pennies scavenged in a field. It's a comfort, God knows, that ignorance of his. And only a young man can give to you.

"Well—," he says after a time.

I roll onto my back. He has on his derby now, and his ivory smoking-jacket. He sighs and ruffles out his feathers.

"I've a hard time thinking—," he says. "I've a hard time thinking that the R—— planned for me to end up like your friend Goodie Harvey, packed under the clay. Or like Virgil Ball, either."

"Oh! You'll end up differently from those two, Oliver."

He squints down at me. "Different how?"

"Go play Indian," I say. "Go on!"

He says nothing, does nothing. I feel his dark eyes picking into me.

"You know what I call you to myself?" I say, for no other reason but to get him gone.

"What?"

"I call you 'the boy.'"

That stops him quick. "Not *your* boy," he spits out. "Not yours, you three-penny flop! Not yet."

The door bangs shut behind him then, and I can take a breath.

NOW THIS ERROR is tucked in with the rest—: all the wide yellow rest of them, so many that the room is bloated up, hard and shiny and tight, like the stomach of a cow. And yet each mistake, taken in the hand, is no greater than a pea.

When I'm sure the boy is gone I go quietly to the window. Virgil is nowhere to be seen. I take a breath. The window has two loose panes, diamond-cut and beveled, the size of my palm exactly. I tip them out with my thumb and the air comes hissing in like nothing. I press my face against the glass. The air gets shriller in my ears. Shriller fiercer colder.

This is how I talk with the R——.

The air comes all in a single sucking. There is no relief from it. When every other sound is swallowed I can begin to ask my questions.

"Is it you, my love?" I ask.

SSSSSSSSSSSSSSSSSSS, the sucking answers.

"Who will it be?" I ask. "Who will it be next?"

It answers quick and spiteful and I know it won't be me.

"What's Virgil's scheme?" I ask. "What's Parson's?" But the sucking has stopped already. A noise from the hall has frightened it. The R—— is gone as quickly as he came.

The noise from the hall reels clumsily about the landing. It comes up in bursts and crashes from the entry-way downstairs. I figure it out in pieces—: scuffling, curses, the voices of three men. One of the voices, high-pitched and coarse, is a new one to this house. I walk to the landing bare-footed and numb.

I'm just at the banister when Virgil appears below me. "Where'd you catch him?" he says to somebody—: Kennedy or the Colonel. His face is red and fretful.

An answer comes. He bobs his head. "There'll be others," he says. "Others behind him—: a whole company, most likely."

Then he's gone under the landing.

I pinch my cheeks to redden them, arrange my hair, and tip-toe lightly down. To the parlor, as usual. Always the parlor. But this time the door has been left open wide.

Let there be others, I think. Let them come and catch us, Virgil. We'll be gone from here then, gone away from this house, and there'll be an end to things. I have no fear of that. The R—— will find me wheresoever I get sent. If the soldiers come I'll bring each of them a cup of cold well-water and kiss them on the lips. Let them come all at once, a power of them, a flood—; let their fury be swift and holy.

Virgil is afraid, of course. But Virgil is an empty bottle.

The first of them I see is Oliver, hanging back inside the door the way men do when they're not needed. He doesn't look at me. In the room are the Colonel and Virgil and Kennedy. And a man in a gravel-colored coat.

"Now!" says the Colonel.

The man in the coat is sitting on the settee the Colonel usually favors. The Colonel is sitting on a busted stool.

"Now, sir! I trust that you are comfortable—"

"Who in Sam Hell are you people?" the man yells. "What you fooling with me for?"

Kennedy scratches at his face. "You was puh!—puh!—*poaching* on this land."

"Poaching hell," the man says. "Ain't nobody cautioned you there's a war on?"

"Yes, young man. We have all of us been cautioned," the Colonel says. "I served in the army myself. We appreciate about the war."

The man looks down at nothing. "Which army you serve in?" he mutters. "Ours or theirn?"

"The army," the Colonel answers. "Back when there wasn't but one. I served under General Sterling Price."

"Price," says the man. "What you messing in Confederate business for, then, uncle?"

"This here is private puh!—puh!—*parpetty*, corn-pone," Kennedy says in a friendly way. "You mistook yourself if you thought of it as otherwise. You must of missed the postings on the trees that said 'Corn Pone Disinvited.' You must of been looking down the fly-hole of your puh!—puh!—puh!—"

"Mr. Kennedy!" the Colonel barks out. "The man before you is a sergeant in the Confederate Army. As such he is doing his fighting best to preserve the prerogatives of our Trade—"

"What damn trade?" the man says, looking round.

"What's your name, corn-pone?" Kennedy says.

The man makes a face at him. "Ain't sayin'."

"I apologize for this gentleman's rudeness to you, son," the Colonel says. "I profoundly regret it. I would, however, counsel you to answer him in full."

The man curses at them both—: queer, butternut-sounding curses I've never heard the like of. Now he sees Virgil tucked away in the corner. Virgil smiles and waves hello.

"Get him talking, Kennedy," Virgil says.

Kennedy looks at Virgil and lifts his eye-brows. "Right! I'll just go and fetch my works," he says. He goes off happy as an eel.

"There's no cause to set up walls between us, Sergeant," the Colonel says. "We are in no way your natural enemies—"

"Ain't *nothing* natural about you, far as I can tell," the man mutters.

I laugh at this—; I can't help it. The man looks at me. He shakes his head once, then again, as if to clear it. Then he looks past me at Oliver.

"You! Boy!" the man calls out. "Maybe you can explain to your masters here. I'm a representative of the Twenty-seventh Tennessee and Mississippi—"

Out in the corridor Kennedy sniggers. Oliver makes a little sound. An instant later he's crouched low beside the man with his knuckles twitching on the floor.

"I'll explain something to you, friend," he says. "We here are the gang off of Island 37. And you're going to spend the rest of the war at the bottom of a barrel."

The man's eyes go round and starting and I'd be telling a lie to say it didn't tickle me to see it. "*Murel's* gang," he stammers.

"Just tell us your name and placement, Sergeant," the Colonel says softly.

The man looks round the parlor, blinking. Then he breaks into a buck-toothed grin.

"Ha, ha!" he says.

"You going to tell us?" says Oliver, rolling back his sleeves. But the mention of the gang has struck the man right dumb. He googles all around him like a fish.

Kennedy comes back now, cradling a satchel. It clanks and rattles as though it were full of cutlery. "Ain't he talking yet?" he says. He says it like a hosanna.

The man's face goes soft. "Eukah David Foster," he says. His eyes go to Virgil. "You the chief? I thought Murel was a old midget."

Virgil's mouth opens.

Kennedy shows his teeth. "Shall I start in?"

"Let's have your company and regiment, Foster," Virgil says. "Let's have it quick."

"Sartoris Company," Foster says. He rubs his nose between his fingers. "No regiment to speak of. We just barn-burners now. Lines done moved to Tennessee."

"Tennessee, eh?" the Colonel says. "What's the latest?"

Oliver jerks his chin at Foster. "You won't get much out of this one, Colonel. He's one of those that fell through the cracks and liked it."

"That's true enough, I reckon," Foster says. He grins. "That what you all hoping to do?"

No-one says anything to that.

"How many of you buh!—buh!—barn-burners you say there was?" Kennedy says, coming up to the settee.

Foster looks down at the satchel. "Twenty-eight," he mumbles.

"They cuh!—cuh!—*coming* up behind?"

Foster shakes his head. "No, sir. It's only me."

Kennedy looks at Virgil. Virgil looks at the Colonel. All of us know Foster won't be leaving on his feet.

"Where'd you find him?" the Colonel asks Kennedy.

"This side of the shanty-town," Kennedy says. "But only just." He sets the satchel down. "Round where Virgil and his muh!—muh!—mulatto picked off that scout."

"That was past the shanty-town," Virgil says.

"Were that a few day back? That were our boys, all right," Foster says. "Didn't none of us cross that creek till yesterday, account of whether it be Yankees."

"Those were *Union* men," Oliver says loudly.

Foster shows us his buck-teeth. "Nope. Those boys were ourn."

The Colonel looks pained. "What can you tell us, Sergeant, about the Union strength up and down the river?"

"Take what you see and reckon it times four," Foster says. He spreads his arms wide. "They more Yankees in the woods than maggots in a pie. Mostly down at Wayte's River, account of the junction there." He sticks his chin out. "That why we come down here—: that rail-way line. We mean to bust it."

"Jesus Muh!—Muh!—*Mary*," Kennedy groans.

Virgil shakes his head. He turns his face toward mine and I see the worry on it plain as cake. Wayte's River Junction is less than three miles from this house.

"Why hit the rail line here, of all places?" the Colonel says.

Foster shrugs. "Hit's the only one we can *get* at, uncle."

"A peach, this Fuh!—Fuh!—*Foster!*" Kennedy mutters.

Virgil looks hard at Foster. "How do you boys manage to keep clear, with all those Federals in the woods?"

Foster shrugs again. "They plenty of Yankees hereabouts. That's all I can tell you."

"I think you can tell us more than that," says Virgil. "A very great deal more."

Foster looks ruffled. "Look here, now. If you all are really part of Thaddeus Murel's—"

"*Ssshh!*" says Oliver. Kennedy puts his hands over his ears.

"We don't speak that name aloud, Sergeant," the Colonel whispers.

Foster blinks at him. "Why the hell not?"

"Superstition, child—; no more than that," Parson says, gliding into the room like a dress-maker's bust on wheels.

Foster stops and gapes. He makes a creaking sound behind his teeth. "Who is *that*?" he says in a small blanched voice.

Parson looks from one of us to the next. We stare down at the floor.

"Why did no-one wake me?" Parson says.

The Colonel squirms a little. "I sent Dodds up to fetch you, Parson. Heaven knows where that blasted nigger—"

"So you've poached yourselves a Yankee," Parson says, cutting him short. "And now you're having trouble with him."

"No, no, Parson!" the Colonel says. "This man is a member of the Sartoris Company— : a Dixie man. One of our own. He tells me—"

"Oh! I think I'd know a Yankee," Parson says. He winks at Foster. "If the wind was blowing right."

Foster's face goes softer still.

Nobody says anything for a good long while.

"Well, dip me in bread-crumbs!" Kennedy says at last, throwing the satchel open with a laugh.

"Why not leave Mr. Foster in my care, gentlemen?" Parson says.

The Colonel shakes his head at this but no-one minds him. Kennedy stops short, looks down at his works, and spits.

"Parson!" the Colonel says. "Please, Parson. This—this boy—"

"Shut your mouth, Colonel," Parson says. The Colonel shuts it.

"Leave us for a bit," Parson says, smiling at Foster. "All of you."

Kennedy gets to his feet and curses each of us and walks out with his bag of tricks wide open in the middle of the floor. Oliver trails out after him. The Colonel looks so old and dried-up on his stool that I expect him to blow away like dandelion-seed. He looks at Parson, then at Foster. He bows his head and shuts his eyes.

Parson rolls up to the settee. The hem of his skirt scrapes stiff as a tea-cup across the parquet. He lays a hand on the Colonel's shoulder as he passes. "Why didn't you wake me, Erratus?"

"Let me stay with this boy," the Colonel says. "Let me stay with you and this boy, Parson." His voice is as thin as an onion-skin.

Virgil helps the Colonel to his feet. "Come along, old smoke," he says. "This boy's no boy of yours."

"Let the old donkey stay," Foster says. "I don't mind." His up-country drawl has been neatly put aside.

Parson lifts his skirts like a lady climbing into a coach and sets himself down next to Foster. Foster's nape bunches up like a kitten's.

I hang back in the room a moment, watching him. If he's a spy, then he must know something about us already. And if he knows something about us already, then he must be wishing to saints above that Parson hadn't woken from his nap.

I turn to leave. "Miss!" Foster calls out. "Would you be so kind as to get me a cup of water from that pail in the kitchen?"

I stop and squint at him. The air in the parlor is close and still. "When did you happen to be in the kitchen, Mr. Foster?" I say.

"Get me some god-damned *water*," Foster squeaks. His face is grayer than his coat. I smile. The wish of a man who expects the life to be sucked out of him drop by drop for a cup of water seems a funny one to me.

"Go on, Miss Gilchrist," Parson says. "Get our prisoner his drink." Parson has always preferred a drop of water in his soup.

I'm away perhaps two minutes. When I come back they're both exactly as they were. Not a word has passed between them, by the look of it. Dew has begun to form on Foster's temples. I set the jar of water at his feet. He takes no notice. Parson is looking up at the ceiling like a spinster thinking of a dirty story.

"By-the-bye, Miss Gilchrist," he says. "Have you seen little Asa Trist?"

I think a moment. "This morning I did, by the orchard fence. Jabbering away at Virgil."

His eyes come down at once. "Talking to Virgil?" he says.

I nod. "It looked to be quite an epic."

His face gives a flutter. "How do you mean, 'an epic'?"

"Just that," I say. "There looked to be no end of poetry in it."

Parson says nothing.

"I was watching from my window," I say. "I couldn't hear them, Parson."

"From your window. Yes. I have no doubt that you were." Parson looks me over. "But then, you hear all sorts of things through that window of yours—; don't you, Miss Gilchrist."

I keep my face shut to him. "Have you and Asa had a fight?"

Parson sits back with a sigh. "You might say that we've had a parting of the waters," he says.

"A religious matter, was it?"

His eyes go cloudy. "You might call it that."

Foster lets out a choked-sounding breath and reaches for the jar. He moves his arms as though they were borrowed from some other. He takes hold of the jar and lifts it to his mouth. He hasn't once looked at Parson or at me.

"I've always considered you and Asa birds of a feather," I say to Parson. "You both make me want to run screaming for the hills."

"Asa Trist is a bird," Foster announces, setting down the jar.

It takes me a moment to recover my voice. "What did you say, Mr. Foster?"

Foster's mouth shuts. His face is like the weather-side of an old frame house.

Parson gathers up the hem of his gown and studies it. He moves his thumb back and forth across a stain. He purses his lips. "Go on, Mr. Foster," he says.

"Asa Trist is a bird," Foster says again. His voice is as unlike the voice that asked me to fetch the water as my own voice is to Parson's.

"A plucked pigeon," Foster says. "A fallen snipe."

I turn stone-faced to Parson. "I've seen this trick before," I say. "It holds no charm for me." But even as I say so a faintness gathers against my skin and I understand he'll do exactly what he likes. He'll do exactly what he likes with me.

Parson sits forward with a yawn. Foster crumples like a cast-off glove.

"Let's chat a bit, Clementine," he says. He pats the empty stool beside him

From Parson's Day-Book.

This in the language of Christ's murderers is _hokmah nistarah_, the clandestine wisdom, passed from one generation to the next since the death of Abraham, to whom it was revealed by G*d. The sin which sequesters us from His boundaryless glory is not that of vice, but of ignorance. Our eyes were given us to see.

The link between G*d and the world is indirect. G*d is a pier-glass from which pours forth a bountiful light. The light is reflected in a second glass, from which it passes to a third, a fourth, and so on until the mortal coil is reached. With each reflection the light loses something of its strength, till at last it falls dimly onto the floor of this our earth, finite and desecrated, that we may look upon ourselves and weep.

At the beginning all that existed was G*d and nothing. G*d sent out into the nothing an emanation of Itself, and from this came a great tumult of emanations, forming a cradle for the emptiness, a quickening grid of light. The ten emanations are called the _sephiroth_, and their splendid lights, properly read, yield up the most secret name of G*d. The universe that grew up in this cradle was made out of G*d, and the _sephiroth_ are no less than the ten facets of Its nature. They are the path by which the soul journeys downward to the world at birth, and the points by which it navigates its return to Heaven.

Death, however, is not a necessary precondition to this journey. The spirit can climb the ladder of the _sephiroth_ while yet in the flesh, and likewise can a man descend the ladder a second time and make himself as a god on earth. Whosoever has ears to hear, let him hear, etc.

Virgil Ball has ears.

Endurance.

I WAS BORN WHITE, Asa says. Shall I tell it?

Under oath, Asa Trist, genuine land-owner's son, learned to brake, cut, card, spin flax, all genuine farming work well learned, mashing potatoes for the horses, pigs, well-watering and slopping cows, milking cows, pulling the legs at birthing, pulling calves, milking goats, separating milk from cream, setting milk to stand in a cool, dry place, making white-curd cheese from butter-milk, from bitches'-milk, making cheese, making a good side of smooth, oval cheese, good God, dousing it with cream, turning over, standing straight, lying bent, for hours *good God* learning words, boiling sugar-beet, then pressing, boiling the juice, preparing for the making of the sweet sugar-beet syrup, giving it out on Sundays to the niggers, letting twenty niggers in to wash, taking twenty cuts, smelling the butter off the skin, early hot milk skimmed, little tear-drops, big pot full of boiled potatoes, watching father hand out the plates, watching mother, one plate sugar-beet syrup, one plate white-curd cheese, one plate bread, planting rice, laying it out in neat white lines on the ground, cutting up the meat, hunks of ham or fat drippings or scrapple, greetings to all honorable childs of niggers

I SEE VIRGIL ALONE, by the orchard fence. Write my biography, Virgil! I call out to him. And I'll write one for you.

Morning, Asa, Virgil says. Careful, now. Clem is watching us from her cat-seat.

Clementine talks with the Redeemer that way, Virgil.

I know.

Listen to me, Virgil. Please. The Redeemer and I share the same idea.

Virgil smiles. What idea is that, Asa?

To make me sick, I answer. That I might learn endurance.

ONE WHIP LAID LENGTH-WISE IN A LINE, front steps of the mansion to the old poplar tree, two whips end-to-end, back porch to the cabins, four whips configured into a diamond, eighteen feet by eighteen feet by eighteen, one thousand diamonds into a net, neighbors and family and children, nets to catch stray birds, strung out across the water, niggers dressed in net-skirts, Heaven a high, cold house with nets strung across the windows, outside the neighbors, the friends, the chattering family, eighteen whips each eighteen feet laid out in a chain, a stable full of horses, hat-box full of bottles, God laughs—Asa!

Then forgives.

THE LIMBS OF THE FRUIT TREES along the fence look like arms and legs. Virgil is offering me a choice—: to tell him the history of my greatest exploits, or to die.

That hat-box you had in Memphis, Asa. He looks me in the face. Asa!

Yes?

That black box. Do you recollect it?

Parson has it, I say, blinking.

Virgil frowns. Parson.

I feel much better now, Virgil. Pray let's make use of it. There's very little time.

First tell me about the hat-box.

I lift my shoulders. Samples. Cuts. A project.

He looks at me. Research?

Yes. That.

What would Parson want with it?

Parson is a castrato! I snicker. A singer in the choir.

Virgil looks me in the eye. Were *all* the cuts from niggers?

No sir. Some were from dirty old white men.

PLACED IN SOLUTION of carbon disulfide sample desiccates, reduces, color of wood-smoke, color of butter, scars, gouges, incision-marks fatten and blister, cat-fish gathered up in nets, family property,

Federal state and district, oil, coal and natural gas, stately ladies of New Orleans tilt and squat over cast-iron pails, quadrilles, quarantine, quadroons, Creole bandy-legs, red-bones, over the cast-iron fathers of New Orleans. Say, Virgil—:

THEY ALL LOOK THE SAME, you see. In that solution.

Virgil is quiet. They all look like nigger skins.

I say nothing, but my heart is flying toward him—: Yes.

Virgil rubs his face. You might be onto something there, Asa, he says. Laughing as he says it in his heart.

Yes.

I still don't see what Parson would want that hat-box for.

Shall I tell him? *He has three locks of your hair*, Virgil. And of mine.

Virgil stops. Takes hold of the fence-rail with both his hands. Whitens. You don't mean. You don't mean to say, those bottles—

I lift a trouser-leg, disclosing a bright rectilinear scar.

He pants. You buggered fool, Asa. Who else did you cut?

Thaddeus Morelle, a lock of hair. Goodman Harvey—generous, obliging—a snippet of hide. Virgil Ball—

Virgil heaves me back against the fence. You never cut into *me*, you son-of-a-bitch. You never—with your limp white lady-hands. You never did.

Allow me to write a brief chapter, Virgil. *Virgil*—:

VIRGIL'S WHITE ARM UNCOILS. I fall sweetly to earth. I wanted to reconcile opposites, Virgil. Occult knowledge and science, black hide and white hide, the healthy and the sick—

By God, Asa. You'd better tell me something I want to listen to.

He keeps it up in his attic, I say.

What?

The box. The cuttings. Everything I took. I look up at Virgil. And I'll tell you something more.

Virgil turns and starts toward the house. If you're only spinning thread, you moon-faced bastard, on my mother's grave, I'll—

Virgil! I moon-face at him. Stop a moment further, Virgil! There's more to tell.

I've heard enough, Asa. You can dribble the rest out later.

Later is an open grave, but Virgil cannot know this.

ASA TRIST, GENTLE-FARMER'S SON, spit on at birth, mother-coddled, good worker, learned well the following—: the Hand of Glory. Cut a hand from a runaway and wrap it in a winding-sheet. Press it thoroughly to drain the fluid from it. The blood, the water, the lymph. Keep it for a week in an earthen jar mixed with pepper and salt-peter under the ground. Dry it in the heat of the sun or if the sun is not ample in a cotton-wood-fed furnace. The fat which runneth from the hand is mixed with wax to make a candle. Said candle is then put into the hand's own fingers. Light from said candle will cure any spell of whiteness. Light from said candle will bring horrors to a child.

MY FATHER WAS WELL-KNOWN TO THE REDEEMER, Virgil, as you know.

Virgil looks back at the house. I know it.

You walk the grounds each day, with Delamare. The same rounds each day, *exactly*. Why?

For Christ's sake, Asa—

EVERY day, I say again. I close my eyes. You've never noticed it?

He curses. What, Asa? What should I notice?

I raise my left hand, holding up three fingers. Thaddeus Morelle, at the privy. Goodman Harvey, beside the stables. Now there's a hole by the tobacco-shed.

Virgil blinks twice. I know, he says. I've seen it.

Dodds dug it. Parson helped him.

Stone-faced now. Not running up the hill. Listening to me. And?

Two holes, connected, make a line. I work my mouth into a grin. Three holes, now. Three holes make a figure.

That's right, Asa. For the birds to look at.

An angel would see it, I say. Looking down from on high. I take in a breath. Or even from the attic.

His eyes get rounder. He fashions the word 'attic' with his lips.

I killed my mother when I was born, Virgil! And my father was born blue-blooded out of me.

He's off and running now, stumbling and cursing. Off toward the house.

Good-bye, Virgil. Good-bye, house!

Take a pencil with you, Virgil! I shout after him. Make a sketch!

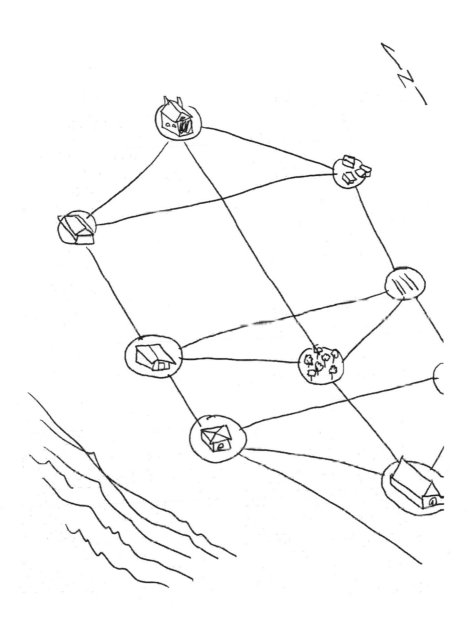

From Parson's Day-Book.

I n using hair or other parts of the body, it is essential to make sure they come from the correct person, as is suggested by the cautionary tale of John Fian, school-master of Saltpans in Midlothian, which is told in a pamphlet of 1591, "News from Scotland."

Fian conceived a passion for the older sister of one his pupils and persuaded the little boy to bring him one of her pubic hairs. When the boy tried to take these hairs from the sleeping girl, she awoke and cried out. Their mother came and, discovering what had happened, took three hairs from the udders of a young heifer and gave them to the boy, who passed them on to Fian. Fian "wrought his art upon them" and in a little while the heifer came to him, "leaping and dancing upon him," and pursued him everywhere, "to the great admiration of all the townspeople of Saltpans."

Last Conference.

Colonel—*You asked to see me, Virgil?*

Virgil—*I've been to the top of the house, Colonel. To the attic.*

Colonel *(PAUSE)—You've been to the attic.*

Virgil—*That's right, Colonel. I made a sketch.*

Colonel—*Hold on a bit, Virgil. You're carrying on like poor Asa, bless him. Sit down a moment and catch your air.*

Virgil *(SHAKES HEAD)—You've been keeping clear of the real business all this time. I know that now—; and I don't blame you for it. But take a look at this map of the grounds I've drawn. It just might give you pause.*

Colonel—*I can't think what you're getting at. The Redeemer himself appointed me in charge of—in head of—you know as well as I—*

Virgil—*What the Hell have you been interviewing us for?*

Colonel *(INAUDIBLE)*

Virgil—*What was that, you old tippler? What was that?*

Colonel—*I—I. Yes. (PAUSE)—He told me to.*

Virgil—*Parson?*

Colonel *(QUIETLY)—Please to leave now, Virgil. Please to let me be.*

Virgil—*You'll damn well look at this sketch I've drawn. (PAUSE)—And I've got something else to show you. (PULLS BOTTLE OUT OF COAT POCKET)*

Colonel—*What's that now, Virgil? (SMILES)—A bottle of perfume?*

Virgil—*Your name is on it, Colonel. There. Just below the stopper.*

Colonel *(PAUSE)—What is it, then? Something pickled—?*

Virgil—*Have you been letting them take the knife to you, you old imbecile?*

Colonel *(INAUDIBLE)—Ah—aah—*

Virgil—*Here! Take a closer look. (SHAKES BOTTLE)*

Colonel—*What is it? Can you tell me? For mercy's sake—*

VIRGIL—*I wouldn't venture more than a guess. It looks to me like the bottom of an ear.*

COLONEL—*Parson never touched me, Virgil! Never!*

VIRGIL—*Lean forward, grand-dad. Lift your hair a bit.*

COLONEL—*Virgil—I'm telling you—*

VIRGIL—*Jesus!*

COLONEL—*Yes. All right. (PAUSE)—Yes.*

(SILENCE)

COLONEL—*What has he got up there, Virgil? Have you seen it?*

VIRGIL—*Enough bottles to open an apothecary. Three or more from each of us. Mine were empty. Yours, on the other hand, were full.*

COLONEL—*It was Asa I let cut me. The bottles were his. (PAUSE)—He's my god-son, after all. I told old Sam Trist that I'd mind him. That I'd see—that I'd see to his education—*

VIRGIL—*I'd say he's taken his degree.*

COLONEL—*You have no idea what that child has suffered, Virgil! None! Even I don't know the half of it. I mean, little Asa—his father, Virgil— you have no idea—*

VIRGIL—*Not yet, Colonel. But I'm learning quick.*

COLONEL—*What do you mean?*

VIRGIL—*There's but one window in that attic. About eye-level to a boy of six.*

COLONEL (PAUSE)—*Yes. The window. Asa told me once. (PAUSE)—He used to go up there to hide.*

VIRGIL—*Have you ever looked out of it?*

COLONEL—*Why the devil should I? I'd barely make the steps in my condition. I shouldn't wonder if I had a pleurism—*

VIRGIL—*Morelle's put us on a grid, Colonel. He's made a trellis out of us for his clambering spirit. Look at this drawing!*

COLONEL—*Give it here. (PAUSE)—Well, Virgil. I see you've sketched the grounds.*

VIRGIL—*It's the Ladder, Colonel. Look at it carefully.*

COLONEL (PAUSE)—*The which?*

VIRGIL—*I've made marks where Morelle is buried, and where Harvey is. And here, where another hole's been dug—: you see? Look at the play of paths between the buildings. Morelle is Malkuth, the top of the ladder. Harvey is Yesod, just below. The hole behind the tobacco-house is Hod. Do you see it yet? Each circle, each building is placed exactly at a sephira, a stop on the path to earth from heaven. Think of it! (PAUSE)—The next hole will be behind the smoke-house.*

COLONEL (PAUSE)—*Perhaps you'd best sit down a moment, Virgil. Take a spot of rest*—

VIRGIL—*What! You mean you actually don't see it?*

COLONEL—*You—you're not making any* sense, *Virgil. What you've drawn is a map of the grounds.*

VIRGIL (MUMBLING)—*The signs were all around me, of course, but I lacked the eyes to see them. It took poor cracked Asa to enlighten me. The grounds are a playing field, a grid, a game of Chinese marbles—; and our cadavers are the pieces. (PAUSE)—The Redeemer's not dead, Colonel. Not in any sense that matters. He'll be back with us directly.*

COLONEL (LOUDLY)—*KENNEDY!*

VIRGIL—*Don't call Kennedy in here, damn you! Just have a look again—here, at the bottom corner*—

COLONEL—*I've looked at it already, Virgil. I see nothing but the grounds. (CLEARS THROAT)—I'll have Parson look it over, if you like.*

VIRGIL (QUIETLY)—*You'll have—you'll have Parson*—

(ENTER KENNEDY)

COLONEL—*There you are, Mr. Kennedy! Please accompany Virgil to his room.*

VIRGIL (REACHING INTO COAT)—*Just you try it, Sluts.*

COLONEL—*There's no call for that, Virgil. Put the pistol by!*

VIRGIL—*Back away from me! (SOFTLY)—You've made an error, Colonel. A right grievous one.*

(EXIT VIRGIL)

COLONEL (PAUSE)—*Well, Mr. Kennedy. (SIGHS)—I'm glad I had you by.*

KENNEDY—*It do seem propitious.*

COLONEL—*What do you make of this whole circus—Virgil and the rest?*

KENNEDY—*Wouldn't cuh!—cuh!—care to hazard, Colonel. (PAUSE)—I could of warned him off that attic, though.*

COLONEL—*You—you've been* there? *To the attic?*

KENNEDY—*Aye.*

COLONEL (QUIETLY)—*When?*

KENNEDY (SHRUGS SHOULDERS)—*Some while back.*

COLONEL—*You saw—all of it, did you? You saw the bottles?*

KENNEDY—*That's why I gone up, grand-dad. To liberate my own. (SMILES)—To Abolitionize 'em.*

COLONEL—*You believe in Parson's pocus, then.*

KENNEDY (COUGHS)—*Superstitious, aren't I.*

(SILENCE)

KENNEDY—*Colonel? Hey?*

COLONEL *(PAUSE)*—*It's so hard to follow, Kennedy—it's so hard to determine who's—dependable—*

KENNEDY—*You can always depend on old Stuts Kennedy, guh!—guh!—grand-paps. You know that much.*

COLONEL—*Thank you, Kennedy. (PAUSE)—I feel worn through, just at present. (PAUSE)—Would you like to sit beside me for a spell?*

KENNEDY—*Be pleased to, Colonel. (SITS)*

COLONEL *(FAINTLY)*—*Asa. I'd—I'd like Asa to come and sit with me. I don't feel well at all. (PAUSE)—Could you fetch him?*

KENNEDY—*Not bloody likely.*

COLONEL—*Mr. Kennedy! I beg of you—*

KENNEDY—*I'd do it straight-away, Colonel, and warmest regards. But it's puh!—puh!—placed beyond my powers, I'm afraid.*

COLONEL *(PAUSE)*—*How do you mean—?*

KENNEDY—*Young Asa's dead as a Christmas goose. I saw him swinging in the orchard not ten minutes gone.*

COLONEL *(RISING)*—*Asa! Asa!*

KENNEDY—*Sit down, grandfather. You'll break your arse.*

Glory.

I AM SINGING IN A CHORUS, Asa says.

Golden and rosy is the castrato's chain that hangs from the masters of this world. If I had never dared to climb onto the stage I would not be singing in this choir of white-gold niggers to either side, this stage-set made of sun, this fire, this glow of flames, this house, this baking-oven. What I have not yet told—: *the nigger's skin is brown because he came too close to G*d.*

Bristly, bistly, silver-and-mossy hairs, glistening and wet, wet eyes, blinking eyes, sack-cloth dresses down about the ankles. Barefoot I stand and without shoes. G*d is passing out the water. It is hot in the oven. All of us waiting in a stinking line making religion. Their religion, religion of cabins and swamp-water and gibbering whispers. Worship of babies and the ovenly future, crossing the Jordan to the heavenly cities, babies sh*tting and weeping and fattening themselves on babies in the cities and my own Dolly who went down too soon under the great nigger-colored river. The brown tumbling-over river, the feeding river, the keel-boats, the working, the Trading, the gray and blue gun-boats tumbling up the river. The War.

G*d moves under it.

Barefoot I stand among them and without shoes. At last I have finished singing, mocked behind my coat, one thousand eight hundred and sixty-three times I sing—: Glory to my f*ther in the highest.

Good-will toward niggers, then pardoned.

V

GEBURAH (5th of the sephiroth; female) Which is the sphere of Mars, and the force appealed to in operations of hatred and destruction. It is the strict and severe authority of the mother, who disciplines and punishes the child. It lies behind all destructive energy, hate, rage, cruelty, war, havoc, retribution; Nature red in tooth and claw.

—Richard Cavendish

"We Are Building a Revolver."

HELL IS A WORD, says Clementine.

Imagine a place where your life's errors hold fast. Hold fast for you to fondle and examine them, then be examined in your turn. Hell is a word that all of us were raised on—; fed and fattened on, then fed back to as we grew. But Geburah Plantation is a place.

The R—— himself has shown me this. It is.

There's to be a marriage, Parson said. He told me on the settee, with the prisoner between us : Someone is to be married, Clementine. Married to the R——.

There will be an end to things that way, he said. The wedding itself will end things. He laughed. A wedding always does.

Today is the day after. Virgil calls on me at last. He finds me at the window as he did on that first day in Madame Lafargue's, with my arms stretched out toward the glass. The R—— is there too but Virgil doesn't see.

"Asa Trist is dead," he says.

"How?" I say. I turn away from the window. Back of my neck I can feel the R—— escaping.

"By hanging," he says. "We've just cut him down. And D'Ancourt's gone missing. Kennedy's searching the grounds."

He looks around him now and blinks.

"Clem," he says to me. "My life—"

Damn you, Virgil! I say. But not so loud that he can hear me. Damn you clear to hell.

It's then that I think—: Hell is a word. Geburah is a place.

"I know what's happening to us," Virgil says. He steps past me as if I were a coat-stand or a potted fern and sets himself down on the bed. He pulls a scrap of paper from his pocket. "Look here at this," he says.

I take the paper and look. "I see."

"You see it?" he says, disbelieving.

"I see the grounds—"

His voice goes sharp. "And the ladder of the spirit? The *sephiroth*, with the paths run between them?"

"Yes," I say. Virgil gapes and gawks at me. The R—— has explained it all but of course he cannot know this.

"D'Ancourt thought I'd gone crackers," he says, passing a hand over his eyes. "So did Kennedy." He lets out a breath. "So did I."

"What can it mean?" I ask.

He coughs. "Look here. Where we buried the R——. The old privy. I've marked it with an X. You see? And Harvey here." He snatches back the paper and runs his finger over it. "Asa will get put here, in Dodds' newest hole. That makes three." He nods to himself. "Someone's following the path. It's all in order."

"The path?" I say.

His head bobs like a pigeon's. "The path from the grave up to heaven," he says. "The ladder of the spirit." He bites his lip. "Only he's traveling the path *in reverse.*"

"Who is?" I say, cursing him.

"The R——," he whispers.

I do my best to laugh. "Him?" I say. "Didn't you and Dodds stuff his body down the—"

"We did. I stabbed him through the neck and watched the blood run out till he was dead." He says this as though I were arguing with him. He shuts his eyes. "Then Dodds and I dug him under."

"In that case, he can't be traveling anywhere."

Virgil hushes.

"Can he, Virgil?" I say, taking the paper from his hands and crumpling it.

"Someone in the house is helping him," he says. "Parson, of course." He looks at me. "Parson and another."

"It's Dodds that buries the bodies," I say. "Not Parson."

"Parson tells him where." The old self-pity creeps into his voice. "But you think *I'm* the murderer, don't you. I'd forgotten."

"I know you didn't kill Harvey."

His brow goes up. "How so, Miss Gilchrist? Did your new *amour* tell you?"

At first I think he means the R—— and the breath catches in my throat. Then I see he only means the boy. I laugh dully. "My new *amour's* not one for talking," I reply.

"Ah," he says. He stares down at the floor. "I see."

"What do you mean to do about Parson?"

He brightens. He's been waiting for me to ask. "I brought down all the bottles with your name on them," he says. "From Parson's coop." He brings four cut-glass vials out of his pocket. "This one here has a lock of your hair in brine." He holds another up to the light, that I can see its yellowishness. "This is yours, too." He blushes.

"You're not the only one raiding my chamber-pot at night, I see."

"These last two have your new friend's name on them," he says, paying my joke no mind. He smiles pitifully. "Or is he your old friend by now?"

I sit down next to him. I run my hand lightly through his hair. "You must mean Oliver Delamare, the gentleman who lifts my skirts," I say.

He does not recoil at this but keeps himself quite still, letting my answer run the length of him. He bows his head that I might stroke it better.

"Until today I thought you wanted him because he was beautiful," he murmurs. "Or to cause me pain. Now I know better."

"What do you know?" I ask. My hand hovers at his neck. His nape is soft and pink, with blotches of red under the hair-line.

He holds up a bottle marked "Delamare." The milky liquor looks so odd inside the glass I can't imagine what it might be.

"Did Parson come to you with this?" he says. "Did he give it to you empty?"

"Yes," I say.

He's above me now, cradling the bottle in his palm. "When was that? After you'd taken your boy to bed the first time, or before?" His hand closes on the bottle. "Did you ask our good Parson what he wanted it for, Clem? Or could it be that you knew already?"

"I know all manner of things," I hiss. "I know more than you know with that fat white eye of yours. I know what Parson does upstairs and I know who's going to be next and I know how little meat-and-bones a man is made of. I learn from *listening*, Mr. Ball. I'm a right good listener. And what I've heard through these walls would turn your blood to vinegar."

"Tell me," he says.

I get to my feet before him. The R—— has explained that he must stay the night.

"I'd thought of this house as our penance," I say. "Worse than any other thing that could befall. I thought of us each as separate, each in a different cell, together in this house only to make each other suffer." I smile at him. "I was such a fool!"

I'm close to him now. I pull my arms out of my shift. "I've been listening, Aggie. Listening and thinking. I'm much better educated than I was before."

"It's true. We aren't separate," he says. His eyes fall to my belly. The bruise at his temple goes livid. "Not you, not me—"

"We weren't brought together as a punishment," I say. I shrug the shift from my shoulders. "The punishment happened by-the-bye. We weren't brought together for our *own* sakes at all—: do you see? We've been so *selfish*, Aggie, and so vain!"

Now the shift hangs from my hips like a bustle. The cloth is damp and patterned with the sweat of long-forgotten hours. Even this past hour, when the boy was beside me. Sunk away and gone.

"You've discovered it too," I whisper. "You went up and looked through Asa's little window. You saw how small we are. Didn't you?"

"Yes," he says. His voice goes tight. "I saw."

I close my mouth. It's done. I look up into his face and wait for him to have me. This time it will not destroy me, not make me into another, not split me into halves. The R——'s breath is full and warm inside of me and it will not subside. My body has no more substance than a cloud.

"We're pieces of pig-iron, Virgil. That's all we are. But each of us has a purpose and a shape." I guide his hand downwards. "If you put us together properly, we make a revolver."

"God, Clem!" he says and brings himself against me. His hand is still closed tightly around the bottle. His mouth opens and his lips push against my own with all the slowness I remember. I feel through his britches that he is ready and I open them at the buckle and bring out his prick and smell the readiness on it. I take it in my left hand at the root and slide my palm upwards. "Clem Clem Clem," he gasps and sinks white-faced to the bed. The memory of it is crashing over me now like a breaker at sea but it finds no spot on my smooth and weightless body to catch hold of. Still I feel that I am ready too and Virgil pulls aside the bustle and feels it on me and pulls me down. The smell of the boy is still in me and run through my skirts and stockings but. In another breath I am astride of him and his hope is up my belly looking to turn me outsides-in, looking for its twin where I've long sheltered it but it finds nothing—! Nothing there at all.

That twin is withered away and vanished. There is nothing in my belly but the R——.

"Oh!" says my mouth.

"Clem!" Virgil says, bucking under me. But Clem is a word.

His eyes fly open, then snap shut. His hand turns and unclenches like a flower.

"We are building a revolver, Virgil," I breathe into his ear.

"Yes," he says. "Yes!"

My right hand closes on the bottle.

"Oliver D. Lamar."

23 May 1863
Geburah Plantation

There are errors or (let us call them as the world calls them) sins of arrogance and pride that even I, wasting hourly as I am, will make no mention of in this accounting. Let that be the measure of how far into the well of hubris I have fallen: to give voice to the preening circus nigger I've become would plant me squarely in my grave. That will be my legacy to the world, and I won't recount it here. Here I will testify, as best I can in this language that has come to own me as a yeoman owns a sow, how I came to trade my existence for a cinder.

I dreamt of grand estates, and made my lodging in an outhouse. I dreamt of virtue, of genteel acts, and indentured myself to treachery. I dreamt of love and poetry, and gave my body to a hussy. First she took it grudgingly, then she took it slyly. She took it from me and she bottled it—a commodity like any other.

The progress of the "grippe" that has claimed me is so ambitious that I'm unable to rise unassisted from my bed, and this less than six hours after I was stricken. A system of welts, in pattern not unlike a skirt of lace, has risen from my ankles to my ribs—where these welts arise, I am a paralytic. That my sex has thus far been spared strikes me as poetic. No better emblem to a history of my follies could have been contrived.

I was born in Vidalia, Louisiana to a woman known as Margaret—; my father was a well-heeled sugar-man from New Orleans. Margaret was too old to bear children and died soon after my début. This I know from the wifey, one Koko Hewitt, who had care of me for a time. Koko herself entertained her share of callers (Mr. Hewitt having died in the Mexican War, leaving her his debts) and as soon as I could button my pants I was hired out to all and sundry.

I was a poor worker, heavy-limbed and listless, but folk approved of me—: I was pleasing to look at, and docile, and in time I discovered this was all it took. I became popular in town, particularly among charitably minded ladies. They took to me with what can only be described as a passion, and often fought amongst themselves for the privilege of putting their sympathies on show—; by the age of eight I was an accomplished gigolo.

It took Mrs. Anne Juvais Bradford, however—of Waterproof, Louisiana—to turn me into a full and able whore.

At twelve I was hired out to "Mother Anne," as Mrs. Bradford chose to be called—; she and her husband, a porridge-faced consumptive who rarely left his bed, ran a profitable still a half-day's passage up the river. Koko referred to this transaction as my "adoption," by which I understood that I was never to return. She wept great oily tears at our separation, the fee for which was seventy dollars in silver. Seventy bits was quite a sum at that time, easily twice my worth. I assumed that Mother Anne was buying herself a worker—; she herself had other notions. Koko couldn't have cared less. We had little Christian sentiment for one another.

The first time Mother Anne saw me she'd caught hold of me by my britches. It was in Koko's shabby parlor, late on a Sunday afternoon—; I'd just come in bare-foot from the street. "You're good and pale, for a half-and-half," Anne had said. "What are you made of, little captain? Quadroon? Octaroon?"

I'd answered matter-of-factly that my father was a Dumaine Street gentleman, white as a winter lily.

"Sure of that, are you?" she'd said, grinning down at me. Her grip, though temperate, was tenacious as a man's.

I'd nodded sullenly. Her hand had remained curled round my belt-buckle. "My mama were black as par-boiled pitch," I'd said. "That's how I'm sure."

Her grin had widened. "You don't care much for your mama's sort, I see."

"I'd like to burn her clean of me with fire."

Her eyes had opened wide at this. "What's your name, little nigger-hater?"

"Oliver D. Lamar," I'd replied, with all the gentility I could muster.

She'd nodded at this with an earnestness that thrilled me to my bones. "Oliver Delamare," she'd said. I'd seen no reason to correct her.

"Can you read, Oliver Delamare?"

My high spirits had vanished at once. I'd shaken my head forlornly.

"I'll teach you," she'd murmured, pursing her lips. "I was a teacher of boys, before Mr. Bradford's time. Back in Ohio, that was." Her face had gone blank for a moment. "Six years of my young life."

"Oh, he's a fine learner," Koko had put in eagerly. "Quick as a cricket. Many's the occasion—"

"Has he any sweethearts?" Mother Anne had said, turning me about. "Any little amours?"

Koko's face had stiffened slightly. "The boy's not yet twelve, Mrs. Bradford."

"Ah! Mrs. Hewitt," Mother Anne had said. "You can't fool me about this one." She'd released me then, and brought out a scuff-cornered purse. "Boys are but men in short pants, after all."

For a year, perhaps longer, Mother Anne partook of my body without asking more than its readiness. I was her plaything, pure and plain—; but the position was not a thankless one. She was kind to me, and repaid my services with genuine affection—; she taught me to read and to dress, and gave me countless little presents. I suffered under her attentions, of course, but no more than I'd suffered under Koko's long indifference. After a parcel of time had passed (enough for me to take leave of my former life, a thing I did without regret) I came to think of Mother Anne's house as my own.

Once her appetite had calmed, however, Anne's face took on a dull-eyed look whenever I was near. The gifts and indulgences continued unabated, but there was an equivalence now between each trinket and the night that followed—: if I'd benefited from her largesse I could be sure that some particular demand would be made of me. I began to fear her, and to escape the house whenever I was able. The purpose of our evenings became less and less the satisfaction of Mother Anne's body than the degradation, the reduction to mud and river-water, of my own.

Once a week, usually on a Sunday, she'd take me down to the cellar, where the whiskey-still was housed, and pull aside an ancient, sodden curtain. Behind it was a narrow alcove—: the walls had a sweet, rancid smell, as though tallow had been rendered there. Anne would undo the silk bandanna she'd taken to tying around my neck, bind my wrists together with it, then attach them to a hook set high into the wall, so that the balls of my feet barely touched the packed-earth floor. Then—cautiously at first, with great affectation of shyness—she'd commence to undo my britches. Once I was stripped and arranged to her satisfaction, she'd take a step backwards and mutter to herself awhile. As she stood there (her lips and jaw working soundlessly, as though she were a toothless beggar chewing on her tongue) she'd work her right hand up under her skirts, then bring it out again, glistening with her sex, and run it back and forth across my face. Within the space of a few breaths, no matter how furiously I pleaded with my blood and bowels, my body would stir in answer. All I could do then was to let my eyes fall closed. At such moments the world contracted into a coal-black pellet, the merest flake of cinder, and I'd watch dispassionately as my body fell away from Mother Anne, away from the house, into an infinite, ghost-like Mississippi. I prayed to Heaven that I would drown in it.

Whenever I could escape from the house (when Anne was tending to her husband, for example, or in the early morning, before she rose from bed) I'd walk the half-mile out to the Mississippi and ease myself into the thick, brown water, at times not even troubling to remove my clothes. My sole wish was to blend in with the river whose color so precisely matched my own—: to vanish into it irreversibly. I'd gulp down great mouthfuls as I swam, picturing the silt passing into my muscles and my blood until my entire body was converted into sediment. I would become as inhuman as the river was, as indifferent, as life-giving, as adored. The river itself was a mulatto, after all—: a hybrid born of the flowing together of three rivers to the north. It would consume my body, given time, as it did the muddy banks that held it. I would carry the filth of millennia inside me and remain pure.

Occasionally, as I lay on the sun-warmed pier, my river-dream would give way before the image of a spectral, gray-faced stranger (sometimes a man, but more commonly a woman) who would appear without warning, like a bolt of stray lightning, and rescue me with one emphatic act of violence. This vision grew more dear to me each time it arrived—: more comforting, more life-like, more extreme. I began to wonder whether I might not carry this faceless, sexless liberator inside of me, and began, painstakingly and cautiously, to conceive a plan of emancipation and escape. Providence, however, had already decreed that my wish be granted to the letter. My liberator was a man of flesh and blood, and he was bearing down on Mother Anne's house with all practicable force and speed.

It happened, as chance (or Providence) would have it, on a Sunday. Dusk was falling, and still Anne hadn't come for me—; I lay rigid and unmoving on my cot. She had never waited so long before. I permitted myself, for the briefest of spells, the luxury of imagining she'd forgotten me. Soon enough, however, I heard her deliberate, heavy foot-falls on the stairs—; a moment later she was guiding me down the hall. Her husband let out his customary warble of despair as we passed his door, propped open, as usual, with an empty mash-bucket. At the head of the stairs the idea came to me, fleetingly and sweetly, of tipping her head-first over the banister—; but I kept passive as a stone. I followed her mutely down the cellar steps, past the filthy, grease-marked curtain, into that hateful alcove. I turned and raised my hands for her to bind them.

"Not today, Oliver," Anne said, her voice high and lilting. It was not a tone I'd heard her use before. She held the bandanna at a distance, as though it were the carcass of some small animal of the field. (Her eyes, too, were more far-away than usual, her face more impassive.) Suddenly her eyes recovered their sharpness, as though a veil had been pulled from them. Her voice fell and roughened. "Turn your self round, boy. Lay your face against the brick." I hesitated, unsure of what she wanted—; the heel of her right hand struck me hard across the chin. When my vision cleared I found myself positioned as she'd directed, my hands held out behind me, my right cheek flush against the wall.

"Cross your wrists above your head. There. Hold them up! Higher, boy."

It had always been important to her to see my face. I shut my eyes and did as I was told, trying to think of nothing but the river.

"Right," Anne said morosely, binding my wrists together. "Right." Her work-chipped finger-nails slid across my brow, lingering there a while—; in spite of myself I let out a sigh as she withdrew them. The world had already begun dwindling away to nothing, to a grain of jet-black coal. Anne was somewhere to my left, perhaps a half a pace behind me. She stripped herself with a few coarse movements, then hurriedly undid my britches and pulled them to my knees. Her right hand planted itself at the base of my spine. I sank my teeth into my lower lip and waited.

Before Anne could act, however, a foot-fall sounded on the cellar steps. After a pause it was followed by another, then a third. Anne stopped short and dug her nails lightly into the small of my back—: a warning to me to hush. As yet the curtain kept us hid.

Nothing happened for a time. Anne struggled to keep her breathing steady, and I, for my part, kept as quiet as a mole. She could do nothing, how-ever, to keep from shivering in her nakedness. The rings of the curtain rattled tinklingly together.

"Annie Bradford? Am I right?" came a voice. (A thick voice, clumsy with its consonants—: the voice of a drinker.)

"_Missus_ Anne Bradford," she answered, her voice steady and severe. "Who the hell are you, sir, to come into my house?" She let go of my nape, now, and crouched to gather up her clothes.

The man proceeded down the steps.

"Hold there! _Hold!_" Anne shrieked, stamping her bare foot against the floor. "I'm entirely as nature made me, sir!"

"*So are we all, Annie,*" the man said sadly, stepping off the stairs. *What I'd mistaken for clumsiness was in fact some manner of dialect—; he wasn't a Dixie man at all, perhaps not even an American. He was no more than three steps from the mash-kettle now, and eight or nine steps from the curtain.*

"*I don't much enjoy trading how-dos with a muslin sheet, Mrs. Buh, Buh, Bradford,*" he said. *He sounded crest-fallen, apologetic.* "*What say you come out, as is, and I avert mine eyes?*"

"*Get you* gone *from this house,*" *Anne said in a hiss. Her breath came whistling against my nape.* "*Get you gone, sir, before I call my husband—*" (*here she took in a frantic, gasping breath, but so quietly that only I could hear it*)—"*or my boy.*"

The man guffawed. There was nothing threatening in his laugh, perhaps, but no politeness, either. "*Your boy'd have no objection, I think, if I tuh, tuh, took you off his hands,*" he said. *He laughed again, more quietly, then raised his voice—:* "*Would you, boy?*"

Anne spat out a curse. "*Let me* caution *you of something, Mister—*"

"*Kennedy,*" *said the man. The mirth was gone out of his voice already.* "*Kennedy's the name I were born into. I'm here on a errand for Mr. T. H. Morelle, gentleman, of Nuh, Nuh, Natchez-on-the-River.*"

A brief, unwieldy silence fell, during which Anne did up the buttons of her shift. The man said nothing, did nothing. Evidently he was content to wait for her to dress. His conduct was unlike any burglar's I'd heard tell of. But in truth I never mistook him for a burglar—; I knew exactly who he was. He was my day-dream of deliverance made flesh.

"*Morelle?*" *Anne said finally, stepping out from the curtain.* "*Does that name excuse a man from ringing my house-bell?*"

"*It should,*" *said Kennedy.*

"*We've a power of customers here, Mr. Kennedy. Quite a number of well-heeled and accredited gentlemen buy their mush from Mother Anne. You'll have to forgive us if a name escapes—*"

"*'Us'?*" *Kennedy said. His voice was suddenly flat as a crypt-cover.* "*What do you mean by* us, *ma'rm?*"

"*Why—just what I said, sir. Us. Me, my husband, and the boy.*"

"*Your husband is upstairs with his guts strung around his ankles,*" *Kennedy replied.*

Anne made a sound at this that seemed stripped of any meaning. It could have been a laugh, or a snort of indifference—; it could have been a cry of pain.

"*You borrowed four hundred State of Louisiana dollars from Mr. Amos Dall, of Vidalia, Louisiana,*" *Kennedy said, as though reading from a receipt.*

He cleared his throat and spat onto the floor. Mother Anne made to answer, but her voice was oddly muffled, little better than a gurgle, as though Kennedy had his hand over her mouth.

"That sum were to of been paid back, with interest, at a monthly rate of three puh, puh, percent, in three-and-one-half years from the time of borrowing," he went on. His stutter seemed to be worsening. He spat again, more loudly still. I decided he was chewing on a tobacco-plug.

"Not that terms *matter much, marm. That money weren't Mr. Amos Dall's to get fancy with. That money belonged to Mr. T. H. Morelle of Natchez-on-the-River, gentleman and financier."*

Anne gave another gurgle, louder and more desperate than before. It was clear from the sound that she was not more than three paces from the curtain, and also that she was kneeling on the floor.

"Let go of my trouser-leg, Annie. No harm will cuh, cuh, come to you today." He went quiet for a moment. "Am I right, little Annie, in saying so?"

Again she tried to answer but could not. "Please," she managed finally. "Please, Mr. Kennedy—I beg—"

"Am I right in saying so," he repeated with great deliberateness. "That no harm will come to you."

Anne gave no answer.

"Where do you keep your profit-box, marm?" Kennedy said smoothly.

He must have turned her loose, for she sucked in a breath and scrambled to her feet. "Under the roof," she said. "Under the roof, Mr. Kennedy. In a linen-trunk."

To this day I wonder what Mother Anne intended. To win a minute's time? To coax Kennedy out of the cellar, away from the profit-box and from me? It makes little difference now.

"That's a lie, Mr. Kennedy!" I said.

Anne cried out, tried to speak, then cried out again.

"Is that you, boy?" said Kennedy. "Speak on up!"

"It's nobody," Anne said quickly. "Don't you mind—"

"That's right, missus! Nobody whatever!" I yelled, thrashing impotently against the wall. "The bills are behind the mash-kettle, Mr. Kennedy! Twined up in a blouse!"

I date my entry into the Trade from that instant. What doomed me was not the betrayal itself, ruinous though it was—; my doom lay in the reasoning behind it. I didn't give the lie to Mother Anne out of a sense of the wrongs done to me, or out of righteousness, or vengefulness, or even out of fear—: I did it out of the simple desire to matter. Friendless and without the least standing in the world, I was nonetheless guilty of the sin of pride. Sometimes I think there is no other.

"Thank you kindly, Mr. Nobody," Kennedy said, and as he spoke there came a sound like that of a boot-heel striking a sack of rice and Anne dropped slackly to the floor. Her milk-colored fist, balled gracelessly together, like a child's hand taken from a railing, fell against my heel and quivered there.

Kennedy rummaged about behind the boiler, cursing industriously under his breath. Anne's white fist held me enchanted.

"Oho!" Kennedy said at last. "Yes."

"Tie me loose, Mr. Kennedy!" I called out. I hadn't yet set eyes on him, but I pictured a squat, hard-featured man—; grave, of course, but with a ready smile. When at last he came, shoving the curtain aside so it fell over Anne's fist and stilled it, he looked nothing like the men that I'd imagined. His long, stooped body and shriveled bloodless face looked like nothing, in fact, that I had ever seen, except perhaps the winged skulls carved by the richer families in town onto their head-stones.

He looked me up and down and gave a laugh. "Mother Bradford's buh, buh, boy," he said.

I stood as straight as I could, struggling to look dignified, but after a spell of time had passed without his saying a single word I began to suffer sorely under my nakedness. When I could meet his gaze no longer, I dropped my eyes reluctantly to Mother Anne. Her shift was ripped open at the breast and a palm-sized bruise was darkening at her temple. Farther down, above her belly, a stain was spreading whose source was hidden by the bunching of her shift. When it was clear to me that she was dead I looked at Kennedy to see whether he had noticed, but he seemed oblivious to all around him. He stood before me awkwardly, breathing through his mouth, with an expression on his face that I knew well enough, though it took me a long, dull moment to decipher it. His right hand clasped the ring above me—; his left twitched restlessly at his trousers. Instinctively I turned to face the wall.

Kennedy took in a rattling breath behind me.

"Mother Bradford's boy," he said.

Stutter Kennedy.

I'M JUST ON MY WAY FROM THE PRIVY, having paid my evening
tithes. The End is waiting for me there with a grin on its face fit for
a monkey's christening. I hang back, quiet as a dove, and bide. So
here it is.

So here it is, says I. I won't be keeping you as I know you're very busy.

There has to be an end, Stuts.

Does there? says I.

You've been no end of help, Stuts, the End says. Truly.

Aye! says I. That I have. And is *this*—you don't mind my asking—
how you shows your appreciation of it.

You know I appreciate it, says the End. I've given you room to play
in, after all. If you haven't made good use of it, the fault is not my own.

I'd of liked to make use of it to whup that niggra boy, says I.

You'd of liked to slip one into his knickers, the End says, giving me
the wink.

I set quiet. The one don't rule the tother out, says I.

No. The one don't rule the tother out, says the End. It grins.

Just you answer me this, says I, before you do me under. Answer
me *this*. Why is that niggra such a bother to my mind?

We are each of us someone's nigger, Stuts. Didn't your mother tell
you?

Each of us a niggra, says I. Each of us—?

The End plucks at a piece of grass.

That's it, then? That's all? You sound like bleeding Asa Trist!

The End shakes its head. A little something to remind you of your
place, Mr. Kennedy. That's all.

I curse and spit. What place is *that*, pray to tell us? Hey?

The End gives a curtsy. The next in line.

A Penance.

VIRGIL COME UP ON ME, Dodds says. Seeking to lay a penance on me.

In broad day-time, while I clambring up the hill with this blankety-blank bucket. Looking at me like he never did make my right features out before. He come up on me all in a sudden and stop me in my tracks and in a voice fit to bring down the Union cannon holler out—

Dodds! I'm wise to your racket after all this time. You and I are going to revisit the scene of our finest hour.

I stand up straight as a picket. Don't follow you, sackly, Mr. Virgil.

That's right—I'm going to follow *you*, old snake-in-the-weeds. Get shambling.

He clutching a long wedge-tip spade, same spade we use to fill in the privy-hole over the Deemer, in he left hand. In he right hand they a bottle full of lantern-oil. I don't say nothing past that. I hunch down and make slow as a mule for the Deemer's hole. I look for Parson or somebody but they ain't nothing doing at that hour.

You're looking for someone to get in my way, Virgil say. I'll confess something to you, Dodds. I'm hoping to see them try.

Can I put the bucket down, I say.

You'd best get moving, you son-of-a-bitch, or you'll be wearing that god-damned bucket for a girdle.

This a error of judgment, I say.

Virgil laugh. One more won't make much difference.

We come to the old privy-hole. Filled in now. Tobacky-house twixt us and the rest the property, woods all behind. Patch show dark on the ground where we put the Deemer under. Part of it glitter against the rest and I pick up a sly old chip of mirror.

Sloppy, Virgil mutter. We were sloppy.

It were dark, I say, watching he hand fingering that spade. I suppose we done it good enough.

I suppose otherwise, he say, chucking the spade down. Get to work.

I look at the spade. This a grave error of judgment, I say. This won't bring no good but evil.

As if you knew the difference, Virgil say. He face gone flat and white and if I didn't know he knew the game before, I know it now. The words get themselves upright, slow and easy, and line up in a row—:

Virgil—knows—the—game.

But that ain't gone help him much at all.

Dig! Virgil holler.

I take the spade and get cutting. The ground good and mealy, praise Jesus. It ain't but a quarter-hour's work. First they water in the hole, then clay.

We sure didn't plant him deep, Virgil mumble.

Another cut and I catch a scrap of cotton.

That's enough, Virgil say. Scrape the clay off of him.

The carcass kept up pretty well, account the clay. First I think it withered some, it so frail and childish—; but that just the measure of the Deemer.

Pull him loose, Virgil say. Put the spade by, Doddsbody. Use your hands now. Get hold of him.

No heavenish way C. B. Dodds gone touch *that* item.

Virgil give a sigh. You're just not afraid of me, are you, Charlie.

I drop the spade. You less to me, sir, than a rarebit of the field.

Step aside, then. Will you step aside?

I do.

He snatch the spade up and bring it down again quick. Worrying the Deemer into bits. The sound of it like a butcher working on a chop.

What you aim to fix that way, little rarebit? I say.

Virgil give a laugh. Fix? he say, and give a laugh again. I'm long past fixing things.

You dug up a heap of dead troubles. That's all you done today.

Virgil don't answer, just hackety-hackety with the spade.

I'd love to know what Parson's promised you, Dodds. If I were you I'd be gone away long since. Gone for good across the river.

Why *you* still here then, Virgil? They the river yonder.

He stop and smile. You know full well.

She not the cause of nothing. You want a old nigger tell you why?

He give a laugh. Yes, Dodds. Tell me why. I'd be beholden.

Nobody ever leave the Trade. Not ever.

I reckon I might be the first, he say. He hush a spell. I'd like to see outside of it one day.

They *ain't* no outside! We floating in it, all of us. Like fishes in a tub.

Yes, that's the gospel, Virgil say, poking at the Deemer. The gospel according to Thaddeus. We all know he was his own archbishop.

Trade eat archbishops for supper, I say.

And archbishops eat bankers, he say. And bankers eat politicians. And politicians—

Ain't no man, woman, nor child *never* left the Trade. Never, Virgil. Not a one.

Let's send this child ahead of us, then, Virgil say, pouring lantern-oil top the pieces. On a voyage of discovery.

I don't say nothing then.

I wish you a safe and speedy transit to the bottom of the Pit, Virgil hisper. Then he let a lit match fall.

I SCUFFLE BACK UP TO THE HOUSE. A week ago it were mischief in every room, but now the house right quiet. Delamare laid up with the shivers. Miss Clem hispering through she window at the Lord Christ Jesus. Parson in he attic laying out for Charlie Dodds.

What is it, I say.

Parson sigh. It's Kennedy.

I know. Kennedy tomorrow.

Kennedy's done, Parson say. Kennedy's done already.

Done? I say. *How* done? Murthured?

Parson set quiet. Done. That's all.

Put in a hole?

Parson shake he head. We'll have to do without.

I hush a spell. Put me in, I say. Put me down in place of Kennedy.

He laugh. We still have need of you, Charlie. Kindly remain alive a few more hours.

You swore a oath, I say. My blood go pricklish. You swore!

Parson give a smile. And the Redeemer will make good on that promise, Charlie, when he comes.

When he comes hell, I say. We short two holes. He gone skip two steps when he come down?

He's skipped two steps before.

Before? I holler. Before *when*?

He hand come over my mouth like nothing. Do you fancy this is his *first* transfer, nigger? Were you not listening when I explained to you the fruitings and the harvestings of the Trade?

Just tell me who come next, I mumble. Tell me who.

Next you take something to the prisoner. Keep his body working.

What you mean, something? Water?

Yes. Water, Parson say, like it he don't care if it be fire.

An idea come to me then. We could use *him*, I say. That Foster. To fill the next hole up.

Parson make a cluck. No, Dodds. The prisoner is set aside.

What for?

He cluck again. A lower purpose.

I FETCH A JAR AND HOBBY-NOB IT DOWN. The cellar door wide open. They the prisoner, deathly quiet. Water! I say. Like talking at a deaf. Mouth hung open, tongue stuck out, lips gone dry and cracklish. I dip two fingers and rub them on he lips. I set the jar down in the dirt. I fixing to go when he hand come up back of my poor bald head.

Dear Lord! he hisper.

I brung water, I say. On the floor, Foster. Drink it.

He hand on my neck. What are you, sir? A slave?

That's right, I say. But I be mancipated soon.

Soon? he say.

Yes sir. My marse coming down. Then I be put to rights.

Now he hand on my throat. Where is he? Up those stairs?

Who? I say. Parson?

It so fierce on me now I can't catch my air. Where is he? Where is he? Where is he?

Parson just upstairs—

Upstairs? Can he hear?

Not if we quiet. Ease up on me, sir!

He say nothing then. Just hide under the steps.

PARSON LAYING FOR ME STILL. Nesting. He look up at me and yawn.

Well?

He awake, I say. Foster.

Parson give a stretch. Well! I should go and see him, then.

You gone pour the Deemer in him, ain't you.

That would be telling.

Virgil burnt the other one, I say. The carcass.

Yes. That's all correct and proper.

His promise, I say. The Deemer's. You aim to keep it, Parson?

Parson in high spirits all up a sudden. He laugh. I haven't forgotten it in the last quarter-hour, Doddsbody.

You aim to keep it?

He give me a whistle. He give me a wink.

I make a breath and groan and drop down on my knees. Let it be tomorrow, I say. I won't bear another hour, sir. I can't. I'll dig the rest they holes tonight. Ah! Let it be tomorrow, Parson. Learn me how to speak the tongue!

Parson study me a good long while with he tom-cat face and he pebble eyes.

It was always going to be tomorrow, Charlie, he say at last. He reach under himself and come out with my bottle. They a powder in it now.

Angel of mercy! I hisper. Sweet righteous angel!

Dig your holes, pilgrim, that you may rest.

VI

A "corporation" is an artificial being—invisible, intangible, and existing only in contemplation of the law. Being a mere creature of the law, it possesses only those properties which the charter of its creation confers upon it. Among the more important of these are Immortality and, if the expression may be allowed, Individuality: properties by which a perpetual succession of many persons are considered as the same, and may act as a single individual. In this way, the corporation is not unlike a church.

—Chief Justice John Marshall of the Supreme Court, 1819

Parson's Witchery.

MY LAST DAY AT GEBURAH BEGINS SOFTLY, Virgil says. I've been sitting in the lampless parlor half the night when the house-door sighs open, delicate as hackled lace. A moment later Parson flutters by. He glances into the parlor as he passes, shading his eyes, but fails to see me slumped over in the dark. He moves on down the hall. The cellar door opens, then shuts, and I draw in a breath. I rise from the settee more carefully than a spinster. A draft curls about my shins, leafy with the smell of coming rain. Something is going to happen. It sits like a clot of river-bottom in my throat.

Parson is quiet as dust on the cellar steps but he can't keep them from creaking subtly as he descends. His oversight has given me an advantage over him, the first in our long acquaintance, and I'm determined not to let it pass. I steal lightly down the hall. He's left the cellar door unlatched. I reach the top of the steps just as he gets to the bottom.

To go any farther would be to lose straight-away, so I crouch at the top of the steps and bide. I see nothing but the rough pine boards leading down into the blackness—; I hear nothing but my own unsteady breathing. I've just begun to wonder whether Parson hasn't vanished through some fissure in the earth when a voice comes out of the gloom, measured and precise, no more than an arm's-length below me—:

"Open your mouth, Mr. Foster. Have a drink."

Parson's voice, talking to the prisoner. Somewhere just beneath the steps. A moment later he speaks again, so close that I fancy I can smell his breath. He speaks as though he and Foster were having a tea-time chat—: there is no cajolery in his voice, no spite, no menace. But Foster hasn't said a word.

"I got this out of the river for you, Mr. Foster," Parson says. "Mr. Delamare, the half-caste, is in the habit of dunking himself in the current, for the performance of his personal ablutions." A pause. "Mr. Delamare was meant as a conduit for the Redeemer. To be what Thaddeus Morelle once was. But Mr. Delamare, unfortunately, is unwell. Mr. Delamare has been taken with the grippe."

Another silence. In my eagerness to hear I nearly tumble down the steps.

"Not at all!" says Parson suddenly, as if in answer to a question. "Mr. Delamare is not the Redeemer's successor—; you fail to take my meaning. The Redeemer is his *own* successor, Mr. Foster."

A low, scudding sound, as of a barrel being pushed aside. Then Parson's voice—:

"How long until the Yankees take this house?"

No reply. Parson heaves a sigh, then asks almost idly—:

"How many men are encamped above the shanty-town?"

This time an answer comes readily, but in a voice I'd swear was Parson's own, grotesquely falsettoed, as though he were acting a part in a traveling theater—:

"Half—; a—; company. No—; cannon. Thirty—; muskets. Eighteen—; rifles. Seventy—; blacks—"

"*Seventy* blacks? Freed-men?" Parson says, interrupting.

Then, in his stage voice—: "Freed-men—; contrabands." Another pause, and the voice resumes—: "Sundry—; blacks—; have—; knives."

"I'd say our time is *dwindling*, Mr. Foster. Dwindling quite away. Is that also your opinion?"

No answer. A bright, dusty squeak, as of wood against wood—: someone is leaning against the steps. Parson clucks impatiently.

"The time is fast approaching, Mr. Foster, when there will be no Mr. Foster any longer. No Mr. Foster—; no opinions. Time enough to be quiet then." He lowers his voice. "We'll *both* be quiet then, you and I. Like school-boys when the master arrives, sets the day's lesson on the table, and hangs up his long gray coat." He hushes a moment. "I, of course, as teacher's pet, may be permitted to raise my hand from time to time. But if I were *you*, Mr. Foster, I'd air your opinions while you may."

Just then a hard, smooth object—glass, or perhaps iron—is run up the underside of the steps. This so startles me that I'm unable to make out the prisoner's next words. I hear only Parson's amused reply—:

"He'll come to you painlessly, through your open mouth. You'll swallow him, Mr. Foster, exactly as you would a biscuit."

A tinkling now, as of glass against glass.

"Why? Because you're *docile*, Mr. Foster. And reasonably pretty." A pause. "The Redeemer has a terrible fear, you see, of awakening in the body of Virgil Ball."

At the mention of my name I recoil from the cellar door as if I've been cuffed. The pantry is across the hall and I scurry toward it. Parson's heard me now—: he must have heard me. I cast frantically about for a hiding-place, make a slow, stumbling circuit of the room, and crawl at last under the cutting-block. The pantry is empty and neglected-looking—; I wonder passingly what's become of Dodds. Out digging a hole for himself, most likely.

No sooner am I settled than I hear foot-falls on the cellar steps. If Parson goes out to the verandah, he'll pass through the pantry and discover me—; if he leaves by the front door, or retires to his attic, I retain my advantage over him. Out of a sense of propriety, a desire to act my part, I gather my coat around me and take in a breath.

He comes to the top of the steps, hesitates, then glides in his ecclesiastic way upstairs. Not bothering to look for me. It must no longer matter what I hear. Does he think me so incapable, so weak?

I listen until I hear the door to the attic shut, or fancy that I hear it. It seems to me that Parson paused a second time—perhaps outside of Delamare's sick-room—but I've no way of telling. I picture Delamare to myself, flushed and wasting on his pallet—; then the prisoner in the lightless, airless cellar. I understood only a fraction of Parson's dialogue with Foster—if dialogue it was, and not play-acting—but it was more than enough to guess at his design. I was right, then, about Dodds' holes, about the map of the grounds, about the Redeemer's return. "A conduit for the Redeemer," Parson said. "What Thaddeus Morelle *once* was." "Redeemer" was an office Morelle held for a time—; that much is clear. An office now come vacant. A position to be filled. I step out into the hall, undo the laces of my boots, and steal in my stockinged feet down the cellar steps.

It's darker at the bottom than I'd expected. Foster's breathing, slow and steady as a sleeper's, comes from every side at once—: if not for the light from the open door I'd be done for. The room has no depth to it, no boundary, no form. But I have no intention of squandering my advantage. I work quickly and methodically, making forays to each side in search of Foster, returning always to the dim square of light at the base of the steps.

I've covered half the cellar, near as I can judge, when the door is quietly pushed shut.

A GROAN ESCAPES MY LIPS as the last light vanishes. The sound is mimicked by the prisoner, suddenly close beside me. A tremendous desire to bolt overtakes me, to exchange the dark of the cellar for the paler dark outside—; but I've lost all sense of where the steps might be. The prisoner's breathing is louder and more urgent than before, as though he meant to guide me to him. I walk in a slow, in-curving spiral, expecting to reach him in a few short steps—; but the sound proves hard to follow, and I soon grow dizzy. I've just decided to stop a moment, to recover my balance and my breath, when my left hand brushes against a sack-cloth sleeve.

"*Aaaah,*" says the prisoner. My hand whips back as though he's bitten it. A body ought to give when touched, no matter how slightly—; but the arm under that shirt-sleeve was as rigid as mahogany.

I stand motionless in the dark, in Lord knows what attitude of terror or disgust, mustering the courage to press on. The prisoner makes no attempt to move. His breathing has grown quieter, more restful. Gritting my teeth, I lay my fingers first on his forearm, then on his shoulder, and then, in the manner of the aged and the blind, lightly on his forehead and his face.

The heel of my palm comes to rest on his chin—; his breath whistles through my fingers, tickling them. My middle finger traces the bridge of his nose, which I remember as high and peaked. The index finger traces the hair-line, the ring-finger the rim of his left eye-socket. The face stays fixed throughout, its breathing regular as clock-work. It's Foster. I'm certain of it now.

"Foster," I whisper, barely opening my mouth. "Can you hear me? This is Virgil Ball."

"*Aah,*" says Foster's face.

"I'm going to liberate you, Foster. I'm going to get you out of here."

No sooner have I said this than the breathing stops completely and his body snaps taut as a cable, flinging my hand away. The silence that follows is so absolute that I can hear his body shuddering. With a great effort of will I bring my fingers back to his face and find it convulsing wildly, as though the blood and ichor under the skin were coming to a boil.

In the next instant the mouth has formed a syllable, a name, and I'm stripped of my last understanding.

"Ball!" it says. It says my name plaintively—imploringly—and I recognize the drawl I first heard under a revival tent ten years ago—: the cane-sugar patois of the Delta flats. The voice that effortlessly, coyly, playfully undid my life.

"Morelle?" I stammer.

The body heaves and spasms. It was Morelle's voice without question. A single word was enough to know it by. My hands make their way from the face to the throat, probing for its hollow. My left thumb finds its mark and my right joins it dutifully. I open my eyes wide—as if to reassure myself of their sightlessness—and drive both my thumbs in with all my strength.

Choked shrieks issue from the mouth, bestial and dull, but the body itself obliges me. Water begins to stream out of its eyes, running down onto my hands, but I do not mistake this watering for weeping. The darkness comes to my aid, helping me to forget the man before me, forget Morelle, forget even myself, and remember only Parson's words—:

He'll come to you painlessly, Mr. Foster. Through your open mouth.

I STAND IN THE DARK for I know not how long, throttling the prisoner. My thoughts begin to stray toward the future, and I see that I'll suffer for this act as sure as I'm alive. The knowledge does nothing to discourage me, however. Every detail of the present moment—the heat, the dampness, the bleatings of the expiring body, the absence of all light—holds the promise of release, of expiation. Only strangling myself could bring me greater peace.

This man has never committed the least crime against me. He's as near to an innocent as can be found in this house. And it's this very fact—the arbitrariness of his killing—that lends the cold beauty of religion to my act. I feel sanctified, righteous—: a latter-day Abraham, holding Isaac aloft to heaven. Is this what the Christian martyrs felt? The knights of the Inquisition? The Union generals? What else could religion be, at its core, but this—: the cold-blooded sacrifice of an innocent, that an entire nation might be saved?

The beauty is enough to sear the lining of my soul. I am ready to wage war against the entire world in defense of this one idea.

A MOMENT LATER I STEP BACK from the body in disgust. The life has gone out of it like wind out of a sheet. The conduit, such as it was, is closed.

I have no time to reflect on this, however. The cellar door flies open without warning, fixing me in its sudden light like a butterfly on a pin. Parson has found me out, as I knew he would—; he's smelled Foster's killing, tasted it on the air, and come scurrying down from his attic to destroy me. I can't laugh at this notion any longer, can't shame myself into dismissing it as I might once have done. I have faith in Parson's witchery now—: I must. If Parson has no power but that of superstition, no gift but that of cunning, then I've just murdered a man on their behalf.

I'm about to step forward, to challenge him at last, when Clementine's silhouette appears in the door-frame. The air spills out of my mouth like water from a jar.

She stands raptly in the light, shifting from one foot to the other, believing herself unseen. Clementine, not Parson. I remain as I am, lifeless as the corpse beside me, cowering from the creature who was once my life.

Clementine Gilchrist.

H E'S THERE, JUST AS PARSON SAID HE WOULD BE. I knew
he'd be there. I didn't need Parson to guess that he'd be drawn
to that cellar like a puppy to its mess.

He stands cowed and huddled, blinking up at me, with his feet in
the light and his fingers in his mouth. Like a babe that thinks itself hidden if it closes its eyes. I wanted to look at him, to uncover him there,
like a worm under a rock. Only that. I knew Parson had won but I
wanted to see it. To have the fact of it before me. And the fact is before
me now, white-faced and trembling, with a bundle of dead rags at its
feet. The last proof I needed of the R——'s return.

Now I see how the rest of it will run. The R—— himself told me.
The R—— himself told me and then Parson showed me proof. Go to
the cellar, Clementine, he said. Open the cellar door and see.

"How Have I Been Used?"

S**HE SHUTS THE DOOR QUIETLY,** Virgil says.
No sooner is it closed than I dash headlong for the steps. I'm just short of them, to my reckoning, when I stumble over Foster's body. A curse escapes my lips before I can stifle it. How the devil did he get there? I kneel and pass a hand over his face—: the nose is flat, the skin is loose and folded, but it takes me a long spell of quiet to admit this isn't Foster. I find nothing in the pockets but tobacco-crumbs and dirt—; but that, taken with the smell off the body, is enough to tell me that this was Dodds.

I never imagined Dodds might go the way of the others, so necessary has he seemed to all the goings-on in this house. But soon this house will be as empty as Dodds' own body. Cradling his head in my lap, supporting its lifeless weight, I feel a slight, cautious wind-change with the knowledge of his death. There was no such change when Harvey died, or Trist, or even Morelle himself. The rest of us grew more spectral with each day we passed at Geburah—; Dodds discovered his great purpose only after he arrived. I find myself regretting his passing not a little. Only Parson can answer the last riddles for me now.

Parson! I say, and give a hollow laugh. Parson is my last remaining hope!

I've just killed a man for no better reason than that he spoke with the Redeemer's voice. One word was sufficient to convince me. My notion of myself as a lantern of reason, a sort of one-eyed Pinkerton Agency, has been put out of its misery at last. My investigation did nothing but confuse my mind and mortify my body. If it was an investigation at all, it was one in reverse, each new clue only stupefying me further. Any of the Gang would have done as well as I did—; each of them, in the end, would have lost their bearings, played into Parson's hands, committed murder.

A thought strikes me now with such sudden force that I'm left breathless—: perhaps each of them did. Not one, but *all* of them, one after another. Perhaps they *did* act as I just have. Each of us was meant to overhear one such whispered conversation, to struggle with himself in bewilderment and panic, and to come to the only decision possible. It would suit Parson's method perfectly. Trist murdered Harvey—; Dodds assisted Trist in hanging himself from the choke-cherry tree—; Foster, perhaps blindly, strangled Dodds in the cellar. And now I, as the next in line, have done the same to Foster.

Parson saw me in the darkened parlor, lingered a moment at the door, drew me after him to the cellar, left the cellar door ajar. The purity of it is staggering. The very grotesqueness of such an idea—its ugliness, its simplicity—bears Parson's stamp like a coat-of-arms in wax.

The floor collapses underneath me. I force my jaws open, desperate for air—; black soil pours into my mouth instead. Blood swells and shudders in the sockets of my eyes. If I choose to disbelieve this theory, what is there to take its place? The only other solution to the killings is a mystical one, and absurd into the bargain—; yet if I choose to *disbelieve* in the Redeemer's return, to reject it as a fantasy, then I've just killed a man for no reason at all. A perfect circle, sleek and impenetrable as a bullet. My sense of religion—of election—is dispatched by it forever. I work my mouth open wider still, as wide as it will go—: soil tumbles into it like gravel into a tomb. What purpose did Foster's killing serve? How have I been used? I have to speak to someone, speak to them at once, if only to hear it said aloud that I'm the Trade's instrument, its play-thing, and was fashioned and favored toward that end alone.

I have to speak to Clementine.

I find Clementine at her usual station, a hair's-breadth from the window with her ear pressed against one of its jewel-cut panes. She seems fixed in place, inanimate, though she stood at the cellar door not ten minutes gone. A smell of sore neglect rises off her—; her hair stands in sweat-stiffened plaits, like a reef of Araby coral, at impossible angles to her skull. When it is that she sits, sleeps, or takes her meals I have no idea any longer. Delamare and I moved into more comfortable quarters as the second floor emptied, but there's been no dragging her out of that cramped hat-box of a room. She eats flock-paper off the walls, and vermin that she picks from among her skirts—; the room has a smell to make you swear off breathing.

"Clem," I say softly.

Her body gives a twitch, then settles. No more than that. Until today I could depend on a flicker of recognition in her eyes, however grudging—; now even that is gone. No matter. I'll use her the same way she uses that window of hers.

"Clem," I say again, stopping an arm's-length from her.

She gives no reply.

"I've been to see Foster in the cellar," I say. "Parson was with him. Parson means to use him as a carrier." I study her reflection in the glass. "Perhaps 'courier' is a better word. For the Redeemer himself, Clem—do you understand me? When he comes down the ladder."

The unlikeliness of what I'm saying breaks over me suddenly, forcing me to hush. But I've said just enough. A rustle of air escapes her lips.

"You remember about the *sephiroth*, don't you, Clem? The ladder of the spirit?"

I wait for an answer, but no answer comes. I lay my hand on her shoulder. "Dodds' holes form a pattern of sorts—; a grid. The geometry they follow is the geometry of the spheres." I take a breath. "I've told you this before. Do you remember?"

Tentatively, almost imperceptibly, she bobs her head. The movement is so slight that I doubt it even as it happens. But her brow taps quietly on the glass.

"I couldn't allow that to happen, Clem. I couldn't just stand by. I took hold of Foster by the throat, and—"

"BALL!" she shrieks, spinning about with such strength that I'm sent tumbling backward. An infant—or a beast, perhaps—could produce such a cry. The Clementine I knew and loved could not.

"Was I wrong to do it?" I whimper. "Tell me, dearest, if you know! Was I wrong to take Parson at his word?"

She hovers in seraphic silence, violence both animating her and holding her fixed above me, as wires both direct and fix a marionette. She shakes her head slowly.

"He's dead?" she says. "You're sure?"

I nod. She brings a hand to her face and passes it from her brow down to her chin, as though she were closing the eyes of a cadaver. Each action she might take next flits past my mind's eye, accompanied by its corresponding shape.

A net of yellow diamonds.

A silver cup, upended.

A ladder of eight stars, one for each of Dodds' holes, over a blood-red field.

An instant later she's away. The L-shaped room is empty. She has stolen down the hall, to him—: to Delamare. I can no more follow her than her bedstead could, or the peeling flock-paper, or the window she so adores. I stand in the center of the room, passive as a dust-mote, listening as her foot-steps fall away.

I've felt it before, this swooning of my will, this collapsing of my spirit like a spider-web in frost. I felt it when Clem was brought to 37, and on that first fatal night at Madame Lafargue's, when she went down to Lieutenant Beauregard. It's happened often enough—God knows!—and Clem has always had a hand in it. The feeling is not one of helplessness or bewilderment, and still less of fear—: it's a gentleness, a modesty, a blushing cooperation in the destruction of all that I hold dear. Were I to follow Clem now— to take a single step in her direction—there might yet be some small hope.

Instead I prefer to remain as I am, dumb-struck in an empty room.

After an immeasurable length of time—perhaps a quarter-hour, perhaps much longer—I'm able at last to struggle to my feet. I find her at Delamare's bed-side, her face dug hard into its quilts. She is sobbing madly, ecstatically—; the quivering of her body makes bright ripples in the air. Delamare seems not to see her. Clem takes up one of his hands as I enter, and passes it abjectly across her face—: without any change of feature, without so much as a sigh, he frees his hand from hers.

For three days now I've known it was Clem who filled Parson's bottles for him, and that Delamare's illness sprang from this act like a tulip from a bulb. Something in her way of clutching at him now reminds me of it.

"I hadn't known you were so fond of Private Foster, Clem," I say.

She answers without lifting her face from the quilts. Her voice, unlike my own, is passionate and clear.

"I'm not weeping for Private Foster. I'm not weeping for you, either, or for this boy here." She raises her head, as if to take my measure, then lowers it again. "I'm weeping for nobody but myself."

I move a half-step closer. A tingling has begun at the base of my skull, causing the palms of my hands to twitch—; I dig my nails into them to keep them quiet. I want to take Clementine by the hair, to scream into her tear-marked face, to drag her bodily from the room. Delamare is watching me now, his eyes full of fire, and I do not mistake his look. He means for me to free him, and so help me God I will.

I mean to take hold of Clementine, to pull her from the bed, but a timid voice, groveling and childlike, stays my hand—:

"Weep for me!"

I recognize the voice, after a brief, unwilling moment, as my own.

"Weep for me, Clem, I beg of you! I'm nearly gone—"

The laugh she gives is so giddy that I find myself breaking, in spite of my best efforts, into an embarrassed smile. Delamare groans and shuts his eyes. Clementine rolls back onto her haunches, laughing in little chokes. But when she speaks her voice is hollow as a well.

"Get the house in order, google-eye! Decorate it for a wedding! There'll be a body in every bed, poor fool, when our Redeemer comes!"

A Single Breath.

VIRGIL TURNS AND GOES, says Clementine.

A look of disgust is on his face, as I'd meant there to be. A few breaths later he is down the stairs and gone. Only Delamare is left, and he's nearly fevered under. I'll serve as sole witness, then, to my own passing. As the R—— promised that I would.

A sound carries in from the hall—: a rasping. Parson is there in the doorway, looking down at Delamare. Virgil's foot-falls sound on the verandah. He's away, then. Gone out of the house. As the R—— promised he would be. Parson looks down at Delamare, waiting on some sign. I'm still shivering from my fit. But Virgil is gone. It's important that he be away, I said. Let him be gone when the R—— comes down.

Promise me that, Parson. Will you promise me?

The room goes quiet as a church. Nobody breathes. Parson keeps his eyes on Delamare. What's he waiting on? I wonder. Maybe Delamare needs to be gone, as well, for the wedding to begin.

Another while goes by. I begin to ask myself if now is not the Time. I stir on the floor and make a wondering sound.

Parson tilts his head toward me. He's not surprised to see me crouched at Delamare's bed-side. He's pleased to see me there.

Get up, Clementine, he says.

I do. Parson stands before me now, or I stand before him. He brings a hand to my face and opens my mouth with two hooked fingers. He lets them rest atop my tongue. He takes a gentle hold of it.

Breathe, he says to me. He says it kindly.

The feeling is like when my Cecilia came, but back-to-front, and quicker. The pain comes sharp, then softens. I expect the change will come up through my belly but—!

But when it comes it steals in through my open mouth. One lonely breath, sucked quiet from day-light, that fills me like a bottle. A ravenous breath, and cruel. As careless of my fears and wants as the world outside my body is. The breath suckles my body, and my body suckles it in turn. The knowledge comes upon me in a swift and certain piercing—:

I've just gotten religion.

The breath trains itself upwards and outwards in every direction like a clambering vine. My bones and blood have nothing more to offer it—; neither does my name.

You may breathe out, Parson says.

I let a small breath loose.

I'M SENT OUT OF MYSELF on that last sigh. I fall straight down from my mouth and scatter like a cup of flour across the floor. My body has no further use for me. Neither does Parson. Neither does this room.

In the space of an instant I'm gone from all three.

I billow upwards through the rib-cage of the house, along the gaps between lath and plaster-work, through the air trapped between the floors, trellising playfully along the beams, running up and over the attic steps—; past Parson's attic with its collection of jars and parchments, round the beveled eaves and gables, off the peaked roof at last and into the violet evening air. It took one breath—: one only. Parson raised two fingers and took my tongue between them. No secret is my secret now, but I might savor that one for a spell. Or I might tell it to Virgil.

Virgil!

I see Virgil below me, crossing the red clay park. I'll follow him a ways. All it took was one breath! No more than that. One coin-purse's-worth of air.

Virgil moves with purpose-minded steps. He's making for the tobacco-shed—; he drags a spade behind him. His head is bent low and his shoulders are set straight and stiff. He walks as though he expects someone to stop him. All of us, perhaps.

In fact he is no danger to anyone—: of course he does not know this. He believes the ball he's set to rolling can be stopped. The ball that by now is become a boulder, a mud-slide, a cliff tumbling into the sea. The event he fears has long since come to pass. Its shadow has a greater weight than he has.

He arrives at the newest of Dodds' holes. He's amazed to find it already filled with dirt. Who is buried there? he wonders. He stares at it awhile, runs a hand over his face, mutters to himself. The soil is damp and rich, brought to the grave from elsewhere. He takes up the spade, glances back toward the house, and commences to dig.

The digging is easy—: the soil has not yet settled. Nothing resists his spade. He's frightened now, frightened of what he might uncover, and his digging gets wilder and clumsier with each spadeful. He's soon past the depth of burying, down in the wet, stubborn clay, fashioning a red sarcophagus for himself. And still he keeps on, hacking away as though the ground itself were between him and some deeper-buried thing, something ancient and indifferent to his fate. Finally he stops, defeated by his own resolve. He looks down into the empty, man-shaped hole.

One day, my son, he murmurs. All that you see before you will be yours.

He stands there a moment longer, mustering his breath. Then he takes up the spade and goes slowly and deliberately from one hole to the next. Some he clears to the red clay bottom—; some he takes down only a few feet. None hold anything but coffee-colored dirt, so fine that it looks sifted through a bed-sheet. At the last of the eight holes, the one in the orchard, he sinks wearily to his knees. It's as empty as all the others, filled in carelessly, hurriedly, a theater-prop whose usefulness is past. He lies down mutely in the grass.

Now he begins to see the swamp belief has led him into. The events since Harvey's death revolve in a wheel of transparent fire before his eyes, but try as he might to take hold of the wheel, to arrest its spin, his dirt-caked fingers find no purchase. The empty graves have bewildered him completely. Harvey's letter, the *sephiroth*, even the name "Canaan's tongue" seem less like clues to a great riddle, suddenly, than the punch-line to a joke. Tears marshal in his eyes.

Poor halved-and-quartered Virgil. Have you never once done a thing, looked upon your work, and been convinced of it? The fault lies in your mulatto self. The Jewish half of your brain flourished under the Trade—; the Protestant saw no fun in it at all. The Jew in you revolted at the abominations it was forced to witness—; the Protestant looked on in casual contempt. Was it this back-and-forth that made you question each idea, each urge, each desire you ever harbored? Was it this that made you late at every turn?

No. You harnessed yourself to a man whose every action was a

certainty. Your R—— was nothing if not a perfect whole. Your R——
was consummate, indivisible. You paid tribute to him for seven years—;
you learned certainty from him, or so you thought. And finally, by way
of proof, you drove a sliver of pier-glass through his neck.

But you were late again, Virgil. You only murdered him by half.

You're lying sideways in the grass, staring ahead of you at nothing,
when a figure appears at the edge the woods. The sight clears your
brain completely, even of thoughts of the R——. You welcome the
sight, ill-omened though it is, for you know straight-away what it
means. At long last something has happened that you can understand.

The figure is a field scout for the Union Army. He's dressed in a
sea-blue uniform, neat and well-tailored, and when he comes level
with the house he looks back over his shoulder, clear-eyed and expectant as a faun. You understand his look at once—: there is a company of
infantry not a quarter-mile behind him. That gives you perhaps ten
minutes, certainly no more, to return to the house and get Clementine
away. This is your only thought, and it arrives in your mind luminous
and fully formed. To your great relief you find that you are fatally
determined. This once, this last time, you will not be late.

The scout moves behind the first of the out-buildings, advancing
playfully, his rifle cradled loosely in his arms. You guess from his stride
that he is very young. As soon as he's out of view you fall headlong into
running.

As you run you curse your muddle-headedness of a few instants
before. You have no pistol, no rifle, not even a scrap of pier-glass. But
the scout has not yet seen you, and the scout is young and full of careless pride. You smile to yourself. That is worth more than a pistol.

You run to a stand of choke-cherry-bushes mid-way across the
lawn. A moment goes by, then another. The scout comes into view
between the stable and the kitchens. You neither move nor close your
eyes nor draw a breath. The scout's face is fixed retriever-like on the
house. He's perhaps ten yards away—: a pebble's toss. You have just
enough time to see the Colt in his left hand before he passes out of
sight.

Left-handed, you think, dashing forward. Bad luck. The scout is
behind the kitchens, the last point of shelter before the house. You
reach the kitchens yourself and lay your hands against the brick. The
solidity of the wall is a balm to you. You rest your face against it. The
weight of the thing you are about to do is on you now and you feel frail
and close to death.

There are windows set into the wall, six in number, with an unhindered view through the kitchens. You're mindful of them as you scuttle forward. As you draw nearer to the scout, you think of him for the first time as a reasoning creature. Is he scouting a route, or a billeting-place? Is he searching for Foster? Will he steal back to camp after circling the house, or will he go inside? You remind yourself that there is no camp, only a power of soldiers on the march. You glance across the lawn at Geburah. It looks benevolent and mild. Its windows are blank and shutterless, oil-colored where they catch the light. No military force is stationed there—; that much is clear. In fact it shows no sign of life at all.

"Damn!" the scout says suddenly. "Hell and damnation!"

He's stumbled over something—: a loose brick, perhaps, or a splinter of crockery. He's no more than three paces off, just around the corner. His voice quiets somewhat but you can still hear him clearly, muttering feverish encouragements to himself. You were wrong to think of him as prideful. He can't be more than sixteen years of age.

Being Virgil Ball, being set against yourself, you feel an urge to embrace the scout when he comes round the corner—: to reassure him, to relieve him politely of his gun, to send him sternly but affectionately about his business. He's as skittish as you are, as easily bewildered, as anxious to please his betters. You can hear it in his muttering, in his cursing, even in the way he breathes. You feel accountable for the scout, indulgent toward him, concerned about his future and his health. And at the same time you know that you will kill him if you can.

The muttering gets shriller now, angrier, more urgent. In a matter of seconds it will carry the scout forward. Your grip on the wall tightens, then goes tighter still, as though you mean to bring it down on top of you. All at once a brick under your right hand comes away, smoothly and without the slightest noise, as though it were eager to be of service. You gaze down at it in wonderment. For a moment it's agreeably heavy in your hand, warm and undeniable and rough, and the next it has dropped the scout to the ground with a sound like wet plaster dropping off a beam. His eyes roll upward, then cross, as if a wasp had landed on his brow. He lies quite still. You bend down, thinking to question him, perhaps, or even to beg his pardon. But his face has gone vacant as a cow's.

You leave the scout where he lies and walk back to the house. The verandah door is three-quarters open, exactly as you left it. You cover your dead eye, as if to ward off further visions, then slip inside.

Good-bye to you now, Virgil Ball. The house has let go of me and I would not return there. An answer of a kind awaits you to the mystery you cherish, the one that sprang god-like from your brow, fully-grown and hungry. I'm high in the air already, curling heavenwards like smoke. Parting from me is as simple as taking in a breath.

The Redeemer's Voice.

A SMELL HANGS IN THE ROOM, says Delamare. When Virgil comes back he doesn't see that anything has changed. I don't see it either. My eyes are closed, shut tight. But I can hear him, him and the others, and picture the abomination clear. My eyes are shut because I don't have need of them any longer. The smell is enough to send me to my grave.

Virgil comes into the room, into the smell of it, like a worm crawling into a cankered fruit. He'll close his own eyes soon enough.

He's distracted, short of breath, and sees nothing out of place. Parson is there but Virgil steps right past him. "They've finally come," he says. "I caught a scout. I killed him."

Nobody breathes.

"I'm taking you," he says. "Get up."

He says these five words, gentle as a thrush, to Clementine's body in the middle of the floor.

Clementine moves. I don't need to see it. Clementine's head turns creakingly on her neck. Virgil stops short. His lips open and flutter. Now he sees it clear.

"What have you done to her?" he says.

Parson hums and clucks.

"Clem!" says Virgil. "Its time for us to go, Clem! Do you hear? There's a company of infantry a quarter-mile—"

Her mouth snaps open.

"You should have seen them *coming*! Shouldn't you, Kansas? With your magical, fantastical, *virginal* white eye!"

Her mouth snaps shut. Her teeth click together like carpet-tacks.

The voice that spoke was the Redeemer's.

VII

You ask my name, and how my trade is ply'd—;
My trade is aulder than the sea is wyde.

—Thomas Cowpers

Belief.

BELIEF IS A RIVER, Virgil says.
Belief is a river and it has drowned me. I was swept up like a bird's-nest in its rushing gray immensity. I vanished into it like a house-boat into a squall.

If I'd truly had a gift, the gift of foretelling, the gift of mystic sight, or even—most impossibly—the gift of natural courage, might I have changed the course of this river? Might it have shifted its banks slightly, carved itself a new chute, and simply passed us by?

No. It never would have passed us by. There is no changing the course of this river. There is no overcoming its current and its weight. This river has no beginning and no end—; it seems, to those swept up in it, to cover the entire world. It seems as final as the sea.

But the river has limits. It has banks. Escape from the river is possible.

To escape I had only to stop believing. I had only to stop believing, but belief is my great and only gift. Morelle said my dead eye was charmed and I believed him, deferred to him, though the whole of my conviction spoke against it. Barker told me in Memphis about the deathlessness of the Trade and I believed in that, as well. I believed Clem's lies and Asa Trist's delusions and Dodds' mush-mouthed testimonials and the Colonel's half-truths. I believed each fiction Parson fed me, till I saw ghosts in every wrinkle of his skirts. Belief was poured into me like water into a weir.

To escape I had only to unlearn what Parson had taught me, what Morelle had taught me, what the Trade itself had taught me to believe. That was all—; but it was inconceivable. My visions, my theories, even my doubts sprang from my belief. My suspicion of Parson—justified though it was—was born of the tricks he played, the illusions he fashioned, the burlesques he put on for our benefit. The more proof I gathered, the more my fear of Parson grew. Such is the nature of enchantment. I had only to doubt him—to say "nay" just once, as Harvey put it in his letter—to be immune to all his witchery. But my faith in Parson had long since grown unshakeable.

I'd just killed a man for him—throttled Foster in the cellar, proved the full measure of my faith—and I must have seemed entirely his lamb, to use as he saw fit. But Parson grew careless in his strength. A final test was put before me. He saw fit—perhaps as a punishment, perhaps simply on a whim—to make me choose between myself and Clementine.

A woman now stands crookedly before me. If I'm to trust my eyes, the woman is Clem, though hideously altered. If I'm to believe my visions, my theories, everything I've puzzled out since Harvey's murder, then the woman is none other than the Redeemer. The Redeemer has been poured into her the same way belief was channeled into me—: violently, mercilessly, wholly. And I've lost my Clementine forever.

To believe anything else is to doubt my own existence—; to disbelieve in Virgil Ball as a sane man, as a man of understanding, as anything but a paper doll. Parson has me stuffed and mounted. But success has made him careless, as I've said. He's forgotten something even Kennedy could have told him. He's forgotten my most sovereign trait, the bed-rock of my character, the secret of my advancement in the Trade—:

I feel no great love for Virgil Ball.

The woman takes a step toward me, hesitates, then lets out a cautious breath. Her face is heavier, slacker, not its earlier shape at all. She teeters subtly on her heels. The thing inside her is uneasy in its new body, unsure of where it ends.

Parson comes forward, cock-sure as a stable-hand, to assist her.

"Tell Virgil about the Trade," he says, smoothing back her hair.

I never saw Parson, never recognized him for what he was, until this day and hour. Never before has he been so vivid, so convincing, so exquisitely detailed. Now I see how many of Morelle's airs and affectations—even his peculiarities of speech—were Parson's own. How could I have mistaken Thaddeus Morelle, even for an instant, for the architect and master of the Trade?

The Trade would have found its way without Morelle. It would have flourished without Kennedy, without Harvey, certainly without Virgil Ball—; without Parson, however, it would never have drawn breath. It was Parson who sheltered it, Parson who shaped it, Parson who gave it suck. Morelle was useful to him, of course, perhaps even beloved. But when Morelle was taken from him—cruelly and prematurely taken—Parson simply found himself another. She stands before me now.

The woman lifts her arms and gathers in a breath, stuffing it into her mouth like spun-sugar at a fair. I begin to see the Redeemer in her face and force my sight away. Delamare lies splayed across the bed, his fists opening and closing, his chest arched off the pallet as though the weight of the sheets might crush him. His eyes are shut but I know him to be listening. For some reason this emboldens me.

Parson has misjudged me. Belief is nothing to me now. I choose Clementine, not Virgil. I have only to take her hand in mine, to depart this house—this revival tent, this medicine-show, this cabinet of horrors—and leave Parson and his witchery to the wolves. I have only to take hold of Clem's hand and away.

"I don't believe in you," I say, stepping toward her.

Parson kisses her on the cheek. "*Tell* him, dearest."

IN AN EAGER, GRACELESS VOICE, a voice still strange to the mouth that shapes it, the woman begins our lesson. Her voice is a river, a hold full of slaves, a high attic window. Her voice is an education. Bright reels of time unspool as I listen, hang between us in the air, then plait together into history. Whole ages pass in a single turn of phrase. The voice is both Clem's and the Redeemer's and I have no defense against it. The lesson is one I've heard before—many times, in fact—but have always failed to master.

The lesson is called "The Future."

The future is made of *passings*, she explains. The passing of slavery, the passing of the Confederacy, the passing of the South. The passing of proclamations, of reconstructions, of humiliations run through centuries. The Trade, however, will not pass. A newer, more resilient strain will issue from the old, fashioned entirely out of breath. Its transparency will be its shelter. It will pass unnoticed, a low and life-long fever, feeding temperately on its host. "The country itself will have this fever, Virgil." She trembles at the beauty of this idea. "The country *itself* will keep it fed!"

She tells me more, far more than this in her euphoria and her spite, and Parson lets her rave, knowing that she grows stronger with each breath she draws. I'm given to see, as if through leaded glass, a future in which the Trade has been mistaken for natural law. Canaan's tongue will be spoken by whores and archbishops, sales-clerks and senators alike. The life of the elect will be the *only* life, she tells me. Their law the only law. Their Trade the only—

"You're proud of your handiwork, I suppose," I say to Parson, cutting the lesson short.

Parson grants me an indulgent smile. "I am, Virgil. Aren't you proud of her?"

I shake my head.

"That hardly matters. She wasn't fashioned to amuse *you*, google-eye."

I study Parson for a moment—: his hands, his mouth, his perfectly opaque gray eyes. Something's hidden just behind them.

"I think she was," I say.

"She was *fashioned*—with no small amount of care—as the vessel for the Redeemer's wandering spirit." Parson toys, as he speaks, with the woman's filthy collar. "I thought you understood that much."

Escape from the river is possible.

"No," I say. "There is no Redeemer, Parson—; Delamare and I snuffed his candle. I took a piece of pier-glass—"

"And yet, you *can't* snuff the Redeemer's candle, as you see." Parson clucks contentedly. "The Redeemer stands before you, hale and full of fire."

I look hard at the woman now, dreading what I'll find—; but the illusion has passed away like winter steam. I see nothing but an empty body.

"You might as well have poured the Trade into a paper sack," I say.

A change has taken place in me—a small but indefatigable change— and Parson knows it. The smile is still fixed on his face, but the naturalness has gone out of it like water from a sponge. We stand facing one another like book-ends, a column of dead air pressed between us. Only Clem's shallow breathing cleaves the quiet. *Her* breathing—; not anybody else's. I don't look toward her yet. I keep my eyes on Parson. To my great satisfaction his face begins to twitch.

"You've been a delightful under-study, Mr. Ball. A proper little bumbler. But that was your *part*, after all, in our Punch-and-Judy show." His grip on Clem's shoulder tightens. "Don't try to write yourself another."

"I'm not writing any part," I say quietly. "Your under-study is leaving the theater, Parson. And he's taking your Judy with him."

So saying, I take Clem lightly by the hand.

As soon as I touch her the floor drops out from under me and a number of things happen all at once. Parson and Clem start hissing like tea-kettles, Delamare thrashes in his corner like a bull at stud, and my vision is flooded by a host of shapes, so many the room is all but set afire. I don't let any of this unsteady me, however. I've been moving toward this moment since the night of Harvey's death, since my arrival in this hell-hole, since my earliest apprenticeship to the Trade. Not toward the discovery of Harvey's killer, not toward an answer to Parson's riddles, not even toward Morelle's murder—; only toward this moment. My investigation failed because I had no idea what I was after. I found answers wherever I looked, all of them to questions that I hadn't dreamt of asking. Now, at long last, I've hit upon my question—: I have only one, it seems. And it carries its answer within it, savory and chaste, like a peanut in its shell.

What is there to keep me in this house?

My vision clears. No more than a few seconds can have passed. Delamare is still splayed across the bed, but he is gripping his Colt Peacemaker now and his eyes are wide and blood-shot. Parson is unchanged, studying me through slitted eyes as though I were a sparrow-hawk he'd previously mistaken for a sparrow. Clem is still breathing in short, brittle gasps. Her hand is warm and spirited in mine.

"You'll have to excuse me, Parson," I say, passing an arm around Clem's waist. "I don't feel the need for a Redeemer any longer."

"*Back*, Virgil! Step away from it!"

Delamare's voice, quavering and wild. He's reached his limit sooner than I'd reckoned. He'll be wanting a clearer shot at Parson—; I don't blame him in the slightest. I bow to him and step aside, drawing Clem along with me. I shepherd her gently toward the open door. Parson hisses and rattles, cursing us all, but his voice barely cuts the air. His outline's gone watery, as I thought it might. He's a jumble of color, no more than that—: a memory, a child's fable, a stray beam of light in an empty room.

Clem grows more Clem-like with each step we take. Her body, formerly so rigid, now bends willingly to mine. As we reach the door it occurs to me that I have won. I allow my eyes to fall briefly closed, then break into a helpless grin, wide as a revivalist's bonnet. No more Trade.

No more shadow-puppetry. No more visions. Clem's body is soft and undeniable against my own. Tentatively, shyly, my eyes come open that I might see her. There she is.

A black globe, spinning silently, crosses my sight from right to left. "B—A—L—L," Parson spells out with his mouth.

A sound is heard. The report of a gun, miles away but fast approaching, overtaken as it comes by its own echo. An instant later it arrives. Clem is torn away as if by a rider on horse-back and hurled against the wall. She falls to the floor flutteringly, like an empty dress. Parson is screeching and thrashing behind me but I can't hear him for the echo. It's the echo of the echo that I'm hearing now. I stand as quiet as an engraving, enraptured by my freedom from the Trade, by my new and perfect knowledge, and by the warmth—already dwindling—of Clem's tender body against my own.

DELAMARE SITS BOLT UPRIGHT on the bed, staring hungrily at Parson. The Peacemaker is unwavering in his right hand. The sight of him, of Parson beating his face and keening, and of the body, not even Clem's any longer, heaped against the base-board, is so very strange that it takes me a spell of time—perhaps a single breath, perhaps a score—to understand that I've been shot as well. There is only sight at first—: the echo still holds everything suspended within it, coldly and transparently, like bubbles in a pane of glass. My hand when it comes away from my shirt-front glistens with blood and bile and a clot of hard, pearly matter that I can't quite identify.

Perhaps it's the last crumb of my belief.

As yet I feel nothing but a round, polished coolness, as though a dinner-plate had been pressed against my ribs. Perhaps my face will soon take on that knowing, self-contented look I saw on Goodman Harvey, that morning back at the beginning of the end. I shouldn't wonder if it did.

The first echo—the bright one—must have been the shot that hit me. Delamare fired twice. I nod to myself, bring both hands up to my belly, then fall twitchingly to the floor.

"Nobody leaves this room," says Delamare.

In spite of the echo I hear those four words plain as day.

The Beginning.

S HE WAS OLD EVEN THEN, Parson says. Old and uneasy in her skin. A nurser of bitter appetites.

She lived in those days on a green forgotten tongue of bayou known as Les Cananes. Red-bones and Creek Indians were her only neighbors, and they kept clear of her affairs. The cottage was a plain one, little more than a room with a wattle-board roof over it, but it was enough. It had only to shelter her trunkful of books, her time-withered body, and her one idea.

A causeway ran out a dozen paces into the bayou and she'd walk to the end of it each morning with a pail, crouch stiffly down and part the duck weed with her hand. The water underneath reminded her of cane syrup. Sometimes she'd bring the water to a boil exactly as it was, and drink it as a tea.

A man was coming to see her. She knew a man was coming, because there always came a man. Women came so rarely, waiting meekly by the door, and she never had the slightest use for them—; they came out of boredom, with little idea what they were after. The men knew what they wanted without fail. It was a matter of coaxing it out of them, nothing more.

Each time a caller arrived, she asked him first the date, then the day of the week, and then, if he was rich and traveled with a pocket-watch, the time of day. Then she took his gift—most often a book, or a small offering of money—and asked him why he'd come.

She passed the time between petitioners by reading. They'd let her take her trunk when they ran her out of the last town—Baton Rouge, sixty miles down-country—and each afternoon she'd open it and take out a volume at random, bound in marble-head or blue morocco, and bring it to the lantern as though offering up a sacrament. But she was not at prayer. She'd seen a fair piece of the country during the long years of her itinerancy, hounded from one village to the next like a devil, and an idea about America had begun to take shape in her mind. Religion was behind it. She'd been met with violence and censure wheresoever she went not for the reasons the deacons and bailiffs gave her, that they disdained her charms and fetishes—: just the opposite. She was made to suffer, she was pilloried in common view, she was cast out from society precisely because her teachings were believed.

There was power in this, if she could just catch hold of it. The steady stream of supplicants that came to her even now, a full day's walk from the nearest town, was all the proof she needed. The country slept under a quilt of superstition, ragged and enormous, stitched together without thought to the design. She had only to map it out, to learn each piece of it in turn, and America would be hers to trifle with.

And so she'd begun her collection. The Bible, *Pilgrim's Progress*, the Upanishads, the Book of Mormon. From each petitioner she received a book, or money with which to send for one—; and with each new book her map grew more detailed. The Lemegeton, Augustine's *City of God*, the works of Swedenborg, *The Rights of Nations*. To believe in anything was to become passive, she discovered—; to believe was to submit. One had only to grasp belief properly, to take hold of it like a hatchet, and one could hack through anything one liked. Violence could be done with it—; great violence, in fact, could be done with nothing else. The country was not yet ready, perhaps, for a great violence. But it would be soon.

Her idea was terrible in its simplicity. It gnawed away at her in her solitude—; it troubled her nights, and made her days monotonous and cruel. She herself could not put the idea to use, as she was old, disquieting to look at, and a woman into the bargain. But a man was coming who would serve her. She had only to sit and bide at Les Cananes.

And while she waited for the man to come, she read.

She had taken lessons in Hebrew from a deaf old milliner in New Orleans specifically to read from the kabala, and the wisdom she drew from it, one morsel at a time, on man as the universe in miniature, was a solace to her in her loneliness. She contained all the universe in her tired body—; she felt this as clearly as the pain that came to her on cold mornings. She chose this book, in secret, to believe in, the way a dressmaker might put aside a fine bolt of fabric for private use. Her copy of the book was ancient and brittle, and she kept it in an old sugar-tin, at the bottom of her trunk, to safe-guard it from weevils and from thieves.

The book was far and away the most precious thing she owned and she thought of it many times a day, reciting whole passages from memory. She held it highest among the forbidden texts, and the Jews highest among the races, on account of the vast suffering it sprang from. Only through suffering could an understanding of life be won and held—; she knew this. She herself had suffered great privations, and by their grace her eyes had been pried open. Now, at last, a man was coming to her. He'd arrive without warning, calm and full of purpose, and she would be struck dumb at once by his entire perfection.

When at last the man came, and the cold flush of certainty broke over her, the disappointment was almost more than she could bear. He was narrow-eyed and dull, little better than a dwarf, and the drawl of the shanty-towns oozed from his mouth like molasses from a bucket. His companion, though similar enough to him to be his twin, was better dressed and cleverer-looking. She'd have much preferred this other—; but he was not the one she'd been waiting for, the one she'd been banished to that god-forsaken marshland to receive. That man stood slouching in the shadow of the porch, leering up at her out of close-set, callow eyes.

She worked her face into a smile and beckoned him inside. His companion made to follow but she turned him away, stifling her regret.

"He been follering me since Natchitoches," the man said as soon as the door was closed. He was already rifling through her books.

"Who is he?" she asked. If anyone else had gone near that trunk she'd have driven them bodily from the house.

He made a face. "My *frère*. Morris Barker."

"Barker." She said the name slowly, getting the sound of it. "Is that your name?"

He laughed. "No, marm. You might say our fathers was unacquainted."

"And your mother?"

"A lady-in-waiting. Nobody had to wait too long, though, that I seen."

He said this flatly, without changing his look, and it took her some time to understand it as a joke. He went on rummaging through her belongings, glancing up now and again to measure her disquiet. She looked on helplessly. His every action was the stuff of her dreams made flesh, but mocked in the fulfillment—; made light of.

With a pick-pocket's sense for hidden things he made straight for the sugar-tin. The breath stuck sideways in her throat.

"What's this?" he said. He prized the lid open with his thumb.

"You couldn't read it." She managed to say this firmly, even defiantly.

"But *you* could, couldn't you, marm." The binding crackled under his fingers.

"What did you come for?" she asked, if only to ask him something.

He regarded her coldly. "Read this book to me," he said.

That he should have sought *it* out, out of everything, was the last proof she needed—; but in truth she needed none. She was at his mercy. It was not a bodily desire—she was too old to care anymore for that—nor a desire of the spirit, but rather a fierce voluptuousness of mind. Her attention was held not by his face or his body or his miraculous presence before her in the room, but only by the book he held. He was proof of the book, after all. Proof of all she'd come over the past decade to believe. Proof, in his sly, remorseless way, of the hidden God within her.

"I can't read it to you," she said. "You'd not understand the words." As she said this she tried to gauge the violence in him—; but he was a cipher to her still, unaccountable and unknown. She hadn't even learned his name.

He grinned at her, showing her his teeth. They were blunt and white. "I'll read it my own self," he said.

She understood then that he was an illiterate.

"It's in Hebrew," she said. "I don't fancy that you speak it."

"*He*-brew," he repeated, working his tongue around the word. "That's a Jewy language."

He guided his improbably slight body to the window and looked out at the bayou. His every act was both naïve and staged expressly for her benefit. "Have you read many Jewy books?" he said at last. The idea seemed to amuse him.

"Only that one," she said. "I learned the language just to read it."

He nodded at this matter-of-factly, as though it were the most natural of things. "A witching book, is it?"

She smiled down at him. "And a great deal else, besides."

"Did you make a proper study of it, marm?" He scratched his nose. "Did you learn it through?"

"I did," she said. She was wooing him now. "I could recite that entire book for you. In Hebrew first, then a second time in English, so that you could understand it. And you'd do well to listen." She took a slow breath, steadying herself. "I could make you king of all this country, if I chose."

"You could do that?" he murmured. There was wonder in his voice.

He held the book at arm's-length, offering it to her.

"I could recite it for you this hour and this minute," she said comfortably. "I carry that book inside me like a babe."

"That must be quite a burden," he said, and tossed the book into the bayou.

She let out a gasp, as the book hit the water, that held the next twenty years suspended within it like a row of wasps in amber. She saw the years arrayed before her, and guessed clear enough what they would bring, but still she couldn't stop them coming. She took a quick step toward him, trembling as though she'd been struck. She knew that she must either kill him at once or give herself to him utterly.

He looked up at her, arms crossed, waiting patiently for her answer.

"It was," she said finally, letting her body and mind go slack.

She would often think, in the years that followed, of that first flawless gesture of his, the act that both crowned him her Redeemer and set the machinery of his death in motion. He was always to treat her knowledge with distrust, learning only what he needed to learn, scorning all the rest. Had he studied that book himself, rather than throwing it into the bayou, he'd have become a sovereign among men—; he'd have pressed an entire nation to the floor.

As it was, he died.

But oh! how she'd adored him then. Her exhilaration was far greater than her pain. He was close beside her now, hands in his pockets, a mock-penitent smile on his flat school-boy's face.

"Those things you done, in Natchitoches," he said. "What they *say* you done." He was quiet a moment. "You do those things?"

The pain was gone as swiftly as it had come. "Some of them," she said.

The smile widened further still. "My name is Thaddeus Hejekuma Morelle," he said, holding out a hand.

She took the hand in both of hers. "Mary Parson," she replied.

Ascent to Heaven.

NOW THERE ARE THREE OF US, Virgil says. A trinity.

There is no Clementine in the room, no Redeemer. I'm still in the room, but barely. The spirit is leaking out of my belly like rose-water. A smell of roses is in the air, as when a saint is to be buried. Morelle smelled of tallow and stale piss when we dug him under. The memory is a sweet one, even now.

"No," I say aloud, mustering my last breath. I'll hold on to my body yet a while. Passing queer things are happening in this room, and I want to make mention of them in my memoirs.

Delamare sits propped against the head-board, his shooting arm buttressed by his knee. The Peacemaker rests prayer-book-like in his right palm. It's pointed straight at Parson. Parson has gone rigid as a cat. There is no concern anymore for the body at the base of the wain-scoting. The Redeemer, such as the Redeemer was, is gone.

"Confess," Delamare says. The Peacemaker is steady as a rail.

"Fool half-caste nigger!" Parson answers through clenched teeth. But fear is writ large across his face. If he speaks through clenched teeth it's on account of not wanting them shot out of his mouth.

"To bring Morelle down the ladder?" Delamare says. "Was that why?"

"There never *was* any damn-fool ladder!" Parson spits. He jerks his chin at me. "That was just a bit of Jewy pocus for Virgil Ball to suck on."

"Talk sense, you old bitch," Delamare says evenly.

"I take what I can *use*," Parson says quickly, holding up his hands. "With Virgil it was the kabala—; with Clementine it was Trist's bottles—; with Trist it was anything at all. You each had some manner of *fright* in you, some superstition, that I was able to make use of." He grins coquettishly. "Belief in anything is a kind of madness, Oliver."

Delamare leans back against the head-board. "Do you mean to tell me you have no beliefs? You, with all your charms and hoo-doos?"

"Not at all," says Parson. "I believe in my charms and hoo-doos, as you call them—: I believe in them absolutely. They would have no power otherwise." He shuts his eyes. "Thaddeus understood that well, God rest him."

"What did *he* believe in, then?"

"Himself."

Delamare hesitates. "But the Redeemer—"

"Is whoever I decide on, Oliver. Whoever *I* should please it be."

"Why play checkers with us, then? Why set us to murdering each other?"

Parson sighs. "You've been desperate for a mystery, you and Virgil, when all along the facts were plain. *Nature*, Oliver, will out. You were thieves and murderers to a man—; I had only to stand aside and let you go to market." He clucks. "If I'd wanted to *preserve* you, on the other hand—"

"But you didn't," Delamare says tightly. "You wanted us to kill each other off."

"I wanted to see what became of you," Parson says. "To see who managed, who was nimble—; who was left standing at the end of it, and why." He purses his lips. "I'd lost my dearest boy, you see."

"That's right," says Delamare. "Virgil and I took him from you."

Parson bobs his head. "I can't make do without a dearest boy, Oliver. It's not in the *way* of things." He clucks again. "Who could I speak the tongue to, with him gone?"

"Don't fret," Delamare says, palming back the hammer. "You'll soon be reunited." But his voice is fainter, more effortful than before.

Parson only shrugs. "I resolved to make the best of it—: to settle on whichever of you was left. Think of it as a *raffle*, Oliver, or an examination at school." His looks demurely at the floor. "I needed a new Redeemer. A new dearest boy. Is that something you can understand?"

Delamare redirects the Colt from Parson's forehead to his privates. "Who murdered Goodman Harvey?"

"Harvey did." Parson all but blushes. "I may have—*encouraged* him, somewhat."

"I suppose you encouraged Trist, as well."

"Not at all, Oliver. I merely held the rope."

Delamare narrows his eyes. "Don't tell me Kennedy snuffed himself."

"Small chance of *that*, sad to say!" Parson titters. "Stuts was a special case. Too stupid to be my dearest boy, too vicious to be let alone. A touch of hoo-doo, as you put it, was required."

Delamare goes quiet. "Foster," he says finally. "That's what you used Foster for."

Parson makes a curtsey.

"Why didn't you use me? I'd have killed him for you gladly."

"Of *course* you would," Parson says dotingly. He hushes a moment. "I had a notion to, at first. But Kennedy was a dangerous man—; and you were precious to me, Oliver." He bats his eyes at Delamare. "Can you not imagine why?"

Delamare bunches his face together. "And Foster? Did Virgil strangle him?" He glances toward Clementine. "She told me that he did."

Parson only clucks.

Delamare curses him hoarsely. "How in hell did you manage it?"

"*Come* now, Oliver! Ball was never hard to manage." Parson cocks his head at me. "Ball was a believer to the bone."

"It must break your heart to lose him."

Parson sucks in a sorrowful breath. "It does."

Delamare says nothing. His face is hid from me now—; Parson, however, can still see it. He looks well pleased by what he finds there.

"It was a *way* I hit on," Parson purrs. "No more than that. But it worked wonderfully well. The slack ones fell away."

Delamare sits forward with a cough. "Fell away, did they? Dropped like peaches from the bough?"

Parson considers this a moment. "Not *unlike* peaches," he says, delighted with the notion.

"What about Dodds?"

"I put Dodds to rest myself," Parson says. "That is to say, I furnished him with poison."

"And D'Ancourt?"

"Ah! The Colonel is a mystery." Parson waves a hand, as if the question were a trifling one. "I suppose he must have doddered off somewhere."

"Obliging of him," says Delamare.

Parson nods solemnly. "I was left, in the end, with just you three. But you were devilish hard, Oliver, to choose between. I needed a *believer*, you understand. A modicum of faith. And each of you cherished certain doubts." He looks down at Clementine. "In the end, to my great relief, one of you chose me."

"Liar!" I shriek with my last breath. "Liar! Pharisee!"

But neither of them hear. Parson watches Delamare, humming quietly to himself—; Delamare fidgets under his bedding as though he were struggling to fall asleep. His skin has turned the color of wet paper.

"So now you're down to none," he says.

"Your reckoning is *off*, dear boy," Parson replies. He glides up to the bed. "Now, after no end of trouble, I'm finally down to *one*."

An instant goes by before Delamare takes his meaning. He gives a low whimper. "If you calculate on using *me*—"

"*Reflect* a moment, Oliver! If you weren't a believer, you'd never have brought out that Colt. You believed that poor tart had the Redeemer in her—; I couldn't *ask* for better proof."

"I could fire again," Delamare croaks, burrowing back under the quilts. "I've got two bullets left."

Parson cackles at this. The fear has gone out of him so utterly that I wonder whether it was ever there. "You *do*, sirrah. But why squander them? Your point's already made!"

Delamare sinks lower still. All that's left of him is the Colt. "Why explain the game, if you love belief so dearly?" he says, so faintly that I can barely hear. "Why reveal your hand to me?"

"Because the hand is *played*, Oliver. It's played—; and you have won it." Parson stands at the foot of the bed now, grinning like a lynx, his arms propped comfortably on the quilts. "What were your first nineteen years of life, after all, but an apprenticeship to the Trade? Have your hopes and ambitions—to say nothing of your lusts—*ever* had a life outside it? Now that tiresome apprenticeship is done. The Trade is ready to receive you, in body and in spirit, as you've so long desired." Slowly, coaxingly, he pulls the quilts aside. "Put your revolver by. Leave the peace-making, dear boy, to those better *qualified*—"

All at once Parson hushes. A shiver runs the length of his body and he jerks his head sharply to one side. He has heard a noise, and no sooner do I harken than I hear it, too—:

Boards are bending down on the verandah.

I drink the sound in, gratefully and slowly, as I would a cup of beer. The hinges of the house-door creak emphatically open. A whispering begins, building on itself and on the silence, and the echo is pushed back before it like water before a broom. The whispers—low, capable commands—slip through clear as notes of music. As the echo recedes I take note of two things—: (I) Delamare's Peacemaker has fallen to the floor, and (II) Parson is taking off his clothes.

He begins at the collar of his stiff-necked soutane, his hairy face rapt with listening. His fingers fly tremblingly from one button to the next. I do not wonder at what he is doing—: I feel content to watch, knowing that time will answer my last questions. Parson himself, given time, will answer them. He is answering them now.

Sounds are soon heard of a great multitude passing the house, and other sounds carry in from the hall—: hushed voices and groaning planks and tentative foot-falls on the stairs. Parson has undone the last buttons of his robe and beneath it I see the pattern and pleats of a faded summer dress. I do not wonder at this. I am rising past wonder. In another moment he has stuffed the robe under Delamare's quilts and taken up position at the head-board, laying one hand next to Delamare's head and taking up the Peacemaker with the other. Calmly and deliberately, with the thumb of the same hand, he cocks it. No sooner has he done so than his body folds in upon itself and there is no Parson anymore but instead an old spinster, rheumy-faced and mild. I've barely taken this in when the first blue-capped head appears around the door-frame.

The head belongs to a bone-thin, whiskered, rifle-clutching ghost. His eyes are sunk so far back in his skull that I can only guess at his expression. It could be righteousness, or anger, or surprise, or even sorrow. The room is filling steadily with blue jackets. I try to bring my hands up, to make a gesture of surrender, but my hands refuse to answer. The ghost looks side-wise at me, then back toward Delamare and the spinster. Now he sees the repeater in the spinster's hand.

"Put that pistol away, ma'am," he says. His voice is clipped and reedy. I guess him to come from Iowa, or Illinois.

"This pistol," says the spinster, "is a Sam Colt .45 Peacemaker."

The ghost looks about the room. He is trying to make sense of the pistol, of the mulatto, of the two bodies on the floor. I can see from his chevrons—two bars, in worsted—that he is a corporal. "Put that pistol away, ma'am, if you please, and explain yourself." He blinks at her. "We heard two shots as we come up."

The spinster collapses a half-inch further and lets the Colt fall—; it lands with a thump against Delamare's ribs.

"I mind the negro," says the spinster. "I can't tell you much."

"You can tell us who you *are*, ma'am, firstly," the corporal says, his voice sharpening. But behind the sharpness there is good-will, of a sort—: I hear it and the spinster hears it. She lowers her eyes to the bed in sham simplicity. Her hands toy idly with the coverlet.

"Mary Parson, gentlemen, if you please."

"Did you fire on these persons, Mary?"

"I did." She gives a fretful nod. "They meant to harm me. Myself and the boy."

The corporal squints at her. "The boy?" he says.

"Yes, sir. This one negro here."

The curiosity of the soldiers shifts to the bed. "What ails him?" a red-faced private asks.

"Yellow fever."

The mass of blue jackets, until that instant pushing forward into the room, flushes clear as though sucked out by a bellows. Only the corporal and the red-faced private remain, looking from Delamare to the spinster and back again. I try to speak, to put the lie to her, but my tongue has forgotten me. The corporal looks down at my body, then at Clem's—; he's trying not to breathe, on account of the fever. The sound of his not-breathing is deafening.

My good right eye shuts, never again to open. All I have now are the shapes. How fitting that they be the last thing.

A red cross, recumbent, over a yellow cloud. "We know this house was tenanted by the gang off of Island 37," the corporal says. "Murel's gang."

"That's two of them there," says the spinster. "One of their whores and Virgil Ball himself."

A violet wheel, spinning slowly to the right. "Ball?" the corporal says, stepping closer.

"A big'un, weren't he?" the red-faced private whispers.

A six-cornered star. "The biggest," announces the spinster. "There from the beginning."

"And where were you, ma'am?" the corporal says, looking back at her.

"I—?" A pause. "Wherever they would have me, Corporal."

"What is it, sir?" the private says.

The corporal says nothing for a spell. "Run and fetch Dr. Hooper."

The private hesitates. "Dr. Hooper, sir? I wouldn't have thought—"

"That man is dead, Corporal," the spinster says. Her voice has gone shrill.

"It's not for him, ma'am," the corporal replies. "It's for that boy of yours."

"I see." The spinster hesitates. That a doctor should be summoned to minister to a dying nigger is inconceivable to her. "I see. As I told you already, Corporal, the yellow fever—"

"I was in Memphis when the Yellowjack last hit," the corporal says. "I saw enough of the stuff to recognize it—; and I saw a good deal else, besides. I'll trouble you, Mrs. Parson, to step away from the bed."

The spinster lets out a laugh at this—: a high metallic laugh, rueful and clear, run through with spite and condescension and defeat.

"It's *Miss* Parson, Corporal. I'm as yet unwed."

IF THE CORPORAL GIVES AN ANSWER I no longer hear it. I'm above Delamare's sick-room suddenly, above the house altogether, spiraling like a dandelion-seed on a cushion of summer air. A vast plain of water lies below me, as though the river were in flood—; Geburah floats upon it like scum upon the surface of a pond. The grid that so enraptured me lies plain to see, but it holds no mystery any longer. The only mystery is on high.

An enormous slate-gray cloud is gathering above me, winding silently about itself like flax upon a spool. The little black ball, my namesake, has appeared at some point without my noticing—: it hovers at my left ear now, chirruping and squeaking, ferrying me upwards. The other shapes—the stars, the cups, the fiery wheels—are nowhere to be seen. I'm free of them at last.

On this, the ball's third visit, I feel no sense of bewilderment. It's familiar to me, an old acquaintance, more genuine already than my memories of the Trade—: realer than Parson, realer than Delamare, realer than Morelle. Realer, even, than my Clementine. I reach toward the ball but it whirls playfully away, whistling heavenward like a shell levered from a rifle.

In the blink of an eye it's gone, swallowed by the cloud.

As the cloud lowers to receive me it grants, by way of welcome, one last vision of the future. The vision is brief, no more than a flicker across my sight—; but what little I see makes me cry aloud in awe.

The future of the Trade is the size of the world exactly. The world will fit into it perfectly, discretely, like a crawfish into its shell. The future of the Trade is made of quartz and salt-peter and burning oil. It will hide where belief hides—in language and in thought—and both will warp and buckle to accommodate it. The visible, tangible, culpable Trade will wither away, and the world will imagine itself cured. The Trade, however, will flourish—: as ever-present as language is, and as unnoticed.

The cloud is parting now into two equal halves, like a gate of wrought-iron, and I rise solemnly between them to meet with my reward. The ball waits above me, spinning giddily in place. It comes gradually to rest, and I see that it's not truly ball-shaped at all—; I begin, as it slows further, to make out a human form. An instant later I've recognized it and let out a gasp of happiness.

It's the child from the battle-field at Shiloh.

The child has matured since then, but it's still no bigger than a fist. Its hair has lightened to the color of new copper and its skin is a deep chestnut-brown. Trist would say it's come too close to heaven's oven, and no doubt it has. Its eyes are white, not like my own poor eye, but white as the driest, coldest snow is white. It takes a gentle hold of my left hand. The touch of its mouse-like fingers calms and saddens me.

The cloud swings shut beneath us now and Geburah is blotted out like a curse-word under a drop of ink. I feel no regret at its passing, no sense of victory, no relief.

The child begins to speak into my ear, softly but with authority, a jumble of jarring notes and sibilants that resolve, as I listen, into a kind of melody. To my astonishment I find that I can understand it. Slowly, easefully, I begin to weep. I am speaking Canaan's tongue at last.

"This was America, Virgil Ball," the child says, passing a forgiving hand over my eyes.

A NOTE ABOUT THE AUTHOR

John Wray was born in Washington, DC in 1971. He graduated
from Oberlin College in 1993 and attended the MFA program at
Columbia University. Since then, he has lived in Texas, Santiago de
Chile, Alaska, and in Brooklyn, where he currently resides. A selec-
tion of his poetry, "The Hat I Wore When I Was Alive," won the
Academy of American Poets Prize from New York University in
1997. His first novel, *The Right Hand of Sleep*, was a Los Angeles
Times Book Prize Finalist, a *New York Times* Notable Book and a
Los Angeles Times Best Book of the Year. In 2001 Wray was given a
Whiting Writer's Award.

A NOTE ON THE TYPE

This book was set in Janson, a typeface long thought to have been made by the Dutchman Anton Janson, who was a practicing type-founder in Leipzig during the years 1668–1687. However, it has been conclusively demonstrated that these types are actually the work of Nicholas Kis (1650–1702), a Hungarian, who most proba-bly learned his trade from the master Dutch typefounder Dirk Voskens. The type is an excellent example of the influential and sturdy Dutch types that prevailed in England up to the time William Caslon (1692–1766) developed his own incomparable designs from them.

Composed by Stratford Publishing Services,
Brattleboro, Vermont
Printed and bound by Berryville Graphics,
Berryville, Virginia
Designed by Virginia Tan